TRIBE

C. VONZALE LEWIS

BOOK THREE
BLOOD & SACRIFICE CHRONICLES

Midnight Tide
PUBLISHING

Also By C. Vonzale Lewis

Blood & Sacrifice Chronicles
Lineage
Zealot
Tribe

Novellas:
Descendants of the Big House

Short Fiction:
The Recipe for Cornbread (Link by Link)
The Soulless Ones (Beyond the Cogs)
An Ax for the Storm (Emporium of Superstition)
Harbinger (This Fresh Hell)
When You Hear Them Scream (The Darkest Lullaby)

Bobby, your support has provided me the way to continue my dream.

And to my incredible mother, thank you for keeping me safe from the dark.

And to Richard Andersen, who is resting in Heaven.

I will show you fear in a handful of dust . . .
T. S. Eliot

An hour ago, I'd made a promise to Devlin that I would not charge headfirst into danger, risking my life and the lives of others. I tended to act before thinking, which, as of late, put me in a great deal of trouble. I also told him I'd work more closely with the team moving forward. I'd made this pledge while eating peanut butter out of a jar. Comfort food always made things easier to deal with.

My utterance to do better and be better came with elation. I'd survived the attempt on my life despite my misguided actions.

I promise to never do this again.

In the past, this sort of proclamation came at the end of the night when the alcohol had turned sour and I was sitting in the consequences of my actions. I'd made a similar remark earlier this week when I woke, head pounding, to learn I'd been attacked while hiding in a bottle of rum.

Now, standing in the middle of Devlin's family room—that I dubbed the war room—I made another declaration.

I was going to kill the person who had dared to disrupt my peace. However, to keep my promise, I'd do so with the team. I considered that progress.

Water dripped from my wet hair and fell onto my bare shoulders. A chill raced down my back, my hand flexing on the terrycloth towel secured around me. I could have tucked it in, securing it firmly to my naked body, but it was probably better if I had something to hold onto. Something to grip while the anger flowed inside of me.

Not more than forty-eight hours ago, I was washing blood off my skin. Standing in the shower while Alek held me, cycling through a myriad of emotions. I'd taken a few lives in the cave underneath The Better Day Church. And had almost ended up being sacrificed in both Gavina Young and her crazed son's fruitless effort to become gods, and now ... now we had another problem to solve. But I had signed up for this. Even when Devlin gave me his bossy ultimatum about how his team worked, I stayed. No one could ever say I'd been coerced.

Even still, was it selfish of me to want to spend just a few days resting? To finally ... *finally* spend time with Alek. The two of us had been circling each other like horny, sex-starved teenagers since we first met. The ache to do something about it was unbearable. At least, it was for me.

My mental state was also a concern. Too much had been piled on me in such a short time: memories of the abuse I'd suffered; my parents' betrayal around hiding my magick from me; dealing with the guilt of not saving Marta and her kids when I knew something at Tribec Insurance was not right; and most of all, letting a sadistic serial killer go free because I didn't listen to the warnings in my gut when I glimpsed his true nature.

I sighed, then swallowed the pain and anger and the childish need to scream *Why me?* I glared at the white slip of paper Alek had taped to the board.

We are Tribe.

It read like a battle cry. Screamed by warriors when they charged the enemy, swords held high.

I stepped closer, examining the blood-stained paper.

Something about those words bothered me.

"Tribe," I whispered, hoping to dislodge the stray thought circling inside my head. It rang like a melody with no lyrics, clarity just out of reach. I shook my head in frustration. No matter how hard I concentrated, I couldn't figure out why that phrase bothered me.

Another concern pushed inside my head.

Why would the killers leave behind this note pinpointing exactly who they were? True, it would take some time to actually locate them on the island. But if they were going to announce themselves, why not simply charge ahead? They'd managed to kidnap two girls and kill their parents. So obviously they had a way of getting close. Yet they had left behind a note they hoped would, what? Scare Petronela?

Not likely. And sadly, without further information, I had no idea what to make of it.

Jonah walked into the room carrying the scent of chlorine with him. I glanced back at him; his eyes trekked over the board while he rubbed pool water from his bald head.

He had told me recently he swam not for fun but to allow himself a moment of rest. In a faith magick ritual gone wrong, he'd created a demon—a mindless being with a thirst for blood and death. And the only way to keep that creature from harming others had been to absorb its essence and keep it locked inside of him. The creature's inability to cross water gave him the respite he needed from having to keep it contained.

"What happened?" he asked, looking at me. He raised an eyebrow, gaze zeroing in on my towel.

I shook my head and turned away. I really needed to put some clothes on.

"We have another job," Devlin answered. "She does want us all working on this, right?" he asked, his question directed at Alek.

I sighed. I'd been avoiding Petronela for years. Ever since she unceremoniously fired me after my short time working at the carnival. I was not looking forward to seeing her again.

"Yes," Alek said, gaze locked with mine. He knew about my misgivings.

"Maybe I should get dressed." I rushed out of the war room and just barely stopped myself from slamming my bedroom door.

Well, really Alek's. I did have my own apartment and even paid the rent. Yet I never seemed to stay there longer than a single night.

I headed toward the laundry basket only to stop in my tracks. It was empty. I let the towel drop to the floor and opened the drawer Alek had cleared out for me to use.

Rachel had done my laundry again. I sighed in relief. I wouldn't have to cobble together some insane looking outfit when I went to see Alek's Aunt Petronela. Muttering a curse at the dread filling my stomach, I pulled on a pair of underwear and slipped on a bra.

After slathering some lotion on, I slid into a pair of tight black jeans and a tank top. I still didn't have a superhero belt like the rest of the team, but I would get one soon. Especially if we were eventually going to war. Well, at least, that's what it felt like thus far—being in a constant state of conflict, wielding magick and weapons. And at the end of each battle, covered in blood.

No wonder I'd developed panic attacks.

At least I had a knife given to me recently that would look nice strapped to my thigh. Made me feel like a badass who knew what she was doing. A lie, of course; I still had no clue how to handle myself in a fight. And I was sure blind rage wouldn't help me for long.

I dug the box out of my purse and opened it to reveal a bone-handled dagger resting on a bed of black velvet. Yep, definitely badass. My hand closed around the handle, and the cool surface sent a hum of energy through me. Was there magick in it? It had belonged to an Old One. Ezra, or as he was known in ancient Egypt, Anhur, God of War and Hunting. I was willing to bet this knife had been used in many battles over the years.

He'd given it to me along with dates to practice wielding it. Sadly, it didn't look as if I'd make those appointments. I took out the brown leather strap and sheath it came with and secured it around my thigh. It would take some getting used to, but I could work with it. At least it let me *pretend* I knew how to use it.

After sliding into my black boots, I looked at my hair in the mirror. An old high school acquaintance told me a few days ago while I was taking a self-help quiz in a magazine that the wildness of my hair really brought out my hazel eyes. I cocked my head to the side, trying to see what she saw. Maybe. I reached up to pull it back and stopped. Wild would definitely project the image of fierceness that I needed. So would some charcoal eyeliner around my eyes and blood-red lipstick. All of it hiding the fear inside of me.

Or it could scream lunatic. Either way, it might give people pause before trying to hurt me.

"Wild it is," I said, then put on some red lipstick to complete the effect. Too bad I didn't have any eyeliner.

I pulled in a deep, calming breath. Now I just needed my own battle cry. *Fuck you* might work.

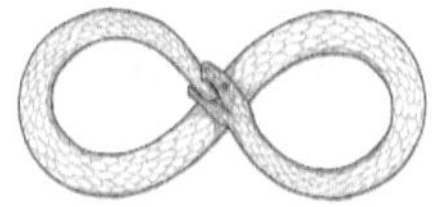

THE SMELL of coffee greeted me when I walked back into the war room. Rachel had taken down the research into the Sinclair family and added the information we had on the Peterson family. Devlin indicated he'd wanted us to do our own research into the families and not rely on what Andrew Snow, the now-deceased former employee of the Stewart family and spy for The Oren Group, had accumulated. We learned the hard way that his data was incomplete. And it had cost us precious time and sent us down many wrong paths with the Young family.

I poured myself a cup of the special coffee and stood in front of the board.

The Peterson's all-girl school crest, a joining of hands circling an open book, had been sketched on the paper above the writing.

"Kara is on her way over," Devlin said, coming to stand next to me. He glanced down at the dagger secured to my thigh. "Nice." He smiled and turned back to the board. "Marta will be here tomorrow." He dipped his head toward the note. "You have any thoughts?"

I glanced at him. "The war cry." I took a sip of coffee. I was becoming obsessed with war. Was it a premonition? Or just the clues lining up to an eventual outcome? "It seems ... odd," I continued. "Why announce who you are?" I tapped the crest. "And what do the Petersons have to do with Tribe?"

"We have to find out," Devlin said.

We both gazed at the images of the Peterson family. Selena's solemn face stared at the photographer. I'd found her journal a few days ago, detailing her account of what went on in the His Holy Need cult run by Lemuel Oren. Or rather, the Old One Khnum, as he was referred to in Egypt.

Like me, the Peterson family were of Creole descent. Selena's mother and father, according to Andrew's notes, no longer lived on Tulare Island. Her younger sister Leticia ran the school. His notes also mentioned they didn't come from money. Yet something about that didn't seem right. Yes, they had taken money from some unknown source—most likely Lemuel Oren—to *not* pursue the people responsible for their daughter, Selena, taking her own life. But they had funds before that. They had been listed as one of Tulare's prominent families.

"Yeah. I just don't want to go on a merry little chase all over the island, being led from one dead end to another." I sounded bitter and on the verge of hysterics. Maybe the wild hair and dagger weren't working.

He touched my arm. "We do this together."

I turned to him. "Okay. Yeah. Together."

He narrowed his eyes. "I'm serious, Nicole. No more running off on your own."

"I promised I wouldn't." Would I break that promise? Crap, I hoped not.

The doorbell rang, and I rushed out to answer it, grateful to get away from Devlin's scrutinizing gaze.

Yanking the door open, I found Kara standing on the porch, a mirror image of me, except she had her long red hair pulled back in a torturous ponytail. And, of course, she wore a belt around her waist with pouches of deadly herbs inside.

"Do you think if I get the belt, I'd feel more like a badass?"

She gave me a half smile. "Is that the knife Ezra gave you?" she asked, eyeing the dagger.

"Yes," I said.

"And that doesn't make you feel savage?"

I sighed, running my finger over the dagger's hilt. "Sadly, no."

She laughed and pulled me into a tight hug.

"I'm glad you're here," I mumbled into her shoulder.

She sucked in a breath, letting it out slowly, then stepped back and stared at me. Worry creased the lines on her forehead. "Devlin and I discussed it and..." She paused, shifting her green eyes away from me. "I told him I would work with you all."

I furrowed my brow. "Permanently?"

She nodded carefully, searching my face.

"What about your teaching job?" I asked, trying to keep the worry out of my voice and off my face. Kara had told me earlier this week that her teaching job helped keep her darker urges to kill at bay. If she was willing to work full-time with a group of vigilantes who looked at murder as a job requirement, then this would not end well.

She took my hand. "You don't have to worry about me. I got you and the rest of the team to help keep me in check." She squeezed my hand. "Besides, this is what I was trained to do," she whispered, sinking heat into the words.

"Your sadistic grandmother trained you to be an assassin." Of course, Kara already knew this. But I thought maybe just saying it out loud would drum some sense into her.

She gave me a sad smile. "Doesn't matter who trained me and for what purpose. It only matters how I use that training. And I think this is a worthy cause."

Cause? She said it as if we were humanitarians out saving endangered species and the planet, not leaving piles of bodies in an avalanche of magick and gunfire. Okay, maybe not an avalanche, but close to it. And I was knee-deep in it as well. But having both my best friends involved in this madness scared the hell out of me. My need to protect them reared its head, sending my thoughts into a death spiral. I gritted my teeth and pushed air out of my lungs. Red fire laced across my arms, the itch making my eyes water.

Kara pulled me into an embrace. "Relax, Nicole. Just breathe normally."

Easier said than done. My vision blurred, and I squeezed my eyes shut. A wall of red rolled across the back of my eyelids. Kara pushed the heel of her palm into my back, kneading the tightness. I sucked in a ragged breath, almost choking on the ball of emotion sitting in my throat.

Alek's familiar scent washed over me; his presence sent a brief wave of calm through my body. But it didn't last long.

"She's having a panic attack," Kara announced.

Warm arms circled me from behind, and Kara moved back, giving us space. Alek's scent engulfed me, and I lay my head against his firm chest. His chest vibrated as he hummed a soft melody, his breath tickling my ear. He'd used this same tune before, when the day's chaos had left me unable to sleep. That familiar timbre washed over me, easing the chaos inside, wrapping every disordered thought in a cocoon. "I'm okay," I said, my voice shaky. I had to get myself under control. Most important, though, was the need to figure out a way to deal with all the mess circling inside my head.

"What happened?" he asked Kara.

She frowned. "I told her I was going to work with you all permanently."

I stared at her. She looked so innocent with the light dusting of freckles and her red hair pulled back in a tight ponytail. Yet underneath that façade was a woman who could pull elements from the earth and crush her enemies. I focused on that. On the times I'd seen her fight. She was formidable. Not some wilting flower I had to protect.

I took a deep breath and gave her a weak smile. "I'm good."

She took my hand again. "Are you sure?" The skeptical tone in her voice had me pulling myself up a little more. I didn't want her to worry about me. I did enough of that for both of us.

Alek still had his arms wrapped around me. I rested my head against his chest and looked up at him. "I promise. I'm okay."

His dark blue gaze roamed over me. "We need to work on this."

I smiled. *We.* "But not now. Now we need to solve this so we can get that hotel room and not come out for a week."

"You have an apartment, Nicole," Kara said, grinning.

I reluctantly stepped away from Alek. "It's haunted." I clapped my hands together. "Now, let's go in there and get our marching orders from Boss Man!" I walked away, hoping they would believe my sudden recovery. All the while, I screamed inside my head.

My assured steps faltered when I walked into the war room and found Devlin holding one of the letters Ronald Stewart had written to me. Devlin's lips thinned, eyebrows drawn into a V-shape as he read what amounted to a sadistic, embellished fantasy of the time Ronald and I had spent together.

Oh, shit. I was not ready to deal with this right now.

For a few months now, Ronald Stewart, a man who hid behind ill-fitting glasses and good looks, had taken to sending me packages filled with mementos of his victims who bore an uncanny resemblance to me. Along with those sick vestiges, he sent, via regular mail, long, disturbing letters of our one and only sexual encounter. He had taken that time and spun it into a dark, morbid fantasy filled with blood and pain, which ended with me being carved up and eaten by him.

While I'd always given Devlin and the team the packages, I'd kept the letters and that particular madness from them, burying the missives in a shoebox under my bed and trying desperately to forget they were there.

Earlier today, in a moment of clarity or stupidity, I had decided to show them to the team. Now, I regretted that decision. Despite me not being the author of those deranged missives, I was the subject, and that was more than a little embarrassing. It also telegraphed my shame and failure at not recognizing a serial killer before I let myself get swept up into his madness.

I rushed toward Devlin. "I was going to tell—"

He held up his hand, stalling my response, then gave me a look, his warm brown eyes filled with concern. "Rachel told me you brought these here earlier. She's read them." He waited, probably letting his words sink in. I closed my eyes, head going up and down. "We will deal with this later," he said, his tone soft. He put his hand on my shoulder. "So get that look of panic out of your eyes. We have work to do."

"Yes, Boss Man," I mumbled, and he winked, setting the letter back into the shoe box. I could have kissed him for not bringing them to everyone's attention. I turned to see Rachel standing behind me.

"We can kill him together," she said, her eyes alight with joy.

I nodded slowly, and she smiled. I was a little bit scared of Rachel. Yes, on the surface, she had a sweet, innocent demeanor—craving friendships and giving out nicknames whether you wanted one or not—but I saw the storm brewing underneath. Rachel was a killer. A person who took great joy in inflicting pain. Was she a threat? I'd like to say no; Devlin wouldn't keep her around if she were. But I was still getting used to the team dynamics. So all I could do was keep a watchful eye on her.

After a brief hello to everyone, Kara took a seat next to Jonah, and Devlin looked at Alek. "Did Petronela mention any connection to Tribe and the Peterson family?"

Alek shook his head.

Devlin took a sip of his coffee and sat on the side of his desk. "Kara has agreed to work with us from here on out." He dipped his head toward her. She smiled, and he continued, "We are going to need a great deal of help with our investigation into the blood magick users. We were caught off guard with the Young family." He paused and looked at the floor. The vein on the side of his neck ticked. A chill settled over the room. Power surged, and Rachel stood up. Devlin shook his head, still staring at the floor.

Rachel took a step back but waited, her eyes locked on Devlin. Something seemed to be bothering him. It wasn't like him to be so emotional. But then again, he had been on edge for a while.

Before I could say anything, he took a sip of his coffee and looked at the team—capturing everyone in his gaze. "Part of that was my unwillingness to do what was necessary. I believed we could find a way to spare some lives." He looked at me. "I told you when you first started working with us that we didn't do black and white. And yet, I went back on my own rule when we were dealing with the Young family. It almost cost you your life."

"I'm ... I'm okay with the gray," I said. The admission felt wrong. I hadn't quite reached that point in my mind. No matter the blood I spilled or the lives I took, I still wanted to look at everything as black and white. Right and wrong. But we couldn't do that. Not when so many lives were at risk.

"The Peterson school is still a priority. And with the slim connection between our current assignment, we can kill two birds with one stone. But we will need to split up to deal with the bulk of it."

I raised my hand to offer a suggestion that would save us a tremendous amount of time.

"Nicole," Devlin said, smirking.

I opened my mouth, but no words came out. My face heated, and I ignored the smothered laughter behind me. "Umm... I agree," I said finally. What I really wanted to say, wanted to do, wouldn't have gone over well. We couldn't, despite what Devlin said, kick down the doors of the school and fight our way to the enemy. We still had yet to confirm they were practicing blood magick.

He studied my face.

"What?" I asked.

"In answer to your unspoken request. No. We can't storm the school."

I really needed to work on my damn poker face.

He raised his hand. "We will need to assess the situation first before we go in." He narrowed his eyes, the lines around his mouth deepening. "But we won't be wasting a lot of time on it. Once we confirm they are practicing blood magick, we eliminate the threat. That is what we are being paid to do."

"Copy that." I emptied my cup of coffee, wincing at the burn rushing down my throat. A tremor engulfed my hand, I set the mug on my desk and leaned back in my chair. *Please don't have another panic attack.*

"We're all on edge," Devlin said, sounding a little far away. I blinked a few times and focused on him. He watched me, constantly assessing with those dark gray eyes. I gave him a minuscule smile. But he wasn't buying it.

"I'm good," I mouthed.

He inclined his head and said, "I would have preferred spending a few weeks training you and Marta, but ..." He glanced behind him at the board. "Sometimes, things just don't work out for the best. Either way"—he stood—"we need to avoid making the same kind of mistakes we made with our last investigation." He gestured toward Alek, standing next to me. "Alek, take us through it."

Alek moved to the center of the room, hands hanging loose by his side. He seemed a little uncomfortable. I didn't blame him. "When I arrived at the carnival to drop off Rae, Petronela informed me they had found the bodies of four people."

Rachel clicked on her laptop and brought up an image of a scanned polaroid. A dark-haired man with brown eyes and creases around his mouth and forehead stared back at us. He stood next to a middle-aged woman with short brown hair and hazel eyes.

"Emil Ardelean and his wife Larissa were the first to be found dead," Alek said.

Rachel pulled up another image. This one was of a teen girl with a huge grin on her face. Her blue eyes danced with laughter. She wore her brown hair short, barely touching her shoulders.

"Their seventeen-year-old daughter Nadia is missing."

Another image appeared on the screen. This one of an entire

family—none of whom were smiling. A gray-haired man with brown eyes and a woman with streaks of gray running through her disheveled brown hair. A girl stood in front of them, anger brewing in her dark brown eyes. Her long black hair had been pulled back so tight, the sides of her face appeared taut.

"Petre Kotzur and his wife Florin were found next, and their seventeen-year-old daughter Sophia is also missing." Alek sat on the edge of the desk near Rachel and continued, "Earlier this week, two other girls went missing. Sisters, Daniella and Ileana Vaduva."

"They're not all Vaduva's?" I asked.

Alek shook his head. "No. The Kotzurs and Ardeleans used to belong to Tribe."

Alek had told us before that Petronela defeated the members of Tribe thirty years ago, yet she agreed to allow a couple of them to stay on the island. There was no way that connection was a coincidence. Someone was sending a message. "So." I paused. The stray thought returned, circling inside my head without any clarity. I was missing something. Something about Tribe's motives bothered me. But I couldn't pinpoint what it was.

"Nicole," Alek prompted.

"Sorry." I shook my head and continued. "The note could just be a way of pointing a finger at the old members," I said. "Outing them, maybe?" *Why would she let her enemies stay with her?*

"No, it wasn't a secret." Alek stared at the images on the screen. "Petronela believes some of the members that fled have returned. Unrie Nevsky, the man she had me locate and bring to her, also had ties to Tribe. Thin, but they were still there." He shook his head. "Something is brewing or has been brewing; it's hard to say what until we find out more."

"Why doesn't she take care of it? She does have people for this," Jonah asked.

Alek harrumphed. "Two reasons. While she does have people to handle issues that arise, she doesn't have investigators." He looked at Devlin. "She needs us for that. And two, when a member of the family dies, a ritual to honor the dead and send them on their journey to become ancestors must be done within three days."

"What kind of ritual?" I asked.

"*Tapiserie Soul*," Alek said. "Translated: Soul Tapestry. It's made with memories and magick, weaving them together into a kind of soul quilt."

"Don't you have to participate?" I asked. The ritual piqued my interest. Especially given my ability to touch another person's soul.

"No," he said, his voice clipped. "It's best I help the team."

I would have pressed the issue, but his body language suggested he didn't want to talk about it. I'd give him that space.

"Rachel. I want you to recheck everything that Andrew Snow accumulated on the Peterson family and cross reference it with what you've found out about the members of Tribe. See if there is a connection between the two groups."

Devlin looked at Alek. "What you've told us about their purpose thirty years ago feels incomplete. Is there anyone else besides Petronela that can give us more details?"

At least I wasn't the only one concerned about the story we'd been given.

Alek leaned against the wall, hands in his pockets. "I don't know. I'd have to ask my cousins. But anytime they've talked about it, it's always the same story. They came to usurp Petronela, and she defeated them. No one talks about how she did it. Nor why they wanted to in the first place."

"Why don't we just ask her?" I asked.

Alek gave me a half-smile. "She won't answer. Not completely. She will give us clues, though." He shook his head. "Can't say I appreciate her methods. But she does have reasons for them."

"Will she at least let us examine the bodies and the scene?" Devlin asked.

"Yes," Alek said. "They're keeping the park closed for today and won't start the ceremony until we've had a chance to investigate. We're expected after sunset."

"All right. You and Nicole head to the carnival and go over both crime scenes. I will examine the bodies when I get there."

"No specifics?" I asked.

Devlin met my gaze. "I trust your instincts."

He trusted me to take the lead? Was he out of his damn mind? I had no experience investigating a crime scene. Before I could question him about his obvious lapse in judgment, Kara spoke.

"Shouldn't we go to the school and see if the girls are there?" she asked.

"We will," Devlin said. "But not without first confirming there is a connection." He glanced at Rachel. "What do you have on the school?"

Rachel brought up an image of a newspaper article from the late '80s. The black-and-white image showed a fair-skinned couple and two children standing in front of a large wooden sign. "Originally named Peterson's School for Troubled Girls, Brett and Gwendolyn Peterson established it in 1986 after their daughter Selena died by suicide."

I gritted my teeth, anger bubbling to the surface. I'd found Selena's diary last week and learned she had killed herself because Lemuel Oren wanted her and the rest of his following to sacrifice themselves. When a reporter got ahold of the story, her parents had the article squashed and took money from some *unknown person* to start their school.

"They built the original school in Alice, and in 2001, their daughter Leticia took over running the school and moved it to Sandpoint." She clicked on another image. "This is the mission statement on their website."

"'To help educate girls who've had a rough start in life,'" I read.

Both Rachel and I shared a skeptical look. Sounded like the school found troubled kids and, given what we'd seen thus far with blood magick users, probably brainwashed them into being willing hosts for their rituals.

I looked at Devlin. "Are you sure we can't just storm the school?"

He shook his head.

"The students live there, along with ten teachers and other faculty," Rachel said. She stood up and posted a picture of the school and a map of the area on the board. "It's located near the border of Sandpoint and South Carolina and is surrounded by trees."

I got up and examined the map. It was near the border on a patch of land that could be dubbed as its own little island. I wondered why Leticia had moved the school to Sandpoint.

"You all notice how every place we end up is hidden from view," I said. "A barn buried in a marsh. A ritual cave underneath the church." I turned to the team. "Maybe that is what we should focus on as well. Finding all the well-concealed crevices on this island." I shrugged. "It might save us some time."

Devlin looked at Rachel. "Keep digging into it and ..." He looked at me. "The hidden places as well."

"Okay, Dev," she said.

"I need to update Opal and let her know we've added new members to the team. Our fee only covered five people; we have seven now."

"Can you ask them to get me a new car?" *Crap.* The request might have sounded reasonable in my head; out loud ... not so much.

"What's wrong with your car?" Devlin asked.

"It's tainted and the air-conditioning doesn't work."

"Tainted how?"

I didn't want to answer that. I'd already put my foot in my mouth asking for a replacement. No need to ram the other one in there as well explaining why.

"She's not happy about how her kidnappers drove her car and locked her in the trunk," Kara responded.

I glared at her, and she smiled.

"We can get the air-conditioning fixed," Devlin said, not even acknowledging my other concern.

"Okay," I said, feeling like a sullen teenager. I refused to drive that car again. Yes, my reasoning seemed ... unreasonable. But just knowing someone else had violated me so easily using my own vehicle rubbed me the wrong way. Made me feel weak and useless. Or maybe I was just behaving like a child and should get over it.

Fuck that. I wanted a new car.

"Jonah and Kara," Devlin continued. "We have been leaving loose ends all over the place. We need to eliminate them." His gaze remained steady on Kara. "Are you okay with that?"

"Wait ..." I started.

Kara shook her head at me and looked back at Devlin. "Yes. I'm ready."

Devlin looked at Jonah. "Recon first. We need to know as much as possible about each of the threats to us. When possible, we will decide as a team what to do. If not, take them down and contact Opal for cleanup."

Opal Katz was an attorney who worked for the Markums. The family who had originally hired Devlin to find out what happened to their daughter. That investigation had him and Rachel working undercover at Tribec Insurance where we met.

"You will need a base of operation. Find a hotel that rents by the week."

"The Brentworth could work," Alek offered. "The manager, Candace Rebel, can be discreet. Just let her know I sent you and steer clear of her employee, Timothy. From what she told me, he spies on her for her father."

"Fancy," Kara said, smiling. "Should we use our real names?"

Devlin shook his head. "No. Check in under assumed names." He looked at Alek. "Put in a call to Candace and make the introduction."

Alek agreed and stepped away to make the call.

"Rachel, set them up with names and an ID. Have your

hacker friend plant a cursory backstory. Nothing too deep. We just need something in place in case someone goes looking." She got to work.

My head spun at the speed at which things were happening.

"Why do they need fake names?" I asked. It didn't make sense to give Kara and Jonah aliases. Most of the key players we'd encountered thus far already knew everyone on the team. Well, everyone except Kara.

"We have too many people with eyes on us for my liking," Devlin said, his gaze on the dagger strapped to my thigh. "For Kara and Jonah to work effectively, we need subterfuge. Not a paper trail of our activities." He continued to stare at my dagger. "Do you really need the knife?"

I lifted my chin. "Yeah. I do."

"When we need to fight, take it. Right now, I need you to use those amazing observation skills to read the crime scenes."

I stared at him, once again trying to find something to say. He was right. I didn't need it where we were going. But I also didn't like feeling vulnerable.

Alek walked back into the room. "You're all set," he told Jonah and Kara.

Rachel handed them a brown envelope. "Here is some money and IDs. I made you a married couple, Jacob and Krystal Smith." She beamed at them.

Kara stared at her, eyes watering as she tried to keep from laughing. "Thanks, Rachel."

I followed them to the door and stepped into the damp evening air.

Kara reached out and squeezed my hand. "Your mind, Nicole. That's what makes you a badass," she whispered as if she had read my mind. I turned, eyes rounding at her using a curse word. She winked at me.

"Thanks, Krystal," I said, smiling.

She smacked my arm and followed Jonah to his truck. Why did I always use sarcasm to hide my feelings?

I watched the truck lights disappear down the street, worry for my friend gnawing at my insides. Damn. I'd turned into a mother hen. Kara could handle herself. And if she got into trouble, Jonah—or was it Jacob now—would be able to step in to help.

No. I didn't need to worry about them. I did, however, have to come up with a plausible reason to keep my dagger. 'Cause I refused to give it up.

Besides, both Devlin and Kara had said my mind made me special. And right then, my mind was telling me to never leave the dagger behind.

I rode in the front seat of Alek's Buick LeSabre with the windows down, letting the humidity engulf me in a wet, warm blanket. We were chasing the sunset. Traveling into those warm orange rays while darkness crawled across our backs.

Alek rested his hand on my thigh. His long fingers traced tiny circles in the denim. He wanted to comfort me. I hated that. Not the gesture. But what it meant. I couldn't keep my shit together. No matter how many inner pep talks I gave myself. Worry and fear always seemed to overcome me at the wrong moments.

Earlier today, a much-needed rain shower engulfed our island, leaving behind puddles of litter-filled brackish water. No one was going to complain. We were long overdue for it. Yet I couldn't help the unease worming its way inside of me. Because it directly connected the sudden onslaught of showers to my mother getting her power back. The magick she had sacrificed to the Old One Hathor in exchange for blocking my memories and magick.

Honestly, I wished they both had remained hidden behind that black seal.

We came to a stop at the intersection. The red light blazed, filling my eyes to the point of pain. Dread settled in my gut, but I didn't understand why. But suddenly, my mind raced. Seeing one horrific outcome after the next. I turned away from that symbol of sacrifice and spotted a woman sitting in a lawn chair in the middle of her yard.

Her pale sundress lay plastered to her sweaty skin. She watched us through a cloud of smoke. Goosebumps broke out along my arms. A cold sensation traveled down my spine. But I didn't look away from the woman. She bounced her crossed leg, the sandal she wore flapping against her bare foot.

From one blink to the next, the orange rays streaking the sky were swallowed up by darkness. Casting the woman into pitch black. The only illumination coming from the red ember on the tip of her cigarette.

Alek squeezed my thigh. "You know her?"

I shook my head, still unable to look away. The light changed, and we drove off. I watched her in the side mirror, trying to figure out why I'd become so fixated on her. I never put much stock in portents. They always seemed like a fancy way to name a gut feeling. Yet I couldn't ignore my preoccupation with the woman. Maybe it was the color? Red light. Red ember. Two instances in a short span of time that caught my attention. Red symbolized courage and sacrifice. Was that a message for me? Would I need to sacrifice something in the coming days?

I rubbed my forehead, warding off a brewing headache.

Alek turned the corner.

A red Jaguar convertible pulled away from the curb and followed us.

Make that three instances of red.

I turned in my seat to get a look at the driver. Long black hair billowed in the wind. I wanted to say it was a woman, but men sometimes wore their hair long as well. And again, I had become fixated on something mundane and random.

"What's wrong, Nicole?" Alek asked.

"I just feel... off. Like the universe is trying to tell me something. Screaming at me to pay attention."

He glanced at me. "Is this because of what happened with the Young family?"

I faced forward and returned my gaze to the side mirror. "Yes. I can't let that happen again."

He squeezed my hand. "I know."

My apartment building once housed not only a mental asylum but a cult as well. Had I known on some level something wasn't right with the place?

The car eased up, tailgating us now. Alek looked in the rearview mirror. "What the fuck is wrong with her?" he asked, speeding up.

I shifted in my seat to get a look behind me. "Do you think she's following us?"

No sooner had I asked than she whipped around us and sped off. Taking the corner too fast and disappearing from view.

"Road rage," Alek said and continued on.

I returned my focus to the homes and neighborhood stores whizzing by as we drove. The engine's constant whine became white noise filling the space. Nothing seemed familiar to me. It was as if I were a stranger in a place where I'd spent most of my life.

Now everywhere I turned, the avenues seemed filled with mystery and foreboding and magick. The recent events had twisted my view of the world around me, and I was slowly coming to terms with just how much the island was still an unknown to me. Like the secret places Rachel was going to ferret out.

Magick had created Tulare. That bit of history was commonplace. Even some of the reasoning why was known although, if I'm honest, not believed.

Our island was the resting place for an imprisoned god called an Old One who had been created by blood magick. His brothers and sisters had locked his soul in an Ark. Turns out, his dark appetite for destruction was too much even for beings created to destroy.

Yet, like all secrets, it couldn't be contained.

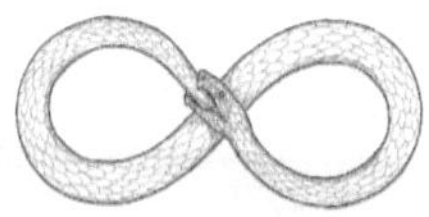

A short while later, we pulled into the parking lot of *Carnavalul de Fear*. Wind pushed against the car, rattling the frame. I pushed open my door and inhaled the popcorn-scented humidity hanging in the air. Trash skirted across the blacktop, wrapping around the light poles, their ends fluttering in the breeze. The entire lot had been cast in pitch darkness except for an eerie crimson light at the front gate. Its illumination barely guided the way.

"This is the first time I've seen this place closed," I said, taking in the empty parking lot.

The carnival had been a fixture on Tulare Island long before my family and I moved here. From what I'd been told, they settled here in 1985, four years before I was even born. Most believed them to be a traveling carnival, but when they purchased the fifty-acre lot sitting off the Tulare River, it remained one of the most popular attractions on the island. Well, the only attraction, unless you counted the museum as a tourist hot spot.

Despite the urgency of why we were there, I couldn't get myself to move forward. Instead, I remained rooted in place, leaning against the safety of Alek's car.

"Do you believe in portents?" I asked, looking for a reason to delay the inevitable. My stomach was in knots. I wasn't as seasoned at investigating as the others, and my last performance was so lackluster, I feared Devlin would change his mind about me working with them if I didn't do any better this time.

But honestly, encountering three instances of red still bothered me.

Alek sighed and moved next to me, gaze on the front gate. He pulled his hair out of its usual tie and slipped the string into his pocket. The wind caught the long black strands, pushing them around his face. "Yes. And no," he said finally.

I turned and faced him. "What do you mean?"

He slanted his eyes toward me. "The mind is a wondrous space. It controls so much of who we are and what we do. Both voluntary and involuntary. If, say for instance, you feared the number three. Eventually, that is the only number you would see. You can view portents as your mind or your instincts using the world around you to solidify something you fear. Giving that worry weight."

"I've seen the color red three times on our way over here. And I know what you're going to say. I'm afraid, so of course I can only see red. But I don't think that's the case."

He shifted around and took my hand. "Tell me about each time."

"The red light."

He cocked his eyebrow in question.

"Okay. That was bound to happen." I swallowed, suddenly feeling like an idiot. "The ember on the woman's cigarette."

"So that's why you were so interested in her. And the next one?"

"The red car that followed us."

"I will give you that one. I was concerned about her too." He paused. "Her mind was blocked."

"You tried to read her mind?"

"Not read it. Get an impression of her intentions. The aggression she showed was ... strange." He gave me a half-smile. "In your case, I think it's okay to be feeling on edge. Everything that happened with the Young family and Logan, as well as you getting your memories back, has to be weighing on you." He leaned down, eyes seeming to penetrate mine. "If you feel on edge, don't hold it in. Let me know."

"I won't have another panic attack. Promise."

"You can't control that." He smirked. "Now, we could have discussed this later. Why do I get the impression you're stalling?"

I smiled with no humor. Pulling a deep breath into my lungs, I glanced over at the carnival. "I got a job here when I was sixteen. I didn't really want the job. I took it on a dare."

"A dare?"

I chuckled. "There was a rumor at our school that the carnival had werewolves hidden on the property."

Alek laughed, and I lightly slapped in arm. "Don't laugh. I was an impressionable teenager."

"Nicole, I really doubt you were ever impressionable."

"Okay, you're right. I was a bit daring. Throwing caution to the wind sort of girl. But the point is, I wanted to see if the rumors were true." I looked up at him. "They're not, right?"

He smiled and shook his head.

I pinched the bridge of my nose. "Yeah. Well, I learned that the hard way. All I got out of those embarrassing two weeks was puke on my clothes and shit on my shoes. And Petronela's finger in my face, calling me a lazy girl."

"Now I understand."

"To be honest, looking back, she was right. I didn't put much effort into the job."

"You were a teenager taking a job to find out if fictional monsters were real. Don't be so hard on yourself."

I frowned. "But the remark still stung." I met his gaze. "Even today, I think about what she said to me. I admit I've had a hard time fitting into any career. Well, until now. But calling me lazy ..." I let the thought trail off.

Alek took my hand. "Was it the comment or the person who said it that bothers you the most?"

I bit my lip, trying to push away the emotions. This was the first time I'd ever voiced these feelings out loud. The fear of never being enough. I'd managed to bury those thoughts for so long, but now ... now, it was too damn hard. "A little of both," I admitted.

Alek's dark blue eyes filled with sympathy. "I understand the feeling. Petronela ... being around her when I was younger, I always felt as if I needed to gain her approval. Maybe it's just part of her magick." He gave me a half-smile. "She's acerbic and deadly. But people love her."

"You think she is using magick to make people like her."

He laughed, shaking his head. "I don't think she cares either way. Her only concern is that people respect her."

"Yeah. I saw that too."

"What did you say when she called you lazy?"

I turned away, face heating. "I flipped her off and stormed away. That's when I stepped in shit."

Alek laughed, his voice echoing around the deserted parking lot. He took my hand and pulled me forward. "Come on. We got a job to do." He leaned down. "And don't worry about it. If she didn't want you here, she would have told me."

As we strode forward, an overwhelming sense of déjà vu came over me. "You know, as of late, I always seem to be walking into danger."

"Danger is part of the job."

"Which is why I hope Devlin honors my request to get a new car. I need something that screams *secret agent* or *badass hit woman*."

"Do you want to be a hit woman?" Alek asked.

"I thought I already was." I glanced down at our joined hands. "Except right now I look like I'm on a date with the cutest boy in school, on our way to make out in the creepy carnival."

He grinned at me. "I'm the cutest boy?"

I laughed. "Yes. Yes you are."

He stopped, taking my face in his hands. "Nice to know." He gave me a soft kiss on the lips and stepped away. If we weren't here for a job, I would have grabbed his head and showed him just what I meant when I said "making out."

Alek pushed open the front gate, the hinges creaking in a horror movie kind of way. At least he'd confirmed there were no werewolves on the premises. We stepped into the carnivorous space and started down the main path leading to the back.

Dust blew in our path, the tiny rocks stinging my arms. Without the throngs of people and bright lights luring carnival-goers to the attractions, the place's true meaning and purpose become clear. Its sole reason for being was to elicit terror.

Prior to my ill-fated, brief employment, Kara, Marta, and I used to frequent it often. We even enjoyed some of the more dangerous rides, like the roller coaster that looked and sounded as if it were on its last leg—the safety bars barely effective. The brownish smears on the cars always reminded me of bloodstains.

But I steered clear of the mind games. Like the funhouse mirror that answered when you asked it a question. Didn't matter what you asked, the answer would always lead to your death. The line for this attraction was always long. As well as the one that led into a hall designed to help you conquer your fear. Everyone that emerged had a look of pure panic in their eyes.

A breeze ruffled the ends of my hair. I rubbed my arm to ward off the warm chill. "Why didn't we go around back?" I asked, giving the antique dark wooden hoops with a head in the center a wide berth.

"Some of the employees kept entering the living space at the back, so Petronela had it sealed off."

Must have been before my time there. The gate in the carnival's rear had always been there. Large and looming and enticing. The Keep Out sign only added to its mystery.

We arrived at the entrance to the back. The door stood ajar, its silver lock and chain dangling from the handles.

Alek pushed open the massive doors, and we stepped into a dimly lit corridor. Large stalks of incense burned in the tall free-standing burners running along the red velvet-covered walls. Lanterns hung from the slat ceilings. Our footsteps made the wooden walkway jump and creak. It gave the illusion of a time long forgotten, where people cooked and told stories by roaring fires.

A short walk later, we were deposited into a field that, if not for the modernized trailers and small buildings, would truly feel as if we had stepped back in time.

A commune had been set up in a power circle. Similar to the one the Stewarts used to drain the life out of their employees.

Just what the hell was Petronela doing to her people?

THUNDER WITHOUT RAIN

Devlin pulled up to a small, light blue house in the settlement of Dulean and climbed out of his truck and took in the posh neighborhood with its wide open spaces between houses, rich green grass, and vibrant flowers and plants. It reminded him of a golf course.

A fragrant, floral mist covered the entire area, mixing in with a salty scent from the Atlantic Ocean carried to him on a warm breeze.

Large oak trees dotted a few of the properties, including Opal's. Acacia plants with their feathery leaves and bright yellow flowers surrounded the front area of her house, and a muted porch light cast its glow along the stone walkway, highlighting a pathway toward the front door.

Devlin cracked his neck and started for her house, only to stop when thunder rumbled. He looked up, searching for the streak of lightning that surely would follow. Yet the sky remained dark, a sliver of the moon barely illuminating its vast space.

Devlin loved the feel of the storm inside of him. Power so potent and orgasmic that he had a hard time denying its pull. His magick came alive, pulsing when the white light finally cracked across the sky. He inhaled the scent of ozone, and power surged through him.

He stood there, letting the energy overtake him as he turned his face up to the sky. Warmth settled over him, and he sighed. So much chaos brewed in his mind, and for that brief moment, he found order in the milieu.

A door opened, its creaking hinges piercing his peace. He let his gaze come down slowly. Opal's front door stood open, spilling more unwanted artificial light onto the walkway. He stared at the woman in front of him.

"Your body is bathed in light," she said, leaning against the doorjamb with her arms crossed under her breasts. Her white blouse molded to her body, showing a hint of red underneath. Feet bare, she wore a short red skirt with the hem set just above the knee. Something in him stirred at the sight.

"You can see the magick in others?" Devlin asked, striding toward her.

She shook her head, dark brown hair spilling over her shoulder. "Were you projecting yours?" He climbed the few steps and stopped in front of her. Maybe a little too close. She stared up at him. "You look a little drunk," she whispered.

He pulled in a breath and stepped back. "Magick sometimes does that to me."

She glanced at the sky. "You were in your element."

He smiled at her. "Yes. You could say that." He pushed down the tension riding along with his lust and cleared his throat. "I need to update you on what's going on."

"You could have done that over the phone," she offered, still staring at him.

She was right; he could have. But he needed a moment to himself. Well, rather, away from the turmoil brewing with a new assignment being thrust at them so quickly. He had wanted some time to properly train both Nicole and Marta, as well as Kara. Get them up to speed on how the team worked. But sadly, it would have to wait. He worried their lack of understanding would lead to mistakes. Ones Nicole was likely to cause. Not because she actively sought them out but because her penchant for charging ahead seemed to be ingrained in her DNA.

And, honestly, a small part of him had wanted to see Opal. He'd never let an attraction impede the job, but he'd been thinking about her for the past few days. The spark of interest between them when they first met had wormed its way inside of him. And despite the many internal admonishments he gave himself about the complications of a relationship between them, he couldn't get her out of his head.

She stepped back, signaling for him to come in. He moved past her, entering the room and inhaling her soft powder scent. "I figured I'd stop by instead," he said, finally responding to her remark. "Hope I didn't disturb you." Despite the casualness in her tone, Devlin still noted a tightness lining the corners of her eyes.

She shut the door and walked around him. "It's fine. Just been a long day." She glanced over her shoulder. "I'm having some wine. Did you want some?"

He shook his head. "Been handed another assignment outside of what the Markums have hired us to do."

They started down the hallway, only for Devlin to stop at the large wall. Black-and-white drawings of religious icons in polished silver frames covered the entire wall. There had to be at least thirty.

"Are you religious?" he asked.

She stared at the wall, a small smile resting on her face. "As a faith mage, I'm drawn to the images." She shifted closer to him as if being pulled. "This is the first one I drew." She ran her finger over the glass. "The Wheel of Dharma. It represents Siddhartha Gautama, the Buddha's path to Nirvana." Awe and longing filled her voice.

"How old were you when you drew it?" he asked, fascinated yet again by this woman.

She bit her lip. "Twelve." She paused, eyes going a little

distant. "The idea of Nirvana seemed so... so much better than what my home life was like. All that preteen anger." She chuckled. "My mother believed I got an extra dose of that hormone. We fought endlessly."

It had to be better than his home life. Hell, he'd have settled for normal teen angst any day.

"I'm surprised you didn't start with the cross," Devlin said, moving away from the topic.

She laughed. "I never did what others expected me to do. Another thing that drove my mother crazy." Her arm brushed his. The smell of her perfume stirred the air. "She's a faith mage too. When I told her I was moving to Tulare Island, she *encouraged* me to plant acacia plants outside my home."

He turned toward her, staring into those gray eyes. The air between them charged with electricity. A magnetism that had him reaching for her with his magick. "I'm surprised you didn't go into that field of study," he said, reigning himself in.

She smiled. "In a way, I did. Faith magick allows you to exert influence." She turned away and frowned. "It helped with every case I tried. My ... power ... magick swayed the jury." She shook her head. "I didn't like not earning those victories because my argument was solid. It felt a little like cheating. So"—she shrugged—"I decided to work behind the scenes instead. The Markums offered me a job, and I took it."

"One could argue you traded one evil for another."

She looked up at him, eyebrows raised. "You believe what you do, what I do... is evil?"

Devlin returned his gaze to the Wheel of Dharma. Did he believe that? He let out a rough breath. "Sometimes."

"Well then. Look at it this way." She placed a cool hand on his arm. "It's a necessary evil. I won't pretend that what we do is legal. But I also know the alternative is much worse. I can live with that." She paused, studying him. "Can you?"

He didn't answer. He *had* been living with it. This wasn't the first time he and his team had had to kill. But previously, they were hunting someone whose guilt had already been confirmed. Now, they were trying to justify the kill. And that was different.

Opal waited for a beat before continuing down the hall. He followed her into a large kitchen. Recessed lighting dotted the slate ceilings. Cream walls flowed into dark brown marble countertops and chestnut wood cabinets. He stepped onto the polished wood floor and looked down at his shoes. "Want me to take my shoes off?"

She glanced at his feet. "Do you plan on staying long?" She gave him a hopeful look that stirred low in his gut.

He grinned; the question was filled with future promise. "Not tonight." He let the comment rest and stepped around her to the bench seat by the window. A laptop sat open on the small Formica table. Pages of legal briefs and law books covered a portion of the space.

"Alek's aunt," Devlin started. "She wants us to investigate two kidnappings and a quadruple murder that's taken place at the carnival."

Opal sat across from him. "I take it Petronela Vaduva doesn't want to involve the authorities." She took a sip of her wine and leaned back.

"No. They govern themselves." He studied her for a moment. "Did your research, huh?"

She smiled, nodding. "I have dossiers on all the important people on the island." She strummed her slender fingers on the tabletop. "Helps to know who's who when we need to dirty ourselves in politics."

"Politics?" Devlin asked, his eyes narrowed.

"You should know better than most that there is always a political obstacle to overcome."

"And what do the Markums really want with Tulare Island?"

She stared at him, her eyes lighting with appreciation. "You ask the right questions. Sadly"—she took another sip of her wine—"I don't have the answers for you. For now, just concentrate on the blood magick practitioners. And the Markums won't care if you are hired by others to work another case just as long as you complete the job they are paying you to do."

Devlin rubbed the stumble on his chin. "The Peterson family might be involved."

She raised her eyebrows in interest. "Well. That definitely helps. You can cross them off your list."

"So you believe what Andrew Snow has implied about them? That they're practicing blood magick? The man's research was sloppy."

She cocked her head to the side. "For now, just assume they are until you can confirm otherwise. It might save you some time. Your dealings with the Young family ..." She trailed off.

"Was a fuck-up. I know." He glanced at the bottle of wine sitting on the counter. "I think I might have a glass."

She grinned and got up. "By the way, we managed to clean up the church." She poured him a healthy glass of white wine. "The etchings on the cave walls were fascinating. I had to document them." She shook her head. "I'm afraid I fucked up in doing so. I was set to have the cleanup crew demolish it, but Gavina's siblings arrived on the island today and took over the building." She brought the glass over to him. "You really need to think about getting rid of all the key players when you do your work."

Devlin harrumphed, then took a sip of wine. "That seems too convenient. Why would her siblings show up today?"

Opal glanced at the papers on the table. "I'm having someone look into it."

"Well, I put Jonah and Kara on it." He set the glass on the table. "I will need another infusion of money to cover both Kara and Marta's salaries."

"I can approve that." She waited a beat, then added, "So, Kara is quitting her job?"

Devlin sighed. "Yeah. Not happy about it, but now she's available full time."

"You're not worried about her spying for The Oren Group?"

He shook his head. "No. We talked about it. Her grandmother has left the island again, and she will inform me the minute she returns."

"She might be able to identify Lemuel Oren," Opal offered. "We know he's an Old One, but they don't necessarily announce who and what they are. It might be a good idea for her to use the connection and at least get a clear image of him. The one Nicole found doesn't help. I've had several people trying to compose a mockup image, but … it's as if the features just won't come together."

Devlin agreed. He started to tell her about the letters from Ronald Stewart that Nicole had showed them today, but Opal would want copies, and he didn't feel it was his place to share those. His jaw clenched when he remembered the few he had read. He could understand why Nicole hadn't wanted to share them with the rest of the team. But he really wished she had. He'd believed the man was only showing a passing interest in Nicole. Turned out, his obsession with her was far more intense and dangerous.

Devlin stood. "We only have a short time to examine the scene for leads."

Opal stood with him. "Let me know what other resources you might need. And did you convey our offer to cover counseling for Marta and her children?"

"I'm working up to it. Marta is complicated. She refused to just accept the money I offered to help her and her kids. She wants to work."

"I can understand that. But please, tell her we can help if she needs it."

Devlin chuckled. "Nicole wants a new car. Says her old one is tainted."

Opal laughed. "I will see what I can do." She stared at him. "How is she handling everything?"

He smiled. "Better. She still's rough around the edges, but her mind … such a beautiful thing. Rachel was right. She sees so much."

"You admire her."

"Yeah. She's also a pain in the ass. Like a little sister I never had."

They both laughed.

"Let me show you out." She walked him back down the short hallway and opened the door. Devlin stepped outside and breathed in the smell of ozone and raspberries. "What does the acacia flower represent?" he asked, turning to look at her.

She leaned against the doorjamb. "It wards off ghosts."

"You believe in ghosts?"

She chuckled. "As a child." She sucked in a deep breath and let it out. "Some lessons stick."

Devlin agreed, reluctantly turning away. "Thanks for the wine," he said, starting down the walkway.

"Any time," she called out.

He didn't turn around. His attraction to Opal had to end. He couldn't do his job effectively and date at the same time. Both required dedication and time. And he wasn't willing to take his focus off the threats coming at him and his team. Besides, Opal was their point person, and any involvement with her would become complicated.

Thunder once again shook the sky. He sent his magick out, sensing the rain. It sat nestled in the dark clouds overhead, waiting. He looked up at the night sky, letting his power pulse, fueling the energy inside of him. In his search, he sensed another being. He jerked his head down, looking out over the neighborhood, trying to find the one who had brushed against his consciousness.

It wasn't the first time he'd sensed this person. They had been there all his life. Watching from a distance. And now, they had followed him to Tulare Island.

J onah recently asked me why the different areas on Tulare Island were called settlements. I told him despite being a city in Georgia, thanks to a road connecting to the land bridge, the locals still used the names first given the different areas. It was a homage to the first six families who were granted permission by the Cherokee to settle here. They called the areas settlements back then. And no one saw a reason to change.

Like him, even with that answer, I never understood the reason the locals held onto old descriptions. To me, a settlement sounded more like a space occupied by rustic buildings and outhouses. Something from a time in the past when there wasn't any running water or electricity. Or even a place where people who wished to live off the grid gathered and made a community.

The Vaduva camp fit that description better, with their mobile homes, outdoor seating, and clotheslines strung up near each of the trailers. Set up in what looked like a power circle, a fire blazed inside a massive pit in the middle of the commune. Light danced in my eyes. If I stood there long enough, staring into those orange, yellow, and red flames, I could see myself becoming ensnared in its heated sway.

Was it by design? The fire being dead center inside the power circle?

An accusatory comment lodged in my throat. I glanced at Alek. He wouldn't readily walk into danger. So there must have been a reason Petronela had set up their camp this way. Maybe it was a protective circle. My knowledge only went as far as power circles for earth magick and prayer circles for faith. Did mind mages use circles in their practices as well?

We'd been running into them a lot lately. But then again, we'd also been facing down families immersed in blood magick and its morbid practices. But between the Stewart family and their use of circles to drain their employees and Gavina Young's hidden circular cave beneath their church, I wondered if that, too, was a path we needed to explore. Find the circles that were used outside of any normal magick practice, and we'd find the ones using blood magick. Because I had no doubt the prominent families on Tulare weren't the only ones using it.

I made a mental note to add that to the search along with the hidden spaces. My boot heel dug into the hard packed earth as I made my way around the settlement. We'd come in between its western and southern points. Four small buildings made of a granite-like substance rested on the four directional points between the mobile homes—each of them painted a different color.

On the southern point, the orangish oblong structure reminded me of a sunset. It seemed to shimmer when the light from the fire danced across its marble exterior. Its brown tiled roof flowed into a long block shape rising out of the center. The outline of a door had been cut into the smooth surface. But no handle was evident. I ran my finger over the Eye of Horus carved into the stone—the Egyptian symbol sat in the center of a triangle.

"Mind magick," Alek said.

I nodded and continued my trek around the area, ignoring the hushed voices that followed me. It was as if I was being pulled to each of the buildings by an unseen force.

The edifice on the western point, painted a dark green, held a large tree, the roots digging deep into the earth. Each of the branches were outlined in gold, red, and brown. The Tree of Life was often used as a symbol for earth magick.

A carrion smell wafted off the building, its thick, pungent scent seemed to crawl across my skin. I closed my eyes against the sting.

"How can a carving smell?" I asked, not really expecting an answer.

"I don't know," Alek said. "But the Houses of Power have always emitted strange smells."

Houses of Power? It sounded ancient.

I pulled my gaze away from the symbol that represented part of my magick and moved north to the next building, a dark blue one that looked almost black. The image on this door was unfamiliar to me. Contained in an intricate circle, in the very center was a ten-point star. Moving out from that, there were ten orbs in varying colors. The image seemed to move inside that marble space, while the stench of ozone drifted off it. I looked back at Alek. "Does that symbol represent elemental magick?" I asked.

He grinned as if he were relishing my unbridled sense of joy and wonder. I'd always enjoyed learning about magick. Of course, I'd kept this pleasure to myself. Hiding behind a mask of indifference to the subject. Due to my own lack of ability.

I went to the last building. It was not the bright shiny gold found in jewelry but the brown starting point before it is melted down and made into adornments. The symbol on its door was recognizable. A large ankh like the one on my charm bracelet—a representation of my father's power.

I inhaled the scent drifting off the building. "Frankincense and myrrh," I said.

"Faith," Alek responded. "I believe it's also mentioned in the bible."

My mind filled with all the things I was learning. Like the fact that my father had access to all the principles of power. Much like Kara. Did that mean I could access them too? Along with the power of the *Nar al-nasaa*, Firewomen, passed down to me through my mother's lineage.

They'd captured each of the forms of magick here. Well, all the forms except the other half of mine.

I turned and stared at the center of the settlement, letting my gaze go distant so I could see the magick. A spectrum of colors flowed from one building to the next. Each of the symbols were alight with their representative colors. The Eye of Horus blazed, its gaze directing the accumulated energy into the firepit.

As I stared, all the noise around me ceased.

Replaced by a strange melody that filled my ears.

The colors engulfed my entire vision, cutting off the world around me.

Power.

So much power being channeled into the ground. I looked at the hard-packed earth and saw a nexus made of gold and silver. Its potent power buffeted my skin—raising the tiny hairs on my arms.

I pulled warm, salty air into my lungs and expelled it in a whoosh. The energy rushed through me, leaving me with only a smile.

A warm hand touched my electrified skin.

Slowly, the sound of rushing water penetrated the bubble of harmony I'd been in. The crackling of fire and the melodious voices of the people standing in the clearing pushed out the rest of that strange, beautiful song. I blinked a few times, and the whorls of colors faded. The humidity returned in a punishing wave, coating my skin with salty sweat. I lifted my hair off my neck while sadness filled me. I wanted to hear that song again.

Alek touched my arm vonce more. "I've been calling your name for the last five minutes." He paused, his gaze trekking down my body. "Your entire body was outlined in red. You looked... like... fire."

I shifted. Uncomfortable with the scrutiny in his eyes. "These buildings are channeling power into the ground."

He nodded. "I know. I can feel it too."

"Why is the community set up this way? Why direct so much power into the ground?"

He shrugged. "No one knows for sure. Petronela says it's for protection. But ..."

"You don't believe her."

He gave me a half smile. "Let's just say, she's not always forthcoming."

People with power and their secrets. And while I wished I could ask more about it, we hadn't come here for this. "We should get to work."

He stared at me for a while, concern etched in the creases around his eyes. Finally, he dipped his chin in acknowledgement and guided me away from the pillar.

"Are they starting the ceremony?" I asked.

Alek shook his head. "Not until midnight." He waved his hand around. "This is preparation."

He tugged at my hand. "Come. Meet my family."

Nervous jitters had bile rising in my throat, but I let him pull me along. Besides, I was still in a daze and needed a moment to orient myself. I glanced up at his face. The light from the fire seemed to shine underneath his bronze skin. For a moment, he looked like a warrior from ancient times. Long hair hanging loose, dark blue eyes narrowed in concentration.

As we approached the people standing in the center of the clearing, they turned and focused on us. Petronela stood in the center of the crowd wearing a red robe with intricate gold lacing woven into the fabric. She turned, her dark gaze landing on me. I expected scorn to paint her features. But all I saw was an open curiosity and so many emotions cycling behind her eyes. Like she was assessing me. Trying to figure out something about me without asking.

I cast my conscious inward, looking at my phoenix protection mark that my mother had placed inside of me to keep me safe from magick attacks. It remained dormant. Which meant

Petronela wasn't using her power to study me. I wanted to ask her what she saw. Then I remembered her comment about me being lazy when I worked here all those years ago and decided it was probably better if I didn't.

"Alexandros," a woman standing next to Petronela said, her eyes also focused on me. "Is this your Nicole?" she asked, cocking her head to the side. The woman was stunning. Long dark hair cascading down her back. Green eyes dancing with mischief.

Alek chuckled. "Yes, cousin. This is my Nicole."

The way he said "*my Nicole*" sent warm shivers through me. I smiled like a damn idiot, and she laughed.

"He is ... too much." She stepped forward. "I'm Bria." She shook my hand. "It is truly nice to meet you, Nicole. I'm sure my cousin never told you about me."

"No. He didn't," I said. "Nice to meet you too."

She leaned in. "He is secretive. Much like our auntie." She glanced at Petronela. "But she has told me many things about you."

"I'm not lazy," I blurted out before I could stop myself. Heat scalded my face, and I turned away. I glanced up at Alek and watched the war of trying to keep himself from laughing play across his face. I narrowed my eyes, and he grinned.

"I would hope not," Petronela said. "I believe Alexandros and your Devlin are pleased with your work."

I turned and met her gaze.

"This... what you do now, it is your calling." She glanced at the knife. "And you are safe here."

Emotions clogged my throat. I blinked to ward off the tears threatening to spill. She sounded so sincere. Alek squeezed my hand, and I smiled.

"Thank you," I said.

A door creaked open, and we all turned toward the sound. Light spilled out of the doorway along with the sweet smell of frankincense. Alek's cousin Cristian stood in the doorway, shirt off, jeans slung low, hair spilling over his chest. Another warrior from a different time. "Nicole," he said, dipping his head in my direction. His cool blue eyes assessed me before he turned to Petronela. "Yes, Auntie."

"I will need you to help your cousin while he is here," Petronela said. "The bodies," she started, gaze returning to us, "have been removed from the trailer. I believe Cristian has photographs for you of how we found them."

"Maybe I should go with them as well," Cristian offered.

Petronela narrowed her eyes. "You will attend the ceremony," she bit out.

"You let our enemies run rampant, Auntie." His voice held more than a hint of scorn.

I sucked in a breath. Silence seemed to fall around us. Petronela cocked her head to the side. "Is this what you all think?" she said, her words cold and challenging. "You think me weak too?"

Cristian shook his head, his hair trailing across his chest. "No, Auntie. But the threat is to all of us." He glanced behind him. "My family ..." He closed his eyes. "Apologies."

A woman came into view and put a hand on his arm. "Cristian. We are safe here." He moved down the steps and took the woman's hand. She stepped carefully onto the first stair, her hand resting on her rounded belly.

Now I understood. He was worried about his family.

Petronela's face softened. "Despite what has happened, I will allow no one to threaten or harm my family. We must honor our dead. If they are to join the ancestors, we must weave their stories into the tapestry. You know this."

Cristian's jaw clenched, but he gave her a shallow nod.

"Where's Rae?" Alek asked, taking the tension out of the air.

Bria pointed toward a trailer near the end of the lot closest to the water. "She's gotten settled."

Alek stared at the trailer. "Look out for her."

No sooner had he said it than the door to the trailer opened. Orange light pooled around the open doorway. A young light-skinned girl with a bald head stepped out. Five feet tall, with a slender build, she walked with an assurance I wished I'd had at that age.

She stopped next to Petronela. "Ms. Petronela," she said after giving me and Alek a quick glance. "I'm done unpacking." She rattled this off as if she were waiting for the next task. Petronela's lips turned up slightly in what I assumed was a smile.

She patted Rae on the shoulder. The gesture looked a little awkward. Like she was trying to determine how much affection she should show the teenager. Judging from the way Rae leaned into the touch, I'd say it was enough.

"I will give you the time you need to conduct your investigation and talk to the people. After that, we will close our doors for three days," Petronela told us. "We won't have contact during that time. If you can, bring those responsible for this tragedy to me. If not, I trust you will take care of them."

"Do you think the girls were taken or left on their own?" I asked.

She grew silent, her gaze going inward. "There is something I'm not seeing. I cannot say for certain. But ..." She glanced at Cristian, who had his arms around the woman next to him. "Some have started to doubt me."

"Auntie—" he cut in, and she lifted a hand to silence him.

Steel infused her voice as she said, "I'm aware of what goes on. And once we lay our people to rest, I will address it."

She walked off.

"Is the rest of your team coming?" Cristian asked, his gaze still on Petronela.

"Devlin should be here shortly." Alek turned to Bria. "Can you wait out front for him?"

"Of course," she said and walked off.

Alek looked at the woman standing next to Cristian. "How are you, Ericka?"

She smiled, rubbing her belly. "My feet are sore, and I want to give birth already." She shuffled forward and gave Alek a hug. "It is good you have returned." She glanced at me. "I have heard of you. The woman who has tamed our Alexandros."

"Tamed?" I laughed and extended my hand. She shook her head and pulled me into a hug. She smelled like warm apples and lilies.

"How long has Auntie been like this?" Alek asked Cristian.

Ericka kept her arm around my waist and answered. "She has been having some troubling visions, and when Daniella and Ileana went missing ..." She stared at Cristian. "We all knew those girls were trouble. They made no secret of their hatred for Petronela. Asking pointedly about Tribe without a care. So, no. They didn't go missing. They left and then returned and convinced two others to join them."

"But they didn't kill their parents," I said.

She glanced at me. "No. Which makes all of this... odd." She moaned, rubbing her belly. "I need to sit." She squeezed my waist. "You have to come back and visit."

I smiled. "I will."

After saying goodbye, Cristian helped her back inside.

I looked at the teenager eyeballing me. "I'm Nicole," I said.

She rushed forward, hand extended. "Rae. Your man here brought me to this place. Said I was needed." She looked at Alek. "Maybe I should have stayed with you until they finished the ceremony for their dead."

"Yeah. I'll check with Auntie. See if she wants you to come with us."

Her eyes rounded. "No. No. Don't say anything." She stuck her hands in her pockets. "Everybody's been real nice. Don't want to fuck that up."

Cristian came out of the trailer with a stack of polaroids in his hands. He handed them to me. "Everything all right?" he asked, gaze going between Rae and Alek.

"You think Rae should be here right now?" Alek asked.

Cristian looked at the teenager. "Up to you. No one will fault you for leaving right now. Things aren't ... ideal."

Rae shook her head. "No. I'm good. I can help."

Cristian gave her a half-smile. "Just let me know." He looked back at the trailer. "You mind grabbing Ericka some food?"

Rae nodded. "I can do that." She started to leave, then paused and added, "If you need me to help you while you're here, just let me know." She winked at Alek and rushed off.

"That one is eager," Cristian observed.

I had to agree. She also seemed skittish. Like she wasn't sure of what she should do and did everything all at once.

"She'll settle in," Alek said.

Cristian dipped his head toward the photographs I had in my hand. "They're not the best. But I figured you all wanted some taken before we moved the bodies to prepare them for the ceremony."

"Thanks," I said, sifting through the pictures.

I gasped, my gut clenching at the macabre display captured in the images. Another occurrence of red filled my vision. Alek may have been able to dissuade my paranoia earlier, but this ... this was different. The crimson stains screamed at me. Blood rushed through my ears, rendering me temporarily deaf. Muted sounds thumped at my eardrums.

I tried to count the wounds on the woman's torso. But the smears of blood obscured them. The jagged slash across her throat and the pool of blood circling her head suggested a great deal of rage. To ram a blade into the soft flesh of a human being repeatedly while they screamed for their life.

Who was capable of such a thing?

As I sifted through each of the pictures, I was reminded of what the color red truly represented.

Sacrifice.

An interspersed row of modern trailers sat between each of the Houses of Power. The three rows on the left started at ten, then tapered off to a line of six sitting near the gate separating the carnival from the living space. On the right, two rows of ten led up to the half-moon wall near the employee buildings.

Cristian led us past the House of Power for faith magick. Directly across from it, people worked in groups intertwining flowers and green vines between the spaces of four wooden structures. Bodies covered in white linen lay atop the pyres.

A few feet away, grills had been moved into a line along with long tables. On the other side of the fire pit, three adorned wooden chairs sat facing the fire. I glanced at Alek, hoping to catch his eye and ask questions about the ritual, but he held his gaze trained ahead.

I wondered about his relationship with his family and why it seemed so strained. But now wasn't the time to talk about it.

We stopped at the second trailer near the northern building. Cristian pulled a key from his pocket and opened the door. A coppery, musty scent wafted out of the trailer, making my eyes sting.

"This is where the Ardelean family lived," Cristian said, moving out of the way so we could enter.

I stepped inside, covering my nose with my tank top, and

entered a spacious living space. Dark- to light-brown furnishings covered the entire area. From the faux-wood walls to the cabinets and tabletops. Two brown recliners sat on the right in front of a large window, curtains drawn. On the left, the trailer flowed into a small kitchen area with a Formica table across from the stove and sink.

I shuffled through the pictures Cristian had given us and found one that matched the room. In it, a man, long black hair fanning out on the table, sat slumped over, hand resting on a green coffee mug. A matching cup sat across from him, along with the carafe directly in the center.

"Did he have any marks on him?" I asked Cristian.

Cristian stood by the door, hands clasped in front of him, his gaze trained on the table. "No. We think they laced the tea he drank with hemlock. His death would have been painful."

I looked at him. "How did you know it was hemlock?"

He stared at me. "John, our healer, confirmed it."

I nodded. He was right. The pain from hemlock poisoning would have been excruciating. Rapid heartbeat, trembling, muscle aches, and a burning in the throat no amount of water in the world could have appeased. I went over to the table. The musty scent grew stronger.

I picked up the teapot and inhaled the flowery scent interlaced with a moldy smell. "I'm surprised he didn't detect it." I glanced at the picture again.

"What kind of power did he have?" Alek asked Cristian.

"Earth mage," Cristian said.

I whipped my head around, eyes rounding. "That doesn't make sense. As an earth mage, he should have known there was hemlock in the tea."

Cristian shrugged. "None of this makes sense. Least of all how the women were killed."

I remembered the picture of the woman lying in a pool of her own blood.

Alek tapped my arm. "You want to take the bedrooms?"

I glanced up at him. "Yeah." I moved away from the table and started down the hallway, passing a bathroom and entering a small bedroom. Again, my assumptions warred with what I was seeing. I'd never been one to put up posters of musicians or actors and have any sort of frills all over my bedroom, and neither did this girl. But my room did have some adornments that screamed *teenager*. Maybe Nadia was forbidden from doing so in this commune-type environment where every move she made was witnessed by all. Or so I believed. Because this room didn't fit with how a typical teenager decorated their space.

She'd covered the mauve walls in neat, orderly rows of archaic magick symbols. The etchings gave me the impression of a barely constrained rage. Each stroke bit into the wall, leaving deep grooves in the wood. Above the twin bed, a row of cabinets stretched across the small space. Each of them stood open, empty save a few random items.

Her pillows lay on the side of the bed near the window, and the beige comforter had bloody handprints all over it. I pulled it off the bed and found torn sheets of paper scattered about. Devlin wanted us to bag everything. I glanced about the room, looking for something to put the scraps of paper in, but there wasn't anything. Not a single discarded purse or bag. Crap.

I went out to the kitchen and found a black trash bag, then returned to the room, passing Alek, who stood in the bathroom, putting the small jars from the medicine cabinet into his own bag. Didn't seem important to bag the stuff in the bathroom to me, but Alek had worked with Devlin longer than I had and knew his routine. Then again, maybe those items could tell us why an earth mage hadn't realized someone had laced his tea with the deadly plant.

Returning to my search, I gathered the scraps, noting the writing. The words "Dear Diary" stood out. What if there was a clue in how Nadia had left the torn diary entries? Pulling my phone from my pocket, I took a few shots of the bedroom and closeups of the markings on the wall. Once done, I gathered the items and placed them in the bag.

A small white dresser sat inside the closet. The drawers were open, discarded clothes hanging out. She had packed in a hurry. Some of her clothes, however, were still on hangers inside the closet. I looked through them, noting the formality of the long white dresses with their embroidered magick symbols and floor-length skirts and blouses that didn't seem to have been touched. They reminded me of formalwear. Not church clothes but something worn during ceremonies. Interesting. I looked at the walls again. Why had she put so many symbols related to magick on her walls yet didn't take any of her clothes used in what I assumed were magick rituals?

The remaining furniture—a built-in desk, a chair, and a small television set—were free from any clutter or markings. I started to leave, yet once again paused. If she had a TV, why not a laptop? I set the mostly empty bag on the desk and went to my knees to look under the bed. A single light green box sat underneath. I pulled it out and opened it.

Inside were stacks of photos and baby memorabilia. I stuffed all the items in my bag to review later and went to the last bedroom. The one I was dreading.

Before I stepped inside, I studied the picture Cristian had taken of the woman's body, once again seeing the rage in the savage way she had been stabbed. Alek joined me.

"Did you find much?" he asked.

I turned and looked up at him. "Yes and no." I pointed to the picture of the woman. "When I first saw this, the ferocity of the stab wounds caught me off guard." I moved around him and signaled for him to follow me inside the daughter's bedroom. He walked in and glanced around the place. "What is the first thing that comes to mind when you see the symbols?" I asked.

"Order."

I nodded. "But it also screams restraint. People who write on walls like this are often knee-deep in fits of madness. Otherwise, why not simply write them in a notebook or journal."

He moved deeper into the room. "She had a lot of anger."

"Do you know what the symbols are? What they mean?"

He didn't respond right away, eyes tracking across the wall. "They look familiar," he said, rubbing his chin. "But I can't place them." He turned to me. "Ready?" He had that look in his eyes again. The one he'd given me when we were outside the carnival.

"You knew I was stalling," I said.

He nodded and reached for my hand. After a quick squeeze, he gently pulled me toward the main bedroom. My stomach twisted into knots as I walked into the room, a complete contrast to the daughter's room.

Ignoring the blood splatter all over the walls, I concentrated on the layout of the slightly larger space. Against one wall, in an alcove with a window on one side and a cabinet on the other, rested a queen-sized bed. Opposite it, a tiny round table had been nestled between two easy chairs. Clothes lay strewn over both.

The closet took up the entire back wall of the trailer and opened to reveal a mahogany dresser.

I took in the feel of the room. Trying to see past the evidence of carnage and murder. This could have been a place of peace for both Emil and Larissa. A place they went to at the end of the day to spend time alone with each other. Feeling safe against all things. Yet that safety had been breached by the one person they should have been able to trust.

Their own flesh and blood.

My hand shook as I stared down at the picture of Larissa. She lay on top of the bed in a pool of blood, her sightless eyes staring up at the ceiling. The multiple stab wounds to her torso and arms and neck had shredded her clothes. How much hate did her daughter have to have done this? If it was Nadia. We were assuming a lot here.

I put the picture away and focused on the scene before me. The bloody sheets were still on the bed. I wondered if Devlin needed us to take them with us as well. There could be an array of biological evidence on them. But we'd need a crime lab to analyze it, and we didn't have that kind of time. And if he did want them, he could collect them himself. Carefully, breathing through my mouth to avoid the stench, I pulled the top layer to the side and searched the mattress. The soaked-through blood had spread into a Rorschach-like pattern. The blood stain formed an image of a snake eating its tail, an Ouroboros.

The ancient symbol depicted the cycle of life and death. I didn't want to outright dismiss the impression. But I did worry my own thoughts of portents and signs could be influencing what I saw. Just in case it was significant, I snapped a picture of the image, then flipped the sheet back over it.

On the right side of the bed, I studied the nightstand. Bloody fingerprints and scratch marks marred the wooden surface. I pulled on the handle, but it wouldn't open.

Alek came into the room, gaze roaming over the space. "Anything?"

I showed him the picture I took on my phone. "This is either important or I'm trying to make it so."

He focused on me. "You want to explain it here or with the rest of the group?"

I thought about it for a minute. I could either look like a big idiot in front of Alek once again by spinning a wild theory as I tried to work out what a random blood stain could mean (another occurrence of red), or I could have several pairs of eyes on me as I devolved into a conspiracy nut.

Decisions, decisions.

"What does the stain look like to you?" I asked finally.

He studied it for a moment, eyes squinting in concentration. After a short while, he shook his head and looked at me, brows furrowed in confusion.

I paused, once again doubting myself, but then shrugged and said, "It looks like an Ouroboros."

He cocked his head to the side and gazed at the picture again.

"Yeah. I could see that," he said, nodding as if trying to convince himself.

"But it's not immediately recognizable." I slipped my phone into my back pocket. "Which means I'm imposing my own ideas on it."

He watched me, eyes roaming over my face. "You keep doubting yourself." He paused. "Why?"

I shook my head. "I don't know."

"The reason Rachel was so adamant that you join our team was because you're so observant." I started to protest, but he raised his hand to silence me. "I know what happened with the Young family was difficult for you. But remember, you have sworn off all your vices and are dealing with a lot of traumatic memories at the same time. You were off your game. Hell, we all were."

He was right, of course. But I was having a hard time accepting it. I turned and studied the accent table next to the bed. "Looks as if she tried to get into that." Deep gashes with streaks of blood marred the wood around the lock.

Alek tried the handle, then pulled a pocketknife from his pocket and jammed the blade into the lock. It popped open, and we looked inside. Empty.

"Why would she try to open an empty cabinet in such a frenzied way?" I asked, searching the space. Maybe there was a secret compartment. After running my hand over the cool wood and coming up empty, I stepped back and once again took in the scene, mind cataloging everything we had learned thus far.

The two methods of death bothered me. It was obvious she'd drugged them first. But with hemlock, her mother wouldn't have had the strength to fight, let alone make it to the bedroom. I went back to the dining table in the front room and examined the two cups of tea. The one the father had drunk was almost empty, yet the other one was still full.

Had she detected the poison? And not warned her husband?

"What kind of power did the mother have?" I asked.

Cristian stood by the front door. "She was a Mind mage," he said, calling over his shoulder.

Alek came into the room. "What are you thinking?" he asked, setting his plastic bag on the counter. Both our bags had little to no contents in them. And I doubted what we had collected would help much.

"Maybe she figured out what her daughter was doing," I said, thinking. I pointed at the full cup of tea. "She didn't drink. Yet her husband did. Why didn't she warn him?"

Cristian turned to us. "Emil was off. Larissa would have come in after her shift."

"So maybe the tea wasn't for her," I said.

They both looked at the table.

"Which means," I continued, "Nadia killed her father and then ambushed her mother."

I thought about the scratch marks on the cabinet. Maybe that's why Nadie had waited for her mother: she couldn't get into the cabinet. But no, that didn't make sense either. Alek opened it easily. I sighed, chastising myself for trying to rush through it. Part of me was still upset with having been thrust into another assignment so soon. Another part was struggling with the strangeness of clues we'd seen thus far.

I wouldn't be able to solve this by shoving the pieces together to fit when I didn't have all the pieces to begin with. It would take time. Coffee. And ... yes, the team. Which meant I'd have to find a way to articulate my thoughts. Yeah. That wasn't going to be easy at all.

After we finished gathering what we could, we left the trailer and started for the next double-murder crime scene. I tried to ready myself for the bloodbath we'd be walking into.

Fuck, I cried inside my head.

Unkindness of Ravens

Devlin pulled into the darkened lot of *Carnavalul de Fear* and parked next to Alek's Buick. He stared at the empty lot while he catalogued what needed to be done. His encounter with the one who watched him had left him a little rattled. It was the first time he'd felt their presence since he'd been on Tulare Island. What did they want? And why were they here?

A well of frustration bubbled inside of him. Closing his eyes, he dug his balled fists into his thighs and pulled in a deep breath. He held onto that deep well of air until the need for oxygen became too much.

On a whoosh, he opened his eyes and relaxed his hands, letting them rest on his lap.

He didn't want to work for Petronela Vaduva.

The main reason for his reluctance was knowing she had people in her employ able to handle what she needed done. Like when she had asked Alek to hunt down Urie Nevsky last week. Being her nephew, Alek had felt obligated to honor her request. Devlin had kept quiet then, hoping it would be a one-time thing, but now, he worried she would continue to demand they work for her. Which meant he'd have to find a respectable way of letting her know it wasn't an option she could rely on.

He sighed, then climbed out of his car and turned his face up to the sky, letting the mist coat his skin. A burst of energy raced down his spine and settled in his center. His heart pounded in his chest; every cell in his body came alive as the potent power of the elements surged through him.

Rachel, Alek, and now Nicole used the special brew of coffee Rachel made to replenish their power. He preferred to use the elements. The power was much more potent. And, honestly, he liked the peace it gave him to connect with his magick in this way.

Debris skittered across the blacktop, catching on the metal trash bins overflowing with discarded food. The stench of it carried on the salty wind. Unease crept up his spine as he stared at the cumulation of trash and overturned traffic cones. At the brooms and dustpans laid on the blacktop.

Something was off.

Alek had learned of the deaths and missing girls when he dropped off Rae earlier that afternoon. Devlin had wanted to head over right away, but they'd been told to arrive later, after sunset. The park didn't open until after dusk. The last time he was here, the cleaning crew had been working during the day. Readying the park before it opened. Yet the evidence suggested they had started, then stopped abruptly and were sent home before they could finish their work.

So why not let him and his team come earlier? What had they been doing this whole time? It felt calculated. Like a game Petronela was playing. Or was he reading too much into it? Letting his distrust of Alek's aunt feed his thoughts? But even Alek had reservations about the woman's true motives.

Whatever the answer was, he wasn't going to figure it out standing in the empty lot. He grabbed his backpack out of the car and started for the gate. A crimson light cast a macabre path along the blacktop. It reminded him of spilled blood. Like someone had fallen and bled out, leaving behind a brutish outline to their demise. He didn't believe in portents. The ability to sense the danger around oneself was ingrained. People just often choose to ignore it.

But like Nicole, his instincts were born from a traumatic past. One where he was forced to find order in chaos. He had watched his mother constantly for any sign of her spiraling.

He cracked his neck, his footsteps slowing. Why did the red path give him pause? Humidity buffeted his skin. He inhaled, pulling in more of the elements. The underlying scent of popcorn and sugar coated his nose. He turned, his gaze trailing along the blacktop, following the path back to their cars.

A gate creaked open, and he whipped around. A woman with long black hair, wearing a dark brown skirt and beige top, stepped out. The wind picked up the strands of her hair, lifting them around her to create a shadowy veil.

"Well look," she called, her voice rich and thick with an accent similar to Alek's. Only hers was more pronounced. "The elusive Devlin Grey."

He spared one last look at the ground, then walked the last few feet and stopped in front of her. "Yes," he said, staring at her face. The woman reminded him of classic movie stars with their natural beauty carved into the features.

"Alek has told you about me?"

Alek wasn't prone to idle chitchat with anyone. He only gave information when prompted.

She laughed, a rich, throaty sound that enveloped him. Her green eyes caught the moonlight. "No. Of course not." She extended her hand. "I'm Bria. And Alek only told me to wait for you." She stepped closer, bringing a whiff of spice and vanilla. "It's Auntie who has mentioned you a time or two. Which means you are important to her for some reason." She smiled, eyes locked with his.

He had been right. Petronela was fascinated with him. Now he just had to figure out why.

"I'll show you to your team," Bria said.

They started forward. Devlin glanced at the red bulb blazing inside its metal canister. "Why use a red light?"

Bria stopped and followed his gaze. "To scare the tourists."

Despite the explanation, he still couldn't shake the eerie feeling in his gut. "I'm sorry for your loss," he said, mind still occupied. She didn't respond. "Your people," he prompted.

She nodded. "Thank you. While it is a loss, few will mourn their deaths."

"You weren't close?" It reminded him of the funerals he attended for fallen officers that he didn't particularly care for. A simple perfunctory act that was expected of him. He loathed having to put on a show of camaraderie when he didn't feel any sense of fellowship. Was it the same here? Did they choose to have a ceremony because it was expected? And if so, by who?

They arrived at a massive wooden door. Bria reached for the handle, then stopped. Her gaze tracked all over him, scrutinizing. "Your magick is strong. The blue is so dark it borders black at times."

"Your aunt was interested in my magick too. She even hinted at knowing my father." Her avoidance of his question made him wonder if he'd touched a nerve.

"That is interesting." She paused, then added, "They did not wish to be close with us." She turned away, then pulled open the massive doors, the silver chains knocking against the wood. "Come. Alexandros and Nicole are already searching the trailers."

The abrupt change in her demeanor threw him for a minute. He didn't know what to make of the Vaduva clan. And it would seem they all had a penchant for obscurity.

They stepped into a dimly lit hallway encased in red velvet walls with large stalks of incense burning in tall free-standing burners. He glanced up at the lanterns hanging from the ceiling. "Interesting," he said. "Feels as if I'm traveling back in time."

Bria laughed.

The hallway led out to a large clearing with trailers and four oblong structures, their surfaces shimmering in the firelight.

"A power circle," Devlin said, gazing around the enormous space filled with people. "The buildings?" He made his way to the orange building as if he were being pulled. Power ran across his exposed skin. He pulled that potent energy into him and sighed as it raced through his veins. He stopped at a makeshift door and stared at the Eye of Horus carved into the surface.

"Mind magick," Bria said walking beside him. She signaled to the other buildings. "Each of the principles has its own House of Power. And yes, we have set the grounds up in a power circle."

Devlin looked at her. "Is it a ritual?"

She smiled and shook her head. "No. It's meant for protection. Also helps to restore our power after work." She gave him a mischievous grin. "Most of us are mind mages, and we use our abilities to scare the ones who come here seeking fear."

Devlin nodded. "I wondered about that." It was then that he saw the four funeral pyres at the edge of the power circle, bodies laid out on top. "They moved the bodies?"

"I believe Cristian took pictures for you all," she said with a note of caution in her voice. "They have already cleaned them so..." She trailed off.

He sighed. "It would have been better to study the scene as you found it before the bodies were removed."

"The pictures won't work?"

He shook his head. They would. But he preferred to get a look at the crime scene intact as well. It wasn't particularly necessary. It wasn't as if they were building a case. But it all went to his way of doing things. Order in the chaos.

"Why study the scene?" Bria asked when he didn't respond.

He glanced at her. "It's how I was trained. You can learn a lot by analyzing a crime scene." He blew out a frustrated breath. "But it really isn't necessary. I just need it..." He trailed off, looking around the clearing again.

Bria touched his arm. "You need the structure."

He looked at her through narrowed eyes. "Are you reading my mind?"

She grinned. "No. Your frustration is written all over your face. I understand the ways of the law. But you are not part of that world anymore." She narrowed her eyes in concentration. "Yet you still find comfort in it. Like we do in the old ways."

He sighed, relieved she understood. "Yes. I find having a system in place makes it easier to sift through all the clues and determine what needs to be done. What gaps in our knowledge need to be filled." He chuckled. "It does drive my team a little crazy, though."

She laughed. He loved the sound of it. That deep, throaty timbre that seemed to come from a bottomless well inside of her. "Did you wish to join Alexandros and Nicole?"

He shook his head. "I still need to examine the bodies."

She nodded and led him to the pyres that sat at the edge of the property, close to the huge bonfire in the center of the community.

Devlin dropped his bag on the hard-packed earth and studied the set up. Thin white linen covered the four bodies. Flowers and colorful ceramic jars lined the sides. "Is this part of the ritual?"

Bria nodded. "The jars hold messages for lost loved ones. Sometimes stories or memories are stuffed inside." She tapped a gold jar with green beads wrapped around it. "I put a message to my father in this one. Along with the ring I'd hid from him." She smiled without mirth. "I believed that as long as he couldn't find his ring, he'd never leave." Bria looked at him out of tear-filled eyes.

"I'm sorry. How old were you when he passed?"

"Twelve. I was young and had time to heal. But the loss is still there."

Devlin stared at the intricately designed jars. "This reminds me of Egyptian burial customs. Putting the organs into jars."

"Yes. It is similar. All rituals for the dead have come from ancient times. They just change as people do."

They stood there for a minute, Bria looking deep in thought. While he hadn't come here to learn about their ceremony, curiosity still stirred within him. "Can I remove the cloth from the bodies?"

Bria gave a quick nod and pulled each of the shrouds down, letting the cloth rest at the foot of the wooden plank. She pointed to the first woman. "That's Larissa Ardelean. The attack on her was especially vicious."

Devlin stared at Bria. "Any theories as to why?"

Bria shook her head and turned away. He waited, hoping she would add more. When she didn't, he pulled a pin light from his bag and studied the woman more closely.

Underneath the stench of death, the smell of jasmine wafted off her clean skin, mixing with a plethora of floral scents.

"Was it difficult to move the bodies?" Devlin asked.

Bria gave him a confused look. "Yes," she said slowly. "Why?"

"Trying to estimate the time of death."

He studied the skin and lifted the woman's arm. "The relaxed muscles say she died within the last twenty-four hours, yet the cold conditions would have slowed the body decomp down," Devlin said more to himself. He would have questioned Bria further but wanted to assess everything first. Besides, he'd rather ask Petronela the tough questions.

He shone light on the wound on Larissa's neck. The cut wasn't in a straight line. Or rather, a clean slice. It had various starts and stops. The entry point was wider, moving into a shallower line and then stopping. As if the person had jammed the knife in then dragged it across the woman's neck, inadvertently removing the knife at the same time.

He moved his attention to the woman's hands and found shallow cuts along her fingers and wrists. She'd put up a fight. The neck wound would have killed her instantly, yet the killer had also stabbed her repeatedly, leaving both deep and shallow cuts all over her torso in what looked like a frenzied attack.

He glanced at the man on the next pyre.

"How were the men killed?" he asked.

"Hemlock."

It was clear from Larissa's wounds that she'd fought, which would have created a spike in her adrenaline, not to mention given her muscle fatigue. He'd had a crash course in forensics when he was working as a detective in Los Angeles. The process of dying started with the depletion of ATP, or adenosine triphosphate. It was what led to the stiffening of the body during the first twelve hours after death. But a few things could impact that. One being muscle fatigue. The other, drugs.

So, if the men were killed using a drug, that would have sped up the rigor process. When they were killed would give them the biggest clue as to who was responsible.

He looked at Bria. "I would think the men were a greater threat than the women. Yet..." He stepped away and examined the rest of the bodies and found the stab wounds on the other woman, but, as Bria had said, they were less severe. That was interesting too. It could mean that Larissa was the main target, or it could mean she was more skilled in her attempts to ward off the attack. But what about the men? Could they have died first?

Damnit. Why did they have to move the bodies?

Devlin pulled his phone from his pocket. "Can I take pictures of them?" he asked.

She nodded consent, and he snapped a few pictures. Repeating the process with the remaining bodies.

"What are you looking for?" Bria asked.

Devlin stepped back and stared at her. "You can tell a lot about a perpetrator by analyzing how they attacked their victim." He pulled up the picture of the wound on his phone. "See here," he said, blowing up the picture. "There are hesitation marks all along this cut. Like someone stopped and started in the process." He paused, studying the image. "Could mean lack of skill. Or remorse. Or it could be that Larissa was able to block the worst of it." He slipped his phone back into his pocket. "Either way, this was personal. The person who killed her was full of enough rage to overcome her."

He glanced at Bria. "All of you are mind mages?"

"Most of us, yes. But we have a few earth and faith practitioners."

Devlin nodded. "Then my question is how no one knew this was happening? It would have been loud."

"That is a fair question." She pointed at the trailers. "We are far enough away from each other that sounds can be muffled. Include the noise from the carnival, and it would be almost impossible for anyone to hear anything. And unless a person is actively looking for a threat, no one would have known." She paused. "Has Alexandros not told you how mind magick works?"

"I know he can see impressions or images of people."

Bria nodded. "He has a lot of control with that. Auntie believes it's because of what his family did to him. He had to hone those skills to better protect himself. Sometimes the enemy can wear a false smile."

Devlin shuddered at the similarities in what he and Alek had endured.

"Because of this," Bria continued, "he is constantly expelling magick." She grinned. "He told us about the coffee Rachel makes for him. Such a sisterly thing to do."

Devlin gave her a half-smile. "Yes, they both use magick constantly. And 'sister' is the best description for what Rachel is to all of us."

"Because of our work at the carnival, we all expel magick continually. It's draining. But the Houses of Power help us." She stared at the fire; her green eyes shone with an inner light. "While some of us see the emotions. Others see glimpses of future events. But that is mostly Auntie. Mind magick mostly works to infiltrate the mind of others. It's a ..." She paused, thinking. "It's an active form of control. That is where the true strength lies." She pointed at the people on the altars. "The only one with mind magick was Larissa."

Devlin thought about that for a minute. About the frenzied way in which they had killed her. Had she been trying to infiltrate her attacker's mind? "Is there a schedule posted daily? A set routine?"

"Yes."

What about the guards? Would they have access to this area?" he asked, ordering the timeline in his head.

Bria's eyes rounded. "Yes. They all do. Dimitri even had a trailer here." She looked away. "I thought it strange that he quit the other day."

"Dimitri was a guard?"

"Yes."

"Was he friendly with the girls?"

Bria scowled. "Too friendly."

Devlin looked around. "Is there only one entrance to this area?"

Bria shook her head. "It can be reached from Petronela's... office."

He'd seen what they considered her *office*, and the word didn't fit. It resembled an area of worship or congregation, with its abundance of artifacts and the red couch with plush gold pillows that looked a lot like a throne.

Devlin pointed to the edge of the property behind the dark blue House of Power. "Can someone use a boat to access the area?"

Bria furrowed her brow. "They haven't before," she said carefully.

"I'd like to take a look."

She nodded. "Of course." She started forward only to stop suddenly. "Dimitri had the trailer near the water," she said as if she were talking to herself. "We gave it to Rae." She turned and looked at him. "He asked if he could move there."

Devlin watched the realization creep into her eyes. If Dimitri had asked for that trailer, it meant he could have been planning this for some time. That is, if he were truly involved.

While he didn't want to jump to conclusions, he also couldn't ignore the obvious.

Dimitri's abrupt departure suggested he was either to blame or figured he might be. Which, in a way, also spoke to a guilty conscience. Living among so many with the ability to, as Bria said, get impressions of thoughts or intentions would have left him exposed to whatever he was trying to hide.

Devlin and his team would have to hunt him down to find those answers. And hope they led to the missing girls and the mystery of their parents' murder.

Agony in the Stony Places

Devlin followed Bria around the bustle of activity. No one stopped them as they walked, which was a good thing, because it allowed him the time to concentrate on what he'd noticed about the bodies. The savagery done to Larissa Ardelean meant something about her was important. Could she have been the main target? Were the others just collateral damage?

While it really didn't matter who had died first, the question still plagued him. This vital piece of information would have helped him understand the motive behind the killings and the kidnappings. He was still getting hung up on the latter. Why kill the parents and take the girls? Had the parents tried to get in the way? That brought him back to deaths. Both fathers were poisoned, and the mothers stabbed. He'd think the men posed the bigger threat. And the deaths felt... personal. Especially Larrisa's.

Mid-thought, a wave of power washed over him. Devlin stopped, his attention drawn to the dark blue House of Power. His body jerked, head thrown back as wave after wave of potent power rushed over him.

He took a step forward.

The sound of thunder boomed inside his head. Lightning cracked as if striking stone.

Another step.

An intricate circle with a ten-point star in the center with an equal number of colorful orbs surrounding the star moved inside the marble surface of the building. He placed his hand on the cool outer wall, and all the sounds around him fell away. He was transported to that storm.

He could hear rain pounding the earth, creating a melodious symphony. A cool breeze wound around his body, then settled in the center of his being.

Voices filled his head.

His breathing slowed.

And a power so primal and ancient burst out of him, setting the building ablaze with a blinding gold light. The scent of rain and ash overwhelmed his senses. His back arched the moment fire lit up his veins. Warmth, but no pain, coursed through him, and he couldn't pull himself away from the all-consuming power. He didn't want to, either. A crescendo of bells ringing and wings flapping sounded alongside deeper, somber notes, all joining the steady rhythm of the storm. Bursts of light heated his eyelids. Elemental magick came to life, showing him all the threads that made up its existence.

"Devlin!" a woman called, her voice familiar and wrong. She did not belong on this plane of existence. He tried to shove that voice away. But she kept calling. Something slithered around in his mind. Pushing at his senses.

"Devlin!" she shouted, her voice like a wave in the storm.

But still the bells rang on.

"Stop!"

He turned toward that familiar voice, his eyes burning with the steady flow of power.

Bria.

Outlined in a blinding white-gold.

Two others moved toward him, arms outstretched. They meant nothing. He turned away and greedily pulled the energy to him, devouring its force. Adrenaline rushed through his body.

"More!" he yelled. His power had never responded in this way before. It was as if he had become one with its ancient power.

Someone knocked him to the ground. His knees bit into the hard earth, sending a shock wave of pain up his thighs. He fell forward and lay there while the world spun around him. Finally, when the dizziness subsided, he turned onto his back and lay there, eyes closed, waiting for normalcy to return.

A hand lay across his chest. The scent of spice and vanilla engulfed him. He smiled and opened eyes.

Bria knelt beside him, hand on his chest, her long, dark hair forming a shield around him. "You are the second person to react to the House of Power today. Alek's Nicole did as well. I know of her lineage. But now I am doubly curious about yours."

"My mother wished me to be immortal," he slurred, trying to ease up. Why had he told her that?

"Careful, you don't look too steady," she said, gently urging him back down. "Immortal, huh?" She smiled. "Was she a loving mother?"

He closed his eyes, not wanting to answer her question. Saying no seemed ... cruel. He didn't know how his mother felt about him outside of her desire for him to live forever. Most of the time, she remained in a manic state. Never showing an ounce of love or affection. But there had to have been some at one point, right?

"I couldn't resist its pull." He filled the sudden silence while, internally, he attempted to work out what had just happened to him. "I heard the elements. Felt them all over me." His tone had a pleading note in it that unnerved him. It was almost as if he'd become addicted to the sudden rush of power.

Bria stood. He opened his eyes and stared up at her. The stars seemed to frame her entire being. Was it the residual influx of magick making him see her this way? When he didn't immediately take her hand, she knelt and studied his face. "Should I call Auntie?"

He shook his head; the movement sent a wave of pain down

his spine. He bit down on it and sat up. She helped him stand on shaky legs. Devlin glanced at the building. It seemed so innocuous. How could the small structure hold so much energy?

He moved toward it. Once again feeling the pull deep in his being.

"Best if you not get too close again," Bria said with a warning note in her tone.

Devlin nodded. She was right. The earlier euphoria was wearing off, leaving him in a state of agony. Yes, the pull had been intoxicating. But the aftereffect was not.

He looked at the crowd. Some still watched him, while others went about their work as if nothing had happened. "Did they feel it? Hear it?" It had been loud in his own hearing. Like he'd been in the eye of a storm, engulfed in a haunting melody. He half expected there to be damage all around him.

Bria shook her head. "The power surge was felt. But no one heard anything."

He looked at her. "Was it the same for Nicole?"

"I was only told she reacted to it. I didn't see for myself."

He stood there, mind filled with questions he knew Bria could not answer. His focus had been thrown, order lost. Bria touched his arm. He glanced at her.

"Devlin," she prompted. "Did you still want to investigate the area near the water?"

He mutely nodded and let her guide him the rest of the way while he attempted to once again stifle the chaos brewing inside his head.

T he area had come alive since Alek and I had been in the Ardelean trailer. I pulled in the scents of cooked meat and spices, letting the smell settle over me. My mind continued to race. Demanding. I scratched at my arm, relieving a sudden itchy sensation as we made our way toward the Kotzur trailer. I should've been reviewing the photos Cristian had taken of the scene before we went inside, but my attention went to the surrounding bustle.

Orange, yellow, and red flames danced in the fire pit, their tendrils reaching for the sky. I spotted Devlin and Bria walking toward the water. He seemed determined. No. Agitated. I wondered if I should go and check on him, then thought better of it. We had a job to do, and he could take care of himself.

Long wooden tables stretched out in front of the House of Power for earth magick, piled with varying fruits, vegetables, and meats. Women arranged the food while others brought heavy-laden trays out of the building. Rae worked among them, seeming lost. She glanced up as we passed, a question in her eyes.

I tapped Alek on the shoulder. "I think Rae wants to help us."

He turned and looked at her, giving her a smile. He shook his head and continued walking. "It's better if she stays away from this."

"She grew up in Greenwood Apartments," I said. "Violence and death are a way of life there."

He nodded. "True. But I still want to keep her out of it if I can."

I smiled at the protective note in his voice. Seemed Alek had fashioned himself as a sort of big brother. Which was a little strange seeing as he was responsible for the death of Rae's actual brother. Maybe he was trying to make up for it.

The Kotzur trailer sat to the right of the House of Power, directly across from the Ardelean trailer. I paused, visually tracing their positions. Once again trying to insert clues into what I was seeing. Logan's accusations about me missing signs right in front of me had really messed me up. I had to get over this. Or I'd drive myself crazy with worry.

Even so, I took a picture of the correlation between the two and walked the last few steps to the trailer, where Alek and Cristian waited. Despite my awareness I might be reading too much into coincidences, I was willing to suffer a bit of mortification when we went over the leads we'd uncovered back at headquarters. I'd be sure I left no stone unturned.

At least, that's how I hoped the team would interpret my effort, not as some raving lunatic latching onto wild conspiracy theories.

The Kotzur trailer was massive. Cristian unlocked the door and stepped aside, letting us go inside first. The droll of the air-conditioning unit greeted us, along with the familiar, coppery, musty scent. It wasn't as overpowering as it had been in the other trailer.

Something, besides an overall larger space, seemed ... different here. Yes, the décor and color scheme differed—the Kotzurs had chosen more greens and yellows and light wood—but something else was off. It was as if I'd walked into a void. Like no life had ever existed in this place.

I turned to Cristian. "Why did the Kotzurs have a bigger trailer?"

"They had two other children." He winced, his mouth

turning down, then added, "Who died last year. Twin boys. They fell asleep and never woke up."

"How old were they?" I asked, wondering if this had been a case of instant death syndrome.

"Ten."

"They were so young," I said.

I studied the place, trying to decipher what I was feeling. Grief had somehow taken on weight, settling inside the trailer and snuffing out all life.

I couldn't imagine what it was like to lose a child. Some parents never recovered.

"Had their space always looked like this?" I asked.

He raised an eyebrow in question.

"Might help if you tell us what you're seeing, Nicole," Alek said, gaze going around the living area.

I sighed, ordering my thoughts. "The place feels lifeless."

Alek and Cristian nodded.

I ran my teeth over my top lip and moved farther into the living room, then pulled the photographs from my pocket. I shuffled through them, looking at the ones Cristian had taken of this place.

At first glance, the crime scenes looked familiar: tea set out on the table, father slumped in a chair, and mother lying on the bed. Only here, the mad frenzy wasn't as apparent. Yes, the mother, Florin, had been stabbed, but not repeatedly. A single slash across her neck and a wound on her right arm was all that had been inflicted. But I still wondered why they would physically attack the women and not the men. "What kind of power did they have?" I asked, studying the pot of tea. Hemlock again.

"Petre was an elemental mage, and Florin was a faith mage."

I halted my search as what he'd said finally sank in. I'd been so caught up in the horror of the last scene, I hadn't readily processed the significance that all four victims were not mind mages. I looked at Alek. "Do all the clans have different magick affinities?"

He nodded. "The Kotzurs were known for having elemental powers, and the Ardeleans practiced earth. Their wives also came from different clans."

I bit the inside of my mouth. This had to be important. I just couldn't figure out how. Why the two distinct types of death? All the people involved had a connection to Tribe. I shook my head and started toward the back. "I will take the bedrooms again," I called over my shoulder.

A pair of bunk beds had been situated against the far wall in the first bedroom. Dark gray walls and navy-blue accents decorated the space, along with posters of cartoon characters and a toy box. A photograph of two smiling, dark-haired boys filled a silver picture frame sitting on a desk near the window. The space reminded me of a museum.

While it wasn't necessary to our current investigation to search the boys' room, I couldn't stop wondering if their deaths were part of what was going on now. Cristian said they had died in their sleep. So how had their deaths been explained? Hemlock had been used to kill the children's father. Could the twins also have been killed with the deadly substance? And if so, why?

I made a mental note to ask, took a few pictures of the room, and then moved on to the next.

Farther down the hall, the main bedroom sat across from a tiny bathroom. The layout of the bedroom was comparable to the other trailer, only this one had bedside tables on both sides of the bed. A smaller pool of blood had soaked the center of the mattress. I yanked the pictures from my pocket and sifted through them.

Florin's body had been found directly in the middle of the bed, limbs splayed out like a star. Why? A ritual? I shook my head and stepped farther into the room.

Much like the living room, the space felt lifeless. I had always pictured grief as messy. Not the emotion, but the impact of the pain on everything around you. Like being unable to maintain one's appearance or living environment. Yet this place was so orderly, it bordered on obsessive. Maybe that *was* a reaction to the loss as well.

A torn piece of paper, stuck between the bed and the cabinet, jumped out at me. It screamed chaos and didn't belong in this soulless space. I pulled it free and stared at the messy handwriting.

I will love you always, Florin. Just trust me and we can ... The rest of the letter had been torn. Was this a love letter from her husband? Had she torn it? I combed through the rest of the room, looking for missing pieces, but came up with nothing.

Standing with my hands on my hips, I looked over the space slowly, taking everything in: a bed, dresser, and single chair; clothes neatly hung in the closet by color scheme; an open jewelry box with only two pairs of earrings and a necklace inside. I went over to the cabinet just as Alek came into the room.

He stood at the entrance and looked around the room. "The bathroom is similar. No sign of anyone really living here."

I opened the first cabinet and found a single box. "It's eerie." I opened the box. Someone had crammed stacks of photos inside. I handed Alek the box and started on the next cabinet. "It's surely a reaction to their boys' death. Like they just gave up and went about life on autopilot. Depriving themselves of any type of joy."

The next cabinet was empty. I turned and looked at Alek. "It's more than that, though. This place just feels off."

He nodded and flipped through the box of pictures. "You want to do the daughter's room?" he asked.

I walked over and stood in front of him, gazing into his eyes. "You okay?"

He gave me a half smile. "I just wish..." He sighed as he set the box on the bed and pulled me toward him. His heart beat steadily, the rhythm soothing in my ear. "I should have been here to stop this," he added.

I stepped back and glanced up at him. "You're sounding like Boss Man now. How could you have stopped this?"

He shook his head. "I'm part of this family. At least, I'm supposed to be. But I fought coming here for so long. Letting my own parents paint an awful picture of my auntie." He closed his eyes. "She'd wanted to help me with my magick when I was a child. If I had been here…"

"You could have stopped four murders?" I asked skeptically.

He smiled down at me, eyes filling with sadness. "Yeah. I think I could have."

"Then you should get yourself a superhero belt," I said and cupped his face in my hand. "Alek, your aunt is powerful, and even she couldn't stop what happened here. I don't doubt your skills. I've seen you fight and use your magick. But evil has a way of slithering into our lives unnoticed. It wears a pretty smile, lulling us into a state of ease. And then striking when we least expect it." I paused, letting my words sink in. "We will find the people responsible for what happened here."

"I thought we agreed the girls killed their parents," he said.

I nodded. "If they did, I doubt they worked alone. This kind of planning takes time, resources, and cunning." I smirked. "Teenagers aren't smart enough to pull something like this off."

He bent down and kissed me lightly on the lips. "Thank you," he whispered.

"For what?" I asked.

He grinned. "Taming me."

I shook my head and turned away. While the levity helped to lessen the heavy sadness saturating the room, I'd much rather finish our search and get the hell out of here.

"Let's finish," I said.

He stepped back, and I made my way down to the last bedroom. Part of me had expected to see the same manic outpouring I'd found in Nadia Ardelean's room. But what greeted me was more order. More absence. A teenager would have rebelled at this forced conformity. Yet, Sophia had allowed it to creep into her private space. Or had they always been like this? Again, I had no way to confirm any of my theories. The inability to confirm even one idea was driving me a little mad.

A footlocker sat at the foot of a single bed. The cream-colored walls were bare of any adornments. I opened the small closet and found a single black dress inside. Had she taken her clothes? She must have.

The footlocker contained a box of pictures and nothing else. I closed the lid and paused. I'd told Alek that evil was sneaky. It hid in plain sight. And struck when you least expected it.

Mind spinning with questions, I shoved the footlocker aside, exposing a hiding place. Sophia had cut a hole in the floor. I removed the carpet square and found deep gashes in the hardwood.

The hole, no more than two feet on all sides, was constructed using wood painted black. Magick symbols were drawn on the surface using a gold marker. Stacks of crumpled letters lay on the bottom, crammed in as if by force. I pulled out a stack of four red journals with the same magick symbols drawn on the exterior covers. I shoved them into my black bag, just realizing I should have used separate bags for each trailer's contents.

I pulled the letters out, smoothing the crinkled paper so I could stack them neatly. Someone had written "liar" across the page, almost covering the words underneath. It seemed to be the same handwriting as the letter I'd found in her parents' room. These letters were addressed to Florin also, yet the writer didn't sign their name.

A commotion out front drew my attention, stopping any further examination of the missives. I set the letters in the bag and got to my feet. Alek walked into the room.

"Devlin's here," he said.

I ran my teeth over my top lip and handed him the bag. "We should probably separate the contents," I offered.

"Yeah." He stepped to the side, and we went out to meet Devlin, my mind filled with questions. The most important being: Who had written those letters to Florin, and why did her daughter have them?

The Cry of Gulls

Devlin stopped at the edge of the settlement, where patches of grass met sand. On the right, a timber wall had been built. It curved toward two buildings and blocked the way to Tulare River. On the left, iron gates encased the carnival. The Ferris wheel, a dark monolith, creaked in the breeze. Its sound was an eerie backdrop to the night sky.

But it was the black water that drew Devlin's attention. Normally, he would pull some droplets to him, letting the raw power in the element recharge him. Although now, he hesitated. Contact with the House of Power had left him ... full. As if an anvil had settled inside of him, grounding him in place. He stared at the current, tiny waves dancing across the surface.

He'd always been attuned to his source of magick. Feeling the cells within the elements gave him comfort and made him feel ... powerful ... connected. His senses were still overloaded, creating an even deeper bond with the sand beneath his feet—regardless of the soles on his boots—the air and its multitude of particles and smells, and the fire crackling in the center of the settlement. All the elements reached for him. But none so much as the large body of water. Its rhythm seemed to flow against itself. As if it were fighting off a disease.

Some bodies of water were like that. Most due to heavy contaminants and debris. But here, it seemed more pronounced—his awareness of it sent tiny pricks across his bare skin. It reminded him of the coffee Rachel made with a concentration of her healing power woven into the ingredients. It gave them not only fuel but a boost in power. Creating a sort of heightened sensitivity to their magick.

He shook his head and blew out a frustrated breath. He really needed to work off some of this energy. Otherwise, he wouldn't be able to do his job effectively.

"You still look a little off," Bria said. "Maybe you should rest for a while."

He turned to her. "No. Just getting my bearings." He turned away from the water and got to work.

After retrieving the penlight from his back pocket, Devlin crouched to study the patterns of footprints leading to the water. "I take it everyone spends some time in this area either laying out in the sun or swimming," he said, following the many impressions in the sand.

"Yes. Mostly the teenagers."

Devlin glanced up at her. "How many teens do you have?"

"Ten. Including Sophia and Nadia."

"What about the other two missing girls, Ileana and Daniella?" he asked, standing. The departure of the two girls Alek had met a few days ago when he'd come to see his aunt about a job in tracking down a man associated with Tribe and the kidnapping of these two girls was too much of a coincidence for him to ignore.

Bria's lips thinned; her eyes filled with unmasked fury. "They left on their own," she bit out.

"Did they mingle with the others?"

She laughed. "Mingle?"

"Hang around," he said, chuckling at his use of such a grown-up word for a group of teenagers.

"No, they liked to believe they were above everyone else. Rebelled against anything and everything." She stopped suddenly, looking back over her shoulder at the encampment. "But most of their fury was directed at Auntie." She rubbed her arms as if she were warding off an unpleasant thought.

"What about their parents? Did they have a problem with Petronela?"

Bria met his gaze. "They don't share their daughters' feelings toward Auntie," she said. He could hear a "but" in her tone.

"But?" he asked, prompting her.

She gave him an amused grin. "They are concerned, like many, that Auntie is losing her power. She seems... weaker." She shook her head. "Softer."

He thought about that for a minute. He didn't believe Petronela was weak. At least, her reputation would not suggest as much. But that was the thing. Reputations were often built on the embellishments of truth. And all the revered had to do was sit back and allow these tales to continue to be told. Then a generation of people filled with cynicism and doubt come along who test theories and find weakness where there was supposed to be strength. Could that be what was happening here? Or had she truly grown softer as she... aged? "How old is Petronela?"

Bria shrugged. "No one knows." She said this not in anger but in wonder. As if the answer could somehow solve a riddle that had plagued her for some time. Bria's reverence of her aunt seemed to have many layers. Sometimes, he heard love in the way she said "Auntie." Other times, fear and confusion.

"So, if they didn't hang out with the other teens," Devlin continued, "then they wouldn't have influenced the other two girls to leave." He hesitated a beat. "I'm trying to see the connection. Your aunt suggested there might be one to Alek. And why the mention of Tribe?"

A puzzled look crossed Bria's face. He probably should have given her the opportunity to answer one question at a time. "Daniella and Ileana often talked about Tribe," she said finally. "But we believed it was to goad Auntie. And I doubt they would have invited Nadia or Sophia to join them. The girls fought constantly."

"What about the Peterson's School for Troubled Girls, did any of them express an interest in going?"

Bria nodded. "Yes. Nadia and Sophia did."

That might explain the symbol drawn on the note left behind by the killer. Implicating the school because the girls wished to attend. But it didn't explain the reasons for mentioning Tribe. They were missing something.

"This area is not secure. It can serve as an entry point and an exit," Devlin said.

She sighed. "We never believed anyone would dare, but now …" She trailed off, gaze on the water.

"Some automatic lights and cameras would be beneficial." Devlin walked farther out onto the sand, eyes roaming the ground. He doubted he'd find a clue. But he had to search anyway. "You said Rae has Dimitri's trailer now. Is she around?"

Bria nodded, and they started back toward the trailers. "She's there," Bria said, pointing toward a long table covered with food.

Devlin stared at the crowd. "Who would have been in this area last night when this happened?"

"Only one other person. But we've already talked with him."

"I will need to interview him myself."

"Of course," she said in a rush. But she didn't move. "It's hard."

Devlin didn't say anything. She obviously had something on her mind and was having a difficult time voicing it.

"It wasn't just Auntie's reputation we relied on," she said after a short while. "It was ours as well. All the power we have, and still, we were attacked. Our young stolen. And some of the powerful among us taken down without us even knowing." She wrapped her arms around herself. A breeze blew through the clearing, carrying the scent of spicy meat. Her hair lifted, once again creating a veil around her narrow face. "I don't know what you'll find." She closed her eyes, teeth grazing across her bottom lip.

"But something ... a small part of me worries the enemy is closer than we know." She opened her eyes and looked at him, seemingly willing him to understand.

Devlin touched her arm. The simplest of contact. She smiled. "Most of the time, that is the case." He stepped closer. "But we will find them." He stared at her, letting her see the determination in his eyes. They would find them. That much he knew.

"Thank you," she said, giving him the barest hint of a smile. "I will let Auntie know you need to speak with him."

Once they parted, Devlin made his way toward Rae. A few whispers reached his ears, but he ignored them. They were probably still curious as to why he had reacted to the House of Power in such a strange way. But no one dared ask. A small part of him wished they would. Then he could ask questions of his own about those strange buildings.

Rae glanced up at his approach, then quickly looked away. It was almost as if she had been keeping an eye on him and got caught doing so.

He chuckled and closed the short distance between them. "Rae," he said. "How are you?"

She looked up at him. "Okay. Just trying to help."

Devlin nodded. "Well, how about you help me out as well?"

"Sure. Sure," she said, bobbing her head up and down. "How much you payin'?" she asked and then shook her head. "No. Never mind. Don't need you to pay me."

Devlin pulled out his wallet and handed her a twenty. "You *will* need money. So, think of this as a fee for your help." He pointed toward her trailer. "Was the trailer empty when you set up inside?"

She looked over at her new home. "No ..." She hesitated. "Dude left some random stuff laying around. I put them in a box and was going to give them to Ms. Petronela."

"Mind showing me?"

"Not at all." She led the way, her steps quick as she weaved around the people. A few made eye contact, smiling at Rae and him—with a hint of curiosity in their eyes.

When they arrived at the small trailer, she turned to him. "You know, they all whispering about you and Nicole. Sayin somethin' about power and those Houses."

"The Houses of Power."

She nodded. "What happened?"

Devlin rubbed the back of his neck. His hair was longer than he'd usually keep it, and it constantly grazed the nape of his neck. He really needed a haircut. "I wish I knew," he said. "Were you nearby?" he asked hesitantly.

She bobbed her head up and down slowly. "You was all lit up. Just like Nicole was."

Interesting.

Rae pulled a key from her pocket and opened the door. "Come on in," she said, moving so that he could enter.

He stepped into the space and glanced around. The place was tiny but efficiently designed. It must have been one of the units used for a single person. Did they have a steady flow of people moving in and out of the area?

"The stuff is right there," Rae said, pointing to a soiled brown box sitting on the table next to the kitchen.

Devlin walked over and flipped open the lid. "Was the stuff scattered or all in one place?"

"Scattered. Like he packed in a hurry," she offered.

Devlin glanced at her. Observant. "Mind if I look around a little?"

She shook her head. "Not at all." She moved around him and picked up a backpack near the refrigerator. "Found this too."

Devlin took it from her. "Where?"

She thumbed over her shoulder. "Shoved in the corner by the bed."

Devlin walked down a short hallway and looked inside the small bedroom. "Is the bedding new?" he asked Rae.

"Yeah."

So he took the bedding but left other personal items behind? Strange. Unless someone else removed the old sheets.

Devlin went back to the box and peered inside. Odds and ends, he noted. Things people wouldn't deem important if they were in a hurry.

He pulled a folded-up map of the carnival from the box and laid it on the table. Several routes leading from this trailer to the three exit points had been highlighted. Scribbled notes with times next to them marred the surface. All three areas had red tracings leading to some of the attractions. Devlin sat down on the bench seat and traced one of the routes with his finger. It went from the funhouse to the guard station leading to the back. A row of times all falling on the half hour had been written and crossed out.

He sat back, puzzled. None of the routes led to the water. But Devlin was almost positive that was the way the girls had been taken or escaped. He couldn't decide which. And without enough evidence, he wasn't ready to make that call.

He would have to study it more with the team.

The remaining contents in the box included a schedule for the employees, a key card, a medallion with an infinity symbol inside a pyramid, and a copy of *Naqada* by Professor Shukuma.

He flipped through the pages of the familiar book. This was his second encounter with this text since he'd been on Tulare Island. It'd been a clue in the last case. Strange how the professor's book kept showing up.

He opened the backpack. It was stuffed with empty plastic bags, a roll of tape, several black sharpies, and a scale. Drugs? Devlin stood up and shoved the backpack into the box. "I'll take care of this for you," he told Rae. He hesitated, then added, "Any clothes left behind?"

She snapped her finger and dug inside the trash. "I should have put this stained shirt in there as well, but I thought he might have used it to clean." She stuffed the dark, soiled shirt into the box.

They stepped out into the warm night air. He turned to find

Bria striding their way. Her gaze went to the box in his hand. "What's that?" she asked, stopping in front of him.

"Dimitri left these items behind. I want to take them with me to study more closely."

Bria's eyes widened. "So you do believe he is responsible?"

"Timing fits. And leaving like he did is suspicious." Devlin set the box on the ground and pulled out the backpack. "Rae found this inside shoved in a corner near the bed. The items inside suggest he might have been dealing drugs."

Alarm crossed her face. "To the teenagers?"

Devlin shrugged. "Or the carnival guests."

Her lips thinned in anger.

"I won't know for sure until I ask him," Devlin said. "Do you know if he has any other family on the island? Maybe an alternate address?"

She shook her head slowly. "I can ask around. But from what I understand, he came straight here when he arrived on Tulare."

Devlin picked up the box and shifted it to his hip, then looked at Rae. "Need your help again. You game?"

Rae nodded.

"You have a phone?"

She pulled one from the back pocket of her jeans.

He turned to Bria. "I want her to take pictures of the entire area and down by the water. Is that okay?"

Bria looked at Rae. "Ask permission before you take pictures of anyone or their personal space. Everything else is fine."

"All right," Rae said. "What am I looking for?"

"Just capture it all."

She nodded slowly, then started off.

"Is it a good idea for her to work with you all?" Bria asked, watching the girl.

"She has before," Devlin said.

Bria stared at him. "When?"

"When we were attacked in Greenwood Apartments." Devlin

chuckled. "She took a man twice her size down using cunning and a switchblade."

Bria smiled. "Damn," she said in an appreciative tone. "I like her. She'll fit in nicely."

"Do you know why Petronela wanted Alek to bring her here?" Devlin asked.

"I'd have to say it was because of her magick."

Devlin lifted an eyebrow in question.

"You can't see it. But her power fluctuates. That is rare." She turned to him. "Auntie is waiting."

They started out. "Alek and Nicole are in there," Bria said, pointing behind them at a large trailer south of the House of Power for earth magick.

He wanted to touch base with them, but he also wanted to get the interviews over with. Another thought niggled his mind.

He stopped. "Can you arrange for Alek and Nicole to talk with the witness?"

Bria stared, eyes narrowing slightly. "Yes. Is there a problem?"

Devlin shook his head. "No. I would like to speak with Petronela ... alone."

She glanced behind her as if searching for an answer. After a short pause, she agreed. "I can have them meet in the employee lounge."

"Thanks," he said. "I'll check in with them first."

They backtracked to the trailer Alek and Nicole were searching and went inside. Cristian stood just inside the door.

"Devlin," Cristian said, extending his hand.

Devlin shook it and glanced around. "Whose trailer is this?"

"The Kotzur family. They've already searched the Ardeleans'."

Devlin nodded, moving farther into the room, noting the absence of any real indications that people thrived in the neatly ordered space. He sat the box on the nearest chair and pulled his phone out and called Rachel.

"Rach," he said when she answered. "Report."

"Jonah and Kara have checked into the Brentworth Hotel and said Candace was helpful. I contacted Opal to let her know they are using aliases. Don't know if it's needed, Dev. Everybody knows who they are."

"Yes, but where they are staying needs to be kept secret."

"Marta's here. She took the kids to Nicole's parents' house and will stay until the job is done."

"Okay, put her in Jonah's room." He paused. "I need you to dig up info on one Dimitri"—he looked at Cristian—"Vaduva?"

Cristian shook his head. "No, Costa."

Devlin repeated the last name to her. "Search for any connection to the properties we found for Tribe. Also, pull the social media for the missing girls. Go back..." He paused, thinking. "How long did Dimitri work here?" he asked Cristian and glanced over as Alek and Nicole walked into the room.

"A year," Cristian said, his gaze going hard. The man must have figured out the guard might have had something to do with the murders.

"Go back a year," Devlin told Rachel. "Have Marta do that." He rubbed his face, trying to think if he had missed anything. He hated feeling rushed.

"Okay, Dev," Rachel said.

He said goodbye and hung up. "I've checked the bodies and have Rae taking pictures of the area. I need you two to talk with the person who found the bodies and Daniella and Ileana's parents."

"You don't want to question them?" Alek asked.

"I'm meeting with Petronela."

They both stared at him for a moment. Waiting for him to elaborate. He'd tell them later, once they were back at the house.

"I want you to work on the timeline. If we can narrow down exactly who was in the area between—" He looked at Bria. "When was the last time you saw all of them?"

"At breakfast Saturday. We all gather to eat early."

"When does everyone leave for work?"

"At four. To get the attractions set up."

"So the area would have been cleared except for those who weren't working?"

She nodded.

"What time were they found?"

Bria didn't answer right away. "At ten this morning," she said softly, as if she were ashamed.

"You all didn't wonder why they didn't show up for breakfast?"

"They don't always join us," Cristian said.

Devlin nodded, thinking. "I need the work schedules for everyone. Since we won't have access after tonight, I also need to know the break schedules. Talk to anyone who would have been in the area between four..." He trailed off.

"What time do you return here after work?" he asked Cristian.

"At two in the morning."

"That's our timeline. Between four in the evening and two in the morning." Devlin sighed. While their deaths could have happened earlier, it was the best he could come up with without an autopsy to confirm a more exact time of death.

Talking to so many people would be a massive undertaking, and their time was limited.

He looked at Cristian. "Any way you can help with the interviews?"

Cristian nodded.

"I have a theory I want to work on," Nicole announced, hesitation in her voice.

"Run me through it," he said, leaning back.

Nicole told him about the twin boys whose deaths shockingly coincided with Dimitri's arrival.

"You think there's a connection?" he asked.

She hesitated. He hated that. Nicole was smart. She just needed to get out of her own way and not be afraid to say what was on her mind. Even if it was laced with sarcasm. Like this morning, when she told them to look in all the hidden places. Even in jest, she found answers to questions they should have been asking all along.

"Follow it," he said, and surprise briefly flitted across her face. "Remember. I told you. Trust your instincts."

She nodded, suppressing a smile.

"We can question the people who fit inside your timeline," Bria said.

"That would help." Devlin stood.

They all said their goodbyes, and Devlin and Bria stepped out of the trailer, then made their way to Petronela's place. They walked in silence. He needed time to think. He wanted to make sure they had all the information they needed to solve this. That meant truly understanding the motives behind the group calling themselves Tribe.

And the only person who could tell him that was Petronela.

Horizontal wooden boards made up a small, half-moon shaped wall running alongside the riverbank. Rising above it, bamboo trees swayed with a soft breeze. A salty scent tickled my nose and deposited grainy residue on my skin. I licked my suddenly dry lips, letting the briny deposits coat my tongue. I should have brought a bottle of water.

The beam from Cristian's flashlight danced across the seagrass and shells lining the narrow walkway toward the wall. The structure appeared solid, but then Cristian stuck his hand behind one beam and pulled a hidden lever. A grinding noise sounded as a doorway appeared, revealing another path lined with seashells.

"I take it everyone knows about the hidden entrance," I said, stepping onto the dark path.

Alek moved in behind me, followed by Cristian.

"Yes," he said. "But we are encouraged not to use it."

I turned and looked at him. "How are you encouraged?" I asked.

"With threats," he said, a half-smile on his lips.

"Seems the threats haven't been effective enough," I mumbled.

We continued down the short trail and came to a fork in the road. Located on the right was a building made from wood and painted orange with a dark brown roof. The structure was surrounded by bamboo plants and water lilies. That was where

Petronela lived. Or held court. I had noticed this building from the window of the employee lounge all those years ago and had even plotted ways in which I could sneak in. Never panned out, of course, but I used to wonder just what went on inside that secret place.

To the left was the employee building. It was a deeply uninspired dark brown edifice with a cream-colored roof and dark windows, an afterthought compared to the other structures at the carnival. Not that the Vaduva family didn't care for their non-family employees. I'd seen first-hand how well they treated them. Well, everyone but me, that is.

We headed toward that ugly structure—the sandy walkway eventually morphed into concrete—and stopped at a large red door with the words "Exit Only" stenciled on front. Cristian pulled a key from his pocket and opened the door. An alarm bleated at us; the sound pounded at my eardrums, threatening to deafen me. "I'd hazard a guess they didn't use this door for their escape."

Cristian raised an eyebrow in question. "Escape?"

I paused, thinking about my choice of phrase. They all believed the girls killed their parents. "Escape" implied they were being held against their will. "After they made their getaway," I offered.

He dipped his head and led us down a dimly lit corridor.

We stopped at the employee breakroom located across from the locker room and showers. Cristian stepped aside so we could enter. I fully expected the room to be industrial looking, but they'd updated the space to resemble a botanical garden, complete with a fountain in the corner.

Lush plants dotted every corner of the room, some even hanging from the ceiling. A rich, earthy scent gave weight to the slightly warmed area. Five long wooden tables were in individualized nooks around the room. Each nook boasted a different tropical theme, complete with ground seashells and moss grass.

A few platters of food had been set up on one table, and the coffeemaker sputtered the last of a percolating brew into the pot. I closed my eyes and inhaled, trying to pick apart the food scents wafting around the room. Definitely beef with lots of spices and the ambrosia of the gods: potatoes. A brief pang of sadness hit me; Jonah, who made the best potatoes, would be absent while he and Kara went off assassinating people.

Not only had my best friend chosen to go into a situation that would require her to use the skills she'd been trying to suppress almost half her life, but our highly skilled chef would not be in residence making those delicious meals that have added a few extra pounds to my waistline. More reasons for me to kill whoever was responsible for this mess, disrupting my peace.

My stomach guided me toward the table, and my feet obeyed. I grabbed a plate, completely forgetting that Alek and Cristian were there. Hell, I even forgot why we were there. My attention had been drawn to the juicy piece of roast, surrounded by baby potatoes glistening with herbs and butter, and the colorful veggies looking crisp and ready for consumption.

"Hungry?" Alek asked, sitting down next to me.

"Please, sir. Don't bother me for a while," I said as I piled my plate high.

They both laughed, and Cristian settled across from us, resting his chin on his fist.

"What's your read on the situation here?" Alek asked Cristian while he added food to his own plate.

Cristian sighed, picking up a baby potato and popping it into his mouth. After he swallowed, he said, "I don't think the true rot has been exposed yet. I've heard whispers and rumors about others being tired of Petronela's rule."

I paused, the fork halfway to my mouth. "You all treat this as if it's a monarchy."

He studied me for a minute, his gaze distant. "It could be viewed that way," he said finally. "All the clans that hold pieces of the great libraries are run this way. Only the Vaduva family have stopped traveling and settled. The rest continue moving." He glanced at Alek. "People have expressed the wish to leave Tulare. Yet Auntie forbids it. Says our power is needed here but doesn't explain why."

I shook my head. It was common for people in charge to do that. Expect people to follow blindly with no explanation.

"Do you really believe Tribe has come back?" Alek asked.

Cristian shook his head. "I can't say for sure. Leaving a note behind and not attacking seems ... off. But the signs are there. And we can't ignore them."

"Why not postpone the ceremony until you all know for sure?" I asked.

He huffed out a breath. "She won't listen." Sadness crept into his eyes. "I can admit, it is important we move forward and sing our people into the Soul Tapestry. But we can do that anytime. She is the one who created this ritual and its timeframe."

I wiped my hands and sighed. "Maybe we should start with the healer." I looked around. "Damn. I need a notebook to take notes."

Cristian got up. "I can grab one from the souvenir shop."

"I need a pen too," I called after him. The one day I decided not to lug my purse around was the day I needed it. Too worried about looking tough. "Maybe I should have left the dagger at home," I said.

Alek swallowed the last bite of his food. "I don't know"—his gaze roamed over my body—"I think you look fucking sexy as hell."

My entire body heated, eyes going round from the waves of lust rolling through me. My hormones, done up in battle paint, sent out a rallying cry, while my stomach turned into a butterfly theme park. I also may have needed to change my underwear. Oh, dear god! How did this man reduce me to a horny teenager so effectively?

Alek leaned in and kissed me behind my ear just as Cristian came back into the room with a novelty notebook and black glitter pen.

The urge to slide under the table was so intense, I had to physically restrain myself from doing so.

Cristian laughed and handed me the items. "I'll go get John for you." He started to walk away, then stopped. "Why are you so worried about the twins' deaths?"

I thought about it for a minute. Why was I? I didn't have enough information to actually form an opinion. Yet something about their deaths and the timing of it just felt... wrong.

"I don't know. Maybe the doctor can set my mind at ease."

"Healer," he corrected.

I nodded. "Yeah, him." I shrugged. He dipped his head and walked out.

Alek rested his arms on the table. "What are you thinking? Really?" he asked.

"I'm thinking someone killed those boys, and the only reason they'd do that is if they knew something or witnessed something." I turned and looked at him. "Am I paranoid?"

He shook his head. "No. Something caught your attention. And I trust you, babe."

I smiled. "Stop flirting with me."

He leaned in. "But I'm the cutest boy. I'm supposed to flirt."

I chuckled, then picked up the ridiculous pen and opened the notebook. Seriously? He couldn't find something a little less flashy? On a sigh, I wrote out my observations thus far. Trying to order my thoughts. We were missing something. But what?

After a short while, Cristian escorted an older couple into the room. Both similar in height, the man looked to be in his early fifties, a few years older than the woman. He gave us a hesitant smile as he strode forward. The woman had flame-red hair worn short, the ends curling to frame her face. She gazed at us out of suspicious eyes.

They both wore green robes with intricate gold embroidery down the front. An infinity knot rested on the left side, positioned over the heart. The woman's robe lacked some of the elaborate design.

The man helped the woman sit and turned his gaze to us. His eyes filled with unvoiced questions.

"John, you know Alexandros?" Cristian said.

The man agreed. "You're not staying, Alexandros?" he said, his accent thick.

Alek shook his head. "No. I have not practiced the old ways for some time."

John gave him a sad smile and turned to the woman sitting next to him. "This is my wife, Dawn."

Alek smiled. "Nice to meet you, Dawn. And this is Nicole."

John leaned back, his gaze steady on Alek. "The last I saw of you was when your mother brought you here. You were such a sad boy. All the light had gone out in your eyes."

Dawn placed a hand on her husband's arm. "John," she said with a faint Irish accent. "You shouldn't speak of these things now. They are investigating the deaths of our family." John turned to her. She placed a hand on his bearded cheek. "You will have time to reminisce with him."

"Alexandros is family, my love. Not ..." He bit off his last words, anger filling his face. "I apologize," he said, turning back to us. "I do not wish to weave the betrayers into our Soul Tapestry. They have their own ways. And should be sent to their own people to mourn them."

Cristian said something to him in Romanian. The man shouted his reply. Then Alek joined in.

Dawn looked over at me as the men argued. "So set in his ways, my husband."

I smiled. "Most men are." I studied her, curious why she didn't have the earth magick symbol on her robe. I let my gaze go distant, viewing the aura surrounding her. "You don't have magick?" I asked and shook my head. "Sorry, I shouldn't have asked that."

"No," she smiled. "It's fine." She leaned back, crossing her feet at the ankles. After sparing her husband another glance, she continued, "I met John at a holistic healer conference over ten years ago. I hated him at first sight." She laughed. "He was so full of himself. Strutting around like a damn peacock." She leaned in and whispered, "But boy was he a fecking fine one." She winked and smiled. "Eventually, hate turned to lust, and a few months later, we married." She stared at me. "But that is not what you wanted to ask."

The men's conversation had grown in volume and urgency. I stood up and signaled her to follow me, and we settled at a nearby table. "I trust your husband brought you here for a reason."

"Yes. Five years ago, he got a call that they needed a healer. So he decided to return." She lifted an eyebrow in question when I didn't respond, then gave a short laugh. "Silly me. I thought you were asking why he brought me to Tulare."

I smiled. "No. But it is a nice story."

She shook her head. "Cristian told him what you wanted to talk about. I am trained as a nurse and help out with the medical needs of the people." Her lips thinned, and she seemed deep in thought. "I was the one who examined the boys when they fell ill." She jerked her attention to me. "We don't have the modern instruments that hospitals have. They very much practice the old ways of healing and treatment. I would have liked to run blood-work on the boys when they were brought in."

"What was wrong with them?"

"According to their mother, they had gone out exploring as they usually did. Getting into all sorts of mischief. And, after being gone for a while, she searched for them. They eventually wandered back to the trailer, complaining of headaches and stomach pain. After dressing cuts on their hands, she brought them to us." She paused, her eyes tearing up.

"Given the wounds on their hands, I first believed it to be toxic shock. They had all the symptoms: red rashes on their bodies, low blood pressure, headaches, nausea. But it was the slowing of their heartbeats that dispelled that diagnosis. So, all I could do was treat the symptoms." She grabbed a napkin from the table and wiped her eyes. "They passed in their sleep a short time later." She grabbed my hands, squeezing. "We did everything we could," she said, as if pleading with me to believe her. Their deaths must have weighed heavily on her.

Slowly, she withdrew her frigid hand and sat back. The men had stopped arguing, the sudden silence deafening. I glanced over and found Alek and Cristian comforting John, who had his head down as if he'd expended too much energy.

I was at a loss for words. I'd wanted to go down this avenue of questioning, not even thinking about my lack of knowledge when it came to medical illnesses. What follow-up questions should I ask? I inwardly cursed myself.

What about their deaths bothered me the most? Timing. It kept coming back to timing.

"You said they often got up to mischief," I said finally. "Can you tell me a little about that?" It was a strange question, but I needed to get to the root of my concern.

She gave me a puzzled look, then wiped her nose. "Well. You know."

"They liked to snoop," her husband interjected. "Always where they shouldn't be."

"Who were their usual targets?" I asked.

Cristian chuckled. "Everybody."

"Was anyone a favorite of their torment?"

They all gave me confused looks and shook their heads. Damn. This was difficult. And definitely not like in the movies or television shows where the person who had the biggest grudge suddenly announced him or herself by cursing the boys' names.

I sighed and pushed the notebook toward Dawn. "Can you list all their symptoms and what you used to treat them, please?"

She rubbed her hands on her robe and picked up the pen. After giving her husband a quick glance, she scrawled down the information I needed.

Devlin had told me to chase this thread, yet I couldn't effectively do that. We would lose our access to everyone once the ceremony began. Which meant every single question that came after we left would not get answered.

Dawn slid the notebook back toward me and stood. "I hope to see you again soon. It would be nice for Alexandros to catch up with John. Maybe you two can join us one evening for dinner."

I smiled. "That would be nice." I glanced down at the neat lines of information she'd written. "I appreciate your help with this."

"Of course. Can't say I see the connection with the boys' deaths and what has happened today. I hope there isn't one. But if there is, you must tell me. I have gone many nights without sleep, worrying if I'd done enough to help them." She gave me a sad smile.

John put his arm around her waist. "Come, love. We must finish our part of the preparation." They walked away, John giving Alek a single nod as they left the room.

"Do you know everyone here?" I asked Alek.

"Most," he said, eyeing me.

I looked at Cristian. "If it's not too much trouble, can you write down the names of everyone here and their interaction with the boys?"

He sat next to me, pulling the notebook to him. "You really believe their deaths have something to do with what's going on now?" he asked, writing.

"Yes," I said truthfully.

His head jerked up, and he stared at me. "How could they be connected?"

I licked my suddenly dry lips. "Timing," I said. "Dimitri's arrival at the carnival and the boys' deaths coincide."

He furrowed his brow, pen posed above the paper. "We hired Dimitri a few weeks before they died."

"But you said yourself they harassed everyone. That, I assume, includes the guards."

He tapped the pen on the paper, then looked over his shoulder at Alek. "What do you think, cousin?"

"I think Nicole is on to something."

I might have preened a little at the praise.

Cristian finished writing down the information I asked for and led us out of the breakroom. My thoughts kept going back to the list of symptoms. A lot of toxins and poisons had similar reactions. I just needed to find the one that mirrored what Dawn had described.

THE WISDOM OF OWLS

A hidden doorway built into the timber wall parted, revealing an area cast in shadow. Muted light lined the seashell walkway leading to an orange building to the right of the fork in the road. Devlin followed Bria down the walkway, spending that quiet time ordering his thoughts. He had been in Petronela's domain a few days ago with Alek. Their impromptu visit had been an effort to try and figure out what game the old woman was playing.

During that meeting, she had shown a strange interest in him and his magick, hinting at his parentage and offering the use of the knowledge she guarded. Did she know he would react to the House of Power? Was that why she had been curious? Either way, it unnerved him. He had to make sure to keep the conversation focused on what was necessary. Despite his curiosity.

Bria stopped at a black door and turned to him. "I'm worried about my auntie. She's been ... ill." She stared at him as if she were trying to say something without words, willing him to understand.

"I don't plan on interrogating her," Devlin said. "Just need to understand some things about the past."

"She might not tell you."

"And you don't want me to push?"

Bria sighed, then acquiesced. "Yes. I know you need the information—" She stopped suddenly, head facing up, gaze distant. "They have arrived."

Alarm raced through him. "Who?" Devlin asked, looking around and letting his magick flow into him.

Bria smiled, pulling a key from her pocket. "You're quick. No need to worry. Auntie sent for the Dacian to keep people away during the ceremony. Their power is"—she pulled open the door; light spilled out onto the ground in front of them—"overwhelming."

Devlin followed her into the corridor and stopped in front of a red velvet curtain. "Dacian?"

Bria thought for a minute. "Like your Secret Service," she said. "They are battle mages who are hired to protect."

"She didn't want to use the guards she already has?" he asked.

Bria shook her head and stared up at him. Her eyes caught the light, creating a spark in their green depths. "She didn't say why they have been called. And the other guards have been sent away."

Devlin agreed, caught up in Bria's gaze. There was more to this woman than she let on. Secrets swam in those emerald eyes. He only wished he had the time to unearth them. He'd have to ask Alek about her later.

They stepped inside. A warm, sweet-smelling aroma circled the room, its vapor hanging in the air. Petronela lay on her red lounge chair, a gold pillow supporting her back. She held a long ivory pipe gripped in her strong fingers. Her wrinkles had settled into a serene mask, while her eyelids pulsated with activity. As if she were in the midst of a terrible dream.

"She's calling the souls of our ancestors," Bria said in a whisper.

Devlin clasped his hands in front of him and waited, letting his gaze travel around the room. Artifacts occupied glass cases in the four corners, each with glyphs etched into the surface. Wards?

Spells? Alek had told him Petronela had part of the Alexandria library. Yet, so far, he hadn't seen a building large enough to contain it. Unless the books were inside the Houses of Power.

"You are welcome to anything here, Devlin Grey," Petronela said, her voice a scratchy murmur. Bria rushed over to a long wooden table next to the entrance. A glass pitcher contained water with floating petals in a deep shade of blue. Next to the pitcher, a single cup.

After pouring, Bria brought the water to Petronela. The elder closed her eyes, drinking the entire thing in one long pull. Perspiration dotted her brow.

"You've told me that before," Devlin said, studying the ashen state of Petronela's complexion. "Are you well?"

Petronela smiled with a whine. "It takes a lot of power to call to the dead." She handed Bria the glass and sat back. "I learned how as a young woman. The souls of the dead always remain nearby. Thirsting for the memories we share of them. They gave all the first this ability."

Devlin raised an eyebrow in question. "Who are they? And what is a first?"

Petronela waved his question away. "You have come to ask me something else. Bria says you wanted to ask about Tribe."

"Yes," Devlin said.

Petronela's brown gaze bore into him. "I have told my people about this before. What happened then is not important."

Devlin shook his head. "I am not your people. And I disagree. Why else would Tribe leave that note on the bodies except to bring up the past?"

"Nothing more than misdirection." She looked away from him.

"I don't agree," he bit out, physically reigning in his anger. If not for the fact that she looked on the verge of collapse, and his word not to interrogate her, he would have called bullshit on the obvious lie she'd just told him.

Bria stepped forward, mouth open to protest, but Petronela silenced her with a look.

"Leave us," she told Bria, her hardened gaze on Devlin.

"Auntie," Bria started.

"Devlin and I have something to discuss." She turned to Bria. "And I need you to show the Dacian where to go. We will be fine for now."

Bria looked at Devlin. "Remember what I asked," she said. "And I will talk with the ones you wished to speak with as well." After one last look at the both of them, she left the room.

"Why do you keep your people in the dark?" Devlin asked, understanding the real reason she'd asked Bria to leave.

Petronela scoffed and gave him a half smile. "You are observant. This is good. Maybe you will figure this out and save me the trouble of killing so many." She waved her hand, silencing his reply. "Please." She signaled to the bench seat in front of a vanity table. "Sit next to me for a while. I don't care to keep looking up at you."

Devlin grabbed the bench, moving it next to her. "You don't strike me as the frilly type."

Petronela gave him a genuine smile. "In my past," she started, gaze going a little distant. "I used to sit at the bench and study every inch of my face."

"Looking for flaws?" Devlin asked, thinking of the way modern women put themselves down daily.

Petronela shook her head. "No. I wanted to memorize the details before I had to choose how I would present myself for the rest of my existence. I will not explain that now. But one day, I may have to. For now, I will tell you about Tribe."

She settled back and took a long pull on her pipe. Blowing the smoke out, she said, "Thirty years ago... no, I will start further back. I'm sure Alek told you about the Historian." She smiled. "You even met her, yes?"

Devlin nodded.

"She is a Goddess. Her and her brother created the whole of humanity."

Devlin had learned what Luisah was when he, Alek, and Nicole went to visit her a few days ago. In exchange for information on Divine Evil, she'd elicited an oath from them to return in ten days. Now he wondered just why she wanted them to come back.

"You don't look surprised by this," Petronela said.

"No. I'm not."

Petronela sighed. "Good. You will need her. I will skip forward, then." She stretched and took another pull on her pipe. The sweet aroma filled the room. "We Roma traveled with her thousands of years ago. Before humanity had saturated the earth. Poisoning it with evil. Our task was to keep the secrets of magick safe. To not allow this great power to be exploited."

"Before or after the creation of the Old Ones?" Devlin asked.

"After. That twisted blood magick ritual that created them should never have been performed. And because of this, because of the easy access to knowledge, it was deemed that the knowledge was too powerful to give away so freely. So, they divided it. Garnering an oath in blood that the secrets would remain forever hidden. Doled out only by the Historian, and even then, she would only give what was needed to overcome obstacles or challenges a person faced. A bargain would be struck, a tithe exchanged."

"How does this relate to Tribe?" Devlin asked.

"Fifteen of the clans who traveled and held pieces of the great libraries did not like my bargain with the Historian. Did not like what she had entrusted me with when I settled my family on this island. Envy is such an evil emotion. But it was more than that. They wished access to this knowledge."

"What did she give you?"

"The Song of Creation. The power that made all things. Including magick."

"You store that in the Houses of Power," he said.

She closed her eyes, leaning back. "Yes. I understand both you and Nicole reacted to the song."

"That's an understatement." He hesitated, then added, "Do you know why? Is that why you're so interested in my power?"

"No. I only wish for you to show more interest."

"Care to explain that," he bit out.

"In time." She opened her eyes and stared at him, daring him to push.

Devlin sighed. "You haven't told your people what's in those Houses, have you?"

"No. They believe the Houses helping to restore their magick is really a ward. Any attempt to remove the knowledge would result in the person or persons' death. The only way around this is if they kill me."

Devlin leaned in. "You are vulnerable. At any moment, someone here, the one you trust the most even, can rise up and take that power."

She gave him a sad smile, a single tear sliding down her cheek. "I knew this when I made my pact with the Historian. I believed the illusion of wisdom and age and a ferocious reputation would stay most hands from rising against me." She touched her face, running her finger down her wrinkled cheek. "I miss my face."

"So your reputation is... embellished?" He had already figured that out but still wanted to ask.

She smiled through her tears. "Yes. While I have no trouble killing when necessary to protect my people, my power is the same as most. Yes, I have had many years to hone my skills. But still, I am only human."

A knock sounded at the door before he could ask her what she meant.

"If we had more time, I could talk to you about your own power." She pointed to one of the glass cases in the corner of the room. "For now, take what little I can give."

Devlin got up and went over to it. The rectangular glass

encasement sat on a marble base. He stared at the jeweled mask inside.

"Push at the base," Petronela instructed.

He did so, and a lock clicked open, then a drawer slid out. Inside was a dark blue cylinder with the symbol he'd seen on the elemental House of Power.

"When magick was first created, the earth and elemental powers were combined. But the raw, wild magick was too much for humans. The magick during those early days had yet to be mastered and tamed. So, the gods split them in two. Now, elemental magick only holds a fraction of creation's song. Making the most dominant of the four principals faith. From nothing ... everything is born."

Devlin stared at her, suddenly recalling the parting words given to them by the Historian when Nicole asked how to kill an Old One. She'd said "with faith." At the time, he believed that meant literally believing in one's ability. Now, he wasn't so sure.

Curious, he tried to open the container.

"No," Petronela said in a rush, eyes wide. "Not here. Our ritual must begin soon, and you have a task to complete. Besides, you won't be able to read it just yet." She grew quiet. He glanced at her; her brown gaze locked with his. "You might even consider it a long overdue bedtime story."

"Bedtime story?" Devlin asked, giving her a skeptical look.

Another knock sounded. This one with more urgency.

"They may break down the door if we do not open it." Petronela chuckled and expertly avoided answering his question.

Devlin didn't move. He didn't care who was outside. He wanted answers.

"Now is not the time," she said firmly. She pulled a bag out from the drawer near her couch. "Put that inside here."

After Devlin put the cylinder in the bag, he went and let in a man standing outside. "Bria says you might need to speak with me," the man said, eyeing Devlin with suspicion. He wore an orange robe with the Eye of Horus, the symbol for mind magick, etched on the front.

"Didn't she question you?" Devlin asked. Curious as to why she sent the man when she had said she would question the people for him.

"Yes. But she also said you had questions as well."

Odd. He stepped back, and the man hustled inside and marched straight to Petronela's room.

Devlin reentered the room and found Petronela had returned the bench to the vanity table and rearranged herself in the same position he had left her in.

The man greeted Petronela. "Bria asked me to tell you the Dacian have taken up position in the prearranged formation." He glanced at Devlin. "Will the ritual begin soon?"

Petronela dipped her head toward Devlin. "You will answer his questions first."

"Of course, Auntie." The man crossed his arms over his chest and spared Devlin a brief glance. Devlin understood the body language. The man didn't want to be here.

"Were you working last night?" Devlin asked.

"I've already told Bria that I wasn't," he said, his tone flat.

Devlin sighed. He couldn't understand why Bria had sent this man to him. Unless she wanted to make sure he had kept his word and not harmed her aunt.

"Did you hear anything? See anything out of the ordinary?" Devlin asked.

The man shook his head. "I don't understand why this is necessary. You and your people have all—" He dropped to his knees.

A wave of power washed over him. Devlin jumped back before the man crushed him.

Petronela stood, strength seeming to flow into her. "Your guilt is screaming inside my head."

The man raised his hands, casting his eyes to the floor. "Forgive me, Auntie."

She bent down, again showing a strength Devlin believed she didn't have. "What. Did. You. See?" The ice in her tone sent a chill running down his spine, his fight-or-flight response kicking in. Her reputation might have been embellished, but her strength and power could never be denied.

The man choked out a ragged breath, a sob wrenched from his lips. "I heard. Not saw. I heard."

"What did you hear?" Devlin asked, kneeling so that he could look at the man.

His gaze came up, and he stared at Devlin. "Just a cry. A single cry. But I didn't... I didn't check." He gritted his teeth. "I didn't want to."

"And why not?" Petronela asked. "They were family."

The man shook his head vehemently. "No. They were not."

"Did I not allow their families to stay." It wasn't a question. "Did I not instruct all my people to show them love." She grabbed his chin, forcing him to look at her. "Shall we weave your soul into the tapestry tonight as well." Again, she wasn't asking.

Tears flowed down the man's face. "Please, Auntie. Forgive me."

"I don't know if I have that in me." She stood, still glaring at him. "Now leave."

"Wait," Devlin said, hesitantly. He didn't want to get ensnared in Petronela's wrath, but he needed his questions answered before they lost contact with the only witnesses to the crime. "Who cried out? And what time did you hear it?"

"It was Larissa. And I don't know what time." He stood on shaky legs and ran out.

Devlin wrung his hands together. Given time, he could have picked apart the man's recounting of events. Found little crumbs of information he was sure would help them. But the man's fear of Petronela would have been too great to overcome.

Yet, he had to admit, despite his need to pinpoint every single thread, the only task before them was to find the girls and the ones who might have aided them in this crime. Understanding it might have been important but not so significant as to hinder their investigation.

He looked at her. "Will you kill him?"

She sighed. "Yes. I fear I must."

"Why?"

"Bria would have sensed his guilt when she started asking him questions. Sending him here was a test. And soon, others will learn of his secret, and if I don't do anything, it will lead to more unrest." A heavy sadness filled her voice.

On one hand, Devlin understood why she must punish him. On the other hand, leniency might go a long way. Or a punishment that didn't result in the man losing his life. "Heavy is the crown," Devlin said.

She wiped a shaky hand across her face.

"Why do you feign weakness?" he asked.

She smiled at that. "I am tired. So, when I don't have to fight through the pain that old age has brought, I allow myself some respite. And yes, Devlin Grey. My crown is heavy. But I am the only one who can wear it."

"One final question," he said. She waved for him to continue. "Why wouldn't you have questioned him before?"

She lay back and picked up the ivory pipe resting on the table by her couch. "The faith in my people is only now being tested," she said, not really answering his question. She closed her eyes, the backs of her eyelids working as if she were in a dream state.

A short while later, Bria returned with Dimitri's employee file in her hand. It was his cue to leave. He slipped the slim folder into the box with Dimitri's other belongings.

Bria escorted him to the gate.

"You sent him to his death," Devlin said, not masking the accusation in his tone. "Why?"

"I must protect my aunt. So many conspire." She turned and met his gaze. "Any sign of weakness, and they will hurt her. Or ..."

"Or?"

"I will ask Alexandros to break all their minds. She must be protected."

"Why do I get the feeling you know more than what you're saying?"

"Because you are intuitive. Find the ones responsible for taking our young. And I will take care of Auntie."

She walked away. And Devlin fought the urge to call her back. Demand she tell him more. He wouldn't allow her or anyone to force Alek to do anything to jeopardize his sanity. He'd pulled his friend out of that darkness before. If Alek slipped again, he feared he wouldn't be able to save him.

He made his way to his car. Alek's Buick was still in the parking lot, but there was no sign of either him or Nicole. They must still be following her lead. He was curious as to what she might find. Maybe the boys' deaths would hold the key. Or maybe it would just be another thread to unravel. A piece of a larger puzzle they'd have to figure out.

He debated if he should wait but then decided against it. He needed to be alone with his own thoughts for a moment.

The creek of the gate stopped him in his tracks. He glanced back and watched a lone figure emerge from the darkness. Rae, carrying her backpack, walked through the gate and made her way toward him.

"Ms. Petronela wanted me to come with you all. Said it was better if I come back after the ceremony."

"Did she give you any sign something was wrong?" he asked, uneasy. His people were still in there.

Rae shook her head. "Nah. Just said you might need me or something."

Devlin inclined his head in understanding and resumed his trek toward his car. Rae fell into step beside him. His thoughts went to the old woman, who had now sent the most vulnerable among them away. There was no question in his mind now that Petronela would not allow that man to live. And from what Bria had said, more people had begun to question her strength as well.

That meant her enemies were still inside. He stood outside his car, staring at the darkened carnival. The Ferris wheel creaked in the wind. Should he go back inside? Was it even his concern?

No. It wasn't. She had asked him to locate the ones responsible for her people's deaths. That was what he would concentrate on. Along with keeping his own people safe.

And if that meant dealing with the other enemies the old woman had hinted at, so be it. He'd told Nicole once they didn't do black and white. They operated in the gray.

Which meant there would be blood.

lek and I emerged from the employee building and made our way back to the living area. I still wasn't completely satisfied with my efforts and wished I could have learned more. Breadcrumbs were all I had to go on. Another puzzle for me to put together. The gate leading to the settlement had been left partially open.

We stepped onto the hard-packed earth and found everyone gathered around the center of the camp. All of them adorned in robes.

My footsteps slowed.

Something inside of me awoke. Like my contact with the Earth House of Power, an all-consuming energy rushed through, igniting every cell in my body. The beating of wings echoed inside my head. I could almost feel the wind from their powerful thrashing.

Alek was talking. He sounded so far away.

I turned in slow motion, as if I moved with the second hand on a clock.

My eyes widened.

A bright patchwork of souls hung over the pyres. The blinding gold and white light filled the entire area. So many souls, all woven together as if fused by an invisible thread. I reached for those beautiful beings. Their cold energy brushed against my feverish skin. I swallowed down the well of emotion that had balled up inside of me. Tears freely streamed down my face while I stared, wide-eyed, my entire being transfixed on the souls of dead.

I'd recently learned that through my mother, I was a *Nar al-nasaa*. Loosely translated, a Firewoman. Our roots gave way to the myth of the phoenix. A representation of which resided inside my core in the form of a protective mark that warded me against magick attacks. And if I looked inside myself, I could see that fiery bird now, suspended in a vast space while its wings flapped.

One of the many benefits of my power—at least, that was how I was learning to see it—was the ability to keep a dead person's soul tethered to their body. This strange power scared me. Because I didn't understand the full extent of it, nor was I ready to ask the one person who might know more about it. Instead, I'd chosen to practice with the team, hoping I'd figure out the reason for this ability.

With more knowledge, I might have been able to keep myself from being ensnared in the Tapestry. Able to pull myself away from the sight and suppress the hunger to pull all those souls to me.

But instead, I held my hand out, willing them toward me as I stared hungrily at those spirits. I watched the tiny threads spin their way down to connect with the threads being sent up from the souls of the recently deceased.

"I can see them," I said my voice barely a whisper. My eyes ached for me to blink, but I couldn't. "They are so beautiful."

A faint harmony of chimes and soft voices rang in my ears. Alek took my hand.

People stood around the bodies, talking and laughing, and with each word, another thread appeared. My heart seized with anguish and love and longing and joy.

"I have to get her out of here," Alek said, still sounding so far away.

"What's wrong with her?" a woman asked.

"She can see souls," Alek said and tugged my hand.

When I didn't move, he covered my eyes, and I gasped at the

absolute darkness engulfing me. He turned my head, keeping a firm grip on me as he walked us toward the entrance. I fought him with every fiber of my being.

"No!" I screamed, my heart breaking at the loss.

I wrenched away from him and looked back at the gathering of souls. My fingers itched to touch them again. I took a step forward, and Alek picked me up and ran for the entrance. His footfalls pounded on the pavement, the jarring motion bringing bile up into my throat. I was going to be sick if he didn't stop. I tried to bring my head up, but it only made it worse. I closed my eyes and fought against the nausea.

Once outside the gate, he sat me down in front of him.

He took my face in his hand, urging me to look at him. "Fight it."

I panted, my heart racing. "What's happening to me?" A deep sense of longing overcame me. I needed to hold those souls. To let them fill the spaces inside of me. The places where all the past events of my life had broken me. Creating holes inside of my very being.

"I wish I knew, babe. I wish I knew." His grip on me tightened when I tried to turn back. "Fight it." His dark blue eyes pleaded with me. "Please, Nicole."

Finally, I closed my eyes and took a deep breath. "I don't understand why I reacted like that. I've seen souls before. I've even touched them. You know this. But this... this was different. It was like they were whispering to me. Urging me to join them." I didn't dare mention the need for them to take away my own pain. It spoke to a darkness inside of me that I wasn't ready to share with anyone.

"With words, or was it more of a feeling?" he asked.

I put my hand over his, letting his warmth ground me. "A feeling."

He pulled me to him, and I wrapped my arms around him. "We must leave. Can you walk?"

"Yes. But it might be better if you guide me until we leave the carnival grounds."

His chest rumbled with laughter. "Okay. We will do this slowly. I will take a step, and you follow. Keep your eyes focused on mine."

I drew my teeth across my bottom lip and inclined my head in agreement.

It took some time, but we finally got to his car. I'd have laughed at the silliness of it if I hadn't been so afraid of my need to join the Soul Tapestry.

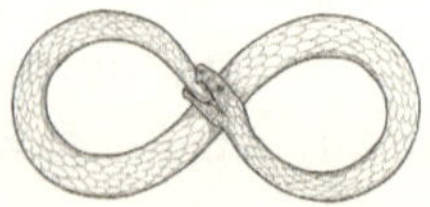

I WATCHED my once familiar island whir by like a montage as we made our way back to Devlin's. Every corner of my homeland seemed filled with magick, mystery, and, sadly, blood. Why had I never noticed these things before? Had I really kept my head buried in the sand? Well, maybe not sand. More like alcohol, cigars, and sex. Still a form of hiding.

To add to this, I now had to figure out why the souls had called to me. Was it part of my abilities? If so, what did it mean? And what about the Houses of Power? So many questions, and yet I didn't see myself getting the answers anytime soon.

I gripped the glitter pen in my hand, running my thumb over its pitted surface. I'd be covered in sparkly stuff by the time we got home. "How do the souls return?" I asked Alek, my voice hoarse.

"Petronela calls to them."

I turned and looked at him. "Does she have power like mine, then?"

Alek shook his head. "No." He paused. "At least, I don't think so." He gave me a quick glance. "But we will ask her. Maybe even talk with Luisah about what just happened." His brow wrinkled with worry. I was sure mine looked the same.

"Why can't I just have a simple power, like everyone else?"

"You're unique. Even without the power, you would be."
Alek squeezed my hand. "We all are."

"What do you—"

Alek slammed on the brakes, throwing my body forward. The
seatbelt cut across my torso and dug between my breasts.

"What the fuck!" I yelled, looking over at him.

He stared straight ahead, and I followed his gaze.

A woman wearing tight red slacks and a blazer with no shirt or
bra underneath stood, leaning against a familiar bright red Jaguar
convertible, blocking the street. Her long, curly black hair fluttered around her, reminding me of a storm cloud in motion. Her
eyes, one emerald and one whiskey, caught in the glow of our
headlights, tracked our movements like a panther's.

She smiled, then ran toward our car. Alek shoved the gearshift
in reverse, and the engine whined as he backed up.

"Just mow the bitch down!" My homicidal rage scared me.
But not enough to retract my statement. If the woman wanted to
run at us, intent on doing harm, well, she'd best be prepared to be
run over.

The woman ran back to her car, slid over the hood, and
climbed into the driver's seat. She had skill. I would give her that.

Alek whipped the car around, tires smoking as he gunned it.
We sped off with her in pursuit.

"It's the same woman who followed us earlier!" I slammed my
hand on the dashboard to brace myself.

The Jaguar's engine screamed at us as if in challenge. Power
filled the car; I glanced over to see Alek bathed in a dark orange
mist.

"Yeah. And I can't break her mind," he gritted out. A note of
fear rang in his voice, and it was then that I realized we were
running from a fight. Alek never ran. At least not in the time I'd
known him. He faced danger in a way that bordered on maniacal.
So why was he running now?

The Buick chewed up the road, taking the streets at more than
a hundred miles an hour. Sadly, it didn't matter how fast we went;

the Jaguar stayed right on our bumper. Our car filled with light. She'd switched on her brights. Most likely trying to blind us.

Alek took the next turn. We skidded across the lane. Just a whisper away from plowing into a parked car.

He gripped the wheel, muscles bulging with the strain of keeping the car from losing control. He yanked the wheel, bringing us back into alignment with the road. The stench of burnt rubber filled the car. Alek slammed his booted foot down. We shot forward down the street, our tires smoking.

"We won't be able to lose her!" I yelled.

The Jaguar crawled up our bumper.

A sea of red rushed at me as the car swerved around, barely missing my door.

She pulled ahead, car rocketing toward the intersection.

She skidded to a stop in the middle of the road.

Alek slammed on the brakes, and we slid, tires screeching. My body rammed into the door when we hit the curb. Blood filled my mouth.

"Fuck this!" I yelled. My tongue throbbed, and I shoved open my door and got out of the car, intent on murder. Alek kicked open his door and joined me.

She waited, lazily leaning against her car. Her red-painted lips parted slightly, as if she were savoring our emotions.

"What the fuck is your problem?" Alek barked.

She didn't respond, only watched us out of those strange eyes. Her stillness reminded me of a feline, a predator waiting for her prey to move so she could pounce.

A gold chain holding a gold ankh with a green cat's eye in the center rested between her breasts, drawing attention to her smooth brown skin.

"Bast," I whispered, and her lips stretched into a smile, showing bright white teeth.

She craned her neck to the side, the movement fluid. "What gave me away?" she asked, her voice a purr.

Alek glanced at me, eyebrows knitted in confusion.

"You went a little overboard with your namesake," I said, keeping my gaze trained on her. Ezra's warning came back, punching me in the gut. The Old Ones had made a pact to either kill or protect people with my unique magick. So why was she here?

She pushed off her car, and I tensed. Alek moved closer to me. She laughed.

"I only wanted to meet you," she said, her voice placating and in no way matching the dangerous look in her eyes.

"Strange way to meet someone, don't you think? I assume you know where I live or stay," I said, thinking about Devlin's. "Why not just stop by?"

"That wouldn't be fun," she said, coming to stand in front of us. She slowly raised her hand, long red fingernails stretching toward me.

The dark orange tendrils of Alek's power lashed out, only to be blocked by a burst of gold light. He froze, body vibrating in place. His power pounded on the gold light surrounding her, trying to find a way in. Sweat trailed down his face; his dark blue eyes swam with murderous intent.

I slapped her. The sting on my hand made me wince. She laughed and caught my hand when I tried to strike her again.

"Now, that's not very nice." She licked her lips and stared down at me. "He attacked me first." She pouted as if she were actually hurt. But those deadly eyes betrayed her. She was toying with us.

I wrenched my hand free and stepped into her personal space. "Leave him the fuck alone, bitch."

"If I let him go, he might attack me again." She jerked, her eyes rounding, and turned to him. "My, he is strong." She licked her lips as if savoring the fight in him. "Umm ... I guess I will have to—" Before she could finish speaking, she flew back, her body crashing into her car.

She laughed again and held up her hands. "Please. I really don't mean any harm."

Alek lashed out once more. Gold met orange as they fought with power. I turned and stared at him. How the hell could he take on an Old One? More importantly, why wasn't I trying? I looked back at her. She laughed, batting at his magick like a cat playing with a ball of yarn. In the center of all that gold power, I found a horde of souls.

She flicked her hand, and Alek fell to the ground. She turned that playful, dark gaze toward me. "I can feel you rummaging around inside of me," she said with a note of awe in her tone. "What do you see?"

I didn't answer. Just stared at the impossibility of so many souls.

She threw her hand back and laughed, completely unfazed at my attempts to harm her. But truthfully, I hadn't even tried.

Alek stirred next to me. I helped him up. He started forward again, but I stopped him. We couldn't win. This was just a game to her. And we were the toys she could bat around when she felt bored.

I shook my head and glared at her. "Like I said, you really are taking your namesake too far. Do I call you Bast, or are you using another name?" I ignored the quiver in my voice.

"You didn't answer my question." She smiled. "So I won't answer yours." She turned her attention to Alek. I tried to move in front of him, but he blocked me. "Your power is delicious. I wish I had the time to savor it some more." She licked her lips.

Her hand went to the ankh around her neck. "I've had so many names. But you can call me Camille." She glanced down at the dagger secured to my thigh. "You know I gave that to him."

It took me a minute to catch up. Her shift in mood was a bit jarring and unexpected. What was she playing at? And why the fuck hadn't I tried to stab her with said dagger? "Are you going to take it back?"

"No. It suits you. And my brother had to have his reasons for gifting it to you. So much blood has coated that blade. You should feel honored to hold it." She stared at my lips. "He's even marked you."

I remembered the searing pain on my lips when Ezra branded me. I'd thought he was kissing me. Turned out he was trying to protect me. But from what? He never did say. And knowing he'd given me his favorite dagger as well, the one his batshit crazy sister gave him, was more than a little alarming. I was getting really tired of the Old Ones and their games.

Her gaze traveled down my body. "So many of my siblings have marked you." She tapped her chin with her finger. "I wonder why." That stupid grin spread across her face. "Maybe I should as well."

"I think I have enough," I said.

"Her mouth stretched into a Cheshire Cat grin. "We three can share a bed." She winked at Alek. Then reached into her pocket and pulled out a red business card and handed it to me.

I looked down at the smooth card. Camilla Rochester, Cooperate Medium. I laughed. "Is this an actual job?"

She grinned. "Yes. You'd be surprised what men obsessed with moncy would pay for." She glanced at Alek. "Before they made me a god, I, too, was a mind mage." She paused, studying him. "There is so much darkness and power in you. How you broke my hold is ... interesting."

"I was motivated," Alek said.

She giggled, and her gaze traveled down my body once again. "I can't say I blame you. She is a magnificent woman." She moved forward, her nostrils flaring. "Jordin. He still hasn't learned his lesson. Giving you some of his power." She shook her head. "Must have been an epic orgasm."

"Umm..." I looked away, my cheeks blazing. She did not just say that about her brother.

"Stop toying with her," Alek said, voice like steel. "So far, you've not given us a sufficient reason for blocking our path. You could have called or even dropped your business card in the mail."

He stepped toward her, pushing her back a little. "What the fuck do you want?"

She studied him, a condescending smile crossing her mouth.

I moved between them. "I got this," I said. "If I had to guess. I'd say you were testing us. Someone has done that recently, and I vowed if anyone ever did that to me again ... I'd make them hurt."

"Not kill them?" she asked.

"Maybe. Or maybe I'll just make them bleed." Oh, how I wished I could simply kill someone for testing my patience. But that way lay monsters and madness. And I wasn't ready to cross that line just yet. But if this bitch kept fucking with my man ... I may just forget I had a moral compass and cut that smug look off her damn face.

She watched me as if I was some strange specimen she needed to figure out. "You are different from your ancestors," she said finally. "How... strange."

"What do you mean?" I asked.

Camilla smiled. "They have lain waste to so many in the past. Fueled by a hatred for those who used them in blood rituals."

My thoughts got hung up on that for a minute. I'd gotten the impression the Firewomen were more ... peaceful. I remembered the dream I had some time ago of my mother reaching for me as she rode on the back of a phoenix. Maybe my understanding of them was wrong.

"Hathor said an Old One can't be killed," I said finally.

Hathor—goddess of the sky, the sun, sexuality, and motherhood. She was responsible for blocking my memories and magick when I was six years old.

Camille's eyes rounded. "Hathor?" She paused, cocking her head to the side. "My sister is here?"

I narrowed my eyes. "Are you afraid of her?"

She stepped back. "Hathor is wrong. You can kill an Old One. And I believe I've found the people who will help me do it." She opened her car door and climbed inside. "You're right, Nicole Fontane. I was testing you. I had to." She drummed her slender fingers on her steering wheel. "It's my nature. One that has been forced on me, much like godhood." She spared us a last look and drove off, barely missing hitting Alek's car.

"Okay," I started. "That was way too strange for me."

Alek watched her taillights disappear down the street. "Her power was overwhelming." He rubbed the back of his head. "I honestly don't know how I broke her hold."

I glanced at him. "What did she do to you?"

"She sent me a barrage of images of what I assume were past events. An Ark sat in a hole in the middle of the desert. Women lay angled so that their blood could drain into a crevice where the Ark rested."

We'd learned recently there were three Arks: one for life, one for knowledge, and one for death. All of them created to store the power of the three Gods responsible for humanity.

My blood cooled. A few months ago, Camille's brother Set had pulled me out of the fight we were engaged in with the Stewart family and deposited me on a mound of dirt, rain beating down on me. He'd wanted my magick and told me I was of the blood. I learned later that they had sacrificed the *Nar al-nasaa* in a blood magick ritual to create the Old Ones, and that Set had been imprisoned by his brothers and sisters shortly after he had been made into a god. His corporeal spirit had somehow been freed, and he could interact with me.

As I lay on that ground, he'd shoved memories inside my head. The same ones that Camilla had just shown Alek.

The blood magick ritual that made them.

We pulled up to Devlin's just after midnight. I stared at the cluttered area in front of the four-bedroom house, listening to the rumble of Alek's engine, noting the four vehicles parked there. A jumbled mass that mirrored my mental state at the moment. Alek climbed out of the car, and, after a beat, I followed him. The pen was in my hand again, clutched between my palm and fingers in a bruising grip. The trash bag of measly, confusing clues was in my other hand, also in an iron grip. It was as if I feared someone would run up and snatch them from me.

The adrenaline rush from our confrontation with Camile had long left my body, replaced with an achy, jittery state.

My bravado in confronting Camille looked more like stupidity. I'd have to avoid telling Boss Man I'd slipped once again.

I yawned as we made our way up the walkway to the front door. The porch light blazed, making my already itchy, tired eyes burn. I wanted to punch someone or take a nap. Couldn't decide which of the two sounded better. Either way, this day had to end soon, or I was going to lose my shit.

Alek opened the door, and we went inside the cool house. An odd array of sounds traveled down the short hallway to us. The television, muted voices, computer keys clacking, all of it scratched at my eardrums, making my brain hurt. I blew out a frustrated breath and walked sluggishly toward the war room. Devlin met us halfway there.

He looked me over and then focused on Alek. "Problems?"

"Oh, we ran into another Old One and had a nice little chat about my magick and her desire to get both Alek and I in bed. I got in her face. Maybe even threatened her a little." I dropped the bag and snapped my fingers. "I reacted to the Houses of Power. Was also drawn to the souls of the dead." I shrugged. "Not too eventful besides that." I could have sworn I wasn't going to tell Boss Man about my fuck-up. Oh well, too late now.

Alek and Devlin stared at me. Both looked a little confused as to how they should respond. I snatched up the trash bag and gave it to Devlin. "Here's your evidence." I walked away from their obvious concern. "Rachel, I need coffee!"

Behind me, Devlin asked, "Is she okay?"

"Probably not," Alek said.

I stopped in the archway and took in the scene. Rae lay on the floor, eyes closed, with a laptop open in front of her, the screen illuminating her pale skin. Marta stood by the whiteboard, holding a pencil near her open mouth. Her eyes rounded when she noticed me. Rachel studied my face and then rushed to the adjoining kitchen. Hopefully to get that coffee.

I'd first had a cup of her dark brew, made to help replenish magick, when we were investigating the Stewart family and Tribec Insurance. It had been only recently that she told me just what she put in it: apple blossom to feed the immortality of our magick; pennyroyal for strength; rosemary to restore memory; yarrow for mental and physical injuries; and caffeine in its purest form. Sounded like a mad chemist experiment, but right now, I could use every one of those ingredients and then some. But one day, when I had enough brain cells to work with, I would ask about the immortality of our magick.

Marta came over and looked me up and down. "Are you doing okay? And why are you covered in glitter with a dagger strapped to your thigh?"

I sighed. "Not really. Fighting delirium and information over-load and losing royally. I forgot my purse, which meant I had to ask for a pen. Alek's evil cousin gave me a black glitter pen, and it shed its nasty, sparkly shit on me. The dagger"—I patted the aforementioned item— "was in case we had to do battle."

"It looks like you had one with the pen and lost."

"Yeah. Well. Shit happens."

Marta had bags under her eyes, and her long black hair looked as if she'd been raking it with claws.

"I thought you weren't coming till tomorrow. Where are the kids?" I asked.

"At your parents' house. I wanted to get a jump on things." Her gaze went hard. "I understand children are involved," she said, her tone deadly.

The fury in her voice reminded me why Marta was truly here. Yes, she needed a job, but her desire to work for what amounted to a group of vigilante mages was not for a mere paycheck.

She wanted revenge against the blood magick users who'd taken her kids and abused them.

I was not looking forward to telling her the daughters might be responsible for their parents' deaths.

"I understand," I said finally. Rachel brought me a steaming cup of coffee. I inhaled the enticing aroma and took a sip. The heat rushed down my throat, soothing me. "I'm sorry to say this ..."

She gave me a pained smile. "I already know the girls who are missing could be responsible for their parents' deaths. Rachel told me when I got here."

"And you stayed?"

"Might as well." She gave me a one-armed hug, then rubbed the glitter off her cheek. "Are you sure you're okay?"

I lifted the mug. "Ask me again after I've had a few cups of this."

Her brow furrowed, like it always did when she was worried. "All right, just let me know." She hesitated, as if she wanted to press me more, then walked back to the board and continued her study of it.

Rae stirred, opening her eyes, and shot up. "Didn't mean to doze off."

Devlin waved away her comment. "No. You need to get some rest. Start fresh in the morning."

"You can sleep in my room," Rachel said, taking the bag I'd given to Devlin.

Rae shook her head. "No. I'm good." She yawned, making a liar of herself. The girl looked dead on her feet. She glanced at the bag. "I can sift through that if you want."

Rachel gave Devlin a questioning look. He paused, then dipped his head in consent.

While Rae took the meager contents out of the bag, I sat at my desk and opened the notebook where I'd scribbled my own notes. Sipping my coffee, I stared down at Dawn's written account of what had happened with the twin boys.

Alek sat next to me. Rachel had given him a cup of coffee as well. "You want to take a break?"

I looked at him. "And look like I can't hold my own?" I signaled to Rae, who was taping the scraps of paper to the white-board. "If she can fight through fatigue, so can I." My words came out a little sing-song. Now I was trying to keep pace with a teenager. I shook my head and finished my coffee. The caffeine should kick in soon.

Devlin sat on the edge of his desk and took a sip of his own regular coffee. "All right. Let's run through it." He looked at me. "Why don't you start with what happened on the way here?"

"My brain cells are on strike right now. Can someone else go first?"

Rae chuckled.

"You get used to her," Marta offered.

"Alek," Devlin said.

Alek took them through our encounter with Camille. I pulled

the red business card she'd given me from my pocket and handed it to Rachel.

"Corporate Medium," she said. "Like a business fortune teller?"

"I gather she mostly charges obscene fees while feeding gullible individuals a line of bullshit." Okay. I sounded childish. And a little petty. I blew out a frustrated breath. "She is powerful."

I rubbed my head and stood up. The caffeine had started coursing through me. I needed to move. "She hinted at being made. Like someone did something to her, turned her into a god. Fuck! I can't keep it straight in my head." Of course she'd been made. All the Old Ones had been. But it was more than that. Like she'd been forced into a persona she didn't want. At least, that's what I was thinking.

My hands shook, and a fiery itchiness raced down my arms and legs. My breaths grew ragged. Every single thought inside my head rammed against my cranium, begging to be let out. If I kept talking, I'd most likely devolve into gibberish. Was it the caffeine? It had never impacted me like this before.

Rachel handed me a pen. "Write it down."

I took the pen from her and stared at it. My grip tightened on the black plastic casing. A loud snap made me jump. The remnants fell to the floor. The world blurred around me, and I dropped to my knees.

"Panic attack," Alek announced.

His arms came around me, and I screamed. Rachel kneeled in front of me and started humming. A warm energy engulfed me. I opened my eyes and watched her soothing green magick caress my skin. I started to tell her to stop. But the words died in my throat. A sense of euphoria washed over me. I looked inside myself and found the phoenix wings fluttering. As if they, too, were in a state of elation.

"My mark is..." I finally mumbled.

"I'm not attacking you," she said, her voice barely a whisper.

"Let the energy heal you. Okay?" Her hazel eyes were filled with so much concern. Out of the corner of my eye, I spotted Marta pacing and wringing her hands as if she itched to do something. I met her gaze. Trying to tell her I would be okay. She finally assented, then sat down in her chair, eyes still on me.

After a short while, my skin cooled, and my thoughts cleared. "I'm okay." Rachel could use her power to heal someone. But because of my protective mark's reaction to magick being used on me, I didn't believe she could use her ability to heal me as well. But then again, Alek had done something similar when he'd sung me to sleep. My mark hadn't reacted to him either.

Come to think of it, it hadn't repelled Camille either. Had she tried to attack me? Or was it just Alek she'd wanted to toy with?

Rachel stood. "Why didn't you tell me you get panic attacks?" she asked with genuine hurt in her voice.

I pulled in a cleansing breath and let Alek help me up. "I thought I could deal with them on my own." Everyone watched me. I turned away from them and sat in a chair. Marta handed me a cup of water, and I drained the glass. "I can deal with it," I repeated, trying to convince myself as well. I wasn't so sure. Especially if they came on with no warning.

Devlin walked over and crouched in front of me. "If you need time. I can give it to you. I don't want you continuing like this." He placed his hand on my arm.

I nodded. "No. I need to do this. I've spent too much time trying to avoid all the uncomfortable things in my life. Which is probably why I'm breaking down now. So, I have to face it. One way or another." I swallowed the lump in my throat and smiled. "If I can get a dose of Rachel's healing power daily, I can manage anything."

"I can make you something to help," Rachel said eagerly.

"Thanks, Rachel," I said.

"All right. Just take a break," Devlin told me, then picked up a file and handed it to Alek. "Dimitri is the same guard we encountered earlier this week when we went to talk with Petronela about the job she gave Alek. He was hired a year ago and could be the one who helped orchestrate the attack." He looked at Rachel. "Anything?"

"Nothing on him. I have several searches running on his family," she said, looking at her computer.

I glanced at the file as Alek thumbed through it. While we'd been investigating the Young family, Petronela had forced Alek to locate a man named Unrie Nevsky. Devlin had been none too pleased about that.

Alek handed Rae the photo of the guard, and she attached it to the whiteboard. The man looked young and a bit cocky too. Like he felt the world owed him a favor and he was going to collect. If not for that off-putting smile on his face, I'd think he was handsome.

"I also found an unguarded entry point near the water," Devlin continued.

Alek shook his head. "Why leave that open?"

"Best guess," Devlin said, "she assumed her reputation would be enough of a deterrent."

I looked at Boss Man. His tone seemed a little off.

"And people have been questioning her rule for a while now," Alek said. "Cristian was right. She is getting soft."

"Give me more on the Dacian. Bria compared them to our secret service," Devlin said to Alek.

Alek pulled his hair back, securing it with the band he always kept in his pocket. "They mainly work for the Roma families. An elite security detail that swears allegiance only to the one who hires them." He paused, then added, "I have heard of them working outside the community, though."

"So they're not connected to any one family?"

Alek shook his head no.

"What are you thinking?" I asked.

"Something more is going on that we're not seeing," Devlin

said. "Petronela is deceiving her people. And she's not getting soft." He stared at Alek with a look of concern. Shook his head, then continued, "Her reputation is built on subterfuge. Most of the stories about her have been embellished."

Alek sighed and scrubbed his hand down his face. "I had wondered about that."

I'd expected more of a reaction from him. His lack of surprise suggested he'd already figured that out. And if he had, others would have as well.

"Do you think she's in danger?" I asked Alek.

He shook his head slowly. "No. She's still powerful. But ..."

"But you worry someone can take her?"

He splayed his hands. "It's not that. It's more of what she's willing to do. She ... hesitates. In the past, this sort of thing would have never happened." He looked at Devlin. "She gave Daniella and Illeana an opportunity to make amends for their transgressions. In the past, she would have killed them without a single thought."

I winced at the brutality.

"So, no. Not entirely without power. Just an unwillingness to use it."

"So, like Cristian said, she's gone soft." *Or stopped being a crazed, bloodthirsty dictator*, I left unsaid. I couldn't be the only one thinking about it, though.

He nodded, then looked at Devlin. "Did she tell you more about Tribe?"

"Yeah." That one word seemed to weigh him down. "We'll save it for the morning."

Devlin gave me a questioning look.

I finished the rest of my coffee and stood. "What I was trying to say earlier," I started, "is that Camilla embodied her namesake to the point of garishness. Like she was putting on a show."

"Her namesake?" Marta asked.

"Bast. She behaved more like a cat than a human, and I got

the impression she didn't like that. She said her being Bast was forced upon her, like her godhood."

"Do you think she's a threat?" Devlin asked.

I shrugged. Was she a threat? "I don't know. But I do get the feeling she's afraid of Hathor. Which is puzzling, given Hathor's state of mind." Hathor had saved my life when her brother Set had tried to dig my power out of me like it was an organ inside my body. She'd also turned up earlier this week at the store I frequented, encouraging me to find my purpose in a self-help magazine. To say she was strange was an understatement.

"Check with Ezra and confirm if we need to be concerned," Devlin said. "Now, take everyone through your thoughts about the twins."

Why had I become so fixated on the twins' deaths? I opened my notebook and stared at the account of the illness that Dawn had written down for me. Swallowing the sudden uncertainty, I plowed ahead, hoping I wouldn't ramble too much. "Cristian said the boys just went to sleep and never woke up." I looked up at them. "It caught my attention.

"Please don't laugh, but it sounds like a fairytale. And then there was their trailer. It seemed... lifeless. Like the family had given up on life. Or had been punished." I held up my hand to stall their comments. I needed to get this out. "On our way to the carnival, I kept seeing the color red. I told Alek I believed they may have been portents. Despite his explanation, it stayed with me. Then I walked into this trailer, and something just felt off. Sure, I could chalk the feeling up to grief. But it was more than that."

The look on Devlin's face gave me pause. His eyebrows had drawn together, gray eyes filled with... worry? Fear?

"Boss Man?"

He shook his head. "What did you learn from the people you questioned?"

"That I might have been right to focus on them. Their deaths didn't happen so quickly. They went through a series of ailments that the healer's wife, Dawn, believed resembled toxic shock syndrome." I gave Rachel my notebook. "Their behavior was also something that helped cement it for me too. The boys liked to wonder and get into things. They sounded like menaces. So, I might be making a wild assumption but what if they overheard something and..." I didn't want to say it aloud.

"You think someone actually killed them to keep them quiet?" Marta asked, her voice filled with anger.

I nodded. It was the only thing that fit and made sense. Of course, I was willing to acknowledge my whole assumption about them was fueled not by fact but feeling.

"Foxglove," Rachel said. "Their symptoms mirror foxglove poisoning."

"Oh man. Maybe I shouldn't be staying there," Rae said, eyes rounding.

"I don't think you're in any danger," Alek said. "And if Nicole is right, we will find the ones responsible."

"This is bad, Dev. They poisoned kids." Rachel looked up at him. "Can't let them get away with this." Her voice sounded small, as if she'd folded in on herself.

Rachel didn't usually exhibit this type of raw emotion.

Devlin had told me her biological father had killed her siblings with poison. And if not for their immunity, Rachel and her mother would have died as well. I'd never gotten the full story. And would never ask. I figured she'd tell me in her own time.

I went over and knelt beside her. She stared at me out of tear-filled hazel eyes. "I'm so sorry, Rach. It was insensitive of me to talk about this."

She smiled as a tear slid down her cheek. "You called me Rach." Rachel had a thing for nicknames. Had even asked if she could call me Nikki. I had vetoed that request, but now, after shoving my foot in my mouth, I was seriously considering letting her. "It's okay. Just make sure you let me deal with the person who poisoned them."

"Deal," I said and stood up. Now I understood why I had become so fixated on the boys. A part of me must have inadvertently associated the similarities in their deaths to Rachel's siblings. Seeing suspicion in everything and everyone. Either way, I did believe someone had hurt those kids. There may have been a connection to the disappearance of the girls and the murder of their parents or not. And I was damn sure going to find out.

I looked at Devlin. "Other than that, just the items I collected from the two trailers." I rubbed my eyes. "Honestly, Boss Man. It's going to take some time to mentally work through that mess." Despite my body now thrumming with energy, I didn't want to explain another one of my theories. That would take too many brain cells.

Devlin nodded. "Then we'll tackle that in the morning." He picked up the cloth bag next to him and pulled a dark blue cylinder out of it. Etched on the front was the same elaborate symbol I'd seen on the Elemental House of Power. "Petronela gave this to me. I don't know why. But I figure we can add it to the other clues."

Alek walked over and took the object from him. "Why would she do that?" he asked, confusion in his tone.

"I'm just as lost on why as you."

We all went silent. Rae blinked and rubbed her eyes. Maybe this wasn't the best place for her either. But then again, she had grown up in South Perry.

Rachel smacked her hands together. "Finally! Found an address for one of Dimitri's relatives." She turned her computer around. "He lived in South Perry."

Of course he did. "Lived?" I asked.

"Yeah. Says here his grandmother left his cousin the house when she died, and six months ago, his cousin was killed in a drive-by shooting. Apparently, Dimitri was the only living relative able to claim the residence."

"Does it say he did?" Devlin asked.

Rachel shook her head. "No. But someone turned the utilities on."

Why would he move into a trailer at the carnival if he had a house? It made no sense.

"Should we check it out tonight?" Alek asked.

"Fuck yeah," I said, heart pounding. I was too damn wired to go to sleep now. "I need to take my frustration out on someone." I picked up Alek's mug and finished the rest of his coffee. "Ready?"

"Will you be wearing the glitter-covered tank top?" he asked.

"Yes. Along with my dagger." I pulled it from its sheath. "Might even get to stab someone with it." It would be better than sitting here, continuing to discuss the case. I'd already given myself a panic attack and brought back painful memories for both Marta and Rachel. At this rate, we'd all end up in a "share circle" crying. And I wasn't ready for that stage in my recovery. If I ever got there. So it was better for me to spend my time stabbing people.

Oh, I needed so much help.

"I know where that is," Rae said, studying the address on the screen. "It's down the block from Greenwood Apartments."

Damn. We were heading into The War Zone.

Devlin went to his footlocker and pulled out a gun. After handing one to Alek, he asked, "Marta, did you bring your gun?"

She nodded. "It's in my purse."

"Good. You and Rachel stay here with Rae." He looked at the teenager. "I want you to get some rest. I need you alert in the morning."

She opened her mouth to protest, then shut it and nodded her consent.

"Should I bring my gun too?" I asked.

Alek and Devlin both said "no" in unison. I wasn't particularly happy with their lack of confidence in me but had to agree. It was probably better if I left it. I couldn't aim for shit.

"Stick with the dagger," Alek said, giving me a look that

reminded me of his earlier comment about how I looked wearing it.

My cheeks heated, and I turned away. He really needed to stop flirting with me. We were heading into battle for fuck's sake.

The three of us walked out into the night, armed with magick, two guns, and a knife.

Looked like I was going to start Monday seeing red as well.

We entered the neighborhood from the north and traveled south down Pascal Drive. The address Rachel had found sat in the middle of the block between two houses with manicured lawns and a few dull porch lights, barely touching the darkness.

A short distance away, Greenwood Apartments rose over the neighborhood, looking out at the homes surrounding it. Its dark mass seemed to swallow the area whole. Its corruptive power crawled all over my skin. As far as I knew, very few residents in The War Zone used magick. They preferred weapons, fear, and intimidation. But mostly, they preyed on those who had given up on life. Much like I had when I ventured into that dark maw, hoping to assuage my pain.

I suppressed both a shiver and the memories of the last time I was there and turned away from that evil building. I had almost lost my life there. At the same place Alek had rescued Rae from.

He'd told me Petronela had seen the teenage girl in a vision of sorts. Said she was a bright light in the murky waters. I was more than a little curious about what that meant. Especially given current events.

How had Petronela not seen the revolt going on around her? How had she not been able to stop the deaths in her own backyard?

Yet, she could find a single girl amid so much darkness. Devlin was right. Something strange was going on with that old woman. I only hoped we didn't get caught in the ensuing war with her and her people.

Alek parked across the street from the house in question. Every nerve in my body thrummed like live wire. Adrenaline flooded me in a nauseating wave. Coupled with the abundance of caffeine, the only thing keeping me from flying to the moon was the residual healing magick Rachel had given me.

The streetlights buzzed, winking in and out, then finally going out altogether. Moonlight barely touched the area. A warm wind blew through the neighborhood, carrying the scent of rain and stale trash. We got out of the car and closed the doors softly. The clicks barely registered any sound.

Before we left, I'd changed into a black T-shirt and blue jeans. Glitter just didn't scream "dangerous" enough for me. Devlin had his superhero belt on—black leather with vials of the four elements floating inside—and his gun holstered in a rig around his left arm.

Alek's mind was his superhero belt. But he had a gun too.

I wished I had a belt as well. But what would I use it for? What I needed was the time to work on controlling my power. Grabbing a person's soul and holding it long enough to cause permanent damage took a great deal of concentration, which left me vulnerable to attack. No enemy was going to stand there while I got my shit together long enough to strike.

I scanned the neighborhood, noting the checkerboard-like picture of it. Some homes had given up any pretense of maintenance. Others maintained their properties as if their very existence depended on presenting an image of order.

The house we were going to sat in a thicket of overgrowth that came to our knees. Once painted beige with dark trim, the house now resembled something found in the bayou. Paint peeling, porch crumbling, and a weak light barely illuminating the wall behind it.

Alek's magick surged, running across my skin. Those orange

tendrils crawled across the cracked walkway and up the wooden porch—seeking.

"Two girls inside." Alek announced. He turned and scanned the area. "A few people are awake in the area. But on the verge of sleep."

I let my gaze go distant and scanned the area as well, noting the souls inside the homes. My fingers fluttered with the desire to touch those balls of light. A few of the people even had some magick. But nowhere near mage level.

"You two take the front," Devlin said, then made his way around the back of the house and disappeared into the thicket.

Alek and I went up the walkway and arrived at the front door. I tried the knob. Locked. "Did you bring your lockpicks?" I asked.

He pulled a slim case from his back pocket and knelt in front of the door. A sense of déjà vu overtook me, remembering a similar scenario when we had broken into Marta's house after her and her kids had gone missing. We'd found that place empty with blood on the walls. What would we find here?

Alek made quick work of the lock, and we stepped inside an overly furnished, darkened living room. The air conditioner droned in the background, kicking out frigid air. I rubbed my arms and stepped carefully onto the worn beige carpet.

Two mismatched couches on the right side of the room, without any space between them. A glass coffee table sat on bricks, piled high with pizza boxes. Two dark green recliners were positioned on either side of the table. An array of magick symbols decorated the opposite wall, alongside an undecipherable language scrawled across its white surface. These were the same symbols I'd found in the trailers.

Devlin came into the room and switched on a pin light. He ran the beam over the area, bringing the dark spots in the carpet into focus.

"Looks like a meeting area," I said, picking my way around the worst of the stains. I glanced toward the dark hallway on the left.

"You said there were two girls in here. I wonder why they haven't come out."

"They're in... pain. High, maybe," Alek said.

My dagger was in its sheath. I'd learned the hard way, in the cave under The Better Day Church, not to be too trusting. I'd assumed the women who had been readied for sacrifice were in a weakened state and needed rescue. Turned out, they had been willing participants and didn't much appreciate Jonah and I trying to save them. So, I'd treat the girls in the other room as a threat just in case. I yanked my dagger from its sheath.

Alek followed me down a long hallway to a room at the end. Soft light filtered out under the closed door.

My grip tightened on the knife handle.

Slowly, I eased the door open. A pungent aroma rushed out.

The click of a gun being made ready echoed.

I froze.

"Who the fuck are you?" a girl yelled, her words slurring.

I looked at Alek, and he shrugged.

"We're looking for some missing girls," I said. "Someone told us they were here."

The girl laughed. "No one here is missing. We know right where we are. Go away before I put a bullet in you."

"Let me go in," I whispered to Alek. Of the three of us, I looked the least threatening.

He nodded.

What I needed was for her to trust me. Not an easy feat, but I had to try. Otherwise, we'd be here all night. "Will you let me come in and talk with you?" I asked.

She didn't respond. I chanced a look around the door and found her leaning against the headboard, forearms resting on her bare legs while the gun hung from her loose hand. She saw me and raised the gun. I darted backward before she could shoot.

"What do you want?" she asked finally.

"Just to talk."

"Why? You don't know me." Her voice held so much pain. "And I don't feel like talking."

She didn't sound sure of her words. Like some small part of her did need to talk, but she refused to admit to it. I was like her, in a way. At times unable to voice the thoughts going on inside my head. And unwilling to allow others to see me struggle. Maybe I could use that connection.

"Then what do you want?" I asked, hoping my assumption was correct.

Again, she went silent. I crouched and stuck my head around the door again, taking in the room. A twin bed rested next to the window. She sat on it, with another girl lying next to her, unmoving. Opposite me, flush against the wall, was a dresser with a single lamp on top.

I eased back and stood. "The other girl doesn't seem to be moving."

"Keep her talking," Alek said and stepped away. I watched him retreat.

"Are you still there?" the girl called out.

I let out a silent breath of relief. This might be easier than I thought. I resheathed my knife and took a tentative step into the room, hands raised. "Can I come in and talk with you?"

"I have a gun," she drawled.

"I heard. And if you feel threatened, you can use it." *Please don't use it.*

She went silent again. Time stretched between us. Was she thinking? Had she fallen unconscious? So many questions ran through my head. I didn't want to chance another look. Not yet. I needed her to talk with me first.

"Do you have a death wish?" she asked finally.

"Sometimes I wonder if I do."

She let out a painful chuckle. "Me too."

Silence again. I wanted to take another step into the room but didn't dare move unless she said it was okay. Despite my answer to her question, I didn't truly have a death wish. Although, I had, as of late, put myself in more deadly situations than I cared to think about. But she didn't need to know that.

"Gracie and I should have stayed at the school," she mumbled.

It was now or never. I steeled myself, heart ramming in my chest, and then took another tentative step. She stayed in the same position. She didn't turn when I walked into the room. Just stared at the wall, gun hanging from her hand.

I slowly let my arms down and studied the girl. Late teens, maybe early twenties, she had short black hair that rested on her shoulders. She wore a black bra and red panties, showing the glyphs that covered most of her light brown skin. She turned and looked at me out of half-lidded eyes. "Who are you?" she asked.

"My name is Nicole."

She licked her chapped lips and nodded. "Never thought I'd end up in a place like this."

The girl next to her stirred. She absently rubbed her bare back.

"Are you being held against your will?" I asked.

She shook her head. "No. Just promises that turned out ..." She sighed. Tears trailed down her cheeks, and using the hand holding the gun, she swiped them away. She bit a loose piece of skin on her lip, and I examined the girl next to her.

Long blond hair pooled around her. She wore a pair of pink silk underwear and nothing more. Tiny scars covered both her calves in a crisscross pattern. Her hand hung over the edge of the bed. I watched the rise and fall of her back for a minute before I refocused on the other girl. She watched me out of those disinterested eyes.

"Why did you come here, Nicole? Why did you come to this place where dreams go to die?"

"I'm looking for some missing teens," I said, my voice catching. *And I've been here*, I left unsaid.

"At least they have someone searching for them." Her voice sounded hollow. Like she'd given up hope.

"Don't you have people worried about you?"

She gave me a half-smile. "Everything I care about is in this room." She paused, eyes going to the girl next to her. "It's my fault Gracie is here."

"Why did *you* come to the place where dreams go to die?"

She slowly looked up at me. "To escape the pain."

I swallowed the lump that had risen in my throat. She sounded like me. Who was I kidding, she was me. Not too long ago, I had lain in a bed next to a boy while his uncle filled his body with bullets. I had lain there... waiting... knowing I would die.

"Who hurt you?" I asked, steeling my voice against the raw emotion threatening to overcome me. I had survived that ordeal. And she could too. I just needed to show her the way.

She shook her head. "Doesn't matter. They lied and left us here to die." A trickle of blood ran down her lip, and she swiped it away. "Who are you looking for?"

"Nadia Ardelean and Sophia Kotzur," I said, hoping I got their last names correct.

She smiled. "Dimitri talked about them. Said they would..." She let out a ragged breath.

I rushed over. The gun slipped from her hand, and she laid her head back against the headboard. "It's getting... getting..."

I placed my hand on her clammy skin. "Don't talk. I will get you help."

She shook her head vigorously. "No. You have to get out of here. They will come."

"Who? Who's coming?" I shook her, and she opened her eyes and swallowed.

"They told us they'd give us more. It's not working... I don't want to... die... Not here... It's not working."

She wasn't making any sense. Drugs? "I won't let you die," I said, unsure if I could do anything. If only Rachel was here. She could heal them.

Her head lolled side to side. "It's my fault Gracie is here," she repeated and started crying. "He said..." She trailed off, eyes closing again. "At least she... at least she... Help us." Her head fell forward, and she didn't move.

Alek and Devlin stepped into the room. They must have been listening outside the door.

I checked her pulse. It beat steadily. I also checked Gracie's and found it to be slightly weaker. "We have to get them out of here," I said.

Alek looked around the room. "Find them some clothes," he said, lifting Gracie to a sitting position.

Devlin helped the other girl while I searched inside the dresser and found a few shirts and shorts. I pulled out a T-shirt and stopped. The Peterson's School for Troubled Girls crest had been sewn into the fabric.

"These girls are from the school," I said, pulling another shirt out of the drawer. I handed Devlin and Alek their shirts and opened the closet door.

"Opal," Devlin said into his phone. "I need a medic at my location." He rattled off the address and hung up.

A few dresses hung in the closet with matching shoes underneath. My imagination got the better of me as I stared at those garments. Had Dimitri been pimping them out? Did he plan on doing the same with Nadia and Sophia? Both girls were obviously in pain. Or angry. Ripe for grooming. Was that why he had gotten a job at the carnival and asked to live there?

Alek and Devlin picked up the girls, and I started for the door, only to stop dead in my tracks when power surged into the room. They set the girls back on the bed and went to the bedroom door.

"Watch them," Devlin whispered.

He and Alek strode down the hallway, magick rising around them both. Their orange and blue power streams intertwined. Heat buffeted my skin.

I seethed at being left out of the fight. I'd brought my dagger for just this reason. I should be out there, damnit. Yet, someone had to watch the girls, and I could grudgingly admit they would be better at handling the threat for now.

I eased up to the doorjamb and strained to listen.

"They are powerful," the girl whispered. I turned and found her eyes open and staring at me. "You should have left."

"My friends are powerful too."

She closed her eyes again. "They will tear your mind apart," she said on an exhale, then jerked up, holding her head in a vice-like grip. "No!" Blood oozed from her eyes, nose, and mouth. She shook her head violently. I ran over and grabbed her shoulders, trying to stop the seizures. Blood coated my skin.

Her friend bucked up, body going into a painful arc. She cried out and then fell... silent. Blood pooled around her head.

I watched helplessly as the veins on her face and arms bulged as if she'd been hit by lightning. One final gasp escaped her bloody mouth.

And then, she fell still.

Her vacant eyes stared up at me. My heart rammed against my chest, the adrenaline rushing through my veins rendering me momentarily deaf while rage roared inside me. I had promised her she wouldn't die. But in the end, I hadn't been able to save her.

A rush of water flowed from the hallway and into the room, saturating the carpet. I went back to the door with the intent of running out to join the fight.

Someone bellowed, the sound filled with pain.

A gunshot rang out.

Two thuds sounded. Like bodies hitting the floor.

"Alek?" I called out. "Devlin?"

Silence.

Someone screamed, and another thud resonated.

I was on my own.

ove, Nicole.

I yanked my dagger from its sheath, then plastered myself against the wall, straining to hear. It was quiet. Too quiet. As if someone were waiting. And by calling out for Alek and Devlin, I'd foolishly announced I was in the house. So why hadn't they tried to kill me yet?

I'd promised Devlin I wouldn't rush headlong into danger. But I couldn't stay here either. The only issue was, I didn't know how many people were out there. And if they were able to take Alek and Devlin down so quickly, they had to be extremely powerful.

I looked back at the girls on the bed. A pang tore through my chest at the waste of life. I wished I could have helped them. But it was too late now. I needed to save myself and my team. The girl's gun was still lying on the bed. I went over and picked it up. Two weapons were better than one. I might not be able to aim for shit, but the people out there didn't know that.

Steeling myself, I crouched, then chanced a peek around the corner. The hallway was empty save a thin layer of water on the floor. Devlin had used his magick. So how the hell had they gotten the better of them? What chance did I have? And then it hit me.

"*They will tear your mind apart*," the girl had said. Which meant whoever had come in was a mind mage, and if both Devlin and Alek were hurt, it had to be more than a few. I'd seen Alek take down over ten people. But, of course, none of them had magick. Still, the fight had been too quick.

Shit.

I looked inward and found the phoenix wings on my protective mark open, fighting against magick I couldn't feel. It had reacted without me knowing. That was new. And something I'd have to think about later. Along with why I couldn't see the attack. Usually when people used their magick, it emitted a color. A common indicator of what type of power the person had. For mind magick, it was orange. Earth magick was green. Elemental was blue, and faith gold and white. I was a rarity. My power had a green hue with red striations running through it.

Either they weren't using their power—my protective mark said otherwise—or their magick didn't emit any color. I checked the hallway again. Still empty. Could they be outside the house?

"Time to put up or shut up, Nicole," I said aloud.

I put my dagger back in its sheath and stepped into the hall, gun raised, tiptoeing along the wall. My boots squished in the flooded carpet. The smell of ozone tickled my nose. I started to move around the corner but then stopped.

No sense making myself a bigger target.

I crouched and duck-walked into the room. Alek and Devlin both lay on the threadbare carpet, not moving. I crawled over to them, water seeping into my jeans, and took Alek's face in my hands. His eyes were open, brows knitted together, seemingly in pain. A smokey, burnt mist of orange magick pulsed around him. His fingers lay stretched out, as if reaching for Devlin. The same energy seemed to circle Devlin as well. But underneath that strange color, another thread of orange circled their heads, and it stretched out toward the door.

Mind mages.

After killing the girls, they must have focused their attack on Alek and Devlin.

Devlin lay next to Alek with his hand over the vial filled with water. The dark blue of his power sputtered in and out, as if losing its charge.

In the corner, near the couches, four men, dressed in all black gear with the Eye of Horus sewn into the collar of their tight T-shirts, lay unmoving. Dacian. Like the ones we'd seen arrive at the carnival. The front door was open, giving whoever waited outside a view inside the house. I hated crawling around on the floor like some weak-willed lady in distress, but I also had enough sense to not announce my presence in the front room without discovering all the key players.

After all, someone had wrapped their magick around Alek and Devlin, keeping them immobile. If they saw me, they'd attack. Might not end well for them, but that didn't mean others weren't out there too, ready to step forward when their partners fell.

Staying low to the ground, I army-crawled, trying not to think of the stains I'd seen on the carpet when we'd first arrived. This close to it, I could detect the faint whiff of piss and vomit in the worn threads. And all of it had been saturated in water that now coated my clothes.

I swallowed the bile that rose in my throat and eased forward.

The front yard came into view. A black car sat in front of the house with two men, also dressed like the downed men inside, standing near it. Their gazes roamed over the home. Another man stood on the walkway halfway between the house and the front door, with orange and red magick pulsing around him. Threads of which stretched toward the house. Making him the one responsible for Alek and Devlin's current state.

The three of them stood out there, seemingly waiting. For what? Reinforcements? It had to be my magick. Someone had attacked me, and I was willing to hazard a guess that it was one of them.

If I could take out the main guy without the others noticing, Alek and Devlin could maybe recover enough to launch their own attack.

Yeah. Not likely.

I moved on. Slower this time.

I said a silent prayer that they didn't turn my way.

I gained another inch, keeping my movements miniscule.

My breaths came out in spurted bursts as I pushed forward.

The man on the walkway moved, and I stopped.

His gaze went to the side of the house, and I fought the urge to scramble forward. No doubt he would see my movements.

Another inch.

My upper body cleared the doorway.

Now, I was blundering along.

Sweat broke out along my hairline. A trail of which ran down and into my eyes. I couldn't move my arms to wipe my burning eyes.

Slowly, I pulled my body forward, then stopped when my feet were no longer in view.

I was such a dumbass.

The people outside were in a perfect position for me to use my power. They had essentially stopped their assault on me, and instead of using that to my advantage, I wasted precious time crawling across the nasty floor to check the men who had attacked Devlin and Alek. And to what end? Why did I need to check them? They were down.

I let out an angry sigh and stood.

I'd have to berate myself later.

Now, time to rip some souls out.

I let my gaze go distant and found their luminescent souls pulsing around them. It turns out I didn't need to have them in my line of sight in order for me to find those bright balls of energy. Once I had a lock on them, one of the men in the room stirred.

I whipped around.

One man on the floor had climbed to his feet.

We locked gazes.

He lunged at me. I scrambled back to avoid his outstretched

hand and slammed my back into the open door. That slender piece of wood bit into my spine, making my teeth rattle. I bowed forward as pain raced down my back. My vision wavered.

The man snatched me up. His eyes roamed over me. "What kind of magick do you have?" he asked, his voice gruff. The side of his mouth had remnants of blood on it.

"Did I hurt you?" I asked, walking my fingers down my leg to get to my dagger. I'd left the damn gun near the entrance to the front room. Stupid.

"Not as much as I'm going—"

I buried my knife in his gut. His grip tightened, eyes widened. He threw me across the room, and I crashed into the wall near Devlin and Alek. My blade was still buried in his stomach. He stared down at the wound as if he couldn't believe I'd stabbed him.

He took a step.

Then another.

And then crumpled to the ground.

The man outside called out to him, his magick attack on Devlin and Alek halted. Alek heaved up, and the smokey, dark orange magick circling him exploded out of the room, flowing outside in a torrent.

Windows shattered, the glass blowing out into the night.

The men outside screamed; their deep bellows seemed to echo.

A gust of wind kicked up inside, and Devlin climbed to his feet, rubbing his head with one hand while the other held the vial filled with air.

They were back in the game.

I eased up, pain making the effort difficult. Alek turned his head slowly; his dark, blue eyes held a storm inside of them. The blue was now almost black. His obsidian gaze raked down my body, as if tallying every single wound I had. I suppressed a shiver at the intensity.

"Alek," Devlin said. "Rein it in."

Alek closed his eyes, and his magick pulsed. Once. Twice. On the third beat, it lost some of its murkiness. His throat worked as he swallowed hard. "Are you okay?" he asked, eyes still closed.

"Other than wading in piss and vomit and getting the wind knocked out of me, I'm fine." It was a lie. Every inch of my body was in pain. Even my eyeballs hurt. I went over to the man I'd killed and yanked my knife out of his gut. I chanced a look outside and found the three men sprawled across the pavement, blood pooling around them.

"What happened?" I asked while I cleaned my blade on the man's pants.

"Two men were already inside when we got in the front room. I put one down before another two entered," Devlin said and looked at Alek. "Alek put two down before someone locked onto us from outside."

I narrowed my eyes. "What's going on?"

Devlin sighed. "If Alek hadn't reacted and put a small protection around us, the man would have killed us." He looked at me. "I assume the third man tried to attack you."

I smiled. "And I hadn't even realized it. My mark acted on its own." I looked at Alek. He still had his eyes closed. I went over and put my arms around him, flinching at the pain in my arms. "Hey. We won."

He opened his eyes slowly and peered down at me. "I lost control."

I shook my head and smiled. "You heard what Devlin said. If you hadn't acted when you did, you both would have been killed. And I would have been left here all by myself, trying to fight off a group of trained mercenaries." I looked at the three remaining men in the corner, who still hadn't moved. "I assume they're dead. The question is, who hired them and who sent them? And why?"

"We'll find out," Devlin said and moved slowly over to them. He knelt, his face constricted in pain, and patted each of them down, searching their pockets.

"Where are the girls?" Alek asked.

I blew out an angry breath. "Dead."

I led him down the hallway and to the bedroom where the girls were. Alek went over and checked their pulses. "I don't understand why they killed them," he said.

I thought about it. It *didn't* make sense to kill them. They weren't a threat. Yet the girl knew someone would return and break our minds. Why? It couldn't have been a trap. I told Alek about my conversation with the one girl, and we both couldn't figure out what she had meant.

A tremor started in my left hand. I gripped it with my right, trying to mask the movement. *Please don't have another panic attack.*

Alek pulled his phone out and aimed it at the girls, only to stop and look back at me. "Doesn't feel right for me to take their picture."

"I understand." I took my own phone out, surprised it hadn't been crushed when the man threw me against the wall, and took pictures of them. Emotions rose in my throat, and I swallowed them. No matter how I felt about the horror of what had been done to them, I had to remind myself they had chosen this life. Yes, they had been promised something greater, but it didn't change the fact they went into whatever this was willingly.

Much like me when I had tried to bury my pain at the loss of one of my best friends by wandering into The War Zone looking for something to ease the pain. A way for me to just forget. The only reason I had made it out alive was because the man who tried to kill me ran out of bullets. And when I had emerged from that brush with death, my parents were there, waiting to engulf me in their love.

These girls had only had each other.

"Well, I think we found our connection to the Peterson's girl school," I said, remembering the crest drawn on the note they'd found on the bodies of the missing girls' parents.

Alek eyed the patch on their shirts. "Yeah. But what does it all mean?"

Before we could ponder it further, the screech of tires pulled our attention. We ran out and found Devlin in the living room, holding a funnel of flames in his hand. The bright ball danced around his open palm. Crackling, spitting out white, fiery sparks.

"We have more company," he announced, eyes glued to the walkway outside the front door.

"Someone is watching us," I said, gripping my blade in my hand.

"Yes," Devlin said, then looked at Alek and me. "No holding back."

Dark orange smoke filled the room.

I peered out into the night and found seven bright souls moving toward the house.

I smiled and let my magick flow.

In military formation, they came. Magick flowed around them and pushed its way inside the house. They moved too quickly. With a precision only seen in movies. A deadly group of mind mages, battle trained, with no sign of humanity in them.

I grabbed the first man's soul and yanked; he fell to the ground, and his team moved around him as if he were never there. I held that icy ball of energy in my hand, willing it to die. Red motes danced around it, creating black holes in the light. My awe at this new development in my abilities rendered me motionless. How had I managed to kill with a single thought? Why had I even tried?

Devlin threw a ball of fire at them. "Get in the fight, Nicole," Devlin bit out.

I let the now dead soul seep from my hands like sand. Alek gave me a questioning look, and I shook my head.

The men outside lay on the pavement. One of them rolled around, trying to put the flames out as they ate at his clothes.

In unison, as if being pulled on marionette strings, they all flowed up from the ground. The man in front sent his magick out, knocking Devlin to the ground. Devlin bellowed, clutching his head.

Alek's power wrapped around Devlin in an embrace. A few

tendrils broke off and flew at Devlin's attacker. The man cried out, and his comrades directed their attack at Alek.

I dropped my dagger and grabbed Devlin's gun out of its holster, then fired out the door. Someone returned fire, and the bullet grazed my arm, knocking me back. The sting made my eyes water.

Alek roared, and his magick darkened—bright orange now black and smokey. His power beat at the multiple attacks coming at him.

Blood trickled down my arm in crimson rivulets, coating my hand. I swallowed the pain, wiped my hand across my jeans, and picked up my dagger.

A man stepped into the room, bathed in an orangish light. Built like a gladiator, his long, dark hair lay slicked back from his brown face and queued at the nape of his neck. He cocked his head to the side, studying me out of cool hazel eyes.

I tried to project helplessness to lure him in. But surely the sneer I felt creeping across my face made me a liar. No matter. I wasn't in the mood to play docile anyway.

Alek's magick pushed at him, but he batted it away, which shouldn't have been possible. And wouldn't have been, if he hadn't needed to shield Devlin.

"I've heard of you, Alexandros Vaduva," one man said, his voice like a melody. "We had wanted to recruit you at one time." He laughed, a dark sound filled with menace. "Didn't think I'd ever get to fight you." He kept his gaze on me, as if Alek weren't even a threat.

Out of the corner of my eye, I saw Alek smile. His eyes had gone completely black.

Devlin's reaction to Alek's overuse of power told me it wasn't a great idea to push him past a certain point, where he could no longer control himself. But this cocky bastard had walked in baiting him. And Devlin *did* say to not hold back.

I had to keep the man focused on me while Alek did his thing.

"Funny," I said. "You haven't attacked me yet. Are you scared?"

He laughed. "Your magick is strange." He shook his head, his power whipping around him. "But you're right. We need to end this."

His power engulfed me.

The phoenix wings unfurled, and a wave of pure power surged out of me, knocking him back against the door frame. I didn't wait to see if he'd recover; I rushed over and thrust the knife deep into his throat.

Blood gushed out, coating my clothes. I stared into his dead eyes. And his soul, a wispy ball of light, detached from his body. I grabbed it and let the cold feel of it writhe around in my hand. His body jerked as I held it, keeping him tethered to the world.

I wanted to punish him. Wanted to make him suffer. But I also had to keep my head in the game. I leaned down and whispered, "Not so tough after all." I let his soul go and stood.

Boots pounded on the pavement outside. I looked up in time to see three men heading toward us. I rushed forward and slammed the door.

I turned and found Devlin and Alek standing, eyes on me.

Alek wiped blood from his mouth with the back of his hand.

"We're cornered in here," Devlin said. "And there is no telling how many more will come."

"Those are Dacian fighters." Alek ripped the bottom of his shirt and tied the fabric around my arm. "They won't stop until we are dead."

"So we need to find the person sending them here and why." I winced as Alek tucked the ends into the folded fabric. "Which means we need to get out of this house."

"Let's move," Devlin said and started for the back.

Before we could, someone kicked open the door and a torrent of power poured into the room. Alek and Devlin dropped to their knees. Dark blue light pulsated around Devlin. Alek's power fell like a blanket of smoke over them.

I dropped beside them as another man stepped into the room.

I pulled Alek's gun free and fired at him. The bullet hit him in the shoulder, and he staggered back.

The men behind him moved out of the way.

I shot at him again and missed by a mile.

When he started for me, I threw the gun at him and scrambled forward, dagger ready, only for him to yank me up and toss me outside. I hit the grass hard, landing on my already sore back. He walked down the steps at a leisurely pace and made his way toward me.

Thankfully, I still had the knife in my hand. I stood up.

His power slithered along the ground in front of me, crawling toward me like a snake.

That's right, idiot. Use your magick.

His power stopped short, licking at the space in front of me. "You can repel magick?" he asked, as if I was foolish enough to answer.

But how the fuck did he know that?

I held the dagger at my side, blood dripping onto the pavement. Lights had come on in the surrounding houses. People spilled out into the streets. Watching but not helping. I spared a glance at the black SUV parked on the tall grass. A man sat in front, bathed in orange light. That explained why Alek and Devlin hadn't come out.

"Are we going to stand here chitchatting?" I asked.

Just attack already!

He huffed and looked behind me. I didn't dare take my eyes off him. "Your friends are powerful. It took two of us to knock them down." He kicked his crawling teammate, whose clothes had been reduced to scorched tatters, skin black with burns. "Die already."

My eyes rounded. "Isn't he with you?"

The man laughed. "He's weak." He pulled a dagger from the sheath on his belt. "So, since I can't kill you with magick ..." He rushed forward without warning, and if I hadn't moved, he would have sliced my neck open. Instead, the sharp blade cut across my chest, just above my breast.

I danced back and swallowed the scream. He kept coming, and I kept dodging. He was toying with me. If I tried to grab his soul, he would get me, so all I could do was keep avoiding his blade. My chest heaved; blood trickled down, coating my skin.

Still, the people only watched. Fucking useless assholes.

The man in the car screamed, and my attacker stopped, looking back at his partner. It was the opening I needed. I let my gaze go distant and found his soul pulsating inside of him. With fury riding me, I yanked it out of his body and willed its death. Once again, black holes ate away at the light, reducing it to sand in my clenched fist.

The man dropped, and his friend got out of the car with a gun in his hand. But before he could fire, a dagger made of water struck him in the chest. He staggered back, falling against the car while the water continued to pound him.

A dark melody filled the night. Its deep timbre caressed my skin.

The water stopped suddenly.

I turned and saw Alek standing on the porch. His magick pulsed, a dark orange tinged in black and gold, the mist eating away at the space in front of him. His hair whipped around him, and his eyes had gone pitch. He looked like a dark god.

Devlin stumbled toward me. "We have to stop him," Devlin said, pain in his voice.

Someone screamed and I turned around.

The man, drenched in water, seized. His body was half in and half out of the vehicle. Blood poured from every orifice on his face.

The bystanders dropped to the ground, clutching their heads.

Dogs howled in the background.

The dark melody swelled.

Devlin moved toward Alek, hands raised. "Rein it the fuck in,

Alek," he screamed over the song of death. Devlin pulled earth from its vial, letting the substance circle his hand.

A slow smile spread across Alek's face, and Devlin dropped to his knees, sending his power out. It punched Alek in the chest.

He didn't move.

I pushed through his power and ascended the stairs. A loud pop drew my attention, and I turned to find the last attacker's head had exploded. I placed my hand on Alek's feverish skin.

"Please, stop," I whispered, moving in close.

Devlin got to his knees, power building. I raised my hand to stall the attack. "I got him," I said.

Alek's dark gaze found mine. His eyes dipped to the wound across my chest.

"I will heal. You are hurting everyone. Please, Alek. Please, stop."

So much power. Rachel's comment about Alek a few months back suddenly made sense.

"If he can take Alek in, he can take you in."

Her statement had suggested Alek was dangerous. I'd seen him fight before, and while he was powerful, this was something much more. Sometimes, it seemed as if he craved death and destruction. Like the demise of others fed his soul.

The torrent of his magick continued to wash over me. And yet, my phoenix wings remained closed. Which meant he had enough control in him to not attack me as well. So why had he attacked Devlin?

I turned to Boss Man, noting the blood smeared all over his face and shirt. "How do I stop him?" I asked.

Devlin stared at Alek, a tic working on the side of his neck. I'd say he was angry, except there was sadness in his eyes. "The only one who has ever been able to is Rachel." He looked at me. "Why isn't your magick reacting?"

I shook my head. "He isn't attacking me."

The people in the street screamed. If we didn't stop him soon, he would kill everyone on the block.

"Alek!"

He didn't respond. His attention now focused on the street.

My first instinct was to slap him. That usually worked when a person was out of control. But this was not a lack of control. This was rage. And hurting him would only make it worse.

So, I pulled his head down and kissed him, pouring as much love into it as I could.

The sound of his dark melody cut off so suddenly, my ears popped.

Alek's arms came around me, and his lips seared against mine. I moaned as his tongue found mine. Twining and dueling and caressing. The urgency sent heat through me, settling low in my belly. I breathed in his scent. Letting the warmth of him engulf me.

It seemed to go on forever. His hunger for me was so intoxicating.

Someone touched my shoulder, and I reluctantly pulled back. I cupped Alek's face in my hand. "Better?"

He nodded mutely and looked over my shoulder at Devlin. "I wasn't attacking you," he said, his voice rough.

"I realized that when the last man's head popped. He would have killed me." Devlin dipped his head in thanks.

Alek stared down at me. "I hate that you saw me like that."

I gave him a half-smile. "Are you kidding? You looked like a god." I swallowed. My throat had gone dry. "But give me some warning next time, okay?"

He smoothed my hair back and nodded. His gaze went to my chest. "It's healing already."

"Yeah. Still hurts, though."

"I should get her home so Rachel can help her," Alek said.

I wanted to protest, but I didn't have the strength to do so. Now that the threat was over, a bone-deep fatigue had taken hold. And the sticky sensation from all the blood coating me was driving me up the wall. I glanced around at the sheer mass of bodies lining the walkway and yard. Why would someone send so many people to kill us? Did they really think we were that much of a threat?

"Maybe we should stay and help clean up," I offered with absolutely no intention of doing so. Seriously, I could fall over at any minute.

Devlin walked away, pulling his phone out as he went.

I glanced around at the carnage left from our attack. Seven men had come for us after the initial assault. All of them lay on the ground—dead—most with blood pooling around their heads.

The bystanders remained on the ground, save a few who stood off in the distance. Was the one who sent the Dacian with them? I searched their faces. "Can you read the minds of the ones still standing?" I asked Alek.

"No," he said. "I'm spent."

I looked up at him and noted the redness in his eyes and the welts on the side of his face. It looked as if blood vessels had broken under his skin. I reached up and ran my finger along the jagged line. His face contorted as he grimaced with pain.

Devlin walked back over. "Opal is sending a team to help clean up. You two head back to the house."

"What about you?" I asked. Devlin looked as if someone had run him over with a truck. Pretty much how I felt at the moment.

"I need to search the house. There has to be a reason they attacked us this way." He looked at the people in the street. "Someone here must have been watching us."

"What if they send more?" I asked.

Alek shook his head. "No. We put too many of them down. If anything, they will use what they learned to devise a better plan of attack." He looked at Devlin. "Still, we should stay and watch your back."

Devlin shook his head, eyes slanting in my direction.

Dead on their feet or not, both Devlin and Alek still looked ready for battle.

Alek nodded. "I'll get her home."

Everything in me wanted to bristle at the implication that I wasn't able to stay and help. Then I looked down at myself. Blood-soaked, with a gash across my chest and a wound on my arm, both of which were still leaking blood, mixing with the gruesome deposits from the people I killed, I wasn't in any condition to help with anything.

As I took a few pictures to document the scene, my mind went to a dark place. Who had killed those innocent people in the street? The Dacian? Or Alek?

At the Violet Hour

Devlin stood at the curb, looking out over the bodies strewn about the street. He waited in the darkness. A hollow ache had settled in his gut as he scanned the surrounding area. The desolate nature of the area explained why, after their lengthy battle with the Dacian, no police had arrived. Even if someone had called them, he doubted they would have shown up in time. He'd seen this in his own work in law enforcement where certain areas in the city were simply not prioritized as much as others. A cry for help would more often than not go unanswered. Leaving the victims to fend for themselves. Oh, the police would arrive. Eventually. But never in time.

The silence was deafening, giving the darkness a frightening weight. He glanced down the block toward The War Zone. Dark tendrils seemed to slither about, ensnaring the area, taking the lifeless bodies as an invitation to pull the neighborhood finally into its web. As if they had sacrificed to it, with their blood.

He sent his awareness out, looking for the one who always watched him, and found only the power of the elements.

He shifted his weight to ease some of his pain. It didn't help. Shoving his hands in his pockets, he glanced up at the sky and used the water inside those heavy rain clouds to fuel his magick. The power rushed through him. Not healing. But soothing.

Soft light pricked his eyes as the sun crested the horizon, spilling its violet rays across the sky. A host of sparrows swooped down and banked right. Their chirping broke the silence. A chill ran down his spine. Sparrows were a death omen.

Devlin pulled in a deep breath and closed his eyes.

Chaos rested inside his head.

They had been unprepared. Had barely escaped death. And he didn't know how to process it. Sure, he and his team had been in some tough situations in the past, but this level of threat was different. They needed a plan. One that involved training Nicole on how to use her power. Because if they were attacked by the Dacian again, their survival would rest on her ability to respond quickly to the threat. It was far too dangerous for Alek to lose control again.

The rumble of an engine pulled Devlin from his thoughts, and he glanced toward the sound. Five green and white utility trucks made their way down the street, parking at intervals along the block. An ambulance, without a siren or its lights on, came next and parked in the middle of the street. Three men jumped from the back of the vehicle and went to check on the people in the street. Workers, wearing green uniforms with Tulare Power stenciled on the front pockets of their button-down shirts, piled out of the trucks and rushed through the open doors of the homes along the street.

The area had come alive with commotion, sending the encroaching dark from The War Zone receding. Orange sunlight trickled onto the street, and the clouds pulled back, revealing a two-toned sky. Despite the sudden flurry of activity, Devlin didn't move. His thoughts had not ordered themselves, leaving him in a catatonic state. It reminded him of his home life when he was a child. How he'd gone inside himself when his mother spiraled out of control, mania taking root inside of her. She'd been diagnosed later as being bipolar.

A sleek midnight-blue Audi turned down the street, its engine no more than a purr. It pulled up and parked behind the discarded black SUV the Dacian had driven. Opal got out wearing a pair of tight blue jeans and a white tank top. She had her long hair pulled up in a bun, exposing her slender neck.

She scanned the area, face a mask of calculation, then walked over to talk with a woman in uniform.

Now that the daylight had penetrated the area, farther down the block, others emerged from their homes and made their way toward the disturbance. He studied them, trying to find a person who showed more than a little interest in what was going on. All their faces held a sickening sort of thrill at the chaos before them. Like moths to a flame. Drawn to suffering.

When he had worked crime scenes in the past, often the perp would blend in with the crowd to admire their handiwork. Even though Nicole had taken pictures of the onlookers, he doubted the ones responsible would be careless enough to show themselves. After all, they'd sent the Dacian to do their dirty work instead of handling the problem on their own.

The question was, why had they sent so many? And in waves? Not to mention the overkill of it. Did they really need elite warriors to take out two girls so high on drugs they couldn't defend themselves?

Opal picked her way around the bodies strewn about and, after retrieving two cups from her car, came over and handed him one. The aroma from the rich brew had him closing his eyes. He took a sip and sighed.

"Thanks," he mumbled.

"How is your team?" she asked, looking up at him.

He glanced at her. "Their wounds can be healed. Their minds ..." He shrugged and took another long swig of coffee. She'd made it just right.

"You look as if you're ready to drop."

He nodded. "I am." He jerked his chin toward the workmen. "What story are you going with?"

She studied Devlin for a minute, then turned and looked at her workers. "Gang violence. Followed by a power outage. The mind mages said it fit the scenario the best."

Mind mages could plant suggestions in a person's head, but they needed to use elements of what the individual had seen or experienced for it to ring true. Otherwise, the illusion would fall apart, leaving the person confused.

The lights buzzed on as Opal's people restored power to the area. Only to switch off again when the sun's rays finally filled the street. It had been a long while since he'd seen the sun rise.

They watched in silence as her team confirmed the dead and rounded up the bystanders. Others gathered the bodies of the Dacian and lined them up in the yard. Once the walkway was clear, Devlin went over and snapped pictures of each of the Dacian. He'd have Rachel try to identify them using facial recognition. The search of their pockets and vehicles yielded no results, so he made his way toward the house to see if there were any other clues as to why this house was so important.

"There are two girls inside," he called over his shoulder. "I'd also like to check out the house again." He couldn't figure out what this house was being used for. The marks on the wall suggested it *might* relate to what they were investigating. But two girls strung out on drugs most likely being pimped out by the carnival grounds security guard Dimitri didn't quite fit with what they had collected so far. Yes, he'd found drug paraphernalia in Dimitri's discarded backpack, but nothing suggested he'd killed the missing girls' parents.

After signaling to one of her men to follow, Opal strode up the walkway behind him and stepped inside the house. Her boots squished in the damp carpet. "What happened in here?" she asked, coming to stand next to him as he studied the symbols on the wall.

"Had to use my power to push them back," he said absently. "What do these this look like to you?"

She moved closer to the wall. "The writing looks Coptic." She moved closer and traced one of the symbols. "Do you have someone to translate this for you?"

Devlin watched as she continued to trace the words. She seemed mesmerized by them. "Yeah. We can handle it."

She jerked her hand from the wall and turned to look at him. "Sorry. Religion and ancient languages were a theme in my household. The two have so much in common."

Devlin cocked his head to the side. "How so?"

She glanced around. "How about we clean this scene up and go for some food to discuss it."

Devlin gave her a half-smile. "After this, I need to debrief my team. So, raincheck?" He wished he had the time for a casual meeting. It would have been nice to just sit for a while and listen to someone else talk. But his life didn't afford him such things.

She smiled. "Raincheck."

After setting their cups down on the crowded coffee table, Devlin showed her team where the two girls were, then he searched the other rooms in the house. He could have kicked himself for not doing so when Nicole was trying to reason with one of the girls to allow them to help. But he had wanted to be on hand in case she needed him.

And then they were attacked.

Aside from the bedroom they found the girls in, there were two other bedrooms down the hallway. Both contained a single mattress and dresser. He found several items of clothing and some men's jewelry. He looked down at the dirty floor, eyes going to the patch of clean space near the window. Something had been there. And removed recently.

Which once again made him think about the attack.

Could it have been the girls they wanted to silence? If so, a single person could have come here to take care of that. Hell, the drugs would have as well.

But one thing was certain: a single attack, overkill or not, should have been sufficient. Which meant somebody, maybe one of the onlookers, had been watching the house. He just needed to figure out who and why.

He stepped out of the hallway and made his way to the kitchen. A few days' worth of dishes rested in the sink, flies buzzing around the crusted food on the plates. Warm air rushed into the room, and Devlin stared at the open back door. The very door he remembered shutting when he entered the house.

Someone had come in after him.

He went through the events of their fight. Given the strategic nature of the ones who came for them, it would have made sense for them to send men through both entrances, effectively boxing him and his team in. Yet, they only came through the front. Keeping them occupied while someone snuck in the back and retrieved some vital element they wanted to protect or steal. Could that be it? Was the attack meant to be a distraction?

Fuck.

He rushed back to the bedroom where he'd found the patch of clean carpet and crouched. Running his hand over the area, he detected a slight difference in the temperature of the clean spot. It was warmer compared to the dirty area. He stood and checked the window. Unlocked. No screen. Which meant someone could have opened it from the inside and passed whatever had been in this spot outside.

Opal walked into the room. "The girls have been taken to the morgue by my team. They'll give a different location as to where they were found."

"They were killed by magick."

"I'll let my contact know to list drugs as the cause of death." She glanced around. "Given the state of this house, we might have to set fire to it to ensure all traces of evidence are gone."

"You honestly believe someone would investigate this?" Devlin seethed with anger. All of this was for nothing. They would find no clues here. Only more questions.

"Eventually," Opal said. "One bystander called the police. We have a man inside, and he will make sure he's on the case."

Devlin looked at her, eyes narrowed. "You have a man inside the Perry Precinct."

She gave him a half-smile "Yes. And you've met him."

"Who?"

"Detective Kneadsome. Barnes's partner. He's been on the island for a year now."

Devlin folded his arms over his chest. "Why didn't you tell me this sooner?" he bit out. Detective Barnes had been harassing him and his team since they started working for the Markums. The man had gone out of his way to insert himself into an incident involving a witness they had wanted to question about the Stewart family, despite it taking place in another area of the island.

"It was my call. The Markums wanted you to know. But I deemed it necessary to wait."

"For what?" Devlin asked.

She averted her gaze. "Until I was sure you all could be trusted."

Devlin wanted to argue with her but also understood why she had been reluctant. Giving away that sort of information had to be managed carefully. Secrets shared by too many had a way of getting out. And if Kneadsome's corrupt partner ever discovered he was there to watch him, Kneadsome would most likely end up dead.

"How long have you all been watching Detective Barnes?"

Opal sighed. "They've had their eye on him for a while." She paused. "I can give you his file. Although, I doubt it has anything to do with your current case."

Devlin nodded. "I'd still like to see it." He pointed to the clean patch in the rug. "I think the ambush was meant to keep us occupied out front while they removed whatever was here. I also believe the girls were killed because they knew too much." Devlin ran his hand down his face. The coffee had given him a little jolt, but not nearly enough.

"What could they know?" Opal asked.

He shook his head. It was the only explanation that made

sense regarding their murders. Why kill them unless it was to protect a secret of some sort?

"So, what now?" Opal asked.

Devlin looked at her. "Now, I debrief my team, and we come up with a plan on how to approach this." He smiled. "Can you give me a ride?"

She nodded, and he followed her to her car.

They had lost a vital piece of the puzzle. One that was sure to come back and bite them in the ass later. But for now, all he could do was figure out a way to protect his team. And if that meant letting Alek off his leash, so be it.

The sun crested the sky when we pulled up to Devlin's house. Climbing out of the car on unstable legs, Alek and I made our way up the walkway toward the front door. At some point today, I'd have to deal with the deaths I'd caused. Try to fit them into my new way of thinking.

But not right now. Now, I needed a vat of coffee and a shower. And after that, I'd burn my damn clothes, because there was no way in hell I was going to wear them again.

The noise from the TV greeted us when we stepped inside. I followed the sound down the hallway and into the war room to find Rachel curled up on the floor with her phone in her hand. She must have been waiting for us to check in.

I took a step back, trying to ease out of the room without waking her, and bumped into Alek. "What's wrong?" he asked, touching my elbow.

Rachel's eyes shot open, and she flowed to her feet, power filling the room. When we locked eyes, she sighed. "Oh. Thought we were under attack," she said, stretching. Her eyes narrowed, brow furrowing. "Why are you covered in blood?"

"Someone bled all over me."

Alek stepped around me, and she rushed to him, placing her hand on his chest. "You got hurt," she said as warm green light pulsed out of her hand.

"Oh, okay. So I come in here looking like Carrie after the prom and you don't even flinch. I could be bleeding out right now! On the verge of death!" I sounded a little hysterical and whiny.

She shook her head at me. "You heal fast. I can help with your pain after I take care of Alek."

I gritted my teeth and walked away. I might have made a lot of unnecessary noise while doing so, but I refused to acknowledge it. Because damnit, she was right. I healed fast. Just another benefit of my power. An aspect that, thankfully, now had a will of its own. Because given my current mental and physical state, I seriously doubted I'd have enough energy to do it on my own. I barely had the strength to walk, let alone wield magick.

I should have got that vat of coffee first.

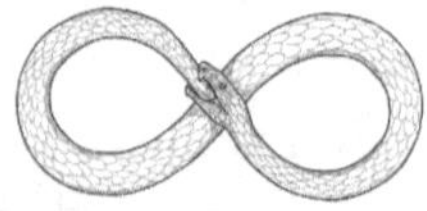

BLOOD-TINGED WATER CIRCLED THE DRAIN. Fatigue rode me like a lover, caressing every cell in my body and whispering in my ear to just lay down. But if I did, I feared I'd sleep for a week. So, I stood there, letting the water scald my skin, wondering why my loofah refused to do all the work for me.

A niggling sensation settled in the back of my head. I stepped back from the drumbeat of water pounding on my skin in hopes of catching that stray thought that kept trying to come into focus. As if absolute stillness would allow it to finally surface in my mind.

I stared at the shower floor, the clear water pooling at the drain while images of the Houses of Power flitted through my head. Could that be it? I shook my head. No. My reaction, as well as Devlin's, while alarming, wasn't something I was particularly concerned with. Yes, it was another aspect of my power that needed exploring, but the time to do so would have to be much later.

Maybe it was our complete failure in saving those two girls. Being in that place. Seeing them like that had forced memories to surface in my mind. Memories I'd long buried.

My chest rose as I inhaled the residual scent of Alek's bodywash mixed with my own jasmine-scented one. I needed to remain calm. Yet something, some stray thought, kept poking at me. Again, I thought of the Houses of Power. And again, I dismissed them.

Maybe ...

The shower curtain whisked open, letting out all the nice, soothing steam. I gave a lackluster yelp and resumed my watchful vigil of the drain. I'd lost my train of thought.

"You okay?" Alek asked, handing me a large mug.

I took it and stared at the dark brew inside, rippling as the water pelted the surface. "The loofah is broken," I said, then took a large swallow of coffee. The caffeine jolt went down smoothly, tickling my fatigue.

He glanced at said item. "It looks fine to me."

"Then why hasn't it washed me yet!"

"You have to pick it up first."

I groaned into my coffee.

Alek stripped down and joined me in the shower. My hormones gave a half-hearted reaction and then rejoined the pity party going on inside my head. I really needed to stop throwing them, but that would require loads of therapy, coffee, sex, cigars, and facing my demons. I had tried to start down a new path. Even vowed yesterday to work on my behavior. Yet, like all declarations of change, it was hard.

As it were, I'd had to shove all the pain and thoughts of the last few hours down deep just so I could peel my bloody clothes off.

Picking up the loofah and my body wash, Alek lathered up the sponge and washed my back and legs. The soothing smell of jasmine filled the steamy space.

"I might have left my bloody clothes on your carpet," I mumbled as he ran the loofah over my stomach.

"Mm... I found them. You want to keep them?"

I shook my head slowly and leaned back against his hard chest, cradling the now empty coffee mug against my breast. "No. I want to burn them. Along with our enemies."

He set the loofah down and placed his hands on my hips, urging me back against him as he squeezed. "We can do that." He ran his teeth over my earlobe, and my stomach tightened with need.

"If I wasn't so tired, I might turn around and have my way with you." I moaned, enjoying the feel of him pressing against me.

His fingers lightly skimmed the curve of my ass. "I'm not tired." His warm breath brushed against my neck. I shuddered, closing my eyes to the torrent of desire rushing through me. The mug slipped from my fingers, and Alek caught it, setting it on the soap holder.

"Can't let you do all the work," I breathed out and took his hand in mine and guided it low, easing it between my legs. His warm hands cupped me; a single finger slid inside of me. I moaned. He pressed against my back, hard and ready.

How long I'd waited for this very moment. And now, after a battle that left me bloody and bruised, I'd get to have him. It seemed strange to make this our first time. But there is something so very heady about danger and sex.

Alek ran his tongue over the ridge of my ear while his long fingers worked up a delicious friction at my core. I felt myself falling, knees weak. His arm tightened around me, keeping me pinned against him. Another finger pushed inside of me, opening me up. My pulse pounded in my ear. The drum of water, now running cold, beat against my feverish skin. I bit my lip against the scream lodged in my throat.

He whispered, "Put your leg on the side of the tub."

My chest heaved as I lifted my leg, letting him dive deeper inside of me.

"You want me?" he asked, voice gruff with his own need.

"Yes," I said, urging him deeper.

I wanted Alek. Needed him, really. Who cared about the sweet romance we'd tried to plan? And at this point, I really didn't give a shit who heard us. All I wanted was Alek buried inside of me. Easing my ache.

"Oh, dear god," I said, letting my leg fall to the side. "I need you inside of me now!"

Alek withdrew his fingers. "Not in here," he said roughly. "In bed." He yanked open the shower and picked me up, throwing me over his shoulder, his hand cupping my ass.

He carried me out of the bathroom, to the bedroom, and laid me on the bed. His dark blue gaze hungrily roamed over me. Devouring every inch of my body. "Tell me you want me again," he demanded. His deep voice seemed to penetrate my soul.

A well of emotions and need rolled through me, settling inside my heart. In that moment, with him staring at me with so much hunger and more in his eyes, the same "more" I couldn't say aloud, I did want the sweetness. But for now, we could satisfy our lust.

I surged up and took him into my mouth, letting my teeth graze against him. He pulled away. "Tell me!" he said, then pressed his lips to mine.

"I want you, Alek," I said.

He shoved me back onto the bed and covered me with his warm, slick body. I clawed at his back as he pushed my legs apart.

"Come when I tell you."

I nodded, and he pressed inside of me.

I arched my back, meeting him thrust for thrust.

His lips grazed over my breast, and he sucked my swollen nipple into his mouth. I tightened my legs around him, squeezing him, wanting him deeper and deeper.

Heat encompassed me, driving me on, fueling my movements. I pulled in precious air as Alek increased his pace, then I locked my legs around him and twisted until he lay on his back. He grabbed my hips, grinding me against him.

I rode him hard, to the point of pain. Letting every single worry flow out of me. This ... this was what I needed. The connection I craved.

Alek reached between my legs and drove his thumb across my clit, quickening the pooling heat at my core. "Come," he said.

I threw my head back and screamed until my throat felt raw. Darkness crept around my vision as wave after wave of pleasure rolled through me.

He pressed harder. "Again," he demanded.

I clawed at his chest, my body writhing, trying to contain the second orgasm threatening to tear me apart. With one massive thrust, a guttural cry tore out of him. He grabbed my hips, keeping me in place, both of us riding the torrent.

My chest heaved; I couldn't catch my breath. The world spun. Bright lights flashed in my vision. Electric heat consumed my entire being. Rivulets of sweat rolled down my body.

I pulled in a ragged breath, then collapsed onto him and passed out.

I came to still straddling him. The rhythmic pounding of his heart echoed in my ears. He ran his warm hand over my back, and I sighed. "I needed that," I whispered, my body trembling. The ache between my legs made me smile.

"That wasn't how I imagined our first time to be," he said.

I eased up on shaky arms and stared down into his dark blue eyes. "Sorry I couldn't wait for the right moment." I smiled. "But damn, Alek. You have some mad skills."

He laughed. I leaned forward and ran my tongue over the side of his mouth, and he turned into me, pressing his warm, plush lips against mine. I breathed him in.

"And if memory serves, it was you"—I sat up—"that started it."

He gave me a devilish grin. "True. But you had no problem taking the reins."

I stared at him. "You have yet to compliment me," I said, teasing.

"I think I might show you just how much I enjoyed being buried in all that heat."

My entire body flushed. "So. Dirty talk as well." I gasped as reality kicked in. "Do you think they heard us?"

He chuckled. "I think everyone on the block did."

"Oh. I will not live this down."

He watched me, a small smile creasing his sexy mouth. I leaned down and kissed him softly on the lips—a total contrast to the animalistic way in which we tore at each other a few minutes ago.

I'd had sex with Alek.

Sure, we'd been heading in this direction. And yes, I missed sex so much, I'd considered getting myself a vibrator to take the edge off. But I never imagined having sex with someone I cared about deeply. To me, sex had always been about the fun. It had been a way to hide from the pain of feeling inadequate in my life. A way to pretend I was okay, when deep down, I was struggling.

Alek ran a finger between my breasts. I suppressed a shudder, watching him out of half-closed eyes. "This is... different," I said, struggling to voice what I wanted to say.

He lifted an eyebrow in question. "In what way, babe?"

I started to move off him, but he held me in place. "Nicole," he said, concern creeping into his voice. Oh great, I'd ruined a beautiful moment with my stupid insecurities.

I sighed. "I've never done anything according to them."

He gave me a confused look and sat up. His arms came around me. "Who's them?" he asked carefully.

"Them. That illusive group of judgmental people who decide social norms." I swallowed the damn lump in my throat and looked away. "I'm not... I'm not good at this, Alek. This emotional stuff." I gestured between us.

"Since when do you give a fuck about what someone thinks?"

"I never did. At least, that's what I believed. But sometimes, they can just get inside your head."

He smiled. "No one can get in your head, babe. Not even me."

I groaned and hid my face on his shoulder. "Can we change the subject?"

He rubbed my back. "Yes."

I moved off of him, and he pulled me against his side. We lay there, sharing a comfortable silence. The warmth of his skin was the only thing keeping me from freezing to death. Pushing the current reality down into my cave of denial, I focused on the attack we had survived.

"I'm sorry I froze when we were attacked."

"Babe, no one is faulting you for what happened. The Dacian took us all by surprise. We just need to hone your skills. Make them second nature." He ran a finger over my arm in the spot the man had shot me. The wound was healed, but the phantom pain of it remained. "Your healing magick reacts on instinct. While we don't understand the battle form of your power, I have to assume it has something to do with your ability to touch souls."

I shivered, remembering my destruction of the soul I'd pulled from one of our attackers. "I killed one," I said. "I held the soul in my hand and willed it to die."

"It scared you?" he asked.

"A little. My magick keeps changing on me."

He ran his hand over my hips. "No. Your magick is waking up, and you're still learning just what you can do." He intertwined our fingers. "I promise you. We will figure it out. And soon"—he touched his forehead to mine—"you will be able to rip souls out without a second thought."

I chuckled. "That's a bit... scary."

He smiled. "But also badass."

I wanted to discuss his power and the striations that had appeared on his face when we fought the Dacian, but it wasn't the right time. Rachel had healed him, and that was all that mattered. For now, I would enjoy him holding me for a little while longer. Because I got the feeling the assault from last night wouldn't be the last. And he was right; I needed to be ready.

Wearing a pair of boots, tight blue jeans, my dagger, and a red tank top, I made my way toward the war room and was happily greeted with the smokey aroma of caramelized fat. Butter filled the air as well, but the fat had my mouth watering.

Marta stood at the stove wearing a pair of baggy sweatpants and a large white T-shirt, with scrunchy socks on her feet. She flipped pieces of bacon over in a pan, taking out a few strips and adding them to an already full plate next to her.

Rae stood next to her, cooking pieces of bread drenched in butter. Or was it butter surrounded by bread? I guess it didn't matter; I was going to eat it anyway.

I smiled at the image of them standing together. While I knew little about the teenager who had clearly made herself at home, the way she gravitated toward affection, first with Petronela and now with Marta, told me all I needed to know. I'd give her the opportunity to share the rest later if she wanted to.

Marta turned and eyed me up and down. "Might want to add an armband and some lipstick to the outfit. But besides that"—she smiled—"looking good, girl."

Rae turned and scrutinized my face. "Yeah. Definitely put some red lipstick on."

I chuckled and poured myself a cup of coffee from the special brew helpfully marked with a new gold-handled pot and sat down at the table. "What exactly are you making, anyway?" I asked Rae. If they wanted to pretend they hadn't heard Alek and I going at it like animals, then so be it. I would pretend right along with them.

She went back to turning the bread. "It's the best way to make toast. Butter both sides and grill it."

I opened my mouth to ask who taught her to make it that way but then shut it. She most likely learned it on her own. "Will there be eggs and potatoes?" I asked.

Marta opened the oven and waved away the heat. "Already made the potatoes. Rae will make the eggs last." She smiled at the teenager and then finished plating the bacon.

Rachel came into the room and set a vape pen and two clear pods on the table along with a bottle of orange-tinted liquid. I eyed the concoction with trepidation. There was no telling what the mad chemist had put in that brew.

Alek walked in the room looking like a Roman god. His long dark hair lay slicked back, and the ends rested on his strong shoulders. He wore black jeans low on his hips with a black muscle shirt and boots. His midnight-blue eyes tracked across my face and down my chest. If he continued looking at me like that, I might have to forgo breakfast and instead indulge myself with another round.

"Should we leave?" Rae asked. "Or at least get out of earshot?"

Alek laughed and straddled the chair next to me. "Mornin'," he said to everyone, still looking at me.

"If they don't stop, we might have to," Marta said, setting the plate of bacon on the table along with plates. "And I'm ordering soundproofing."

I flushed and took a long drink of my coffee.

"They always look at each other like that," Rachel said, filling one pod. "But at least they had sex." She looked at me. "This stuff is a little strong, so you have to be careful until I can adjust it for you," she told me, clicking the pod into place. She extended it toward me.

I didn't know what to react to first. The casual way she discussed my sex life or the experimental liquid she wanted me to smoke. "Umm ... what's in it?"

She shrugged. "Elderberry mixed with burdock root. I might add vervain later, but for now, I want you to try this."

Both elderberry and burdock root could be used for anxiety and stress. But they weren't potent enough to have an immediate impact.

"Why isn't the liquid purple?" I asked.

"Had to infuse it with my magick to get it to work right."

I should have figured that out on my own. I'd grown up learning about earth magick but was never able to make the power work for me. I'd believed it was my lack of strength. Turned out my parents had decided to block my abilities and never told me why. I was still trying to come to terms with that betrayal.

I took a tentative pull on the mixture and let it coat my throat. A slight buzz wormed its way through me, until I settled into a mild euphoric state. I glanced around the room, eyelids heavy. Everyone was watching me.

"You're glowing," Rae said. "It keeps pulsing." She turned away and finished making the eggs.

Alek glanced at her. "Rach." There was a warning note in his tone. Rachel and I turned to look at Rae. "Are you all seeing what I'm seeing?" he asked.

"Her magick is fluctuating," I said.

A mint-green light stuttered around Rae, morphing into pale blue, then flowing into a burnt orange color that looked like the sunset. She eased back, eyes darting around at everyone. "Hey. What did I do?" she asked, hands raised.

Marta rushed over and stepped in front of her. "Stop scaring the girl," she chastised. She ushered Rae to the table. "Now. Let's all sit and eat before the food gets cold." She scowled at each of us before placing the rest of the food on the table.

We tucked into the feast, eating in companionable silence. Every once in a while, Rachel would glance at Rae. But the teenager's magick had settled. I wanted to ask questions about it but doubted even she understood what was going on with her.

After eating enough to feed the entire house, I pushed my plate away and sighed. "I think I might have gained about fifteen pounds."

Marta got up and opened the refrigerator. "Inhaling five pieces of toast, two servings of potatoes, maybe four eggs, and enough bacon to recreate a pig might do that." She set a can of ginger ale in front of me. "I've seen you eat a lot before, but seriously, girl, that was too much." She stared at me over the rim of her coffee.

I ignored her tally of what I'd eaten and instead focused on the overflowing fridge. It had never been so full. Also, I was a tad bit embarrassed by just how much I'd eaten.

"She needs to replenish her magick," Rachel offered. "And the herbs in the coffee and tincture are working against each other." She examined me. "Might need to adjust what I made to account for the coffee."

She'd turned me into a lab rat.

"Who stocked the fridge?" I asked, taking a pull on said mixture of herbs. It really did have a calming effect.

"I just bought a few things to tide us over."

"I believe we have two different definitions of 'a few things.'"

"Also, there is a teenager here." She looked at my plate. "And you. So we might need more."

Alek chuckled and got up to put his plate and mine in the sink. "Nicole will even out once her magick is replenished." He leaned against the counter, smiling. "I actually enjoyed watching you suck down all that food."

I would have given him the finger, but the way he leaned against that counter, looking like every woman's fantasy, rendered me immobile. All I could do was drool.

Devlin walked into the kitchen, handed Rachel his phone,

and made a beeline for the coffeepot. "Download these images and do a search on the rest of the guards that work for Petronela. I also need you to print the images of the girls." He took a sip of his coffee, then grabbed a piece of toast. "Let me grab a shower. Then I need you all in the meeting room in ten." He strode out, taking his coffee with him.

"He's bossy," Rae said.

I saluted her with my can. "That he is."

I polished off the rest of the ginger ale that did, thankfully, help ease some of the discomfort in my stomach. Rae and Marta left to get dressed, and Alek joined Rachel in the war room. I watched them for a minute, thinking about Alek and Rae's magick.

The more I learned about magick, the more I was convinced I hadn't been the only one misled about it. Everyone's power seemed to step outside the norm. Kara with her ability to harness the elements when she was an earth mage. Jonah's ability to both create a demon and keep it locked inside of himself. Said demon had responded to me in an unnerving way we still needed to figure out. Alek's magick had been more than what a mind mage could do. Rae's abilities seemed to shift between the principles. Was that what Petronela saw when she sent Alek to get the girl?

I looked at my palm. How had I been able to destroy a soul with a mere thought? Did I have mind magick too?

Devlin strode back into the room, hair wet, and sat on the edge of his desk. He'd pulled on a pair of black jeans and a blue T-shirt. His wet hair sat on the nape of his neck. It had grown out since the first time I'd met him, seeming to give him a more relaxed look. It wasn't true, of course; he still had a bossy, rigid demeanor. But he looked nice with his hair long like that. Approachable, even. He sipped his coffee, red eyes fixed on the ground. He looked worn down and ready to drop. The three of us had gotten little to no sleep. We'd have to rely on Rachel's special brew to keep us up and alert for the rest of the day.

Devlin's eyes met mine, and I stood. It was time for us to

make sense of what we'd learned at the carnival. And for Devlin to give us our marching orders. I'd have to worry about magick later. Most likely when it came back to bite me in my ass.

W hile the discomfort of too much food being forced into my belly had eased, a sort of euphoric high had settled over me, leaving my mind in a strange place. It wasn't normal intoxication; I'd been there before, where the world became clear, giving way to some loud and assured proclamations. This tincture Rachel had given me left my mind in a jumbled mess, a montage of questions floating around.

Despite my mind buzzing with what I wanted to say, I slouched in my chair, waiting for drool to slide down my chin. Rachel really needed to adjust the stuff. Otherwise, I might end up sprawled in the corner while my thoughts ran a marathon around inside my head.

Rachel had uploaded the pictures from Devlin's phone and projected the images of the Dacian onto the projector screen. Thirteen men, all laid out on the grass. Some had died from obvious wounds, while others seemed to have simply fallen asleep. It made me think about the power Alek had unleashed. That dark melody that sang the attackers' death song. How could he wield so much power? But the quiet deaths couldn't be set at his feet alone; I was responsible for at least one of those deaths, having willed their soul to die.

Stress lines surrounded Devlin's mouth and eyes. He ran his hand over the shadow of a beard on his face and then launched into a recounting of the night's events. My recollection of what had happened differed from what Alek and Devlin experienced. The attack on them seemed loud and brutal, yet from my position in the bedroom, it had been a sort of quiet assault with an occasional thump.

I'd assumed one of the men waiting outside was responsible for the attack on me. But Devlin confirmed it'd been the first wave of men who entered the house. After Devlin finished, I turned to Alek. "I didn't know mind magick allowed you to shield another person."

He nodded slowly. "It was a skill I learned when I was younger."

I waited for him to go into detail. But he didn't.

"Detective Kneadsome in the Perry Precinct is working for the Markums," Devlin said. "He's been watching Detective Barnes for a while."

"Why are the Markums interested in Barnes?" I asked. "He's a corrupt cop. You can find one of those in most precincts." The more I learned about the Markums, the more I wondered what their true motives were. We'd dealt with the Stewart family, the ones responsible for their daughter's death. So why have us focus on the blood magick users? And now we learned they were watching members of law enforcement too. It didn't make sense.

"Opal didn't say," Devlin responded. "But I plan to find out."

"Should we be concerned about Barnes?" Alek asked.

"No. We wait and see." Devlin looked at me. "Why don't you take the team through your end of the attack."

I nodded and tried to narrow my thoughts into a chronological order, made difficult since every single one of those thoughts wanted to go first. Damn Rachel!

Finally, after a rather long pause, I took the team through what I'd experienced. Of course, I didn't tell them about my slow belly-crawl across a piss-stained floor. It was too embarrassing. While I told the story, my mind kept getting hung up on the absolute force of it. I looked at the pictures of the Dacian. Thirteen warriors for two strung-out girls. It was overkill. Then again,

Devlin believed someone had been watching the house. But how would they have rounded up so many in such a short time? Something just wasn't right about the entire encounter.

"Did you see anyone suspicious when we left?" I asked Devlin.

Devlin shook his head. It made little sense. Even if, as he suspected, the people responsible for sending the Dacian wanted to retrieve something important, why so many? I glanced at Alek. "One of them knew you," I said.

He nodded. "More like they know my reputation." Given the potency of his power, I didn't doubt he had one.

"You think it might have been drugs in the trunk?" Marta asked.

Rae scoffed. "If that were the case, they'd send in a few people with guns. Sending in magick users means they were aware people with magick were inside."

She was right. The question was, who could have warned them?

Devlin retrieved a box from the floor and set it on the table. "Rae found this backpack in Dimitri's trailer." He laid the contents of the bag on the table. "Rach, I need you to see if there are any trace substances on the bag or these items." He paused, then added, "My gut instinct says yes. So we'll go with that assumption for now until we find out otherwise."

Rae shook her head. "No one keeps everything in one place. You have lookouts and stash houses and a decoy house too. If everyone in the neighborhood was killed, you can bet a few of those people had been part of the setup."

Devlin nodded. His eyes glued to the board and the pictures of the scene. "Rach. When you're done with the bag, I need you to check the records for all the houses on this street. Any mention of the neighborhood needs to be flagged. The drug angle is a possibility, which means we need to figure out what kind." He looked at Rae. "Anyone in your old neighborhood buy or sell to anyone on this block?"

"No. They didn't trust anyone outside of the Zone. That block ran exotic stuff like opium and blue lotus and belladonna. Heard they sometimes cut it with fentanyl."

Devlin nodded. "Then we need to find the supplier or the grower."

Rae nodded. "I heard once that they worked out of an apothecary shop."

"But they're still classified as drugs, so would be heavily regulated." Devlin looked at me. "Would your father have more information on this?"

"Yeah. I know about a few of the shops. But I don't know who their suppliers would be. My father grows his own supply for his shop at home," I said, hoping they wouldn't want me to ask him. I wasn't ready to talk to my parents yet.

"I found three online, Dev. Beauty Rose, Inner Strength, and Angelique."

"Beauty Rose has been in business for a while," I offered. "Inner Strength opened last year in North Perry. It's run by a man calling himself Mr. Shim. Angelique is more upscale, overpriced beauty and healing products. Never been to any of them. Just heard about them from my father."

Devlin looked at Rae. "Did anyone mention which shop the dealers were working out of?"

She shook her head.

Devlin sighed. "Marta and I can talk with Henri and then visit the shops." He took down the pictures of the girls and handed them to me. "You and Alek take these to the Peterson school. We know one of them is named Gracie. It would be good to identify the other girl and, if we can, notify their parents of their deaths."

"Are we assuming the Petersons are involved?" Alek asked.

Devlin rubbed the back of his neck. "Rach, upload the pictures of the other girls and the note, along with Dimitri's photo, to everyone's phone." He looked at Alek. "Show them the photos and see if they react."

We sent Rachel the pictures.

"And if they do react?" I asked.

"I'll leave that up to you," he said. "But before you cause too much damage, see if they're willing to provide a list of the girls Gracie and her friend associated with." He looked at Marta. "Set Rae up on my laptop." He smiled at Rae. "You up to searching social media?"

She cracked her fingers. "Can do," she said and grinned.

Devlin looked at me. "Walk us through the evidence you found."

I stood and walked over to the board, where the scraps of paper had been taped. I started to walk through it, then paused. "There are pictures of the crime scene on my phone. Can you upload those to your computer and everyone's cells too?" She nodded and plugged my phone into her computer.

I took a deep breath to center myself and let it out slowly. "I found the same magick symbols we saw in the house last night on the wall in the Ardelean trailer." Rachel found the picture and sent it to the screen for the group to see.

Devlin moved closer to the board. "Rach, pull up the images I sent you of the wall in the house from last night so we can compare." She clicked a few keys, and both images filled the screen. Devlin pointed to the image he'd taken of the wall in the house. "Opal believed the writing could be Coptic."

I studied the words, cursing myself for not identifying the dead language when I searched the trailer and later in the house where we found the girls. I'd spent so much time trying to do everything right that I completely missed one of the teachings from my past.

"Luisah introduced me to this language. Along with the others from ancient times," I said.

"Can you translate it?" Devlin asked.

I shook my head, eyes still on the words. "I do know it's derived from ancient Egyptian and Greek." I glanced at him. "Sadly, it wasn't something I wanted to spend too much time learning. I..." I took a deep breath. "I was more fascinated with magick." I'd never admitted that out loud. I didn't want to draw too much attention to my inadequacies. Turned out, it wasn't something I was able to hide anyway. My friends knew. And now the team knew as well.

"I can look for a translation," Rachel said.

I sighed. "I had believed it was the mad ramblings of a teenager."

Devlin gave me an understanding look. "We all miss things, Nicole. It's why we take pictures. Document the scene. You did good. Okay?"

"Yes, Boss Man."

He smiled.

Marta flipped open one of the red journals I'd found in the Kotzur trailer. "These have similar markings in them too. Along with entries about Dimitri."

"Bria said he had been a little too friendly with the girls," Devlin said.

I gritted my teeth. "I think he was trying to lure them away so he could pimp them out. The girl last night implied she'd been promised something. Even said the other girls wouldn't come if there wasn't more."

"More what?" Marta asked.

I shook my head. "She didn't say. But everything points to drugs." I glanced back at the board. "Okay. So, the Ardelean trailer also had the bloodiest scene. Larissa's murder was savage. And her being a mind mage means she probably tried to fight back with her power." I glanced at Alek. "You told me pain can stop a mind mage from attacking. Whoever killed her had to know this."

"Whoever?" Devlin asked.

I pinched the bridge of my nose. "Something just doesn't fit. If all the girls wanted to do was leave, like Daniella and Ileana, they didn't need to kill their parents to do so." I pointed at the scrap of paper I'd found. "This piece of a love letter was found in Petre and Florin Kotzur's bedroom. The remaining letters were hidden in a hole in the floor of their daughter's bedroom. The letters had been written to Florin. Unless Dimitri was sleeping with both Florin and her daughter, why would they be in there?" I paused, then said, "The diaries all talk about Dimitri." I stared at the team, willing them to follow my train of thought despite me not making any sense.

Everyone grew silent, staring at the evidence on the board. "Given what little we know, I doubt Dimitri would be interested in an older woman," Devlin said. "And you're right, they could have left with Ileana and Daniella." He reached into the box and pulled out a familiar book. "He left this in his trailer too."

I took the book from him. *Naqada*, written by Professor Shukuma. "This book again," I said. Luisah had pointed out this book to me—twice. Once when I was investigating the Stewart family and again last week when we were investigating the Young family. We'd already talked with Professor Shukuma, and he'd said nothing about blood magick. I doubted he would have info on Tribe. So what was the significance of this book?

"Doesn't fit," I told them.

Devlin sighed. "We'll revisit the book later. Maybe talk with the professor again. For now, I want to follow the drugs and the school. Which brings me to Tribe." He went through his conversation with Petronela.

"The Language of Creation," I said. "Why... why would Luisah entrust her with that?"

"She didn't say. Just said some wanted the knowledge and will kill to get it." He paused. "But she also believes what's going on now is nothing more than misdirection but then refused to explain why she feels that way."

"She's like that," Alek said. "It's infuriating. But she always has her reasons."

Devlin nodded. "She also implied we needed to stop her from taking a drastic step."

Alek stared at him. "You mean kill," he said finally.

Devlin nodded. "Bria gave me another lesson on mind

magick. She said you would have to actively be looking for a threat in order to stop what just transpired."

"Yes," Alek said. "This all happened on their watch. So now, everyone will be consumed with guilt and sorrow."

"Meaning the killer or killers could still be among them."

A chill ran down my spine. What if we had missed that?

Alek shook his head. "No. The risk would be too great."

Devlin pursed his lips. "For now. We do the job we were hired to do. Since she brought in Dacian to guard them during the ceremony, I assume they're safe for now." He looked at me. "When you finish at the school, talk to Ezra about Camille. And then I want you and Alek to work on your reaction times. I know we were caught off guard last night. And given what the Dacian can do, our survival could come down to you and your ability to repel magick and rip out souls."

"Yes, Boss Man," I said. Alek and I had already talked about this.

Rachel picked up the container Petronela had given Devlin. "I can't open this, Dev."

"Leave it. She said I wouldn't be able to read it anyway, and it could be a long overdue bedtime story. Which means it's not important right now."

I froze.

Last week, I'd met another Old One when I went to see Ezra about the Firewomen. His name was Killion, and he had reminded me of Devlin. While Killion had darker coloring, they still shared many similarities. Which led me to believe he could have been related to Devlin. And, if I was right, possibly Devlin's father. Which meant I'd have to track Killion down and ask him.

Hell, I should have brought it up yesterday when we were sharing peanut butter in the kitchen. But it wasn't the right time. The focus then had been my pledge to not run headfirst into danger and ease the worry of a man who wore the weight of the world on his shoulders.

Today wasn't the time either. It would be an indelicate thing to ask about. Especially in front of everyone else. Plus, we had a quadruple homicide to solve.

I studied Devlin for a minute. He'd told me once that his mother had named him as a play on Dorian Grey. She'd wanted him to live forever. Now, I suspected it was because she knew his father was immortal.

"Nicole," Devlin prompted.

Damn. I'd been frozen, staring at Boss Man for a while.

"You want to add something?"

"No. Not right now."

"How is the stuff working?" Rachel asked with a note of concern in her tone.

"Fine. Fine. Mind is alert and ready for the day. My body, not so much."

"I might need to adjust it."

I wasn't particularly comfortable with Rachel experimenting on me. But I appreciated her effort and concern. After gathering my things—a notebook and pen without the glitter—Alek and I headed out. Marta and Devlin trailed behind us.

I stared at my best friend. She had braided her long black hair, the ends resting below her waistline. She wore dark blue jeans and a black T-shirt, a gun secured at her side, and a bag thrown over her shoulder, which I was sure contained water and snacks. All she needed was a hat and I'd say she was heading for a duel.

I took her arm before she could follow Devlin to his truck. "And just when did you buy this getup?"

She smiled at me. "When Devlin hired me."

"Do you plan on challenging anyone to a duel?"

"Only if they get in my face. Will you be stabbing anyone today?"

I nodded. "Probably." I sighed. "We have so deviated from the career plan the guidance counselor helped us with."

She laughed. "If I recall, you wanted to be an actress."

I stepped off the porch. "Nay. I just wanted the lady to shut up." I glanced back at her. "Give my parents and the kids a hug for me."

She came down the steps and gave me a half-hug. "I will. Try not to get hurt again."

I winked at her. "You too."

I made my way to Alek's car. When I got in, he asked, "What were you two talking about?"

"Boys." I looked at him. "And killing people."

He nodded. "So. Girl talk," he said and pulled away from the curb.

I sighed, settling back into the seat. If only my life consisted of girl talk and boys. I thought about it. No. I liked the danger. I looked at Alek, the man I was riding toward it with.

Vials of Ivory

Devlin looked out at the world through itchy, tired eyes. Gray clouds covered the sky, threatening to rain. The landscape before him appeared washed out and dull. It reminded him of the movies from the seventies that his mother used to watch, where everything seemed as if it were being shown through a dirty brown-and-yellow lens.

Maybe it was the uncertainty of their lead that gnawed at him. The gut instinct of something being askew and not quite in focus was having an influence on his vision.

Or maybe he was just too damn tired.

He yawned, his jaw popping, and rubbed his eyes.

Marta cracked the window, letting in a burst of humidity, and retrieved a bottle of water from her bag. She opened it and passed it to him. "Might help wake you up," she said.

Devlin took the offered item and drained the contents. The cool liquid rushed down his throat, soothing and waking him up a little. He pulled some of the moisture from the air as well to replenish his power.

He slanted a glance at the mother of four. She was reviewing something on her tablet.

Marta had integrated herself into the team in a way that

surprised him. No hesitation. No fear. Just a dogged determination to do the job right. Her reasons for being there might be based on revenge for what had been done to her and her children, but it didn't affect her work in a negative way. Still, he couldn't help but worry for her safety. Should he have brought her along with him? She had no magick. The .380 resting on her hip might not be enough. What if the Dacian attacked them again?

She glanced at him. "You look worried," she said.

He nodded. "Trying to determine if bringing you along was a good idea."

She turned away. "I can understand that. I don't have power like the rest of the team." She paused, then pulled another bottle of water out of her bag. After taking a few sips, she continued. "When Isabel was born, I turned into the worst kind of helicopter parent. Every single item in my parents' house looked like a death trap to me. I couldn't shake the sheer panic that something bad might happen to her if I didn't control everything in her environment. I didn't listen to my parents when they tried to stop me from over-obsessing about her safety. It took having two more kids before I finally relaxed."

"That had to be hard," Devlin said.

She shifted in her seat. "You remind me of me. Always trying to put safeguards in place. Trying to keep your team from the worst of it. The thing is, Devlin. You can't control everything. You have to allow others around you to do their part. I know, with my limited abilities, I can be a liability. But magick isn't the only strength that will help us."

He sighed, hearing the truth in her words. He wanted to keep his team safe. But he feared he might fail in his efforts. And that worry kept him up at night.

"Can you call and see if Henri's at home?"

She smiled. "I can."

Marta confirmed Henri was working from home, and they set out in silence.

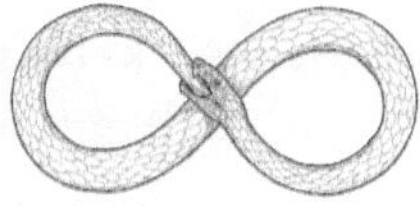

They arrived at the Fontanes' house a short while later and pulled into the driveway. The front door opened, and Maria came running out holding the Fontane dog, Fi', in her arms. A bell, secured around the dog's neck, jingled, giving a cheery sound to their approach. Anne appeared in the doorway, watching the five-year-old with a smile on her face.

Marta got out of the car in a rush and went to her knees in front of her little girl. "Maria, we have talked about this," she said, smoothing the little girl's hair. "You can't run outside without someone with you."

"Fi' is with me," Maria announced. "She wanted to play."

Marta shook her head, a patient smile stretched across her face. "Maybe you should let her walk, then."

"Hi, Maria," Devlin said, grinning.

Maria turned and beamed up at him. "Mama is going to get me a doggie!"

"Just when did I say that?"

Maria turned back to her mom, eyes wide, with a devilish grin on her face.

Devlin smiled at their back-and-forth conversation and made his way to the front porch. "How are you, Anne?"

"I'm good," she said, continuing to watch mother and daughter discuss puppies. "That one is a handful."

Devlin turned toward the two. "Yeah," he said, remembering the conversation he and Marta had. She may have stopped hovering when her third child was born, but it obviously never stopped the worry. He wished his own mother had been able to show some kind of concern for his well-being, his safety.

"I stopped by to speak with Henri," Devlin said.

Anne turned to him. "Yes. Of course. He's out in his shop." She stared at him for a minute. "How is my own child doing?"

Devlin smiled. "Stubborn." It felt strange to entertain

discussing Nicole in this way. She was his employee, not his ward. Yet, he understood the concern Anne felt for the determined woman who could work every one of his nerves. She went at danger without a care in the world, and he feared one day, she might just go too far.

Who was he kidding? She'd already achieved that.

Anne nodded, eyes misting over as she stared off, deep in thought. "I wish she would come to see us," she said. "Oh. This is not appropriate." She waved him toward the front door. "Go. See Henri. I will talk with Marta for a while. His greenhouse is around back."

"Thank you, Anne," Devlin said, glad she'd stopped the awkward exchange before he had to. She smiled and turned back to Marta, who had finally managed to coax her daughter into putting Fi' down.

Devlin stepped into the cool house and found ten-year-old Jose standing in the family room, looking out the front window. He held a baseball bat, his grip on it so tight, his tiny hand had turned red from strain.

"Hey, Jose," Devlin said, walking over. He crouched beside the little boy, trying to figure out what to say to get him to let go of the bat. He was out of his element. Honestly, he was probably overstepping. But walking away was not an option he was willing to entertain.

He started to reach out and place a reassuring hand on the boy's shoulder but stopped. After the horrific things that had been done to them by the Sinclair family, a casual touch by a relative stranger was not a good idea. So, he waited. Hoping the little guy would relinquish his grip on the bat enough to ease the obvious pain in his hand.

"Mom works for you," Jose said, gaze still fixed on his mother and little sister.

"Yes," Devlin said.

"Does that mean you're safe?"

Devlin didn't respond right away. How could he? It was a

question posed by a child who shouldn't have to worry about such things. It did, however, make him think about the work they did. It wasn't safe. But that's not what Jose had asked. "Yes, my team and I are safe."

Jose turned and looked at him. His eyes held a well of emotion and confusion and questions. So much of this young man's childhood had been taken from him. His first thought was that Marta should be here. Helping her son feel safe again. Making sure he didn't have to stand vigil with a bat in his hand.

But it wasn't his place. He'd have to trust she knew what was best for her and her children. And support her when she needed it.

After a brief pause, Jose nodded, and the grip on his bat eased. But he didn't move from his spot at the window.

Devlin stood. Again, the instinct to reach out to the little boy overcame him. But he resisted the impulse. "I'm gonna go talk to Henri," he announced.

Jose nodded again, his only acknowledgement that he'd heard Devlin.

Devlin started down the short hallway connected to the kitchen and made his way outside and to the door leading to Henri's workshop. He went inside the aromatic space and wound his way around the free-standing plants. Isabel, Marta's twelve-year-old, stood near the back window, rag in hand, while her little brother Juan sat on a stool with a drawing pad on his lap. They looked up and saw him.

"Hello," he said, stopping at the worktable. A drying rack filled with herbs hung above the large table.

"Hi, Mr. Devlin," Isabel said, staring at him.

Henri came from around the back shelf and smiled. "How you doing, Devlin? You bring my baby girl with you?"

Devlin laughed. "No. She's out chasing down a lead with Alek."

A grin stretched across Henri's face. "Isabel. I do believe this old worktable is clean enough."

She gave him a small smile.

"Tell you what. Why don't you and your brother head inside and see if Anne needs some help with your sister."

"Your mom's here," Devlin interjected.

Juan looked up. "She is?"

Devlin nodded, and Juan slid off the stool and rushed out of the room. Isabel hesitated.

"Go on, now," Henri said. "Say hi to your mama and then come back and help me bundle up some of these orders." He paused, holding her gaze. "That okay with you?"

"Yes, Mr. Henri," she said, then placed the rag on the table and left the room.

Devlin stared after her, unsure of what to say.

"It's hard not to want to comfort them," Henri said, pulling some herbs down from his rack. "But you have to let them come to you." He picked up a bone-colored vial. "Just like this vial made of ivory. Durable. But with enough pressure, it will break."

"I found Jose standing at a window holding a bat and watching his mother and sister."

Henri sighed. "It's what gives him comfort. He needs to know he can defend his family. For Isabel, she needs to feel like she's needed. Juan can't voice what he's feeling like the rest of us. But he does seem to work it out in his art." He paused, eyes growing sad. "It's Maria I worry about. She reminds of my baby girl. Burying that pain. Hiding from it. The others will get to a point where they can heal." He shook his head. "Maria will take longer to reach that place."

"But shouldn't Marta be with them?" Devlin asked before he could stop himself. It wasn't his place to have this conversation. Yet, he couldn't ignore it, either. It was a delicate rope to walk. But in the end, he knew he would one day have to. It was better to talk with someone who seemed to understand.

Henri looked at him. "Being a parent is not easy. You feel all the joy of bringing this tiny little being into the world but have no clue what to do next. So much of the time, Anne and I did our best and made up for the things we got wrong." He stopped and leaned against his worktable. "I started my baby girl on cigars to get her off drugs." He let out a dry chuckle. "I can see now how wrong that was. But then"—he lifted his hands in placation—"it seemed so right. Marta is doing what she can. Her need to provide for her family. Her pride. Her own pain. All these things at war with one another."

Devlin shook his head and joined him, leaning against the worktable. "Maybe this is something I shouldn't even be discussing."

"You're human. And you care about the people who work for you. That much I can see." Henri smiled. "And anyone who can put up with my baby girl deserves a medal."

Devlin laughed, crossing his arms. "She can be... I wish she would talk to you all about her power. It would help her a great deal."

Henri's body shook with laughter. "Easy is not my baby girl's way." He sobered. "But I agree. She needs to talk with us."

They shared a comfortable silence for a while. Devlin felt a small measure of relief at knowing someone else shared his concerns. And Henri was right. Parents did what they could. His own mother probably had too. He just wished he could see it and feel comforted in that knowledge. But sadly, all he remembered was the sense of loss and confusion.

"We're looking into the sale of a few plants that have been classified as illegal," Devlin started. He filled Henri in on what he could, careful not to mention the encounter with the Dacian.

"The sale of those plants is illegal without a special license. They are mentioned in Title 26 of the Food, Drugs, and Cosmetics code. Belladonna, specifically, is classified as a poison. But Tulare has amended this code and gives out special licenses to apothecaries to use these products for beauty and ritual requests."

Henri pushed off the table and pulled more herbs from his rack. "In both cases, the apothecary has to register with the Heka commission if they plan on growing any of these plants. Pay a hefty tax on it and agree to random inventory searches." He frowned. "I grow all three here." He pointed at the plants on his rack. "But I don't sell them in the store. I only provide them to clients who have registered to use them under the Religious Benefit clause."

"They classify magick as religion."

Henri laughed. "Yes. It was the only way they could legally circumvent Georgia's laws. Freedom of religion."

"I have to say, I'm a little surprised Nicole didn't know about this."

"My baby girl couldn't be bothered about laws and restrictions. She knows about the plants, though."

Devlin pulled his phone out and showed Henri a photo of Dimitri. "Has this guy ever come into your shop?"

Henri shook his head. "No. But then again, I'm not really open to the public. I serve the magick community, and all my customers have been with me for years." He paused. "Did you check the other shops?"

"They're on our list to check out."

"If I had to guess, I'd say that new one, Inner Strength, would be your best bet. The man running it, Mr. Shim, don't seem like the honest type to me."

They grew silent again. Devlin wanted to ask so many more questions. Mainly about Nicole and her power. She needed to understand it. But like Marta and her children, the relationship between Nicole and her parents was not something he should intervene in. He could encourage her to seek out their support. But he could never make her.

"I will keep my ears open," Henri said.

Devlin thanked him for his time and went out to collect Marta.

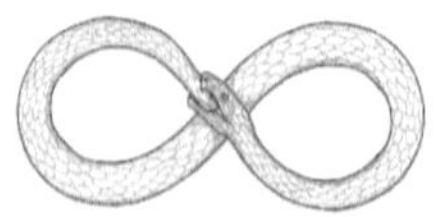

Once they were back in the car, Devlin filled Marta in on his discussion with Henri.

"Do you think we should check with the Heka commission about any illegal activity with the drugs we're looking for?" Marta asked.

Devlin thought about it for a minute. While they would have some knowledge of any irregularities between what was reported and sold, he doubted they would be forthcoming with the information.

"Let's see what we find out from the shop owners first," he said. "Talk to me about Beauty Rose."

Marta pulled her phone out and read through the information she'd found online. "Started fifteen years ago by one Rita Saint Claire. Her shop specializes in beauty and skincare, as well as everyday aches and pains." She scrolled through the page. "Only one of her products contains belladonna. It's used for arthritis pain. Nothing containing opium."

Devlin drummed his fingers on the steering wheel. Part of him wondered if they were wasting their time talking to staff at each of the three Apothecaries. He seriously doubted they would be upfront about any illegal sales outside of their regular business. But they needed to start somewhere.

It was midafternoon when we arrived at the demarcation point between Alice and Sandpoint. Marshland lined the road. I glanced over at the waterlogged trees that led to the Stewart family barn and wondered if it was still in use. Devlin was right. We'd left so many loose ends when we stopped that twisted family's Harvest ritual over a month ago. We should have burned that barn to the ground. Now it was Kara and Jonah's responsibility to clean up the mess. I felt a little guilty about that.

Until I remembered my own loose thread: Ronald Stewart. I would take care of that sadistic bastard all by myself.

Humid air settled on my skin, with an occasional breeze blowing over the accumulated sweat. I could roll up the window and turn on the air-conditioning, but the last dregs of Rachel's brew had finally left my system, and I wanted to enjoy the fresh air for a while, allow it to cleanse my lungs.

We stopped at a light.

Savory scented smoke pumped into the air from an outdoor barbecue pit, making my stomach rumble. People congregated around picnic tables and the grill, smiling and laughing. I caught brief glimpses of the ocean as we drove. Its majestic blue water sent a salty breeze into the car.

The sight and smell dislodged a memory in my mind.

"You hear the water? Set can't cross it unless he's inside a host. Why do you think I built my temple here?"

When Gavina had told me this, I'd believed someone had lied to her. Especially since Set had attacked me on the Stewarts' small patch of land surrounded by the marsh. We didn't learn until later there was a way to get to their ritual space without wading through the mucky water, but that was beside the point. My assumption had still convinced me he could travel across water.

But what if she had been right? If the land bridges hadn't been there when The Old Ones first created the island, then who created them? The connection to both Georgia and South Carolina had been made by extending a bridge, or in the case of Sandpoint, a footpath, to the island. So not part of the original making.

Which brought up another point: Who had let Set's soul out of the Ark? Yes, the Cherokee were supposed to keep the Ark safe. But someone had taken it from them and given it to the Stewart family. If that was truly the sequence of events. And how did the protection work? It wasn't mentioned in the poem.

I touched Alek's arm. "I need to investigate a theory not related to our current case," I said.

He glanced at me. "What theory and why?"

Alek made a sharp turn down a narrow street. Large cypress trees lined the path, their moss fingers sweeping the ground and casting the roadway into shadow. The school's front gate loomed ahead. Its gothic structure rose up from the ground like some twisted nightmare.

"I think Gavina might have been partially right about Set not being able to cross water. But I need more information." Mainly, I needed to see the progression of the land bridges. Had they grown since their creation? Why populate them with protectors if the entire island was supposed to keep Set from escaping?

Alek drove slowly around a fork in the road, the car jumping with each bump on the dirt road. The route segued into a flooded driveway. Water splashed up; droplets hit my arm and face.

We left the waterlogged path, and the ride smoothed over as it segued into a red brick driveway.

"They don't have a parking lot," I said.

The brick path circled around a patch of manicured grass. A single cypress tree sat on the lush yard with an abundance of vibrantly colored flowers encircling the base. Alek stopped the car near the school, and we climbed out into the warm, fragrant air.

I stared up at the enormous building. "I knew about the school but never thought to see it for myself." The entire property was surrounded by a wrought iron fence. "Why would they build it here? Hidden away from everyone and everything?"

"If they're practicing blood magick, it's the best place to hide." Alek said, joining me on the passenger side of the car. "You want to tell me what you were thinking about on the way over?"

I pulled my gaze away from the building and looked at him. "I need to go to the Rothman Museum in Alice."

The Rothman Museum, run by an eccentric woman named Abigail Meadows, had one of the most extensive collections of island history.

"Why?" Alek asked.

"I need to see past maps of the island." I paused. "If the island was created to keep Set contained, then why were the land bridges created? It's as if someone used magick to forge a path for him."

"The same person who let him out," Alek said.

I nodded. "Yes. And I'm starting to believe that's Khnum. But I have to be sure I'm right. And if I am, how would he have the power to do achieve it on his own?" It took twelve Old Ones to create Tulare Island. I assumed it would take all of them to shift the island as well. Which meant there was a possibility they were working together. Camille's appearance on Tulare gave this idea some weight. Or did it? She had implied she was being coerced in some way.

I lifted my hair off my neck, letting the breeze dry the sweat. Too many clues to sort out. I would need to write this new information down, along with all the other ideas. Because in my head, they felt like wild assumptions, and I didn't like that. Which meant I needed to gather more information to fill in the holes in my thinking. Sadly, I just didn't have the time to sit with it long enough to connect the pieces.

A dark-skinned man with close-cropped hair and wearing all black walked out of the building. "Can I help you?" he asked, his brown eyes scrutinizing us.

We stepped forward in unison. "We need to speak with Leticia Peterson about two of the girls who attended this school," I said.

"What girls?"

I gave him a tight smile. "It's best we speak with her."

He glanced down at the dagger strapped to my thigh. "You'll need to make an appointment."

Alek shook his head. "No. I don't think we do."

The man stepped forward, hands raised, as if he was going to physically move Alek. Alek stood there with a smile on his face, almost daring the man to touch him. I debated whether I should step between them but decided against it. I'd let them sort it out.

"If you don't move, *sir*, I will have to move you," the man barked.

A short Creole woman wearing a light green suit jacket and skirt walked out of the building. "I will handle this, Randall," she said. Leticia Peterson. I recognized her from her photo. She glanced between Randall and Alek. "Randall," she said, a note of concern in her voice.

Randall looked over his shoulder at her. "They don't have an appointment." He jerked his chin toward me. "And this one has a weapon on her."

She examined my knife. "I said. I will handle it," she said slowly, as if speaking with a child.

Randall swallowed and turned on his heel, then stormed away.

"I apologize for that," Leticia said. "Randall can get a little ... overzealous in his duties to protect the students in our care. How can I help you?"

"We understand," I said. "I wonder if you have some time to talk about two of your students." I kept my tone casual, so as not to alert her that anything was wrong. It would be a little tasteless to show her the photos of the lifeless bodies of her former students out in the open. Besides, we needed to get inside the school.

"What's this about? Which girls?"

"It's a sensitive matter, Ms. Peterson," Alek said.

She let out a heavy sigh. I could see the indecision warring inside of her.

"I would not normally allow you into my school. But I will trust my instinct on this and hope you don't prove me wrong. Randall is never too far away." She looked at my dagger. "However, you will have to leave the weapon in your car."

Alek looked at me. "Nicole," he said, making it my decision.

I stared at Leticia. A bright green aura surrounded her, indicating she was an earth mage. Since we suspected her of using blood magick, I'd assumed she would have a tinge of red as well. It was what the other blood magick users had. But hers didn't have any. Again, the color of one's aura wasn't always a guaranteed indicator of a person's power. However, it was a starting point. And so far, all I had detected from Leticia was earth magick.

Still, I didn't want to enter the school without some form of protection.

"That's fine," I said, unstrapping it from my thigh.

After locking my blade in the trunk, we followed Leticia down a short concrete path that led to a massive double oak door with wrought iron handles. She pulled it open and signaled for us to enter.

Cool, sweet-smelling air rushed across my skin. We stepped into a long, dimly lit hallway that seemed to go on forever. Leticia shut the doors, casting us into even more darkness. The echo reverberated along the hallway's dark, glossy wood flooring.

Gilded framed portraits lined the mahogany walls. I counted thirty faces, all illuminated by picture lights mounted above them. It reminded me of a museum. Potted acacia plants sat between each painting.

I walked over to the first portrait.

"She sang from her soul," Leticia said, joining me by the painting. "I put these up to show the girls who come here, broken and lost, that so many strong women existed and paved the way for all of us."

I'll tell you what freedom is to me. No Fear.
- Nina Simone

The artist had captured her dark skin and soulful eyes in a way that made the rendering seem almost lifelike.

"My mom used to listen to her music a lot when I was younger." I smiled at the memory. "When she was working on her pottery, she'd have 'I want a Little Sugar in My Bowl' on repeat." I laughed. "I can't stand sugar."

"Because of the song," Leticia asked.

"No. I just ... It's too sweet."

I turned away and continued down the hall. Curiosity led me from one portrait to the next, reading the little gold nameplates: Nellie Bly, Margaret Sanger, Anna May Wong, Indira Gandhi, Katherine G. Johnson, Ella Fitzgerald. So many notable women whose impact on society often went unnoticed. I could admit my own failing at learning about these powerful women. But I did recognize most of their names.

I felt Leticia's presence next to me along the way, quietly following me down the hall. It was as if she were waiting for me to ask questions.

Had our assumptions about the Peterson family been wrong? Maybe they were just educators. This hallway suggested an emphasis on empowering young girls. For someone to curate this, they must have a vested interest in their pupils' futures. Why spend so much time and money educating the young girls to simply end up using them in blood magick rituals? It didn't make sense.

"I have to apologize again for Randall's behavior," Leticia said as we stopped at a portrait of Rosa Parks.

To bring about change, you must not be afraid to take the first step.
We will fail when we fail to try.
- Rosa Parks

I turned and looked at her, and she continued, "He is vigilant in his duties to protect everyone here. A few years back, someone managed to get onto our campus and assault four of our girls."

"I'm so sorry."

"Thank you," she said and looked at Alek. "You are powerful. So, I had to be sure you weren't a threat."

His gaze roamed over her. "I can say the same about you."

She smiled. "I only attack when I know I have the advantage. If you had used your magick on Randall, I would have killed you. But you didn't." A dark green light pulsed around her.

"I can respect that," Alek said, smiling. "It would have been an interesting fight, though. Nicole is no lightweight."

She looked at me. "No. She's not."

"We really just want to talk," I said.

She nodded. "Fair enough. Let's go to my office." I didn't know what we'd done to earn her trust. But I was happy we had. It would make the next part so much easier.

LADY OF THE ROCKS

A short while later, Devlin and Marta arrived at Beauty Rose. The apothecary rested between a bar and a sandwich shop. Its dark red awning hung over large bay windows, highlighting elaborate displays of beauty products. They drove down the side street and spotted a small patio in the back.

He looked at Marta. "Might be where she grows her herbs," he said, circling back to the front of the store.

Marta pointed to the space above. "An apartment, maybe?"

Devlin nodded.

"Should I leave the gun?" Marta asked.

Devlin studied the storefront. "If we had time, I would have preferred to go in as customers to see if we could get some information out of them more discreetly. But direct also works." He looked at the gun on her hip. "The gun might put them on edge. But if there's trouble, I'd rather you have it on you." He jerked his chin toward her bag. "Put it in there."

"Got it," Marta said and shoved the gun into her bag.

They climbed out of the car and made their way to the entrance. A woman stepped out, and Devlin held the door for her. She gave him a beaming smile that faltered when she saw Marta standing by his side.

"Maybe you can charm them," Marta said.

"Not one of my strong suits," Devlin said.

"You're a handsome man. Just smile a lot. That usually works."

Devlin smiled and shook his head.

They stepped inside to find cream-colored walls with rose trimming. Display units that held soap, candles, little satchels of herbs, and glass bottles of elixirs covered the highly polished hardwood floor. A conglomerate of scents swirled in the small space, making it hard to pinpoint any one fragrance.

A woman in her late sixties wearing a rose-colored dress and a cream scarf around her neck stood behind the register, chatting with a customer. Two other employees, a man and a woman, were helping customers. Each of them wore a pair of charcoal pants and a cream top with the words "Beauty Rose" stenciled on the front.

Before they could make their way to the woman, the young man stepped into their path with a practiced smile lining his youthful face. He had long, red, curly hair tied back in a queue at the nape of his neck, and his blue eyes stared at them out of gold wire-rimmed glasses. His name tag read "Eddie."

"Welcome to Beauty Rose. What can I help you find today?"

"We need to speak to the owner," Devlin said.

"Is there a problem?" he asked, a line forming between his brows.

"It's something we would rather discuss with your boss, Eddie," Marta said, smiling. "Besides, there are a few other people in here who could use your help. Am I right?"

He nodded; his eyes narrowed. He obviously didn't appreciate being dismissed.

An elderly woman made her way to them with concern in her eyes. "I'm the owner. How may I help you?" she asked.

"Yes, ma'am," Devlin said. "My name is Devlin." He pulled a card from his pocket and handed it to her. "And this is my associate, Ms. Hernandez. We're private investigators working on a case involving two young ladies."

"Okay," she said, studying the card.

"I wonder if there is somewhere we can talk in private?"

"What is this regarding?" she asked, clutching her throat.

Marta smiled. "It's best we do this in private, ma'am."

The woman stood there for a moment, eyes full of worry and fear. Eddie touched her elbow. "I can handle it for you, Ms. Rita, if you like."

She fluttered her hand at him. "No. No. You go on and help the customers." She extended her arm toward the back of the store. "We can talk in my office."

Devlin and Marta followed her to the back. As they walked, the other employee gave Eddie a questioning look, and he shook his head. So, the man was not overly interested, just showing the usual casual curiosity Devlin had seen when he worked in law enforcement. No doubt as soon as they left the room, the rumors would start. He thought about leaving Marta out front to listen, but he doubted they would talk openly in front of her.

Rita led them past the patio room filled with various plants. Devlin stopped, hesitated, then stepped into the room. Rita followed soon after.

"You grow your own plants?" he asked.

"Umm... yes, of course. It's all legal."

Devlin glanced at her. "We're only here gathering information." He looked around the room. "I don't see belladonna. Or opium." He glanced at her. "Do you grow either of those?"

Her brow furrowed, and once again, she clutched her throat. "Well, yes. I do grow my own belladonna." She walked down the aisle and signaled to a potted plant on the floor. "This is all I have."

Devlin walked over and studied the pot. It was a small amount. "What about blue lotus? Do you grow that here? Or do you have plants at another location?"

She shook her head. "No. Only here. The elixir I make for

arthritis doesn't take much belladonna, and I don't carry any products with blue lotus or opium."

Devlin straightened. "Do you sell the plants wholesale?"

She didn't answer right away, just stared at him out of eyes filled with confusion. "I must ask again what this is about?"

He debated how much he should tell her. While the events of last night hadn't appeared in the news, him giving her too many details could pose a problem.

"We're looking into the deaths of two girls who both had drugs in their system. And we've reason to believe an apothecary shop supplied them. Their parents wanted us to find the dealers."

Her face filled with outrage. "Why on earth would someone accuse me of dealing drugs?"

Devlin shook his head. "They didn't name you. Just said an apothecary shop."

"I'm not the only one on the island!"

Devlin gave her a warm smile. "We know that, ma'am. We have to check all of them." He pulled his phone out. "We also learned that this man could be involved. Have you ever seen him before?"

She looked at Dimitri's picture. "No. I've never seen him before."

He paused. "Do you think your staff might have any information regarding the selling or buying of these items? Maybe they've been approached by this man?"

She shook her head furiously. "Of course not," she said, her voice a deadly whisper. "My employees have been with me since they were teenagers. I trust them completely," she bit out. "I would suggest you visit the shop in North Perry. They are close enough to that evil residing in the south. The owner is sketchy. Just like his trash employees."

The anger in her voice gave Devlin pause. Was she an employer defending herself and her employees, or was this the adamant denial of a guilty woman?

Marta stepped forward and smiled at her. "No one is accusing you or your employees, ma'am. All we want to do is cross you off our list so we can question the other shops." Marta stared at her with a warm smile on her face. "It might speed things along if we can ask your staff if they've ever heard of the people in the North Perry shop selling any of these drugs to their customers. I'm sure they would know, right?"

The woman pulled a tissue from her pocket and dabbed her eyes. Again, Devlin was struck by her emotions. Why was she so upset?

The woman sucked in a breath and let it out slowly. "I apologize for my behavior. It's been hard lately. The North Perry shop opened a year ago, and it has been undercutting me ever since." She nodded as if she were trying to reassure herself. "I can let you ask my staff." She stared at Marta. "I can assure you, though. They won't know much." She sighed. "I tried teaching them how to grow the plants." She shook her head. "Let's just say, it's a good thing they are so good with the customers." She wiped her nose. "Here. You can use my office, and I will send them back one at a time."

She showed them to her tiny office crammed with products and mountains of invoices. "Can I get you any tea or water?"

"No." Devlin smiled. "We're fine. We wouldn't want to take up too much more of your time."

"It wouldn't be much trouble. But, if you're sure?" She paused, and Devlin and Marta nodded. "Okay. Let me send one of them back, and you can ask your questions." She gave them a tight smile and walked away.

"You think it was wise to give her so much information?" Marta whispered.

"We wouldn't have got much out of her if we didn't," he said, looking around at the cramped office.

Papers and product samples covered every single surface. He pulled his phone out and took a few shots of some items on the desk along with the paperwork. While his brief interaction with Rita wasn't setting off any alarm bells, he wanted to make sure he had enough information in case she did turn out to be the one responsible for supplying drugs to Dimitri.

Marta moved some stuff off one of the chairs. "Not enough chairs for us to sit," she said.

"It's better if we stand." Devlin listened to the footsteps coming down the hall, his mind still trying to puzzle out Rita's reactions. Maybe the new store had cut too far into her profit margin. And if that was the case, wouldn't she look for other avenues to supplement the loss of income?

A young woman in her early twenties with short brown hair and bright green eyes stopped in the doorway. "Ms. Rita said you needed to speak to us about some drugs," she said, her tone casual. But it was the worry and fear in her eyes that interested Devlin.

"Yes," Marta said. "Please come in. We have just a few questions."

"Okay," she said in a rush, then sat down in the only available chair and rested her hands on her thighs. "I can't tell you much. We don't sell drugs here. Per se." She chuckled. "I mean we do ... sell drugs. But they're homeopathic. Most people just buy them for aches and pains. Some use them for hair growth. We have one customer who comes in and cleans out all the walnut soap." She laughed. "I mean, who needs that much soap?" She rubbed her hands down her legs. "But other than that. I don't know... Okay. Please don't tell Ms. Rita, but I took some of the juniper oil for my bloating last month. I was going to pay her..."

Devlin put his hand on the woman's shoulder, and she sighed.

"I'm sorry. I just talk too much when I'm nervous."

"Why are you nervous?" he asked.

She bit her lip, chewing at the loose skin. Then rubbed her hands on her legs again. "Because I don't always pay for the things I use." She whipped around, eyes widening, and looked at Marta. "It's not much. Honest. Just a few items. See, college is so expensive, and I can't always pay right away." She hung her head. "Ms. Rita is so good to me. Please don't tell her."

Devlin crouched and looked her in the eyes. "We won't. You can do that when you're ready. And I get the feeling she'll understand."

The woman nodded.

"What's your name?" Marta asked.

"Oh, sorry. Yeah. I'm Crystal." She let out another nervous chuckle.

"Well, Crystal. My name is Marta, and I'm a private investigator."

"Oh, wow! I would have sworn you were cops."

Marta tilted her head to the side. "Why cops?"

The girl shrugged. "I don't know. You just seem so official, and you came here asking about drugs."

Marta nodded. "I can understand that." She paused. "Has anyone else ever come in here asking about drugs? Maybe asked you to sell them some plants or seeds?" She showed Crystal the picture of Dimitri. "Maybe this man?"

Crystal studied the photo. "No. I've never seen him."

"What about outside of work?"

Crystal shook her head furiously.

"We're looking for any information related to belladonna, blue lotus, or opium specifically," Devlin added, surprised she hadn't asked them which drugs they were talking about.

Crystal's eyes widened again. "No." She shook her head. "I would never mess with that stuff. It's bad." She continued to shake her head as if she worried that they wouldn't believe her.

Marta patted her shoulder. "It's okay. We believe you. We just had to ask."

The girl nodded and stood. "Can I go back out now?"

"Yeah," Devlin said. "Do us a favor and send Eddie back."

She laughed. "Oh, Eddie would never do any drugs. He's too much of a"—she leaned in—"mama's boy." She smiled. "But I like him. He makes me laugh."

"That's good," Marta said, giving her a reassuring smile. "Remember. Tell Ms. Rita what you've done."

The girl nodded, eyes growing sad. "I will." She rushed out of the room without a backward glance.

"What do you think?" Devlin asked.

"She would have told on herself if she were guilty."

Devlin agreed. "Yeah. Definitely not cut out for a life of crime. I'm surprised she's been able to keep her stealing from Rita at all."

"Maybe she hasn't," Marta said, a grin on her face.

A few minutes later, Eddie came into the room and stopped at the doorjamb. "What'd you do to Crystal?" he asked, eyes narrowed. "She's out there crying her eyes out."

Devlin eyed him. "Not something you should concern yourself with." He jerked his chin toward the chair. "Why don't you have a seat?"

Eddie shook his head. "No. I'm good. You have questions about drugs?" He pointedly ignored Devlin and instead looked at Marta when he asked the question.

Marta, without hesitation, asked him the same questions she'd asked Crystal. Devlin watched the young man, wondering about the misplaced aggression. Unless Crystal had told him they'd hurt her in some way, his defensiveness about the young woman seemed a bit over the top.

Eddie turned to Devlin, eyes going hard. "You honestly believe Ms. Rita would sell drugs here?"

Devlin didn't respond. Just let the silence grow between them. He'd used this same tactic before, many times, when interviewing a perp. Eventually, they'd give in to the need to fill the void with protests of innocence.

"Ms. Rita is an honest person," Eddie said finally. "I don't know who in their right mind would tell you she's selling drugs here, but they are lying."

His insistence on Rita not selling drugs was... interesting. Unlike his coworker, he didn't plead his innocence; he focused on his boss instead.

"What about you, Eddie? You ever sell some stuff on the side?

Ever have any dealings with this man?" Devlin showed him the picture of Dimitri.

Eddie shook his head. "No. I don't know the guy, and I wouldn't do that." He stared at Devlin as if waiting for the man to call him a liar. A simple "no" would have been enough.

Devlin studied him for a moment. Finally, he nodded. "Thanks for your time."

"Sure thing," Eddie said, mood suddenly shifting to one of jovial cooperation. He left the room as if he hadn't just spent the last few minutes in a rage.

Marta shook her head. "I'm starting to wonder about the people working here. Could they be sampling the product? If so, what?" She moved the papers back to the chair. "But honestly, I'm not getting the whole drug-ring vibe from them."

"Neither am I," Devlin said. "But Eddie is really concerned about Rita. I wonder if she is doing something illegal."

Marta stared after the young man. "Yeah. He was a bit over the top. It might be a good idea to circle back to them later and see what Ms. Rita is really getting up to."

Devlin agreed, and they made their way back to the front. After saying goodbye, they went outside and climbed into their vehicle.

"Dulean next?" Marta said, fastening her seatbelt.

They had discussed saving the North Perry location for last. Part of the reason being the proximity to the original crime. He had wanted to cross the least likely places off his list first, just in case his assumptions were wrong. Most drug dealers worked in areas they were familiar with. Places they had connections. But everything about the people they were dealing with suggested they were cunning and smart. And probably knew better than to work in the same area they lived.

He sighed. "Let's deal with North Perry first."

Marta nodded. "I'm thinking that's a good idea."

Devlin started the car. "You did good in there."

Marta smiled. "Thanks."

"What have you got on Inner Strength?"

Marta pulled out her phone. "Nicole was right. It's run by a man calling himself Mr. Shim. His photo is plastered all over the website." She showed Devlin the picture of a white man with dreadlocks. "And he sells some of everything."

"Does it mention any products by name?"

She shook her head. "No. Just says, 'We sell everything.'"

Devlin harrumphed. Maybe they would find what they were looking for at Inner Strength, or, judging from the proprietor's image and name, just a charlatan selling snake oil to his customers.

Eventually, we came to a set of offices near the end of the corridor. Leticia opened the door to the one at the end, and we stepped inside. The cool air held an earthy scent infused with vanilla and ginger. I inhaled, and my entire body relaxed. All the turmoil, worry, and rigid alertness to danger just seeped right out of me. I glanced at Alek. A peaceful mask had settled over his face. His dark blue eyes seemed filled with tranquility.

Magick?

I looked inward and found my protective mark dormant. Which meant it wasn't an active spell. But something had impacted my mood. I looked around and found an array of flowers and potted herbs on top of a long cherrywood cabinet underneath a large window. I went over to study them.

"I use them to help keep the students calm when they're sent to see me," Leticia said, easing up beside me. "My mother used to have stations like this all over the house." She chuckled. "Us kids were a rowdy bunch. Always into something. The only way she could keep us from tearing into each other and destroying the house was to infuse the air with calm."

"Do you use magick as well?" I asked.

She shook her head. "No."

I recognized the flowers she had grouped together: lavender, jasmine, chamomile, passionflower—and blue lotus. A few of them were used in teas. Chamomile was especially popular to aid in insomnia. But I'd never heard of them being used to adjust the mood in the room without the use of magick.

I started to turn away, then paused. "You grow blue lotus here?" I asked.

"Just a small supply for my plant boxes."

"Do the students have access to the plants?"

She shook her head. "I'm aware of the potential for abuse. Which is why I don't grow the plants on site."

That was a relief.

Across from the plant display was a wall of books. Those cherrywood shelves held so much knowledge on magick and history that my fingers itched to touch the worn spines. To run my hands over the covers as if I could absorb the information through osmosis.

I used to devour all knowledge about power. But only in secret. I'd been too ashamed of my lack of skills to openly display my hunger to learn. And I'd believed that if anyone became aware of my obsession, it would look like desperation. Turned out, I hadn't been so successful in keeping it secret.

But even more worrisome was learning my parents and Luisah had carefully censored all my studying on the subject. That glaring lack of expertise had been on full display since I started working with Devlin and his crew.

I gave myself a mental shake. "Sorry," I said, knowing that they were waiting for me. Nothing would come from dwelling on the past. I had a job to do, and it required all of my attention.

"Why don't we sit over here?" Leticia made her way to a desk tucked into the corner. A laptop sat on its highly polished surface. She signaled for us to sit in the chairs in front of it. Alek and I took a seat. I set my notebook on the desk and pulled out the pictures of the girls.

"I don't know a delicate way of doing this." I paused. "So please forgive me if I blunder." I handed her the pictures. "Did these girls attend your school?"

Leticia sat back with a heavy sigh. "Yes," she said, clearing her throat. "This is Gracie and Cecilia." She slid the printouts back to me. "What happened to them?" A crease formed between her eyes. Anger and sadness dwelled in those dark brown eyes.

"We found them in a house near The War Zone. An associate of ours transported them to Perry General Hospital."

"Were they able to help them?" she asked, hope in her tone.

I shook my head. "I'm sorry. We couldn't save them."

She stood up and went over to her plants. "I'm familiar with that area." She shook her head, her finger skimming the petal of the blue lotus. "Was it drugs?" she asked, her voice seemingly thick with sadness.

"No," Alek said. "A mind mage destroyed their minds."

Leticia whipped around. "What? Why?"

"We don't know," I said. "We were hoping to find the answers to that."

She nodded; tears spilled down her cheeks. She came back to her desk and sat down. "I told you four of our students had been attacked two years ago. Well, Gracie and Cecilia were among the two. They were unable to recount all the details of what had happened to them. But from the bits and pieces we did get from them, and the state in which we found them, we guessed that someone powerful had managed to get onto our campus and subdue all four girls. He tied them up and abused them for several hours." She stopped. Tears continued to trail down her cheeks. I quickly wiped away my own as my heart broke over and over again.

"Their teachers believed they had skipped their classes," she continued. "That maybe they were sick and just hadn't notified us." She looked up. "We do ask that students let someone know when they aren't feeling well. But they don't always follow this rule." She blew out a breath. "It wasn't until dinnertime later that day that we found them bound and gagged in their rooms. Bloody... broken..." She shook her head and pulled in a deep breath. "We never found their assailant."

"What about law enforcement? Did they ever find..."

She shook her head. "The law enforcement officers on Sandpoint only took the report and gathered evidence. Since there are only three precincts on Tulare that actually have detectives to investigate these crimes, the request for assistance went to the precinct in Perry."

I let out an angry breath. The Perry precinct was so corrupt, I was surprised they continued to call themselves officers of the law. More like a crime family with badges. Oh, there might be a few officers in there who did wish to do their job, but the ones in charge would hardly let them do it.

"Why would Sandpoint send the request for assistance to Perry?"

"They didn't. Any requests from the smaller precincts are sent to the liaison officer who works out of the government building in Alice. He assigns the cases."

"Of course," I said, frowning.

"You understand. To those useless bastards, this school is for drug-addled, highly sexual teens and young adult girls who can't cut it in the world. And no matter how many times I try to explain our program and what we do, they refuse to change their bias. They took the report, asked a few questions, and dropped it."

"Did the parents demand answers? Or at least insist the case be transferred to another precinct?"

"They tried. I tried. In the end, bias won."

"What happened to the other girls?" Alek asked.

"They left a few months after the attack. I haven't heard from them since. I did, however, find out they stayed on the island. But that was over a year ago. I don't know where they are now." She shook her head. "Up until a few days ago, I believed Gracie and Cecilia might turn themselves around. They had decided to stay, and despite the change in them, they were still working towards their goals." She gave a humorless laugh. "Cecilia wanted to be the next Madame Curie. And

Gracie was going to be a teacher someday. Those girls were so bright."

The image of the two girls drugged out and half naked on a dirty mattress coalesced in my mind. Two girls whose future had been bright until one horrific act tore their world to shreds. Could they have been saved? Maybe.

"Why did you come here, Nicole? Why did you come to this place where dreams go to die?"

"Did you offer them help? Therapy?" I asked, as if I was an authority on the issue.

Leticia nodded. "Yes. But the girls refused all of it."

I knew firsthand you couldn't save anyone who didn't want to be saved. My parents tried relentlessly to pull me back from self-destruction. In the end, I had to decide to save myself.

"Will you tell Gracie and Cecilia's parents?"

"Yes."

I swallowed the emotion clawing at my throat. I had to ask about the girls who had gone missing from the carnival, but it just felt like the wrong time to do so. She was grieving for her students. Piling more onto her right now seemed too insensitive. But again, we had a job to do.

We'd come here expecting to find blood magick users, and instead, we'd discovered that Leticia Peterson was a woman working tirelessly to educate those who would have otherwise been thrown away to fend for themselves.

"You have more questions," Leticia said.

"Yes." I pulled the printouts of the other girls and handed them to her. "Have you ever seen these girls before?"

She studied the printouts of Nadia and Sophia. "No," she said, scrutinizing the photos. "I don't believe I have." She gave the images back to me. "What makes you think they're here?"

Alek pulled out his phone, and after scrolling through the images, he showed her the screen. "What about this man?"

She shook her head slowly, eyes glued to the screen. "I'm positive I've never seen him before, but... something about him is familiar." She looked at Alek. "Is he responsible for what happened to my girls?"

"We believe so. But we also think he's tied to the disappearance of the other two as well." He didn't say anything about the parents' deaths. I glanced at him, trying to get a read on the situation. His face held no clue as to why he chose not to mention it. But I would follow his lead.

Leticia stared at the picture as if she could force the memory to the surface. Finally, she shook her head and said, "I wish I knew why he seems so familiar."

"Did the girls ever give you a description of their assailant?" I asked.

"No. They said he wore a balaclava." She paused. "They did say something strange."

"What?" Alek asked.

"They said he smelled like evil." She splayed her hands on the desk. "I didn't know what to make of that. They didn't give a specific scent... just evil. It could even be just their impression of him. Because he was—is evil. But it stuck with me. And when I asked about specific scent notes like sweet, spicy, pungent, overpowering, they couldn't pick any one smell. They remained steadfast in their assessment: He smelled evil."

Alek sighed. "I want to show you something else. It might be connected, or it might not. But we have to find out." He scrolled through his phone and showed her the screen.

Leticia's eyes narrowed. "We are Tribe," she said and looked up at him. "Why would someone draw our school crest on a note I'm assuming has blood on it?"

"You speak Romanian?" Alek asked.

"I'm familiar with the language." She sat back, eyes still on him. "I'm also familiar with the group."

"You have a connection to Tribe?"

"Yes. When I was thirteen, a man and a woman came to visit my father. This was right after my sister had taken her own life. We were grieving, of course, and these people just showed up. I was surprised that my father welcomed them inside. I didn't hear all of their conversation, just bits and pieces of it. I do remember them uttering that phrase." She paused. "They also mentioned Petronela Vaduva."

I tensed.

Waiting.

"Yes, I do know who you are and what you've done."

"And you still let us inside your school?" I asked.

She smiled. "I have learned to trust my instincts. And like I said, if you had posed a threat, I would have no problem killing you. While our family does share a troubled past with the Stewarts and the Youngs, we are not friends. I did not mourn their deaths. As far as I'm concerned, they are responsible for my sister's ... pain. Them and Lemuel Oren. We share common enemies. So, yes, I allowed you inside my school. Because I trust that you are being honest about the reasons you are here." She stared at us. "Am I right?"

I nodded. Unable to speak. I refused to bring up blood magick. Because despite Alek's abilities and my own, I believed she could kill us.

"Good." She stood up. "Someone is taking great pains to tie my school to your investigation. I want to know why. So I will allow you to search the girls' room and talk with their instructors. It's our summer program, so only three teachers are here. I need to contact the hospital and claim my girls. And notify their parents." She walked over to the door and opened it.

Randall stood outside waiting.

"Escort them to Gracie and Cecilia's room." She looked back at us. "If you need to remove anything, please let Randall know."

"Of course," I said.

"Once they are done with the girls' room, they will need to speak with Professor Shukuma, Thornton, and Carter." She glanced at the clock on the wall. "Class lets out in an hour. I will let all of them know to expect them."

"Professor Shukuma teaches here?" I asked.

Leticia nodded. "Yes. You know him?"

"I've met him recently," I said. Maybe it wasn't the book that was important. Maybe it was the man himself—the author. Was it a coincidence that he and his book happened to show up in our investigation?

"Yes, well, he gives instruction on the Principles of Magick." She hesitated, gaze still fixed on us. "I provide lunch for my staff, and you are welcome to help yourself. I would like to see you before you leave." She turned and walked back to her desk.

We had been dismissed. We'd also lost control of the interview. But that was okay. At least we got some answers. And possibly discovered a thin thread that connected Tribe to the Peterson family. And maybe one person who just might be at the center of it all.

A Rat Crept Softly

Devlin parked across the street from Inner Strength and stared at the brick building with green vines slithering across the red stone. Large blacked-out windows kept the inside hidden from view. One dark window had the Eye of Horus drawn in gold paint, while the other contained a life size drawing of the Buddha. A green canopy hung over the entrance, with the tree of life sewn into its fabric. It seemed as if Mr. Shim couldn't decide which cultural direction best suited his shop.

"It's a little... much," Marta said.

"Yeah. I was thinking the same thing." He put his gun in its side holster. Marta followed suit, taking her own gun out of her bag and sliding it into her belt.

"Are we going to tell them who we are?"

Devlin shook his head. "No. Let's see how much we can get out of them first."

Marta nodded, and Devlin pushed open his door and climbed out into a pocket of heat. He glanced up at the sky. The sun had finally emerged from the clouds, giving light to the oppressive warmth.

Several cars drove by, the bass from their speakers rattling the store windows. A few of the passengers eyed him and Marta with interest. He glared back, and they sped off.

A line of people wrapped around the building, most seeming lost and confused. A dark-skinned man dressed in white robes and sandals made his way down the line, handing out clear cups of magenta liquid.

When Devlin stepped onto the curb, the man turned. He took them in, gaze lingering on the gun strapped to Devlin's hip, then tracked up to meet his eyes. "What can I do for you, officers?"

Devlin let the assumption stand. "We're here to speak to Mr. Shim."

The man shook his head. "Nobody skips the line." He jerked his chin to the end of the crowd. "Gotta wait your turn." He offered them a cup of magenta liquid. "While you wait."

"We don't plan on waiting," Devlin said. "We're here to ask questions about a crime."

"Mr. Shim is legit, and he's tired of having to tell you people that. So why you keep harassing him?"

"You assume we're here to harass him?" Marta asked. "Why?"

Devlin looked up at the camera pointing at the line. Chances were, Mr. Shim already knew they were here. He only hoped the man wasn't smart enough to insist on a warrant. If he did, things would get violent. Because Devlin had no plans on leaving without asking a few questions.

The employee's dead eyes crawled all over Marta. "You think bringing a pretty lady with you will get you in the door? Look behind you. Line is full of beauty." The man continued to stare at Marta. Not a single flicker of emotion registered in his brown eyes.

Devlin glanced at the customers. They, too, had this faraway look in their eyes. He'd seen the same expression in the employees' eyes at Tribec Insurance. Only there, they'd been draining their employees with a ritual meant to steal their vitality.

"What's in the cup?" Devlin asked.

The man didn't respond. Simply thrust the tray toward him. Devlin looked at Marta. She shrugged in confusion.

It was time to switch tactics. Otherwise, they'd be out here all day.

"We're trying to locate two missing girls," Devlin said. "Now, we can stand out here arguing with you, possibly send a few of your potential customers away. Or you can let us in to ask our questions so we can be on our way." Devlin glared at the man. "Your choice."

The man studied him for a minute as if he were trying to read Devlin's mind. After a few beats, he jerked his chin toward the front door. "Go on in."

"Before we do," Marta said. "Do you all sell belladonna, opium, or blue lotus?"

The man turned away and started walking. "Don't know. You'd have to ask Mr. Shim," he called over his shoulder.

"Maybe he's just in charge of refreshments," Devlin offered.

"I'm wondering what's in those cups."

"Yeah," Devlin said, pulling open the door. "We'll have to get one on the way out and have Rachel test the liquid."

"Good idea," Marta said.

The door opened to a warm, cavernous space. A pungent smell lingered in the air. The inside mirrored the outside, with floor-to-ceiling brick walls. Ivy vines trailed down them, interweaving between black metal shelving. Large glass jars with amber liquid sat on the shelves next to large painted rocks. Incan, Egyptian, and Japanese ceremonial masks hid behind the vines. Colorful designs stretched across the polished concrete floor.

In the center of the store, customers surrounded large bins filled with vials of liquid, soaps, incense, bags of herbs, and brightly colored gris-gris bags. They clawed through the wares in a feverish sort of frenzy, while others roamed in front of the shelves, picking up the merchandise hidden behind the vines.

"I'm going to go out on a limb and say Mr. Shim is doping his customers," Marta said, gaze darting around. "They remind me of zombies." She looked up at him. "Like the employees at Tribec Insurance."

They both glanced down at the floor. Devlin followed the intricate lines, trying to see if they had etched a power circle into the surface.

"It's not a power circle," Devlin said. "Maybe some sort of aphrodisiac?"

Marta touched the arm of a man standing over a bin near them. "Sir. What's in those cups they give you outside?"

"Inner strength," the man responded, staring at them, eyes out of focus. "It revitalizes you," he whispered.

"How?" Devlin asked.

The man shrugged and returned to his shopping. Alarm raced through Devlin. Something was definitely off here.

Mr. Shim, wearing a dark green Kimono and brown sandals, walked into the room. He raised his arms and carried a huge smile on his face. Only five feet, nine inches tall, with brown-blond dreadlocks flowing from his scalp, the man exuded an oily jubilance that pissed Devlin off. He wished he could see magick like Alek and Rachel. But Elemental practitioners couldn't see that energy. He could feel it. The man definitely held power behind all that inauthenticity.

"Welcome, officers," Mr. Shim said, his voice scratchy. "I understand you're looking for some lost lambs." He eyed them out of cold, gunmetal-gray irises.

"Do you need to drug people to convince them to shop here?" Marta asked, tone deadly. "Or do you do it for your own amusement?"

Mr. Shim stared at her out of those cold eyes. "No need for insults, officers. We're all friends here." He smiled, chipped tooth on display.

"Your soldier outside must have got the wires crossed. We're not officers," Devlin said. "But why don't you answer my colleague's question anyway."

"Hmm..." Mr. Shim tapped his finger against his bearded

chin. He'd covered all his fingers in silver rings. "I don't drug people. My prices are such that I wouldn't have to. I simply provide them a refreshment while they wait in all that heat."

"It's a little warm in here too," Marta said, looking around. "And do you think you appropriated *enough* cultures?" Marta asked. "I mean, there are so many out there. And you have all this space."

Mr. Shim's lips thinned, eyes dancing with anger. "I can get you a glass if you like," he said through clenched teeth. "But I'd much prefer you ask your questions and be on your way. I wouldn't want you to run off all my customers." He curled his lips into another fake smile, eyes lighting with challenge.

Devlin crossed his arms. "Tell you what, Mr. Shim. We'll ask our questions when you tell my colleague what's in the shit you're serving to those people outside." Devlin stepped forward, getting into the man's space. Looking down at him, he said, "You wouldn't want us to do any damage to your store, now would you? You must have spent so much time decorating it."

Mr. Shim's eyes hardened, and a nerve ticked in his neck, his face turning red. "Why don't we take this conversation to my office."

"Is that where you keep the recipe?" Marta asked.

"Follow me," the man barked and stormed toward the back of the store, shoving customers out of his way as he went.

"I think we rattled him a little," Marta murmured with a mocking frown. "Might have even hurt his feelings."

"He'll get over it," Devlin said and started for the back.

Mr. Shim waited for them at the door leading to the back room. He tapped his sandaled foot with impatience. When they entered the dimly lit hallway, he slammed the door and marched, sandals squeaking, toward a room straight ahead.

Marta nudged Devlin, and he looked down at her. "Could be a trap," she whispered.

Devlin shook his head and kept walking. No. The man might have been hostile, but he wasn't stupid.

By the time they entered the office, Mr. Shim was sitting behind his massive desk, lighting a cigar that had a pungent woodsy scent. He took a long drag, blew out the smoke, and glared at them. "I'm trying to run a legitimate business here. I don't appreciate being harassed every other day!"

"The formula," Devlin said, ignoring his outburst. The man sounded like a petulant child.

Mr. Shim's chair squeaked as he rocked back in it. "Fine. Blue lotus and pinot noir," he yelled. "Happy?"

Devlin tensed, and Marta shifted next to him.

"Well, I guess that answers one of our questions. You obviously have a supply of blue lotus. Do you also sell belladonna and opium?"

Mr. Shim's eyes rounded, head jerking back. "I don't grow the shit here. And no, I don't sell any of those. They're too damn expensive. I get the wine from a supplier."

"Your website says you have everything."

Mr. Shim rubbed his face and rested his elbows on the desk. "Oh man," he said, sounding put-upon. He let out a loud sigh. "That's a fucking gimmick. Get it? If you advertise you have everything, people will come," he said. "Once they get here—" He splayed his hands.

"You drug them," Marta said.

He exploded out of his chair. "I don't force them to drink anything. I just offer it. It's not my problem if they drink too much!" He slammed his hands on the table. "I thought you were looking for two missing girls?"

"We are. But we're also looking for people selling the drugs my colleague mentioned. Can you give me the name of your suppliers?"

Mr. Shim seethed, then yanked open his desk drawer and rummaged inside. "Here," he said, producing a crisp white business card. "It's all legit. The wine is sold in stores, even."

Devlin took the card: Mason's Wines and Spirits. He almost groaned at having to add yet another location to his search. After pocketing the card, he pulled his phone out and showed Mr. Shim a picture of Dimitri. "Has this guy ever been in here?"

The man shook his head. "Haven't seen him."

"Do you grow your own plants, Mr. Shim?" Marta asked.

"No. I send an associate to the other shops to get my supplies. I make the product myself, though," he said, puffing up. "So, like I said. I'm legit."

"You keep saying that. And yet you ply your customers with an aphrodisiac to get them to buy from you."

He spread his arms. "A man has gotta make his money."

"A man, huh?" Devlin said. "We'll leave you to it, then."

Mr. Shim saluted him. "Thank you. And fuck you as well." He plopped down in his chair and turned his back on them.

Before leaving, they asked the two female cashiers the same questions. And just like the guy outside, they didn't know much.

They left the store, stopping only to grab a cup off the tray, then made their way to the car. Once inside, Devlin turned to Marta. "What do you think?" he asked, pouring the liquid into his empty water bottle. He didn't trust Mr. Shim.

"All he needed was a sign that said, 'we are the criminals you seek'," Marta said.

Devlin raised a brow. "Star Wars?"

She chuckled. "A favorite in our house." She glanced over at the building. "Honest opinion? I think Mr. Shim is a flimflam man. I doubt his products have much potency." She shook her head. "And while I get some really bad vibes from him, I don't know that he's the one we're looking for."

"I want to agree. But I also want to come back when he closes and follow him. The only thing behind his store is an alley, so either he really is getting his products from the other shops, or he's growing them off-site. And since I don't believe a damn thing that comes out of his mouth, I want to confirm everything myself."

"Might be a good idea," Marta said. "What about Ms. Rita from Beauty Rose? You want to do the same for her."

Devlin sighed. "We'll have Jonah and Kara look into it if Alek and Nicole can't." He glanced at her. "Were you channeling Nicole in there?" he asked with a smile.

She chuckled. "Yeah. I had a choice between sarcasm and outrage. I settled on sarcasm. The guy rubbed me the wrong way with his slick attitude." She looked over at the store. "I feel sorry for the people who work there. They didn't seem happy."

"They're just trying to make a living," Devlin said, starting the car. "Now, tell me about Angelique."

I could say one thing for Leticia Peterson: she was a formidable woman. Not only had she managed to steer the conversation, but she'd also effectively rendered me mute. I had so many questions swimming inside my head, and yet I'd found myself unable to utter a single one once she took over the conversation.

Was it strategic? Possibly. But I didn't get the impression she had ulterior motives. If anything, I believed her concern for her students was genuine. Just like her desire to help us. And yes, I was a little afraid of the woman.

The very loose thread that connected Tribe to the Peterson family was something we had to explore. It was thin, but maybe it could hold a key as to why someone had implicated them in the first place. And hopefully, Leticia could give us that information.

We arrived at the second-floor landing. Made up like a recreational room, several girls occupied the space. Some lounged on the plush green couches, while the others lay on the area rugs in front of the muted television, staring at their phones. Large bookcases loomed along the walls. Tinted bay windows with cushioned seating were located directly across from the staircase. A lone girl sat in the window seat, reading a book.

They all looked up at our entrance, and their attention immediately lingered on Alek. He gave them a smile I was sure they would discuss later. Complete with giggles and high-pitched voices.

Randall led us to the dorms. I counted ten on each side of the hall.

"Do the girls share rooms?" I asked.

Randall turned and looked at me. "Yes. Except for a few students who don't do well living with others."

"Did Gracie and Cecilia interact with any of the other girls here?"

We stopped at a door on the lefthand side of the hall. After opening it, he answered, "Maybe Angela." He dipped his head toward the room opposite. "She was the only one Gracie and Cecilia cared for. The other girls can be…" He trailed off.

"Difficult," I answered.

He nodded. "That's a nice way of putting it. It's not all of them," he said in a rush. "But a few have given themselves the title of queen bee, and most seem to fall in line."

"But not Gracie and Cecilia," Alek said.

"No. Those girls—" He shook his head. "Before the attack, they were laser focused on their studies. Nothing bothered them."

"Did you see them when they left?" I asked.

"Yes. On the cameras."

"Was someone waiting for them?"

"Not that I saw."

I glanced at the closed door across from us. "Would Leticia mind us talking with Angela?"

"She'd leave that up to Angela to decide. It might be a little difficult. Angela has a hard time being around people."

Randall walked over to the door and rapped on it softly. After a beat, it opened a crack, and a young woman peered out.

"Hey, Angela," he said. "Are you doing okay today?"

"Yes," she said, her voice soft. "What's going on?"

He jerked his head toward us. "These people have some questions about Gracie and Cecilia. Are you up to talking to them?"

"No. But they can call me." She shut the door.

Randall turned to us. "Sorry about that. I can give you her number before you leave."

"Okay." I turned to Gracie and Cecilia's door. "Is this the same room they were in when they were attacked?"

Randall shook his head. "No. The layout is similar, though."

Well, that was a relief. I wouldn't want to stay in a place I'd been violated either. I looked at Alek. "Let's check out the room."

He nodded, and we stepped inside.

Painted a whisky color with yellow trim, the spacious dorm room had two twin beds with a single nightstand between them. A long wooden table with a rollaway cabinet and two chairs were located beneath a window. They had a single bookcase situated near the bathroom. And a large multi-colored rug covered the hardwood floor.

Both bureaus stood open with empty hangers inside. All their garments lay strewn about the floor and beds. As if they had been sifting through their clothes, looking for something specific. I studied those items for a minute, trying to marry them to the ones I'd found in the house they died in. And suddenly, I couldn't breathe.

"Why did you come to this place where dreams go to die?"

"Nicole," Alek prompted.

I swallowed the emotion. "I'm struggling," I said. "It's like I don't know what the next step is." I looked at him, hoping he understood what I could not. It felt as if a massive ball of emotion had suddenly settled on my chest. I couldn't find words or figure out the steps I should take.

He came over and took my face in his hands. "It's painful to watch someone die. Even more painful to sift through the remnants of their life."

I nodded; he understood. It was difficult. I should have been able to return them here. To the place where their dreams could have flourished.

"Remember when we searched Marta's house after she went missing?"

"Yes."

"You look at everything. Like we did in the trailers. Analyze what you're seeing. What kind of clothes? What kind of jewelry?"

It was just what I needed. A little help focusing. I let out a ragged breath and got to work. I couldn't save Gracie and Cecilia, but I would find the one who had set them on the path. Connection to our investigation or not, I would find the man who had violated them and make damn sure he suffered.

Picking up garments from the floor—a knee-length skirt, a white blouse with a low neckline, and dark, dressy jeans—I laid them out on the bed and examined them. Putting pieces together. Something she'd wear to school, or maybe a date—but nothing too provocative. I sifted through the rest of the clothes. "School clothes. And maybe a few items to wear out. She liked to dress nice."

Alek laid out clothes on the other bed. "Same here."

Of course, there was no way of telling which set of outfits belonged to who, but it looked as if the girls dressed similarly. "The clothes we found in the house with them were more... seductive."

Alek agreed.

Next, I studied the jewelry spilling out of their cases. All the pieces were stylish and fancy. Not too expensive. Simple and pretty. Pieces to match the clothes.

I went into the bathroom and found a trashcan full of makeup. Examining the items, I noted the muted tones in the eyeshadow and lipsticks. No bright colors. Just pretty shades to accent their faces.

I went back into the bedroom and looked at the bookshelf: history, language studies, economics, math, government, and a myriad of science texts. Cecilia had wanted to be a scientist, and Gracie a teacher. All their books leaned heavily into the goals.

I stood in the middle of the room, hands on my hips, and processed it all. They left the place that would help them accomplish these objectives and took up residence in a house filled with sex and drugs. What could have possibly lured them there? "They were discarding their old life," I said. "Leaving behind their dreams."

"Maybe they were running," Alek offered. "From their pain, the trauma of the attack."

I opened the nightstand drawer and pulled out a green diary. Another journal of someone's secrets. I wondered what people would think of me if they ever found mine. Ones I'd filled with so much pain and anger. I opened the journal and scanned a few of the entries. All of them outlined daily goals. Compromises either Gracie or Cecelia made with their time and how long it would take to achieve a certain task. There wasn't any waxing on about boys or anything even remotely personal. That is, until the last entry two years ago.

A single line of text written in big letters, taking up the entire page: *I should have fought back.*

That was the last time she'd written in her journal. I closed the book and sat down heavily on the bed. "We won't find evidence of their attacker here. Only the aftermath." Tucked into the pages was a picture of four girls. Two of them we already knew; the other two must have been their friends. I handed the picture to Alek. "Think these are the other girls who were attacked?"

He stared at the photograph. "Yes. Most likely."

I got up and went into the bathroom. A door connected this room to the next. I put my hand on the cool knob and sucked in an emotional breath. Randall had said they'd changed rooms, but knowing their attacker would have used a similar entry point had my heart hurting. I couldn't wrap my head around how he had managed to subdue and rape all four girls. Did he have an accomplice?

I took one final look around the room.

There wouldn't be any clues in this bedroom. No drugs. No physical evidence of an attack from two years ago. We had no evidence to bring back to Devlin and the others. Because it was the room itself that was the clue. The aftermath of trauma inflicted on them. They'd dreamed of a better place. One to escape that pain.

Maybe they'd assumed they needed to change themselves to find peace. Only that transformation had become an illusion. One that was shattered while they lay dying on a dirty mattress. The only question was, what had happened recently that could have prompted this change?

Into the Rose Garden

Devlin pulled up to a waterfront shopping plaza in Dulean and parked. Well-dressed people milled about, traversing the long wooden walkway in front of various boutiques. Angelique's sat at the corner, near a small parking lot and a jewelry store. They watched a few patrons leave the store carrying silver gift bags with white mesh tied around the handles. The store logo, a single rose with wings rising behind it, was embossed on the front.

They climbed out of the car and into the warm afternoon air. A peaceful energy thrummed through the crowd. He pulled fresh air into his lungs, righting himself. Marta came to stand next to him. A few strands of her dark hair had escaped the braid she wore, fluttering around her head in the breeze. She closed her eyes and turned her face up to the sun.

Sunlight glinted off the bright blue water of the Tulare River. Couples sat on blankets, staring out at the calming waters. A seagull banked overhead and landed on a wooden post by the car.

Marta opened her eyes and stared at the bird. "Why does this feel like the calm before the storm?" she asked.

Devlin wished he had an answer. Because he, too, had an unsettling sort of feeling brewing in his gut. He couldn't decide if they were wasting their time going from one shop to the next or if they were, in fact, on the right track. Unfortunately, it was part of the job. That tedious minutia of following leads, hoping to find one clue that would solve the case. But here, it just seemed strange that this case would start with four dead and two missing and morph into tracking down drug dealers. It just didn't fit.

"Well," he said. "Let's get this over with."

Marta pointed to a small coffee shop a few stores down. "When we're done, I'd like to grab some coffee and maybe a sandwich."

"Deal," Devlin said.

A soft chime sounded when they walked into the store. A sweet floral scent swirled in the air; the soft smell eased some of the tension in Devlin's shoulders. Bamboo floors and white and silver displays with accents of red made up the small boutique. Unlike the last shop they visited, Angelique's shelves were artfully arranged. Minimalist presentations featured a single item on each shelf. An array of mesh and roses surrounded the product. Locked cabinets sat underneath each display.

A light-skinned woman wearing a white, form-fitting sundress and red heels smiled and walked over to them. Her curly auburn hair fanned out around her carefully made-up face. She stared at them out of light brown eyes. "Can I help you?" she asked, her voice a melodious whisper.

Devlin smiled. "Are you the owner?"

She nodded, a small smile on her face as she discreetly looked him over. "I'm Angelique."

Devlin extended his hand. "My name's Devlin Grey." He shook her soft hand and dipped his head toward Marta. "This is my associate, Ms. Hernandez. Is there somewhere private we can talk?"

She gave him a quizzical look, then nodded. "Of course. Follow me." She led them past the cashier and into a small employee breakroom in the back. After shutting the door, she sat down in one of the chairs and took her shoes off. "Oh. I really hate wearing heels." She signaled for them to sit. "Can I get you anything?"

Devlin and Marta sat and exchanged looks of confusion. Angelique stared at them, waiting.

"Umm, water would be nice," Marta said after a brief pause.

Angelique nodded, then got up and retrieved two bottles from a mini refrigerator sitting on an immaculate counter. After giving them each a bottle, she leaned on the table next to Devlin and stared down at him. "You have questions," she said.

"Do you normally get people coming in here asking questions?"

She smiled. "No. Why do you ask?"

"Your reaction to us is a little strange. Almost like you were expecting us."

She nodded. "I was. Rita called me an hour ago and said someone had come to her shop asking about belladonna, opium, and blue lotus."

"That was helpful," Marta said. "Do you sell them here?"

"No. All my products are shipped from my distributor in Los Angeles. This shop is one of nine that I own."

"So, you're from California?" Devlin asked.

She shook her head and stood. After turning on a teakettle, she leaned against the counter and continued, "I was born on Tulare. My family and I lived in Perry for the first fifteen years of my life. When some misguided bureaucrat got the bright idea to herd all the islands criminals into one location, we moved." The tea kettle whistled, and she pulled a mug down from the cupboard over the sink. "Tea?" she asked over her shoulder. They both declined. She sighed. "Anyway, I started my first boutique when I was in my early twenties."

"Did you grow your own products then?" Devlin asked.

She put a tea bag in her mug and came back to the table and took a seat across from them. "I did at first. But by the time I opened my third store, I had to rethink my strategy. So, I hired a family friend. An earth mage who runs a community garden."

"Does he grow any of the plants we're looking for?"

"He does. But I only use belladonna in my products."

"Does he ship the plants or the product?" Devlin asked.

"Neither." She took a sip of her tea. "The products aren't made here."

Devlin nodded. She had said a distributor sent her the products she sold. "You know Rita. Do you also know Mr. Shim?"

She burst out laughing. "That walking stereotype?" She rolled her eyes. "Yes, sadly, I do. He came to my shop a few weeks after he opened, passing out flyers and trying to poach my customers."

"Was he successful?" Marta asked.

She laughed again. "My customers would turn up their nose at anything that cost less than $250. His bargain basement crap isn't worth the bags he puts them in." She took a sip of her tea and shook her head. "I went to his store once. Bought a few of his 'home remedies,'" she said, using air quotes. "Mostly sweet grass and seeds of the plants he claims are the principal ingredient."

"Do you know of anyone else who might grow the plants we're looking for?"

"Henri Fontane grows his own product. He has an apothecary shop in Coeur d'Alene."

"We've crossed him off our list already," Marta said.

Angelique nodded. "Well. That's the only people I know about. Sorry I couldn't be more help."

"Did Ms. Rita also tell you we're looking for someone who might be associated with the sale of these plants?"

She frowned over her mug. "No. She didn't mention that. She was just worried about the plants."

Devlin pulled his phone out and showed her the picture of Dimitri. "Have you seen him before?"

Angelique wrinkled her brow. "He looks ... familiar." She sat back in her chair, cupping her mug of tea. "Of course," she said, setting the mug on the table. She got up abruptly and left the room, only to return a few minutes later with a laptop in her hand. "Let me think for a minute. What day was that?" she mumbled. "Yes." She stared at the screen. "A few weeks. Sun out. Corrine and I working... right. Sun ... Here!" She flipped the screen around, pushed it across the table, and showed them what she'd pulled up on the screen.

Devlin and Marta leaned in and saw Dimitri at the register, standing next to a familiar woman. He stared at the blond young lady wearing sunglasses too big for her face—Gracie.

"Yeah. That's him," Devlin said. "Did he pay with a credit card?"

She sat down and shook her head. "Cash. And a lot of it. Told the woman he was with she could get whatever she wanted. Just as long as it fixed her face." She scowled. "I know men like him. Abusive, then so apologetic afterwards. The girl was a mere shell of a person. Kept checking with him when she took an interest in something."

That explained the shades, Devlin thought.

Devlin stared at the screen, thinking. Like Angelique, he'd seen scenarios like this before at his old job. In those instances, the abuse was at the hands not only of partners and spouses but also pimps. Which meant Dimitri could be involved with not just drugs but prostitution as well.

"Could your employees have seen him before or have any information on the sale of the drugs we're looking into?" Marta asked.

Angelique got up. "We can check," she said and led the way back out front.

They waited as a young woman rang up a customer. When she was done, Angelique asked her about Dimitri as well as the drugs.

The woman shook her head. "I haven't heard anything about illegal drug activity, but ..." She stared at the photo of Dimitri that Marta showed her. "I have seen him in here a few times with different girls." She frowned. "He was slimy and wouldn't let the women out of his sight." She shivered. "He even hit on me a few times."

"Did you, by chance, overhear any of their conversations?" Devlin asked.

She shook her head.

"Thank you both for your time." Devlin wrote his number down on the back of a flyer for the store and gave it to Angelique. "If you see him in here again, please give me a call."

She took the flyer. "I will. And I hope you find what you're looking for."

Devlin and Marta thanked her for her time and walked out into the cool breeze.

They'd reached the last of their leads. And while they had learned Dimitri frequented the shop, they hadn't learned anything about the person who was responsible for supplying him. Unless they could get another lead on anyone else growing on the island, the thread would go cold.

"What do you think?" Marta asked, looking back at the shop.

"Can't decide," Devlin said, scanning the area. Something seemed off.

"Well, the only thing I think Angelique is guilty of is over-charging. Unless she's hiding in plain sight. No criminal would truly broadcast who they were. Outside of cheesy gangster movies, that is."

She was right, Devlin thought. No one would announce who they were. Unless they were a serial killer looking for fame. And that wasn't what they were dealing with here.

It all started with the deaths, the missing girls, and the note.

We are Tribe.

It just made little sense. Unless that had been the point. Kill the parents, take the girls, and then leave a note behind pointing to an old enemy to divert their attention from his true motives. But if drugs and prostitution were his motives, why leave a back-pack filled with drug paraphernalia? They were losing the thread.

"What's next?" Marta asked.

"Still want to get that sandwich?" he asked her, eyeing the black Honda Accord idling a few cars down from them. Dark tinted windows obscured his view inside. The hairs on the back of his neck rose. He could have sworn he'd seen that vehicle before. But where?

"Might be better if we find a more reasonably priced place to eat." She paused, then asked, "What are you looking at?"

"Did you notice that Honda when we went in the store?"

Marta stared at the vehicle, eyes narrowed. "Now that you say it, maybe?" They kept walking toward Devlin's SUV. "What do you want to do?"

Devlin had a decision to make. He'd been trained in defensive driving, so it would be better if he was the one behind the wheel. But that would also put him at a disadvantage. He couldn't use his magick and drive. And Marta had just started training to use her gun. She was better than average, which was a great benefit, but would she be able to hold her own if they were attacked? Magick would have to be the answer.

He handed her the keys. "You drive."

They climbed into the car. Devlin reached behind his seat and retrieved his belt. Vials of elements hung from the loops. Nicole had called it his superhero belt. He had to admit, it was what he himself had thought when he fashioned it, along with the one Marta wore with her pockets of herbs. One day, he'd make one for Nicole.

After securing it around his waist, he looked at Marta. She seemed so small sitting in his seat. "You okay?" he asked.

She stared out the windshield. From their position, they could barely make out the car. "Yes," she said. "Any particular route you want me to take?"

"No. Just try to avoid any heavily populated areas."

She turned to him. "Okay. I'm just going to say it out loud since you won't. Chances are, the people in that vehicle are here for us. I assume they have either magick or guns. And since their windows are blacked out, we don't who has started following us or how many are actually in the car."

Devlin nodded. "Still okay?"

She smiled. "I guess it's a good thing I brought my gun."

"Did you bring any extra ammo?"

She closed her eyes and shook her head. He could see the tension in her shoulders. He put his hand on her arm. "Take it slow. We have to be sure they're here for us." He pulled his gun out and laid it by her side. "In case you need it."

"What about you?"

He pointed to his belt. "I'll use magick."

"Right." She started the car and backed out of the spot.

Marta drove onto the main highway and kept the car at a steady pace. The Honda remained three cars behind them.

"Who do you think it is?" Marta asked.

He shook his head, eyes on the side mirror. "Angelique said Rita had called her," he said, trying to work the puzzle out. "So, was it Rita who sent someone? Or did Angelique simply know where we were headed and had someone follow us?" He paused. "No. Mr. Shim. Has to be him. The car was waiting for us. If Angelique were involved, she would have handled it when we were inside. And if Rita had sent someone, they wouldn't have waited until we got here. They could have ambushed us along the way."

"But why?" Marta asked.

"We're asking the right questions."

Marta got off the main highway. "Where to?" she asked.

Before Devlin could respond, the back window exploded.

Once we finished searching the girls' room, we made our way to the faculty lounge. We walked into a room decorated in warm yellows and browns. Four round wooden tables took up most of the space. A long counter with a sink and cabinets underneath sat directly across from the door.

A buffet of food was spread out on the countertop. I walked over to it and inhaled the scent of herb-crusted roasted chicken. A pan of dirty rice and vegetables with an array of fruit rested next to the chicken. Two trays sat at the end with a variety of sliced meats, cheeses, crisp lettuce, and tomato. Bags of chips filled a bowl next to it.

Leticia had told us we could help ourselves.

After we piled our plates with food, we sank into the plush chairs surrounding the table and dug in. Alek was unusually quiet. His face a mask of contemplation. His dark gaze turned to mine, and he lifted an eyebrow in question.

"What do you think about the connection between Tribe and the Petersons?"

He wiped his mouth and leaned back. "It's thin."

"Yeah. But it's there. What would have brought them here all those years ago?"

"If I had to guess, I'd say they could have been looking for information."

"Petronela doesn't strike me as someone who brings her affairs to the public."

Alek shrugged. "She's not. But that's the only thing that makes any sense with what Leticia remembered. If they had come to threaten her family, she would have said so."

"Why didn't you probe her mind?" He'd told me once that one of the abilities of mind magick was what they referred to as scope—the ability to look inside someone's head. I'd wanted to find out why my magick had been blocked. But when he attempted to look, the protective mark inside of me lashed out at the intrusion.

He chuckled. "I don't have a death wish. The woman's powerful." He glanced at me. "And why didn't you ask her more questions? It's not like you."

"Funny," I said, staring down at my empty plate. "And I also don't have a death wish." I turned and faced him. "But seriously, you could have helped her remember."

Alek shook his head. "No. It's better if she allows the memories to surface on their own. They're more reliable that way. Otherwise, people just fill in the gaps with assumptions."

"What?" I asked, confused.

"Memory is a tricky thing. It's why eyewitness testimony always varies from one person to the next. They may recall some of the details, but not all. So, they make up the rest." He paused. "If she gave me permission to probe her mind, I would only see what she recalled. If I pushed her further, her mind might break."

Damn. I was really hoping for an easy route to the information. "I'm resolved to solve this case. But I'm still trying to figure out how everything is connected."

Alek picked up a slice of kiwi and popped it into his mouth. "Well," he started, "it can be overwhelming to see all these threads but no logical pattern." He smiled at me. "But we'll get there." He glanced down at my empty plate. "Did you want seconds?" he asked with a teasing glint in his eyes.

"Please don't tell Marta what I ate. I get the impression she's keeping tally." It wasn't true. But I did believe she was worried about me.

He laughed. "I like Marta. So"—he leaned over and kissed my cheek—"if she asks, I'm not gonna lie."

I smacked his arm lightly and looked at the buffet table. I did want seconds. Especially the rice. But I'd control myself. Being prone to addiction, I had to watch myself. Because lately, I noticed I had traded food for my usual cigars and alcohol. And if I wasn't careful, I'd end up eating myself to death.

I got up to walk off some of the food.

A wall of framed group photographs covered the back wall of the faculty lounge. I went over and studied the images. Staff and students huddled together, wearing matching shirts, their hands held high and huge grins spread across their faces. A few of the pictures had young men and young children in them, standing next to teachers. I read one of the engraved plaques underneath: Family Festival 2014.

Voices carried into the room, and I turned. Three people walked in, Professor Shukuma leading the way. Behind him stood a dark-skinned woman in her late sixties wearing a pair of navy slacks and a white-and-navy polka-dotted top. Her salt-and-pepper hair framed her narrow face. She stared at us out of honey-colored eyes.

The man who followed could have been a relative of Alek's. Long black hair shot through with strands of gray rested in a curly mass on his shoulders. He wore a beige tunic with an intricate red, green, gold, and brown design around the collar and hem. A pair of dark blue jeans encased his powerful legs. Brown-framed glasses adorned his face.

"Ms. Leticia told me you were here," Professor Shukuma said, coming over to me. "It's nice to see you again."

I smiled. "Nice to see you too. How are your grandkids?"

He chuckled. "Rambunctious as ever. Little Erila is always asking after you."

I grinned, remembering the little girl. "You teach here?" I

held up my hand before he could answer. "No. Of course you do. I'm just surprised to see you." I was more than a little surprised. Especially since his book kept turning up in conversation.

"Yes, I teach a class during the summer. I was on my way home for lunch when Ms. Leticia asked me to stay and speak with you all."

"Thank you for staying." I glanced behind him and found the other two professors introducing themselves to Alek.

We walked over and joined them.

I introduced Professor Shukuma to Alek. He smiled and turned to his colleagues. "This is Ms. Nicole Fontane." They nodded their greeting. "Nicole, this is Professor Pearl Carter. She teaches the English Literature and the Origins of Language. And this is Professor Lionel Thornton. He teaches Government and Power Structures of Ancient Civilizations."

"You all teach a lot of history," I said.

"It's a good foundation for learning," Professor Carter said, her eyes sparkling. "I find most of my students enjoy learning how things began." She leaned in; a soft floral scent wafted off her. "Honestly, I think they're more fascinated with the blood and gore from the past." She chuckled. "I see you both have already eaten."

We both nodded.

"Let me grab you both a coffee, then. Maybe some dessert?" Professor Shukuma asked.

"Just coffee," I said.

"What's for dessert?" Alek asked.

Professor Thornton set a folder stuffed with papers on the table. "Louise usually makes banana pudding." His accent was a little hard to place.

"Where are you from?" Alek asked.

Professor Shukuma set two cups of coffee in front of us and walked away.

"Originally, Romania. But I've traveled so much, picking up

accents as I go along." He smiled. "Vaduva. I've heard of your family. You stay here on the island?"

Alek shook his head. "I came here on business."

Lionel raised a brow. "Business?"

"I work for a private investigator."

Lionel nodded and looked at me. "You work as an investigator as well?"

I smiled. "It's a recent career change." I took a sip of my coffee and sighed as the rich, nutty vanilla brew slid down my throat. Now this was some damn fine coffee.

"I see," Lionel said. "It is a taxing profession." He laughed. "But so is teaching." The others had returned to the table with plates of food. "Let me grab some lunch. I won't be but a moment."

"Is there really a lot of blood and gore in the study of language?" I asked Pearl, then added. "Oh shit, I'm sorry. That's not the right question to ask when you're eating."

She covered her mouth, laughing as she tried to finish chewing her food. "No," she said, swallowing. "I'm not squeamish. And to answer your question, yes. There is a great deal of blood and gore in language studies."

She took a sip of water and continued, "When warring nations conquered their enemies, languages often changed. New words emerged to replace the old."

"Do you know Coptic?" I asked, remembering the writing on the wall at the house where Gracie and Cecilia were killed.

She leaned back in her chair. "Yes, of course I know of its origins. Early Egyptian dialects from the third century BC. No native speakers today, although it's still used as a liturgical language of both the Coptic Orthodox and Catholic churches. I can read some."

I guessed this would have to be our segue into the conversation about Gracie and Cecilia. "We found this scrawled on a wall where two students, Gracie and Cecilia, had been staying." I showed her the picture.

She squinted at the screen. "Hmm, that's interesting."

"What?" I asked.

"It says, 'Speak of dreams. Blood has been spilled. I will die someday.' I can't imagine why anyone would write this on the wall." She frowned.

That was odd. I'd expected some sort of incantation or spell. Something to indicate what, besides drugs, had been going on in that house. Why write that on the wall?

"Did either of them take your class?" I asked.

She nodded. "Gracie did. During the regular semester, I teach English Literature. language origins is for the summer months."

"Was she enrolled in your class for this summer?" I asked.

"Yes, she was."

Professor Thornton set a plate of banana pudding in front of Alek. "You must tell me what you think," he said, sitting down with his own mountain of food.

"Did you teach Gracie and Cecilia?" I asked the professor.

He nodded, chewing a mouthful of food. "Cecilia was in my class for a while." He wiped his mouth and looked off as if in thought. "She dropped out after ..." He shook his head. Pearl sighed and wiped her eyes. "She said she was no longer interested in learning about government structures."

Pearl pushed her plate away. "Those poor girls," she started.

"Did they ever talk to any of you about what happened? Give a description of their attacker?" I asked.

They shook their heads no.

Professor Shukuma drummed his fingers on the tabletop. "I got the impression they feared someone. Like maybe they knew who had attacked them."

"Could it have been someone at the school?" Alek asked.

"No. But we did wonder how the person got in," Professor Thornton said. "It's not easy to sneak through the halls. And their attacker would have had to traverse the entire school before reaching the dorms."

Pearl shook her head. "I... I had a theory. But I couldn't prove it."

"Mrs. Carter," Professor Shukuma said. "We talked about this. I seriously doubt the girls here would go that far."

She waved him off. "No. It needs to be said." She looked at me. "Those four girls—Gracie, Cecilia, Carrie, and Danielle. They were not like the other girls here. They had goals. Dreams. They didn't let boys or drugs or anything distract them from their learning. Some girls here could be catty ... vengeful. I think ... maybe another student wanted to knock the girls down a peg."

My eyes rounded. I knew women could be competitive and, yes, a bit catty. But I was with Professor Shukuma on this. Letting someone into the school to rape the person you hated was a bit too far.

"What made you think that?" I asked.

"I overheard a group of them talking about it. Flat out said they got what they deserved."

Anger rose inside of me. "Are those girls still here?"

She shook her head. "When I told Leticia about it, she confronted them. And a few weeks later, they left the island and returned to the states."

Fucking bitches.

"Leticia said Gracie and Cecilia left a few days ago. Did either of you get the impression they wanted to leave? Did they say anything about it, even?" I asked.

They all said no.

I looked at Professor Shukuma. "Your book keeps turning up in our investigations."

"Is that so," he said, taking a sip of his coffee. "Most researchers start with my book when tracing the origins of the Old Ones. Other books have been written on the subject as well. But they don't have all the Old Ones' depictions. Where did you find it this time?"

"In the trailer of a man we believe is responsible for the deaths of four people and the kidnapping of two young girls," I said carefully.

Pearl gasped.

Professor Shukuma's eyebrows shot up. "You think my book is related to what this man did?"

"We don't know," Alek said.

"It's just odd it keeps showing up," I said. "Besides the Stewarts asking you about the Ark, has anyone else contacted you regarding your research into the Old Ones or blood magick?"

"No. You and your other associate are the only ones who have reached out to me about my book in years. When the book was first published, there were endless requests to give talks on the subject. Now, it seems my book has been replaced as a reliable source by others with more instances of embellishment and half-truths. People seem to like a sordid tale of conspiracy more so than facts." He took a sip of his coffee, then continued, "Do you think Gracie and Cecilia might have been involved with this man?"

"That's what we're trying to figure out," I said.

We showed them the pictures of the other girls and Dimitri. None of them recognized them. Nor did they have any contact information for the other two girls who were attacked.

I sat there as they talked, trying to marry the image of the girls I'd found to the ones they described. I couldn't do it.

Gracie and Cecelia had managed to work past their trauma and stay focused on their goals. Their dreams. Yet something took place a few days ago that made them leave school. I just needed to find out what that was. And the person responsible.

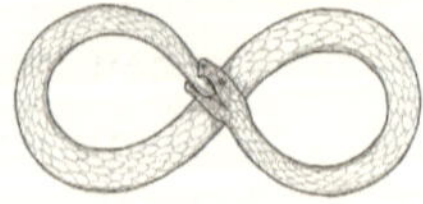

RANDALL LED us down a hallway on the western side of the school that faced the water. Sunlight filtered in through the tall windows, casting a beam of light onto the highly polished staircase. Dust motes danced in the rays like tiny funnel clouds of smoke. We climbed the stairs leading up to the third floor. The wooden planks creaked under our footfalls. An oily lemon scent, mixed with the barest hint of salt and sea, hung in the air. I glanced up. A white curtain fluttered in the breeze, blowing out over a tiny window at the top of the stairs.

On the third floor, a red and gold rug stretched out along the floor. Decorative sconces lined the narrow space, spilling their muted light over an overflowing array of plants set atop polished end tables. Leaves draped over the sides of the tables, nearly touching the floor.

Family portraits hung in the spaces between six large doors, three on each side of the hallway. "Is this part of the dorms?" I asked.

"It's the staff's family quarters," Randall called over his shoulder. "No students are allowed up here."

"Who all lives here?" Alek asked.

Randall stopped and turned to us. "Leticia's brother Anthony stays when he comes to the island. And her parents have a room, although they haven't been here in years. Her Uncle Benjamin and Aunt Louise also stay in this wing." He smiled. "I believe you've had some of Louise's cooking."

We both smiled and nodded.

"And the groundskeeper and his wife stay too, along with Ms. Pearl."

"Where do you stay?" I asked.

"There's a small cottage behind the school. I like the privacy, and it allows me to keep an eye on things."

"You've been here since the attack on the girls?" Alek asked.

Randall continued forward. "I've been here since Ms. Leticia relocated the school to this area." He stopped at the wall in the back. "I told Ms. Leticia we needed more security. I can't cover the entire grounds on my own. She installed cameras and floodlights. But I keep insisting that she hire another guard to watch the front entrance."

"Do you have a theory on how the perpetrator got in?"

He reached under the table and pressed a button. Gears grinded as a wood panel slid to the side, exposing a dark cavern behind the wall. A coppery scent rose from the cavity, filling the hallway.

"Ms. Leticia wants you to know that you're safe here. She realizes showing you this might scare you a little. And she, along with myself, wanted to reassure you with the truth." He handed Alek a flashlight. "Go on down."

We started forward, but before we could take a step, he put his arm up and blocked our path. "To answer your question, I believe the person who attacked those girls was let in."

"By who?" I asked.

He shook his head. "I can't say for certain. But I did suspect it might have been one of the girls bullying them."

Professor Carter had suggested the same thing. It made me wonder if there *was* a connection between the torment and what happened then and now. After being kicked out, could they have returned to the island and met up with Dimitri?

"Can you get us the contact information for the ones who were bullying them?" I asked.

He nodded, then signaled toward the concrete steps. "Make sure you watch your step. I'll be back in a short while." He pulled a piece of paper from his pocket. "This is Angela's number. I will get the others from the admin office."

Alek took the scrap of paper. "Do you think she witnessed something?" he asked.

I wondered the same thing about the shy girl across the hall. Otherwise, why would she give us her number?

Randall rubbed his chin. "She is observant. But doesn't volunteer information readily. So you'll have to be gentle with her if you do call her."

I thought about that for a minute, then wrote my own number down. "If it's easier, she can call us." He took the paper and shoved it in his pocket. I looked down into the dark hole. "What's down there?"

"It's better if you see for yourself," he said and walked away.

After a brief pause, we entered the cool, dry space. My senses became overwhelmed with a plethora of smells wafting up the stairs. With each step, my heart raced and adrenaline filled my cells. Blood rushed in my ears, rendering me temporarily deaf. Alek moved the weak beam over the rough concrete walls. It felt as if the stones were closing in on us, making each step more difficult.

Power surged up, pushing at my body. I looked at Alek. He was bathed in an orange light. "Do you sense anyone?" I whispered.

He turned and looked at me. "Just pain," he said.

We continued forward. Everything in me screamed to stop and run away. That power was so thick in the air, it was becoming difficult to breathe.

Finally, we reached the bottom and froze.

A levitating funnel of blood swirled in the air. In the middle of that storm, a man lay strapped to a metal table. His body jerked with each twist and pull of the stream of blood flowing out of him.

Leticia Peterson stood in that maelstrom of red. Green light streaked with notes of dark crimson engulfed her entire body while she twisted the blood in the air in front of her like some mad conductor at an orchestra.

Her head turned slowly, and she stared at us out of red-rimmed eyes.

Alek's power lashed out and was met with a wall of blood.

Leticia smiled.

A Dead Sound

Shards of glass sliced into the back of Devlin's head. The sting brought tears to his eyes. Marta stomped on the gas, and the vehicle rocketed forward, eating up the road. A pop sounded, and Devlin pushed Marta's head down.

"I can't see!" she yelled.

Another bullet flew by, embedding itself in the dashboard.

"Stay low!" Devlin howled over the blaring of horns and the rush of wind.

The gust sent another onslaught of glass toward the front seat. He glanced at Marta. Tiny cuts dotted the side of her face; blood trickled from her hairline.

"Where are you hit?" he yelled over the rush of the wind.

She shook her head, her knuckles white on the steering wheel as she swerved around the cars in their way. "Just ... glass ..." Sparks flew up as she grazed the side of a vehicle. The car rocked threatening to slide sideways. Devlin grabbed the wheel and helped steady the vehicle.

"Okay?" he asked.

She nodded mutely, eyes trained on the road ahead.

Devlin scrambled to the back seat, shards of glass biting at his palms. The slivers dug into his skin. He swallowed a curse and pulled on his magick, letting the power build inside of him.

A cyclone encircled his hand, power building, cresting. The howl of the wind rendered him momentarily deaf. Anger coursed through his body, fueling his magick. The SUV shook as if an earthquake had struck. Devlin pushed all that power out the window at the oncoming Honda.

The power hit the car, denting the front and shattering the windshield.

The Honda's tires squealed, smoke coating the air, as the driver tried to stop the backward motion.

Cars swerved around it, horns blaring. The scene grew smaller as Marta pushed their car to its maximum. When they had gained enough distance, Devlin climbed back over the seat and searched Marta for wounds.

"Should I stop?" she asked, her voice shaky.

"Turn onto the street up here," Devlin said.

She slammed on the brakes; the car drifted to the side. He pulled wind from the vial on his belt and let the element flow out of him, buffering the car and pushing against the skid. Marta yanked the wheel in an effort to stop the skid. A parked car loomed ahead, its shiny black paint filling his vision. He let out a growl and poured more power out.

Tires smoked.

Metal buckled.

The car slowly righted itself. Marta let out a cry of relief.

Devlin glanced back.

The car was gaining on them.

"Park," he barked.

She swerved the car to the curb and stopped. Her body heaved, breaths coming fast. He touched the back of her head, quickly inspecting her scalp. Tiny cuts, no holes.

"They'll be here in a second."

She patted the seat, surely looking for her gun. Both had

ended up on the floor. Devlin retrieved them and, after handing them to her, jumped out of the car and pulled on his magick again.

Just as he stepped free of the SUV, the Honda shot around the corner. The muzzle of a gun appeared out the passenger-side window.

"Down," Devlin barked and sent another wave of magick at them.

The front passenger door of the Honda crumpled.

The Honda slid to the side, slamming into a parked car.

A woman screamed, and Devlin turned and saw a lady standing in the doorway of her house. Before he could tell her to get back inside, a bullet whizzed by and sent her staggering backward. Devlin cursed. They should have kept going and led the car to a more secluded area.

Marta jumped out of the driver's side, turned, and squeezed off four shots before she ran to the woman's aid.

The neighborhood filled with the stench of gunpowder as the occupants in the Honda continued to spray bullets out the window.

Devlin kept the wind flowing, cycling through the area, while shells rained down on the blackened asphalt. He kept his power flowing, waiting for the enemy to run out of ammo. Or a stray bullet would find another victim. He wanted to check on the woman who'd been hit but had to trust Marta was taking care of her.

The onslaught continued until suddenly, an eerie stillness filled the street—dead sound. The Honda barreled forward, then flew down the road. Devlin ran. Letting his magick carry him forward on the wind. Legs pumping and lungs burning, he ran. Thankfully, he'd done enough damage to the car to keep it from going too fast.

Sparks flew as their bumper skidded across the blacktop.

A tire blew out. The car slowed, careening toward the curb.

Devlin stopped and sent another burst of magick at them. The car slammed against the curb. A loud hiss filled the air. White smoke blew out both windows. The airbags had deployed.

The passenger door flew open, and Eddie, one of the clerks from Beauty Rose, stepped out of the car. He raised his gun and pulled the trigger.

Click.

He was out of bullets. Eddie's eyes went wild, then he took off down the street.

Devlin went after him, his mind reeling at the impossibility of it. He'd expected one of Mr. Shim's goons to be inside that car. Not Eddie. Not the young man who had seemed more concerned about his employer than his own self. Not the boy who had made Crystal, the nervous shopgirl, laugh.

Devlin stopped at the Honda and peered inside. He needed to make sure the driver was down; otherwise, he might end up with a bullet in his back.

An unfamiliar man looked over at Devlin and raised his gun. He wouldn't take the chance that the man was out of bullets like Eddie. Devlin sent a ball of fire into the car and started after Eddie.

The screams of his assailant pierced his ears.

But he pushed on, ignoring the pleas for help.

Eddie had made it a short distance. Stumbling along, head swiveling to keep an eye on his back. When he spotted Devlin, he pushed forward, crying out in obvious pain. He left the safety of the sidewalk and shot out into the street.

A car raced forward.

Devlin shouted at him to stop. Eddie turned, stopping in the street. And a white GMC plowed into him, sending the man airborne. Devlin sent a gust of wind out, trying to buffer the impact. But it was no use. Eddie landed with a crunch, his leg twisted at an impossible angle.

The Escalade stopped. The driver, a teenager, jumped out of the car. He stared wild-eyed at Eddie's body in the street. He turned and looked at Devlin. Then, without a word, rushed back to his car, jumped in, and peeled out.

Devlin stopped and went to his knees in front of Eddie. He stared at Devlin out of wide, fearful eyes. His mouth moved, but no sound came out.

"Hold on," Devlin said and pulled his phone out of his pocket. Traffic had slowed, people looking out their windows but not stopping. He waved them on as he dialed Marta's number. She answered on the first ring. "Is the woman okay?" he asked.

"Yes. The bullet just grazed her. I called for an ambulance."

"Load her up in the car and come pick me up around the corner." He paused. "Is the Honda still on fire?"

"No. Some people came out with extinguishers. We're on our way," she said and hung up.

A yellow VW Bug pulled up to them, and a woman, some Good Samaritan, climbed out. "Is he okay?" she asked.

Devlin nodded. "Thanks, ambulance is on the way." He tried to give her a reassuring look, but she was not having it.

She walked over and crouched next to Eddie. "I know first aid," she offered.

"I don't think it will help," Devlin said, hoping she would take the hint.

She didn't. This wasn't good. A witness to what happened could be a problem. One Opal would have to handle.

Devlin studied Eddie. He was still awake, chest moving up and down, tears running down the side of his face. His eyes darted around, then focused on Devlin. "Hang on," Devlin said, still searching the man's body for obvious wounds. But the blood was making it difficult.

A few minutes later, Marta rounded the corner and made her way to them. She came to a stop in the middle of the street.

The woman stood when Marta got out of the car. "He said he called an ambulance already," she said as if she were Devlin's spokesperson.

Marta gave him a look of confusion before continuing toward

him. Devlin stood and looked at the bystander. "Okay. We could use your help getting him in the car."

The woman who'd been shot stuck her head out the back window, eyes wild. "Is he the one who shot me?" she yelled.

The bystander backed up, hands going up. "I... I just wanted to help."

Devlin shook his head. He didn't have time for this. "It's okay. They both need a hospital, and the ambulance is taking too long. Now, please," he said, softening his tone. "You offered to help. Can you, please?"

She looked between him and the woman in his car, nodded, and stepped forward. "Okay. I can take his feet. Do you have something to help support his neck?"

"Yes," Devlin said. "Marta. There's a first aid kit in the back. Grab the collar out of it." His blood was pumping, adrenaline flooding his body. The longer they stayed out in the open, they risked the chance that someone else would stop. He was sure his photograph had already been taken. Couldn't be helped.

After securing Eddie's neck, the bystander helped them load Eddie into the back seat, and Devlin climbed in after him. The injured woman had moved to the front. Before walking away, the witness gave Devlin her number and asked him to call and let her know if his friend lived, then they set out.

"Where's the nearest hospital?" Devlin asked, holding Eddie's head in his lap.

"Petal is a few blocks south," the woman offered. "My name's Jess. Thank you so much for helping me." She turned in the seat, holding a red-stained towel to her shoulder. "Are you sure we should help him?"

Devlin nodded. "It's the right thing to do."

She nodded and turned around. "I don't feel so good," she said, then passed out.

"Shock," Devlin offered. He looked around, noting the familiar area. "Forget the hospital. Head to the house. We need to get to Rachel." He dialed Rachel.

"Dev," she said, answering.

"I need you to contact Alek and have him meet you at Petal Memorial Hospital. Have Jonah and Kara come and keep an eye on the house. And meet us outside; we'll be there in five." He hung up and looked down at Eddie again. His breaths were shallow, blood seeping out of his nose.

"Stay with me," Devlin said.

"Grandmother... help... safe..." Eddie choked out.

"Ms. Rita?" Devlin asked.

Eddie turned his head slowly to the side. He coughed; a spray of blood coated the seat in front of them. "No... Grandm—" He closed his eyes.

Devlin patted his cheek. "Wake up, Eddie. I need you to stay with me."

Eddie opened his eyes.

He needed Rachel's healing magick now, or the young man wouldn't make it. "How's the woman?" Devlin asked when Marta turned onto his street.

"She's breathing. Probably shock, like you said." She guided the car to the curb, and the door opened before she could put it in park. Rachel climbed in and put her hand on Eddie's chest. Power coursed through the car.

Devlin got out of the car and opened the driver's door. "I'll drive," he told Marta. She got out and got in the back seat with Rachel.

He gunned it. Sending out a prayer that the young man would make it. They needed answers, and the only person who had them lay dying in his back seat.

"He's bad, Dev," Rachel said, her voice strained. "I don't know if I can keep him alive."

He slammed his hand against the steering wheel. The engine whined as he pushed the Escalade past a safe speed. "Do what you can, Rach. Do what you can. But don't push yourself past the limit."

He chanced a look at the woman sitting next to him. An innocent bystander caught in the milieu of his mistake. Why hadn't he steered them somewhere else?

"It's not your fault," Marta said as if she were reading his mind. "So wipe that look off your face."

He caught her gaze in the rearview mirror and gave her a pained smile. She kept surprising him. He'd expected her to freak out. Maybe go catatonic. But she remained steadfast. Even managed to hit the driver when she'd got those four shots off.

"You did good back there," he said. "Real good."

"As did you," she said.

While he appreciated her words, he didn't believe them.

A few minutes later, Devlin leaned on his horn as he surged up the drive toward the emergency room entrance. A man and woman rushed out with a gurney. He'd had Marta call ahead and let them know the situation. Rachel had kept the man breathing, but even she seemed doubtful that he'd live. He just needed Eddie to stay alive long enough for Alek to get here and read his mind.

Once they'd loaded Eddie onto a gurney and put the woman into a wheelchair, Devlin called Opal and gave her a rundown of the situation. She assured him she'd take care of it. Didn't stop his worry that someone had captured the incident and would post it online; then it would make its way back to Detective Barnes. A headache he really didn't need now. But there was nothing he could do about it.

Rachel looked worn down and on the verge of collapse. "You okay to stay and wait?" he asked.

She reached into her bag and pulled out a thermos. "Just need to replenish, Dev."

He nodded. Every cell in his body was urging him to move, but he remained rooted in place, watching the buzz of medical activity move around him. He needed order. A sequence to follow. But he couldn't find it. Too much sensory overload. Marta touched his shoulder, and he jerked.

"What's next?" she asked, looking up at him.

Right. She needed him to decide.

"We need to get to Beauty Rose. Either Rita is responsible or an unwilling accomplice."

Marta tugged his arm. "Let's go."

He took a step. Then another. And soon, he was moving toward a goal. Marta got in the driver's seat. And he climbed into the passenger side. He pulled out his phone, readying to text Alek about what he needed to do when he arrived at the hospital. His fingers felt heavy, and a wave of exhaustion coursed through him as his adrenaline waned. Closing his eyes, he sifted through the events of the day.

Out of the three shop owners they'd questioned, he never would have guessed Rita Saint Claire was involved. But as he'd learned over his brief career in law enforcement, more often than not, it turned out to be the one you least suspected.

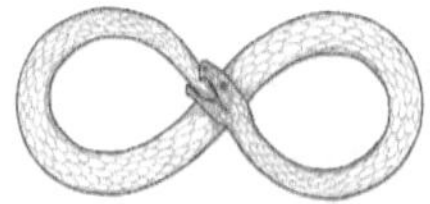

Three police cars were parked haphazardly in front of Beauty Rose, their red and blue lights pulsing. The squad had blown the front window of the shop out; glass lay scattered on the ground. Four covered bodies lined the sidewalk. Blood marred the white sheets. Onlookers stood behind the crime scene tape. A few bystanders had their phones out, pointing at the sea of activity.

Devlin got out of the car and made his way toward the store, heart in his stomach. Maybe he'd been wrong again. Because it sure looked as if someone had attacked the store.

A gurney came out of the building. Crystal lay on it, body covered in blood. A paramedic straddled her body, administering chest compressions. They wheeled another gurney out carrying Rita.

"Oh, shit," Marta said.

Devlin nodded, then walked over to the officer. "Hey," he said. "Where are they taking her?"

The officer studied him, gaze roaming over his body. "You need an ambulance, sir?" He signaled to the paramedic.

"No. No," Devlin said, raising his hand. "Just a little banged up. I have a ride. I just wanted to make sure Ms. Rita was okay."

"Did you see who shot up the place?" the officer asked, pulling out a notebook. "We will need a statement."

"I already gave it," Devlin said and walked away.

He could feel the man's eyes on his back, but he kept going. Walking around the corner, he cursed himself. He'd completely forgotten about his own wounds. And now he'd drawn the attention of law enforcement. He couldn't go back to the car. He called Marta.

"Where are you?" she asked.

"Make your way slowly to the car and head in the opposite direction. I will meet you around the corner."

"Got it," she said and hung up.

Adrenaline flooded his body once more as he hurried up the street.

"Sir?" someone called after him, but he didn't turn around.

He fought the urge to run. If he did, the officer would chase him. So he kept walking. *Breathe*, he told himself when panic wormed its way past the adrenaline. Too much chaos and not enough order. Devlin couldn't think.

An image of his younger self surfaced in his mind. He sat balled up in a corner, the only clean spot in the house, watching his mother, knife knuckled in her hand, as she tore into the sofa. White cotton stuffing circled in the cold air as the ceiling fan sent it flying around the room. When a piece had landed near him, he'd snatched it up and thrown it out into the madness.

Devlin pulled in a breath. He wasn't that lost little boy anymore, suffering through one of his mother's episodes. He was in charge. And he would fix this. Make it right again. Find the order he needed to function.

He chanced a look behind him. He was alone on the street.

Marta turned the Escalade around the corner and made her way toward him. His SUV had taken a serious beating.

Marta stopped beside him, and he made his way around to the passenger side. After climbing in, he turned to her. "Sorry about that."

She shook her head. "Where to?" she asked.

"Home," he said.

Leticia's fingers twisted and turned, as if she were playing a melody only she could hear. The miasma of blood followed the flow of her hand. She looked like a mad conductor orchestrating a macabre symphony. Alek and I stood there, watching this morbid display.

Burnt orange tendrils crawled across the concrete floor, wrapping around Leticia's head.

"Are you probing me, Alexandros? Or do you mean to attack?" Her dark brown eyes, rimmed in red, locked with mine, despite the question being directed at Alek. "And what about you, Nicole? Do you wish to attack as well?"

The man on the table moaned, his naked body writhing as more blood gushed out of him.

"You have a death wish?" I asked, letting my magick pour out of me. I sought her soul in all that gore and found its bright light shrouded in a mist of green.

"Not at all. If you planned to attack me, you already would have. Tell me, Alexandros, what is keeping you in check?"

He cleared his throat. "You haven't attacked us yet."

"So, you're waiting for me to make the first move." She looked up at the curtain of blood she had created. "Blood magick is so intoxicating." She paused, her red-rimmed eyes darting all over the construct she'd made: a funnel with specks of gold. "Do you see the gold?" she asked.

"Yes," I said.

"That is his power."

"Faith magick," I said, eyes glued to the conduit.

"Now listen. Let all other sounds go. And tell me what you hear?"

I did as she asked. The rush of blood had no sound. But other sounds were present. The drip of a faucet. The thrumming of my heart in my ears, pounding with fear and excitement. And the groaning of the man on the table. His moan was filled with both pleasure and pain.

I looked at him. Pale skinned, with a slight build. He had an erection. It reminded me of the first time I'd seen someone use blood magick. The willing donor had a look of pure joy on her face.

"What am I supposed to hear?" I asked, confused.

"Keep listening," she said. "Try to find the song."

"Bells," Alek said. "Faint bells. But also, a whisper of wings." I glanced at him. His eyes were narrowed in concentration. "Could that be what I'm really hearing?" he asked.

"Those are symbols of Faith," she said, sounding weak. "No matter your religion or belief. Faith magick always has the same sound." Her fingers stopped dancing, and she pointed at the grate embedded in the floor. The blood drained into the slots and disappeared. The man on the table exhaled and went still.

"Is he dead?" Alek asked.

She nodded and grabbed the towel off the metal cart next to the table.

"I couldn't hear it," I said.

She stared at me for a minute. "Do you practice your magick every day?"

"Why does that matter?"

She sighed. "It helps." She continued staring. "For some, it's easy to hear the song in the blood. Others can see its power." She licked her chapped lips. "When you saw the gold, what is the first thing that came to mind?"

"I needed to pray," I said.

"That can mean a few things. Since you don't practice using your—" She swallowed and walked over to a sink near the far wall. After filling a glass with water, she drank deeply, then continued, "Power every day, you will need more time and practice to hear it." She paused. "But you did see it. Which means you are attuned to it." She leaned against the sink. "Something to think about, at least."

I had to stop myself from mentioning my reaction to the Houses of Power at Petronela's camp. I'd heard their song. So why couldn't I hear the blood?

I looked at the body on the table. "Maybe we should talk about this man you just killed."

She glared at the man on the table. "Meet Chester Newberry. He killed twelve children in the span of two years." She pushed off the sink and walked over to the body. "Two things kept him from paying for his crimes: a clever attorney and overzealous detectives planting evidence. They didn't need to do this. But they wanted to make damn sure Chester paid for his crimes. My brother Anthony confirmed his guilt, then brought him here for me to use." She looked at me. "We can discuss what I do here. But I need to sit. Working blood magick takes so much out of me."

I didn't know how to respond to that. On one hand, she'd just admitted to having her brother kidnap a man so she could torture him to death. On the other, said man deserved to die. She and her sibling had become judge, jury, and executioners. Yes, the man was a monster, but was she one as well?

Not waiting for us to respond, Leticia started for the open doorway at the end of the hall. I wasn't ready to join her. I needed a minute to collect my thoughts and come to terms with what we'd witnessed.

Alek touched my elbow. "Nicole," he said. "What do you want to do?"

"I don't know yet," I said, staring at the man on the table. "I just..."

A red rash surrounded the man's eyes and mouth, and veins stood out on his stark white skin. Had she pulled all his blood out? I moved closer to him. Tiny holes had been drilled into the crooks of his arms. I found similar holes near his kneecaps. My breathing grew shallow.

Alek pulled me to him. "Breathe, Nicole."

My heart rammed in my chest; too many thoughts competed for dominance inside my head. Damn. This was all I needed. To have another panic attack in Leticia Peterson's dungeon of horrors.

I stepped away from Alek and finally took in our surroundings. "This room looks strange," I said. The stairs behind us spiraled, meaning we were facing away from the living quarters. Sections of the wall jutted out, cutting into the room. They looked like hallways. One side of the room had two small, rectangular windows near the ceiling. The other side held more carved-out spaces. Were we in the walls? A basement?

I let out a frustrated breath. I'd stalled long enough. "Well. We came here to determine if the Petersons were practicing blood magick. Looks like we found our answer." I stared down the hall. "Better go get some more."

We found her in a small office, sitting on a couch, holding a rolled cigarette in her hand. An overpowering scent of clover permeated the air.

She looked up at us, letting smoke trail out of her open mouth. "Sit," she said, signaling toward the couch opposite her. "I need a minute to calm my nerves. Anxiety is the worst kind of emotion."

"It really is," I said, sitting.

"You get anxiety as well?" she asked.

I nodded and pulled out one of the liquid vials Rachel had given me. "A friend made this concoction for me."

Before I could load it in the vape pen, Leticia said, "Can I see it?" She took the vial from me and studied the liquid. "Do you know what she put in it?"

"Elderberry and burdock root."

"I used some of those same herbs when I was first diagnosed." She pulled a brown case from her pocket. "Try these," she said, handing me the case.

"Thank you," I said. "What are they?"

"Clove cigarettes. I make them myself."

I opened the case. Inside were five cigarettes rolled in brown paper. "How do they work for anxiety?"

"According to ancient texts, anxiety disrupts the harmony in your soul and spirit. Clove was used to restore that harmony."

I looked at her. "Where did you learn this?"

"I can't tell you that."

I could press for the information, but really, it wasn't important.

Now how to segue into her use of blood magick. "Aren't you worried that what you do here will one day make you a monster?" I asked her.

"Sometimes you have to become a monster to fight a monster."

"That would make you a monster," Alek said, gaze focused on her.

She smiled at him. "And given what I've seen in your power, I wonder if you're a monster as well."

I cleared my throat. I didn't like her scrutinizing Alek that way. Nor did I like the image of him being a monster in my head. She may have glimpsed the strength of his power, but I'd seen it firsthand and knew that his effortless breaking of another person's mind could be viewed as monstrous.

I took one of her cigarettes out, and she handed me a lighter. After lighting it, I pulled some of the smoke into my lungs and immediately went into a coughing fit.

"They take some getting used to. I should have warned you."

I nodded, staring at the brown cigarette. "It feels ... strange." I looked at her. She watched me out of eyes filled with trepidation. "Why are you being so open with us?"

"You mean honest," she said, then sighed. "I became aware of you and the team you're working with when Lisa and Thomas were killed along with other members of their cult. Gerald Stewart sent his henchman ... I believe you know Logan Magellan?"

I nodded, and she continued, "Well, he came to the school to warn me there was a threat to our families. Gerald even instructed him to offer protection." She laughed, the sound filled with menace. "They still think my family is weak because we don't go along with their misguided rituals to become gods. The Stewarts with their Harvest Ritual and Gavina Young stealing power from the young women she lured into her sect." She paused. "I have to thank you for killing that bitch. I would have preferred to get her on my table, but that would have drawn unwanted attention to myself—" She stopped suddenly. Her gaze went unfocused, as if she were reliving a memory. Then she stood and walked into the other room.

Alek and I shared a confused look and then followed.

"They believe that our shared connection to the past is a reason for us to forge an alliance," she continued as if there hadn't been a pause or change of location in the conversation. "They have destroyed many lives in their pursuit to kill Lemuel Oren and free themselves from his grasp." She covered the dead man's body with a sheet. "I will never sacrifice an innocent in my quest to master blood magick." She dipped her head toward the body. "This is the best way."

"But you can already wield blood magick," I said, trying to plead to her sense of logic.

She gave me a confused look. "Wield? Blood magick wasn't meant to be a weapon."

"Why was it created?" I asked, remembering Luisah's promise to my father not to teach me about it.

"To heal the brokenness inside those who can't use magick."

I looked at the sheet. Blood had started seeping through the fabric. "But he wasn't broken? Was he?"

"No. I wasn't trying to heal him. I was... practicing."

I waited to see if she'd show any signs of regret, or embarrassment, even. But her gaze remained steady on mine. Like she was almost daring me to question her methods.

"Who taught you how to do this?" I asked finally.

She didn't respond.

"Is it the same person who told you about clove? A remedy found in ancient times, you said. Which means someone who is familiar with those rituals..."

She held her hand up. "I get the feeling you won't give this up."

Alek chuckled. "No. She won't. So you might as well tell us."

She stared at me for a while, eyes dancing with admiration. "Thoth," she said, watching me. "But I get the impression you might have already figured that out."

I hadn't. But I wasn't going to admit it. "Do the other families know the true purpose for blood magick?"

"No. And I'm not going to tell them, either. Besides, I doubt it will make a difference."

I stood there, wanting to ask so many more questions. Finally, I'd found someone with answers, who was willing to share them with me, and I wanted nothing more than to stay in this space, learning. But we had a job to do. And that had to take precedence.

"You can visit again," she said. "I wish us to be friends."

I smiled. "It's like you're reading my mind."

She laughed. "No. You wear your emotions all over your face. You might want to learn how to hide them if you wish to continue hunting monsters."

"Good advice." I started for the stairs, then stopped. "Is Thoth on the island?"

She hesitated. I didn't dare look back at her. She'd see the eagerness in my eyes. "Yes. But that must remain between us."

Fair enough. If he wanted to remain hidden, I would respect that.

"When you're done with your current case, I'd like to hire you to find the monster who attacked my poor girls."

"We'll find him for free," Alek said. "Will he end up on your table?"

I turned and watched her face for any sign of shame.

She grinned. "Yes, he will."

She was completely at ease with what she was doing. And, truth be told, I didn't feel any one way about it. Because one day, I may end up with same twisted view about my own acts of violence.

After thanking Leticia for her time, we climbed the stairs and made our way outside. By the time we emerged from the building, the sun was setting. My phone buzzed in my purse, and I pulled it out.

"Well damn," I said, staring at the missed messages. "We need to get to Petal Memorial. Devlin wants you to read a suspect's mind."

"Okay," Alek said.

We jumped into his car, and I filled him in on the way.

The sun had set by the time we pulled into the emergency room parking lot of Petal Memorial Hospital. Where, just a few days ago, Logan had shoved me out a window and abducted me, all so he could feed me a riddle about my heritage. To say the man was elusive would be an understatement.

Alek circled the lot.

Our investigation into the deaths of four people and two missing teenagers had morphed into a drug and prostitute ring. Everything we'd learned today only added to the massive pile of situations we needed to look into. How did these things relate to Tribe? How were we even on the right track? Sadly, the only way to answer these questions was to return to the carnival and interview everyone there. But we didn't have that option. So we had to continue following the clues as they presented themselves. I only hoped said clues didn't lead to even more things we'd have to investigate.

I glanced out the window. "Didn't we pass that car a minute ago?" I asked.

"Yep," Alek said with frustration in his voice. I glanced over at him—lips thinned, eyebrows knitted in an angry downward slash. He needed a break. Hell, I did too.

After his third attempt at finding a parking spot, Alek sped toward the emergency room entrance. "I'll park here and go in alone," he said, resigned. "If anyone comes out and says anything, just move the car."

I sighed. "Might be our best option. What the—"

Rachel stood outside the entrance holding a file folder in her hand, with a backpack slung over her shoulder. Blood coated her jeans and shirt. She looked as if she'd been in a fight. A nurse stood next to her, arms extended as if she was ready to catch her if she fell. The nurse looked as if she was pleading with Rachel. But our friend gave the woman no response. Rachel's head turned our way, and she shuffled over to the car.

She opened the door. "Eddie didn't make it," she announced, climbing inside. "And Opal gave me this file on that corrupt detective, Barnes, before she left."

"Okay," I said, a little lost.

Rachel laid her head on the back of the seat and closed her eyes. She held a file firmly in "I gave him as much as I could, but it didn't work." Her voice was flat. "Dev was hoping Alek could read his mind, find out what he knew, who he was protecting."

"You okay, Rachel?" I asked.

She cracked open an eye. "Used too much magick."

"We need to get her home," Alek said and punched the gas.

"Can we get something to eat? I'm starving. Also, we need to go by Beauty Rose and see if the police have left. Might find evidence in there," Rachel said in a whisper.

Why had Devlin left her at the hospital in this state? "Rach, honey. We need to get you some of your coffee first."

She rolled her head back and forth on the seat. "No. I'm okay. We have to take care of..."

"Rach?" I asked, reaching over the seat and shaking her shoulder.

She didn't respond.

"Oh shit!" I climbed into the back seat and checked her pulse. Her skin was pale and clammy, but I detected a steady heartbeat. "Her heart's still beating." Panic rushed through me. "What do we do?"

Alek's magick filled the car. He swerved, car horns blaring as he parked at the curb. "You drive," he said, then got out of the car and held the back door open.

I scrambled out, heart pounding, and got behind the wheel. Shifting the car into drive, I pulled back onto the street, barely missing an oncoming car. I needed to calm down or I'd kill us all before we got home.

I glanced in the rearview mirror. Alek had pulled Rachel onto his lap. She lay there, limp and unresponsive. He had her backpack open, thermos in hand. "Her thermos is empty," he said.

Sweat slid down my face. I could feel Alek's magick inside the car. Filling it to the point I could barely take a breath.

"Are you healing her?" I said, voice shaky. *Please let Rachel be okay.*

I took the next turn too fast, braking at the last minute. Alek and Rachel flew forward. "Sorry. Sorry," I said, righting the vehicle.

"Yes," Alek said finally. "By expending power." He paused. "She's gotten like this before. She'd used too much magick and passed out. Since we both use our magick constantly, I tried feeding her some of mine. It helped. That's when she created the coffee."

"Didn't she tell you all she was not okay?"

"The opposite. She kept insisting she was fine."

I glanced in the rearview mirror at Rachel lying across Alek's lap. She looked pale.

Finally, I skidded to a stop in front of Devlin's house. Rachel's eyes were open, but she wasn't focusing on anyone. Just kept mumbling something to herself. Alek got out of the car, holding her in his arms, and rushed up the walkway. I swerved around him and, with trembling hands, opened the door. He swept past me and into the kitchen.

Kara, Jonah, and Rae sat at the kitchen table with half-eaten food in front of them.

"What happened?" Kara asked, standing.

Alek set Rachel in his lap, and I grabbed the coffeepot. Only a small amount remained in the pot.

"I'll explain in a minute," I said.

While Alek held Rachel up, I put the pot to her lips. "Drink, Rachel," I demanded. She smiled and took the pot in her hand, downing it in one gulp.

She sat there, staring into the empty pot. I let my gaze go distant, checking her aura for her magick. A pale green light shimmered around her. She was weak. Her magick was usually dark green.

She sighed and rested back against Alek. He ran his hand over her forehead, his magick still pulsing around him. I stared at her aura, willing it to heal. Dark green spots appeared, widening with each second. But not fast enough. I looked around the kitchen. "How do I make the coffee?" I asked, panicked.

"Give it a minute," Jonah said.

Time stretched while I paced the room, racking my brain for ways to help. Alek started humming, his dark melody filling the kitchen. I looked over at Kara. Her green eyes were glued to Rachel, brows knitted in concern.

"Better," Rachel said finally, and I let out a sigh of relief.

I knelt and took her face in my hands. "You scared the shit out of me! And you will teach me how to make your coffee. Also, you scared the shit out of me."

"You said that twice," she said, beaming at me as if nothing had happened. "There are pre-made packs over the sink. Forgot to tell everyone."

I shook my head, resisting the urge to smack her face.

"Still want something to eat," she said and moved off Alek's lap. Her legs shook a little, and she sat down. "Dev wants us to go to Beauty Rose and search it for anything the police might have missed. Can I have a burger, Jonah?"

She was rambling. I looked at Alek and Jonah for directions.

Alek shook his head, took the coffee pot, and started another pot.

Jonah smiled at her and went over to the stove. "You wanna fill us in, Rach?" He started assembling a burger. It would have been rude of me to ask him to make me one as well, so I waited, salivating at the mound of fries he added to her plate.

She shrugged. "Used too much magick trying to keep that Eddie kid alive, and I ran out of coffee."

"How much did you pour into him?" Alek asked.

"Enough to stop his death rattle. It didn't matter in the end."

"I need you to explain what happened to you. How can you use so much magick you almost die?" I asked.

She furrowed her brow. "I wasn't going to die. Only passed out for a minute." She leaned back, and Jonah set a full plate in front of her. Rachel bit into the burger and chewed. After swallowing, she said, "My magick always remains active. I think it's what protects me from poison. Like your mark protects you. Eddie was essentially dead when Dev and Marta showed up. I poured too much of myself into him. I should have stopped, but I knew Dev needed information from him."

"We talked about this, Rach," Jonah said. "You promised you wouldn't push yourself so hard anymore."

She didn't look up at him, just nodded and continued eating.

"I won't do it again," she said after swallowing a bite.

I suspected she would do it again. And I'd pull her aside later to drill into her just how important it was for her to take care of herself. Like I was the authority on mental well-being and self-care. I usually found my solutions in a bottle of Captain Morgan.

Deciding I'd waited long enough, my stomach and I went over and fixed a burger. I glanced back at Alek, holding up a bun. He smiled and nodded. After fixing our burgers, giving him a few fries, and dishing up a mound for myself, I sat down and tucked into my food. Oh, dear Lord. I might have to marry Jonah.

I looked at Kara in her dark green bikini top and white shorts. "So, how was the pool party?" I asked between bites.

"Quiet and invigorating," Kara said, with humor in her tone. "We didn't want to make *too* much noise."

I side-eyed her. Her mouth twisted into a knowing smile, green eyes lit with laughter. I sighed, face heating, and shoved a few fries in my mouth. "What are you two doing here, anyway? Shouldn't you be off playing superspy and vixen? Not getting an earful about my activities from the teenage snitch?"

"Is Jonah the vixen in this scenario?" Kara asked. "That must make me the teenaged snitch. Rae, you must be the superspy." They all laughed.

"I don't like you right now," I said, getting up to fix Alek and myself some coffee and avoiding eye contact in the process. I didn't know why them knowing about Alek and me having sex bothered me so much. I wasn't exactly prudish about my love life. But being with Alek was different. There were feelings involved. Something I was not used to.

"We're here to keep an eye on Rae, and Devlin wanted us to stay for the debrief," Jonah said.

"Where are Boss Man and Marta?" I asked, looking at Rae. She smiled at me, and I winked.

"Marta got a picture of the license plate of the car that chased them before Devlin torched it. They found an address and are going to check out the house before the cops do," Rae said.

"What happened at the school?" Jonah asked.

We filled them in.

Kara's face morphed into an angry mask. Jonah looked like he was two seconds away from letting his demon out. Rachel looked intrigued.

"She has a lab?" Rachel asked. "For blood magick?"

"Did you hear the part about the torture?" I asked.

She nodded. "Yeah. That's the best part. When we find the ones who hurt those girls, maybe she will let us practice on him." Her eyes widened at the thought. Well, at least she was back to her normal crazy self.

Kara kept shaking her head. "I want in. We can hunt down the stragglers from the last two cases another time. I want to find the sick son of a *b* who raped those four girls." She shared a look with Rachel. "And yeah. Maybe get a magick lesson at the end of it."

Well, okay. Things had taken a dark turn. Honestly, I didn't blame them. I, too, had entertained the same idea. Even though I wasn't ready to admit it out loud. "How is your investigation coming along?"

She sat down. "Slow. We could use someone to do research."

"I can help with that," Rae said. "Ms. Marta and Rachel have been teaching me."

I smiled at her use of an honorific for Marta. "Have to ask Boss Man."

"I'll tell him we're taking her with us," Kara said, smiling sweetly.

"Okay. Well, just make sure I'm here when you do," Kara and Boss Man going head-to-head was bound to be entertaining. Kara was stubborn as hell. I got up, patted my stomach, and looked at Alek. "We better go check out that apothecary before Boss Man gets back."

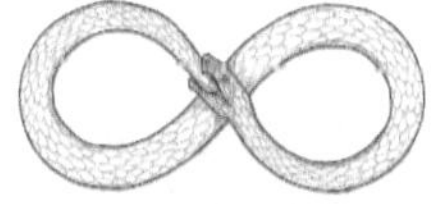

A BLUE STROBE LIGHT, intermittently cut into the darkness, illuminating the bystanders milling about in front of Beauty Rose. One end of the yellow police tape trailed across the black-top, fluttering in the breeze. Officers stood in front of the crowd with bored looks on their faces. Patrons loitered outside the bar next door, drinks in their hands, staring at all the activity. The sandwich shop had a large handwritten sign on the door proclaiming it was temporarily closed.

"Well. Looks like we'll have to come back later," I said.

Alek scanned the area. Drumming his fingers on the steering wheel, he glanced at me. "I'm going to see if I can pick up any impressions." He climbed out of the car and strolled toward the crowd.

I watched his magick roll over the people gathered around, circling the heads of the officers walking in and out of the Beauty Rose. Why were they still here? Was Rita Saint Claire really selling drugs out of her shop? I'd met the lady once with my father, and she didn't seem the type.

Alek walked back to the car and got in. "They can't find anything. Got a lot of impressions of confusion and frustration among the police."

"What about the crowd?" I asked.

"Mostly confusion and curiosity. Speculation and wild theories are mixed in there as well." He sighed, pulled his phone out, and started a call. "Rach," he said. "Did you get an address for Eddie?" He started the car and put it in gear. "Text it to me." He handed me the phone and pulled away from the curb.

A text came in, and I read off the address, thankful we didn't have to go to North Perry again.

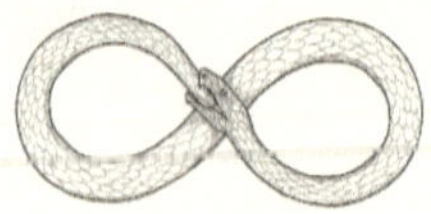

Alek pulled to the curb in front of a two-story apartment building in Brunswood, a few blocks from my own unused apartment. Two police cruisers were parked in the gravel lot across from the building, near a densely wooded area.

Alek surveyed the area. "Not enough people here for me to blend in." His magick rose, pushing out the car and crawling up the steps of the complex. "Same emotions as the crime scene, mixed with concern from the neighbors."

"So, they have nothing."

Alek shrugged and stared at the building. "We'll have to come back tomorrow to be sure." He glanced over at me. "Still want to visit the museum to research your theory?"

"No. They closed at five. I'll stop by after Marta and I take the kids to therapy."

Alek threaded his fingers in mine. "What do you want to do now?" he asked, smiling.

I moved closer, and he wrapped his arm around my waist. "I would like to have sex in the shower, but there are too many people at the house."

"Your apartment isn't far from here." He kissed my neck, and I shivered.

Was I ready to return to my apartment? Where Set had attacked me last week? I stared at the bracelet secured around my wrist.

"I'm surprised my bracelet didn't break during the skirmish with the Dacian," I said, probably killing the mood. But I *was* surprised.

He ran a finger over the bracelet and made a noise of agreement.

A permanent fixture on my wrist since my father had given it to me when I was nine, I hadn't bothered to check if it was still there when we'd dragged ourselves home, bloody and broken from that last fight.

The gold charm Ezra had given me joined the tiny symbols of my mother's power, a fleur de lis with a phoenix flying behind it, and my father's, an ankh.

The charm, a shen ring circling a trinity knot, was supposed to repel Ezra's brother, Set. To keep him from attacking me. His soul—at least, that was what I assumed his manifestation was— could find me anywhere. And, somehow, actually interact with me. Even attack. It was funny how the same symbol Set had carved into my bedroom dresser, and also branded on my wrist, was supposed to deter him.

Alek was waiting for an answer. Possibly giving me time to work through the fear of having to return to a place where I would have lost my life had it not been for him coming to check on me.

I swallowed the sudden sense of dread and smiled. "I think..."

"I know," he said, taking my hand again. "I'll wait till you're comfortable going back there."

"You mean no more sex until then?" I asked, eyes rounding.

He laughed and started the car. "Didn't say that. We still have that weekend date to go on."

"I bought a dress for the occasion. Sadly, it's still in my tainted-ass car."

He smiled. "We won't be wearing any clothes on this date."

My stomach quivered, and I blew out a breath. "Sounds like a good plan. Now, get me home so you can wash the day off for both of us."

He slid his hand up my thigh. "On it."

I'd have to face that place again one day. Probably the day rent was due. And pick up the sick care package from Ronald Stewart detailing his twisted proclivities and pictures of his latest victim. I was sure one of those waited on my doorstep.

Fuck.

Corpse in Your Garden

Oscar Vasquez, the driver Devlin had killed, lived in a middle-class neighborhood on the border of Pleasanton and Brunswood. Devlin drove his damaged car down the short street, with Marta in the passenger seat, toward the house nestled at the end of a cul-de-sac.

The streetlights created round pockets of illumination on the sidewalk. Oscar's house was the only one without its porch light on.

Devlin ground his teeth. He wished he hadn't cooked him alive. If both assailants died, they wouldn't get the answers to their questions and would have to continue searching, hoping to find enough threads to get them to the truth.

And what was the truth? They had ventured so far from their original investigation, he wondered if they were even still on the right track. So much about this case made little sense, and without a living witness to interrogate, he doubted it would become any clearer soon.

He parked at the curb and cut the engine. "There's a flashlight in the glove box, along with plastic trash bags," he said, pulling his phone from his pocket. He sent a quick text to Rachel to see if

Alek had arrived at the hospital in time. He read the response and bit off a curse. "Damnit."

"What's wrong?" Marta asked.

He glanced at her. The interior lights illuminated her face and the many cuts on her skin. "You sure you're all right?" She'd cleaned and bandaged the worst of her wounds, but he still wished he'd had Rachel heal her before they set out again.

She shook her head, eyes narrowing. "No. We already had this conversation. I'm fine. We're all just fine, if a little banged up. Now, tell me what's wrong."

He pushed open his door. "Rachel used too much magick and passed out. Alek took her home. They didn't get there in time to read Eddie's mind—he's dead." He got out of the vehicle and breathed in the warm air, pulling the element inside of him. The cuts on his arms and scalp tingled with the surge of magick inside of him.

"Can I help you?" a man asked. Devlin turned and watched an elderly gentleman make his way toward them.

"What's the play?" Marta asked.

Devlin looked at her and mouthed, "The play?"

She shook her head, and Devlin turned back to the approaching man.

"Evening, sir," Devlin said.

"Evening," the man said.

Devlin extended his hand. "My name's Devlin Grey." He dipped his head toward Marta. "This is my associate, Ms. Hernandez."

"Miss," the man said with a nod. "Name's Willie. You all lookin' for Oscar?'

"Yes, sir," Devlin lied.

The man crossed his arms. "Well, he tore out of here in that Honda of his a little after lunch and hasn't been back since."

"We're private investigators looking into a possible drug connection between Mr. Vasquez and another man."

The man furrowed his brow. "Drug connection?" He rubbed

his bearded chin, looking skeptical. "Seen no sign of that." He paused. "He always has a parade of women coming through here. Made me think he was running prostitutes." He shook his head. "Didn't figure on drugs, though." He leaned in as if to whisper, sneaking a glance over his shoulder. "Wife used to watch him when he was a baby. She'd swear he was an angel. More like a devil to me. Bit too cocky."

Devlin chuckled. "Yes. Well, we have to be sure." Devlin pulled his phone out and brought up the picture of Dimitri. "Have you ever seen this man over here?"

Willie studied the photo. "Yep. Him and another fella used to stay here with Oscar until about a... year ago, I believe. They cleared out of here when the other guy—" He stopped, rubbing his chin again. "Believe his name was Michael something. Never got a last name."

"Do you know why they left?"

"Can't say for sure. Didn't ask, either. Just glad they were gone. The neighborhood got quiet. Fewer parties being thrown."

"Can you describe Michael?" Marta asked.

Willie chuckled. "Dark skinned. Believe he was Romanian. That's what Oscar said, at least. Wore his curly hair a little too long. Looked like a damn woman. Pants too baggy. Just a bad element all around." He laughed. "A week prior to him leaving, an older fella—maybe his daddy?" He shook his head. "Couldn't be sure. Anyway, man came around and pulled Michael out into the street and gave him what for."

Marta and Devlin laughed. "So, not a nice young man, then."

Willie shook his head. "Waste of space." He jerked his chin toward the house. "You looking to take a peek inside?"

"It would really help," Devlin said.

Willie eyed him for a minute. "I suppose if I go with you, might be okay." He pulled a key ring from his pocket. "He never asked for the spare key back his parents gave us when they first moved in here. If he hasn't changed the lock"—he started up the walkway—"we should be able to get inside."

Devlin stopped, staring at the man's back. "I have to say, sir. I'm a little surprised you're helping us. Letting us inside, even."

Willie stopped in front of the door. He sighed, letting his chin drop to his chest. But he didn't turn around. "I used to be an MP in the army." He turned and said, "I take it you know what that is?"

Devlin nodded. "Spent ten years in law enforcement myself."

"Figured as much." He sighed. "I figured the only reason you're here and comfortable with what I will assume is breaking into Oscar's house is because something has happened to him." He stared at Devlin. "Am I right?"

"Yes, sir."

He frowned. "I always hoped he'd pull his head out of his ass. I thought"—he unlocked the front door—"when those friends of his left, he'd get himself together. He told my wife he was even getting a job at the carnival." He pushed open the door and signaled for them to enter. "I'd appreciate it if you let me break the news to my wife and his parents. Might ease some of the sting."

"Of course, sir."

He blew air out of his nose and switched on the light. "Go on in. Just shut the door behind you. I ... I can't bring myself to go in there right now." He walked away, making his way back to his house.

"I think he really cared for Oscar," Marta said.

Devlin stepped inside the house. "I do too."

The front door opened to a sparsely furnished living room. Dark brown carpet covered the floor. A faint smell of bacon and weed permeated the air.

"What are we looking for?" Marta asked.

Devlin sighed. "Willie already confirmed the connection to Dimitri. And gave us a lead on another guy. So, photographs. Maybe an address book. A laptop." Devlin pulled two pairs of latex gloves from his pocket and handed her a pair.

Marta nodded, pulled on the gloves he gave her, and set out.

Something was gnawing at him. Why would Michael's father come here and make the young man leave? He'd said he was Romanian. Was he connected to the carnival? Was that their connection to Tribe?

He shook his head and got to work. The sooner they searched the house, the sooner he could get home and check on Rachel. And figure out their next move.

The house had only two bedrooms, a single bathroom, a kitchen, and a living room. Marta found a few photo albums, but a cursory glance showed they were mostly family pictures. They bagged them anyway, just in case.

While Marta continued going through the house, he stepped out into the backyard and took in the area. Despite what Willie had said, it was still possible for Oscar to have been growing and selling drugs. No doubt the young man knew he was being watched by the older couple. Probably something his parents asked them to do. So he'd have been on his best behavior, especially around Willie's wife. But the old man had seen through that.

A storage shed sat in the center of the yard. Devlin walked to it and found the door slightly ajar. Stepping inside, he found items thrown about as if someone had come in and trashed the place. And given the orderly row of garden tools and yard fertilizer, he was betting that was the case. Wooden shelves lined the walls. He sifted through a plastic bin and found only discarded extension cords and odds and ends. Mostly junk. A footlocker underneath the bottom shelf had a lock dangling from its latch.

Inside, he found an array of firearms and ammo. Maybe Eddie had alerted Oscar. Told him he and Marta had come around Beauty Rose asking too many questions. It must've spooked them. They'd decided to team up and run him and Marta down. Which meant Eddie had to know what path they would take. But how? How did some random store clerk from an apothecary shop have the means to track them?

He shut the footlocker and locked it. The police would identify Oscar's body eventually. Best to leave the evidence behind for them to find.

He rejoined Marta. She'd gone through the entire house. After handing him one of the bags, along with a laptop, they stepped outside and pulled the door closed. The neighbor, Willie, stood on his porch, drinking a bottle of beer. He dipped his head in their direction, and Devlin returned the gesture.

He felt bad for not being totally honest with the man. At least he'd confirmed that Oscar was, indeed, gone. But Devlin would not tell him it was his fault, that Oscar had been cooked alive by his magick.

When my attempts to convince Alek I was still dirty failed, I got out of the shower and pulled on a pair of shorts and a sports bra, leaving my hair to air dry. All I wanted to do was crawl into bed with him and sleep for a little while. Who was I kidding? I wanted to sleep for a week. Right after I worked out some of the frustration running through my system like live wire.

I pulled out the brown case Leticia had given me and stared at the four rolled cigarettes inside. Should I show them to Rachel? Would she feel betrayed if I told her the clove had worked? No. I'd wait.

Sticking the case back in my purse, I retrieved my vape, my notebook, and a pen, as well as my phone, and went out to the war room to go over the copious details we'd uncovered. Hopefully, I'd find the thing that connected them all.

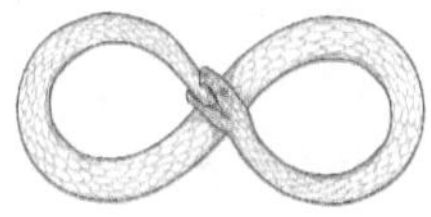

When I walked into the war room, I found Devlin sitting in a chair, arms on his thighs, with the file folder on Barnes lying open on the floor. Tiny scabs marred his handsome face. He'd changed into a pair of loose-fitting gray track pants and a black tank top that molded to his muscular frame. It was the first time I'd seen Devlin so ... relaxed. And, yes, I'll admit, looking damn yummy.

Marta sat at her desk, scribbling in the notebook in front of her. Strands of hair had escaped the braid she'd worn earlier, creating a hornet's nest around her head. She'd put on a pair of leggings and an oversized T-shirt. Tiny scabs stood out on her pale face.

Kara and Jonah sat huddled together, each of them with a journal in their hands. Rae lay on the floor next to Rachel. They both had laptops open in front of them.

And everyone except Kara, Jonah, and Rae looked on the verge of collapse.

Someone had put more information on the board. Papers of all different shapes and sizes were tacked up in a dizzying pattern. A crazed jigsaw puzzle that didn't fit. I groaned. Were all our cases going to be like this? A confused mess with an abundance of clues that seemed to lead nowhere?

Alek walked up and wrapped his arms around me. My eyes widened at the public display. I wasn't used to this. All my encounters took place behind closed doors. I'd never shown romantic affection to anyone. Then again, I'd never truly been on what would be considered a date. Well, except for the time I'd spent with Ronald Stewart.

Damn. Too bad I couldn't erase that memory.

Trying something new, I sank back into his embrace. "You think we can sneak out?" I whispered.

"And go where?" he said, lips next to my ear.

"Your car."

He laughed, swatted me on the butt, then took a seat at his desk.

Devlin looked up and stared at me. "You ready?"

I nodded and took a seat next to Alek.

Devlin handed the Barnes file to Alek and polished off a can of Dr. Pepper. "Okay," he said. "I know everyone is tired. So, I will make this brief." He stood and walked over to the whiteboard. "We have found no evidence that Tribe is actually behind the killings at the carnival. Nor have we found any link between the girls that have gone missing and the ones we found in the drug house last night. But what we do have is a possible link between Dimitri and a drug and prostitute ring." He paused. "So, for now, we follow these leads and see if we can connect all the events.

"Oscar Velasquez is the name of the young man I killed today. His neighbor said Dimitri, along with another young Romanian man, used to live with Oscar until a year ago." He looked at Alek. "The same time Dimitri moved to the carnival. The neighbor said Oscar had gotten a job at the carnival as well. Sadly, we have no way of confirming that until the ritual is over."

Marta placed two photo albums on the table by the whiteboard. "We got a description of the other man." She chuckled. "According to that same neighbor, the guy we're looking for is a pretty boy with curly hair and baggy clothes." She looked at Devlin, and they shared a smile. "I will have to go through the albums we found in Oscar's house to see if I can find a picture of him." She handed Rachel the laptop. "Also found this in his bedroom."

Rachel opened it. "I can go through it."

"In the morning," Devlin said, his gaze steady on her. "And we need to talk about what happened today."

She looked up at him. "I'm okay, Dev. Nicole already yelled at me."

"I didn't yell," I said, thinking back. Had I raised my voice?

Devlin nodded. "He was dead, Rach. You could have told me that."

"You said you needed him, Dev." She stared at him, her eyes filled with shame. Why would she feel that way?

He crouched in front of her. "Rach, I need you more. We all push ourselves past the limit. But that has got to stop." He smiled at her. "And tonight, I want you sleeping in a bed, not on the floor."

She mumbled her consent and rested her chin on her folded hands.

"What about the Dacian?" Jonah asked. His tone suggested someone had already filled him in on our encounter and he was none too pleased at being left out. Kara's look suggested she felt the same way.

Devlin studied him for a minute. As if he were running a scenario in which Jonah actually did take out the Dacian in his head. "Only way for you to help is if we know in advance they're coming and clear the area for you to work. But I don't think it will come to that."

"Why?" he asked.

"The Dacian are hired assassins. Which means either someone spent a lot of money to take out two girls and create a distraction big enough to remove a footlocker from the house undetected, or they came after us specifically, providing a distraction for someone to retrieve their goods. I found a footlocker tonight with guns inside."

"Do you think it's the same one they removed from the house?" Alek asked.

Devlin didn't answer right away. I could tell from the confusion in his eyes he wasn't so sure. Hell, we really didn't have any definitive proof of any of this.

He let out a rough sigh. "For now, let's go with the assumption that it is the same one they removed."

"That attack was overkill," I blurted out. "In order for the Dacian to come for us like that, someone would have had to hire them prior to us going to that house." Given the force of the attack, it was the only thing that made sense.

"Which gave Dimitri and his crew the opportunity they needed to remove the locker. But it doesn't answer why they weren't attacked by the Dacian," Jonah offered.

"I believe they came for us. Maybe even followed us," I said.

"And the girls?" Kara asked.

I paused. It didn't fit. At least not neatly. "We don't know the exact timeline for everything."

"Table it for now," Devlin said. "It doesn't get us any closer to finding the missing girls. So let's stick with the leads we have and worry about the Dacian later."

We all reluctantly nodded.

I glanced at the board. Then I pulled my notebook out and wrote the translation for the Coptic we had found in the house. "Forgot about this," I said, affixing the paper to the whiteboard. "It doesn't make much sense." I stared at the phrase.

Speak of dreams. Blood has been spilled. I will die someday.

"It's almost poetic," Marta said. "Like their dreams are filled with blood." She paused. "Could it be in reference to blood magick?"

"No." I kept staring at the words. Dreams.

"'Why did you come to this place where dreams go to die?'" I said aloud. "Cecilia asked me that. I keep wondering if the phrase meant more. Honestly, I don't know. But I will figure it out." I glanced at Boss Man. "Tomorrow."

He dipped his head in acknowledgement. "Why don't you take us through what happened at the school."

I repeated the events we'd shared with the others earlier. Devlin at least looked a little mortified at the mention of torture.

"Blood magick." He shook his head. "We table it for now. As long as you're both sure she's not using innocent people to experiment on."

Alek and I nodded.

"Four girls." His mouth thinned. "I get the feeling it's connected." He stood up and growled. "I need some theories."

"Dimitri used his job at the carnival to lure girls away. But Sophia and Nadia killing their parents makes little sense. Ileana and Daniella left without incident. I'd say Dimitri, Oscar, and the unknown guy were involved in pimping out girls. We just need to find the connection to the school and how they lured Gracie and Cecilia into their fold," I offered.

"So, the only connection to the carnival is Dimitri. He is too young to have been a part of Tribe. However, the girls' parents were old enough. Petronela said she didn't believe it was about that old group, though." He laced his fingers over his head and stared at the board. "Rach. I need you and Rae to sort out this board. Put all the connections together and all the loose threads on their own. Remove the Peterson info."

I handed the contact information Randall gave me for the bullies at the school to Marta. "Can we rule these girls out too?" I explained the theory both Randall and Professor Carter came up with.

She stared at the paper, lips thinning in anger. "I will."

"We need an investigator, and I wanted Rae to work with us," Kara said. "She offered, and I agree she could help. And before you say anything, I understand she is a teenager, and it might not be the best idea. But it's summer. She needs a job."

Devlin turned and stared at her. "I can't spare her right now. We have too many leads going in all different directions but the one we were hired for." He stopped, staring in turn at Jonah and Kara. "Any updates?"

Jonah shook his head. "Did manage to find Gerald's sister, Helena, the one who belonged to His Holy Seed. She has a place on the island. We'll start with her."

"You're going to kill her?" I asked.

Kara turned to me. "If necessary, yes. But right now, we just want to learn more about her. They started the Harvest Ritual in an effort to help her. We need to see if she had any direct dealings with it. And if so, chances are, they will start again. And she could be at the center of it."

"That's a good start," Devlin said. "For now, I can ask Opal to supply someone to help you with research." He grabbed his phone and sent off a text. "Alek and I will return to Eddie's house tomorrow. See if we can locate any drugs. They could lead us to the other two men involved."

"What about me?" Marta asked. "I can come back after I take the kids to therapy."

Devlin's face softened. "Take the day. The kids will need you. And if you get restless, go through the photo albums." His concern for her was written all over his face. I could tell she wanted to protest, but after the briefest pause, she nodded.

Devlin looked at me. "Alek said you wanted to get some maps of the island."

When had Alek told him that? "Yeah. I've got a theory forming, but I need proof first."

"Take care of that after you and Marta are done at therapy. Then go see Ezra. We need to get a read on Camilla before she becomes a problem."

"Yes, Boss Man."

Devlin sighed, head going up and down. "All right. Let's get some rest. We need fresh eyes on this."

We all got up and said our goodbyes. Opal had responded and said she'd send someone over to the hotel in the morning. I stared at the board one last time, trying to pinpoint the thing that was bothering me about the message. It just seemed like such a random thing to write. In a dead language, at that.

Marta walked out of Jonah's bedroom with her bag. "I'm going to go get the kids and stay at my place tonight," she said, then paused. "I know I asked you to come with us. And I really want you to. But I also think you should work on your theory. If I know you, you'll probably have the whole thing figured out before lunchtime."

I pulled her in for a hug. "I want to come with you and the kids," I mumbled into her hair. "And I really doubt I will solve this before lunch. It's too ... complicated."

She pulled away and smiled at me. "I have faith in your skills. And if you need me, please call." She sighed. "I was going to tell Devlin I wanted to stay with the kids tomorrow. I'm just glad he said it first." She glanced over to where Devlin and Rachel stood. Boss Man had her face in his hands, staring down at her with love in his eyes. "He really worries about her." She turned back to me. "You think it's romantic?" she asked in a whisper.

I shook my head. "No. More brother and sister."

She glanced back over at them. "You're right." She chuckled. "Looks like you'll have to drive the tainted vehicle tomorrow."

Oh crap. "I can ask Kara to let me use hers. Or walk. I'm not getting in that car."

Marta patted my face and kissed me on the cheek. Rae walked up, and Marta pulled her in for a hug. "I'll see you later," Marta said, kissing her forehead. The teenager smiled and walked away.

After Marta left, Alek and I made our way to the bedroom. After pulling off our clothes, we climbed into the bed and just held each other. He'd been quiet for most of the debrief.

"What's on your mind?" I asked him, my head on his chest, listening to his heartbeat.

"The Dacian," he said. "I believe they were sent for me."

I eased up and looked into those dark blue eyes. A storm was brewing in their depths. He'd said the one thing I didn't want to say aloud. The only thing that made sense about the elite warriors.

"Do you know why?" I asked.

He closed his eyes. "No. But we will find out."

I laid my head on his chest. "As long as we get to kill them together."

"Of course. That's a part of any healthy relationship."

I smiled. "I know. That and copious amounts of sex."

He squeezed me to him, chest rumbling with laughter. I was serious. My life had been reduced to blood and now, finally, sex. And I was really okay with that.

Shadow at Evening

Devlin sat on the edge of the sofa bed, listening to the ghostly sounds of the house. A faucet dripping. A floorboard settling. The whispers of another episode of *SpongeBob*, Rachel's favorite show. His mind had yet to follow the slow progression to rest. He still held onto that chaotic noise that started earlier that day.

He got up and went into the strategy room. What Nicole had dubbed "the war room." He smiled at that. She did have a way of putting things into perspective; they had been plotting what amounted to a war on blood magick. A part of him understood the need for their continued efforts in that area. He'd told Nicole they didn't do black and white. They lived in the grey. Yet even he could admit he was having trouble following this path. And he was sure his team knew it too.

Devlin found Rachel lying stretched out on the floor, the television light dancing across her skin. A laptop lay open near her shoulder, and one of Nicole's notebooks sat near her outstretched hand. He let out a sigh. Was he pushing her too hard? Rachel, without input, tended to go too far. They'd seen it before. He shouldn't have asked her to keep that young man alive. Careful not to wake her, he picked her up and carried her into her bedroom. After putting her on her own bed, he eased the door shut and began his nightly ritual.

He went into the kitchen and fixed himself a peanut butter sandwich. It was a comfort from childhood that he couldn't do without.

Their assignment had gotten away from them. What started out as an investigation into four murders and a potential kidnapping had now morphed into a two-year-old rape of four girls, a drug and prostitute ring, and a thirty-year-old mystery that seemed to be at the root of everything.

How were they all connected?

He went to the window and stared out at the backyard pool. Its waters rippled. He thought of Jonah and the demon he kept inside of him. They were no closer to learning how to rid his friend of that unwanted evil without risking losing Jonah in the process. And the way things were going, he had doubts they ever would.

After he finished his sandwich, he checked the time. Three hours behind them would make the time in Los Angeles just after ten in the evening. If he was lucky, his mother would already be asleep. He dialed the caregiver's number and waited.

She answered on the third ring. "Devlin," she said in a rush.

"Hello, Ruth. Just checking in." He steeled himself for bad news.

"We've had a bit of a day today. But otherwise, everything is fine." She paused, and Devlin waited for the question he hated the most. "Do you want to speak with her?" She knew he'd say no. But it didn't stop her from asking each time he checked in.

"Not tonight." His usual answer. "Do you need anything?"

"No. I got your last check." She sighed. "The new meds are working. I just have to go through a lot to get her to take them."

He felt terrible for not stepping up and taking care of his own mother. Despite this being Ruth's vocation, he couldn't shake the sense of wrongness in letting someone else endure his mother's rantings and abuse.

Ruth updated him on a few other things, then got off the phone.

He made a mental check mark in his head and made his way to Jonah's room.

Rae had left the door ajar. He found her intertwined in the blanket, clutching a stuffed animal to her chest. She was fine. At least, that's what he kept telling himself. The issue with her was much more complicated than simply providing a safe place for her to sleep. Alek had technically kidnapped the teenager when he took her from her home and delivered her to Petronela. And by having her here, they were all complicit in that crime.

They'd have to answer for it one day. But thankfully, not tonight.

Check.

He walked over to the murder board and studied the many leads that led nowhere.

A part of him had assumed Nicole would find the answers. She was good at seeing the connections between things. Or the missing pieces that led to those connections. And yet, even she was having a hard time finding that missing thread. In the midst of everything, he found a single note.

Something's missing that should be there.

The writing looked like Nicole's. She had seemed preoccupied. He'd have to ask her about the note in the morning. Add it to tomorrow's list. He also worried about the anxiety she was dealing with and worried this line of work might not be for her. But she was so damn good at it. Better than him at seeing threads. Like the issue with the Dacian. Her health must come first, though. And they'd talk about it soon.

For now, he was just happy she was staying vigilant in dislodging the truth. And he had no doubts she would continue.

Check.

He glanced around at the workstation Marta had created. She had her own idea of order, and he could appreciate that. A pang of regret raced through him, thinking of her. She'd been injured.

It was his fault. He knew that. But she'd also held her own. An impressive feat he couldn't help but admire. Her sole purpose in joining his team was to exact revenge on those who'd harmed her children. And when the time came, he'd help her achieve it. Now, she was safe. Healed. And with her children.

Check.

Alek's hold on his magick was worrisome. As of late, the dark part of his nature had begun to leak out. But it also coincided with the man's need to protect Nicole. Would it become a problem? He'd managed to reign in his friend before. Now, he wasn't so sure. He glanced toward the bedroom Nicole and Alek shared. If it became a problem, he'd deal with it.

Check.

Kara was a larger issue than he cared to admit. Her grandmother's ties to The Oren Group could both hurt and help his team. It was a toss-up which way that situation leaned. But she was willing to help. That was all he needed for now.

Check.

He went back into the front room and sat down on the sofa bed. He'd have to buy furniture for the fourth bedroom eventually, but for now, he'd stay out here and stand watch over his team. Before he lay down, he sent his awareness out, looking for the one who always watched.

All he found were the elements.

S trange dreams kept me from a good night's sleep. I woke every hour on the hour with a crippling feeling that something was missing. That I had misplaced what was supposed to be there. I had gone through the house in a sweaty panic, checking on everyone. At first, I'd believed it was Jonah's absence that had me worried. Then Kara's, followed by Marta. But that wasn't it. When I did manage to fall asleep, well after four in the morning, I dreamed of a blank page in a notebook sandwiched between two other pages filled with text.

That white page had glared at me, taunting me with a message I couldn't decipher and leaving me in a state of unrest.

When I finally woke up, Alek and Devlin were gone, and I'd slept till noon, while the rest of the house had been in motion for hours. Rae and Rachel, having rearranged the board, lay on the floor with their laptops in front of them.

Not wanting to disturb their rhythm, I fixed myself a turkey and cheese sandwich and grabbed a family-size bag of plain potato chips and two bottles of water along with a bottle of ginger ale. With a cooler full of food and a thermos of Rachel's coffee in hand, I set out for the museum, feeling every bit like a teenager going on a field trip.

While it had been my idea to check out this lead, I still felt as if Devlin had agreed only to make sure I would be somewhere with little to no danger. He'd also made sure Marta was out of harm's way. But that didn't explain why he didn't just send Rae with Jonah and Kara. Maybe I was just paranoid.

Or still looking for the thing that should be there.

I ARRIVED at the Rothman Museum in Alice just after one in the afternoon and pulled Kara's car into the first available spot.

Made from black and gray bricks, the three-story building looked more like a community college than an actual museum. The main building sat sandwiched between two adjunct one-story structures that had been added on a few years ago. The two additional areas were built to accommodate visiting lectures and book clubs. They even hosted a wine and cheese gathering once a month. If not for the people, that might have been something I would attend.

Four large daycare vans were parked near the entrance, with toddlers spilling out the doors in a flood of sugar-induced madness that had me debating if I really needed to follow this half-formed idea about the island. I mean, I had come up with this idea after a night of no sleep. And several cups of Rachel's special coffee, and a few hits of the concoction she made to help with my anxiety. So my belief that Tulare had moved since its creation could just be a chemically-induced fantasy.

I'd give the field trip kids some time to get inside. I sighed and polished off the rest of my ginger ale; the stuff wasn't so bad. After finding a napkin wedged between the seats and wiping my hands, I pulled my notebook out and started with a fresh page.

My theory about Tribe's true purpose had become a jumbled mess in my mind, and all of it centered on water. Well, maybe not the start of it. Learning more about His Holy Need was where it truly began.

From what I understood about cults, the founder set themselves apart and required absolute obedience from their flock.

They lured followers in with a promise: the fulfillment of some need. Most cults twisted religious doctrine and made a new set of sacred laws that only the leader could decipher or interpret.

I would never know what Lemuel Oren told his followers or promised them in order for them to pledge their lives to him, but what I did know as that whatever he said had to be so enticing, it convinced young girls to sacrifice themselves.

And that fact had unlocked my theory.

The five women who fled Lemuel Oren's cult before they could be killed told us two things. One: something special was in the blood. And two: Set, the god, could not cross water. I believed Lemuel had sold them a half truth.

Because Set could cross water. He'd been able to attack me on that small marshland where the Stewarts built their barn.

So what if Lemuel Oren meant Set couldn't cross the ocean? The Old Ones had created an entire island to store his soul. Why do that when they could have simply kept Set in Egypt?

Sadly, all of these were merely assumptions. I'd pieced together this thin idea, and without more information, I couldn't prove my theory. One of the things I was sure about was that the sacrifices Lemuel asked for had played a major role in the movement of the island. All I needed to do was find more points in our island's past where mass killings had been reported.

But first, I needed to see the maps.

I looked up from my notebook. The children were still running around outside. Funny how I was able to face down an elite squad of mind mages, but wading through a bunch of children scared the hell out of me.

I pulled out my phone and called Marta. I needed to kill some more time.

She answered on the third ring.

"How was therapy?" I asked.

"Hey! Just a second, Nicole. No, Maria. One cookie." She sighed. "Sorry. We're at lunch, and Maria didn't eat all her food because she had a stomachache that is immune to cookies." She paused. "Where are you? I hear a lot of noise in the background."

"Sitting outside the museum watching a million toddlers spill out of a bus."

"Must be summer camp. Therapy was good. I... I will tell you later. But I'll be back at Devlin's tonight." She sounded a little sad.

"Did you notice how Devlin gave us jobs that would keep us out of danger?"

Marta chuckled. "I did," she said carefully. "But I also understand why he did. He looked bad yesterday, Nicole. Like at any moment, he was going to lose it. I think he's scared I will get hurt again. That you will get hurt again too."

"I knew it was that. But what pisses me off is, he has no problem with Kara putting herself in danger."

"Kara was also trained for this type of work, remember?"

I nodded even though she couldn't see me. Yes, Kara was better suited for what we'd been facing. Didn't mean I liked the idea of my skills being called into question. As limited as they were, I did manage to save all three of us when the Dacian attacked. Well, I helped with the saving. Alek going supernova had done much of the heavy lifting.

"Tell me about your idea," she said.

I ran down my theory.

"So, you believe the island is moving?" Marta asked.

"Yes. Which is why I want to find some older maps for Tulare. If I'm right, it might also explain something that has been bothering me about Petronela and why Tribe tried to usurp her thirty years ago."

"So. It's related to Tribe. Do you think she lied to Devlin about why they wanted to kill her?"

"I think she told a half-truth."

She was silent for a moment.

"I wish I could be there to help you with this. Maybe I can do an online search on past mass murders."

"That would help."

"I did manage to cross the bullies off our list. Two of the girls are in prison, and one is in a mental health facility."

"Oh, good," I said. That sounded horrible. But those girls deserved it.

I stared at the kids milling around, pushing and shoving one another. "I've already procrastinated long enough," I said as if we'd been discussing it. "I need to get this done so I can go home and stare at the whiteboard and figure out what's missing. I might need to grab another bag of Lays. I polished the chips off on the way over here."

"Couple things," Marta said carefully. "That was a family-size bag of chips. And what whiteboard are you talking about?"

"The one with all the clues tacked to it."

"You mean the murder board?"

I sighed. "Is that what it's called?"

Marta laughed. "You might need to take a nap."

"I've already slept most of the day away. I need to pull my weight and get some stuff done. We've been working on this case for too long."

"It's been two days."

"I'm hanging up now. I called you for support, and all you can do is make fun of me. Please kiss the kids for me ... Stop laughing!"

"Maria, no! Sorry, Nicole. I better tend to them. They wanted me to take them back over to your parents' house ... They like it there." The sadness was back in her voice again.

"Are you all right?"

She didn't respond right away. "I will be. Talk to you later. Be safe."

"You too," I said, hung up, then grabbed my purse and headed for the entrance. If I timed it just right, I could avoid the horde of children and the curator, Abigail Meadows, trekking to the nomad exhibit. I'd once witnessed her fornicating with the lifeless replicas of ancient man and really didn't wish to relive that experience.

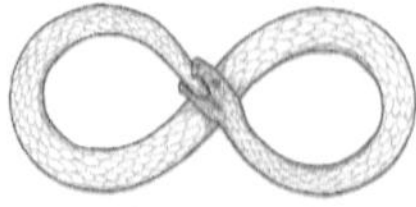

My eye twitched when I walked into the museum and was immediately assaulted by the stench of too much sugar commingling with the smells of old paper, sweat, dirt, and floor wax. A hundred screaming toddlers wearing bright yellow shirts jumped, skipped, and ran their way around a handful of harried adults and museum staff, who fruitlessly shushed their way through the milieu.

The first few floors had exhibits dedicated to world history. Not as extensive as the more advanced museums in the world, but it did have enough of the basics to entertain most audiences and give children a good foundation. Last I checked, they had even added a small exhibit on dinosaurs. Which was probably where the children were headed.

I quickened my pace toward the elevator, hoping I didn't attract attention. While I loved kids and their sweet little faces, the energy coming off the group in the lobby had a horror movie vibe to it, complete with images of sticky-fingers and violence.

The third floor was dedicated to world maps. In this, the island's museum rivaled some of the larger ones across the globe. It was also, as I'd been told in high school, a pet project for the curator of the museum.

The fourth floor was dedicated to the History of Magick and had a small public library on the different subjects. I'd spent some time as a child immersed in the books and exhibits on that floor, only to learn later that the knowledge there had been watered down for public consumption and, sadly, to keep those who viewed magick as the work of evil from picketing the museum.

After a short ride up to the third floor, I was deposited into a cool hallway and complete silence. I sucked in a cleansing breath and made my way past the student study rooms, toward the main exhibit.

A large map of the world covered the entirety of the walls. Every inch of our planet was done in intricate detail, making it appear as if you were surrounded by a globe.

A single employee looked up when I entered. She smiled as she came around her small desk. "Can I help you find something?" she asked in a hushed tone.

"Yes, I need to look at all the maps you have of Tulare. Starting with the oldest date."

She furrowed her brow and tapped a finger on her cheek. "Umm ... I believe the oldest we have is from 1756, if I'm not mistaken." She started walking, and I followed. "I have seen one as early as 1600. But not here." She stopped in front of a long wooden cabinet with three drawers. Opening the middle one, she pulled out a worn map with frayed edges and discoloration on it. "Hmm, this one is from 1827." She looked around the room. "Let me check with Abigail; she might have something older in her private collection." She handed me the map. "Are you okay to start with this one?"

"Yes, this is fine." I started for the table, then stopped. "Sorry," I called after her. "Do you have a ruler?"

She cocked her head. "A ruler?" She raised her eyebrows in shock. "Oh, please don't write on the maps."

"No. No. I just want to jot down some measurements in my notebook. I promise not to put a mark on any of the maps."

She nodded. "Well. Okay." She tapped a series of long cabinets. "Just look through these drawers here while I check with Abigail."

I thanked her and, after setting my things on one of the empty tables, retrieved all the maps for Tulare. They had created fifteen in total.

The lady came back once I'd sat down, carrying a large wooden cylinder. "This is the oldest map we found." She set it on the table and handed me a pair of white gloves. "While the artist did a beautiful rendition, they created a fictional representation of our island."

"Why do you say that?" I asked, staring up at her.

She unrolled the container, revealing a painted map of Tulare. I didn't need her to tell me why she thought it was fictional. The painting showed, in vivid detail, that my theory about Tulare had been true. Sitting in the middle of the Atlantic Ocean was the place I'd called home for close to twenty years. Traced in gold and painted in startlingly rich color, Tulare Island sat a much greater distance from North America than it did today. I didn't even need the ruler.

My fingers shook as I ran my gloved hand over the parchment.

"Because," the woman started, "the artist positioned Tulare more than a hundred miles from the shore of North America."

"What year was this map drawn?" I asked, heart racing.

"Abigail said it dates back prior to the start of known Egyptian society."

I looked up at her. "How does she know the date?"

The woman handed me a small magnifying glass and pointed to a tiny black line in the right corner. Careful not to get too close, I peered through the glass and found the date written in elaborate script.

Tetu.

"So, Thoth himself drew this map. Or the artist believed he was Thoth."

"What does Abigail think?" I asked. Every cell in my body had come alive. They had the first drawing of Tulare. And, unlike the lady next to me, I one hundred percent knew it was Thoth who drew it.

"She believes he drew it. But Abigail is a bit ... out of touch." She rolled the map up. "I'm sorry I can't leave this with you."

I nodded, mind racing. "Do you have a copy? Or a pamphlet with it inside."

She furrowed her brow, gaze going from me to the map. "What is this for, anyway?"

"Just wanted to trace the roots of my home," I lied.

She looked around. We were alone in the tiny room. "I trust you have a camera phone?"

"Yes."

"Well. As long as you don't use the flash, you can take a quick picture of it."

After getting a picture of the map, I sifted through the stack I'd pulled out and found one from the 1700s. Using my ruler, I measured the distance from Tulare to North America. I repeated the process for a series of maps leading up to the creation of the land bridges. Over the course of a hundred years, the island of Tulare moved a few miles at a time. Until finally, in 1875, it stopped. In 1980, when Lemuel Oren established his cult, the land bridges grew, stretching toward the mainland. Then, in 1985, when Petronela moved to Tulare, the bridges stopped growing. Leaving the states of Georgia and South Carolina to complete the connection to Tulare.

I rubbed my sore hand as I stared down at the notes I'd taken. Petronela had lied to Devlin. But then again, we all knew she had. In 1986, when Tribe arrived on the island to usurp the old woman, they hadn't come seeking war. They'd come to remove her from the land so that Lemuel Oren could complete his work of shifting the land toward North America.

And if I was correct about the cult he'd created, somewhere in the past, we'd find large sacrifices or deaths that coincided with each movement.

Now we just needed to find them.

I stood outside Ezra's dojo, peering into the darkened room. I'd been in this position before. Standing in this very spot, hoping I could speak to the illusive man. Only this time, I'd tell him what I knew and dare him to deny it. The maps proved that Lemuel Oren, working alone or with others, was trying to move Tulare Island so he could help his brother, Set. Why hadn't any of the other Old Ones stopped him? Combined their power to move the island back to where they had originally intended it to be?

Blowing clove-scented smoke into the warm wind, I pounded on the glass once again. Still no response. I could go around the corner to his favorite pool hall, but I feared I wouldn't be able to contain my accusations in a quiet conversation outside.

No, I was in the mood to hit something. Preferably Camilla or any one of the Old Ones.

My phone dinged, and I glanced at the display—Rachel. Checking up on me. I fired off a reply, then stomped back to Kara's car. I needed a drink. And I knew just the place to go to get both the answers I needed and some alcohol to drown out the frustration.

Pulling out of the parking lot, I shoved down the guilt trying to rear its ugly head. Alek wouldn't appreciate me going to see Jordin Cisco. None of the team would. I slammed my hand on the steering wheel. "Fuck!" Why did this revelation bother me so much? Why couldn't I shake the feeling of being betrayed? The Old Ones didn't owe me an explanation. They didn't have to interact with me at all. But they had. In some twist of fate or deliberate mechanisms, they had thrust me into their world. Attacked. Marked. And threatened.

And for what? Were they playing some sort of sick game? Did the boredom of their long lives drive them to meddle in the affairs of regular human beings? Wasn't that what the gods of ancient times had been known for? The very gods the Old Ones were said to represent.

My phone rang, startling me out of my inner rant. "What?" I yelled.

"I'm sorry, is this a bad time?" the woman said, voice filled with hesitation.

I looked at the display and didn't recognize the number. "Who is this?" I asked.

"Is this Nicole Fontane?" she asked.

"I know who I am. Now, who the hell is this?"

"I'm sorry. I... Angela gave me your number. My name is Deidra. Deidra Palmer. I used to attend the Peterson's school." Her voice shook as she said each word carefully, as if she were trying to assess the situation for danger.

Fuck, Nicole.

I pulled over and parked. "I am so sorry," I said. "I didn't mean to be rude. It's been a long day." While it was the truth, it didn't excuse my behavior. Angela. I'd completely forgotten I'd given her my number.

"Are Gracie and Cecilia really gone?"

"Yes, I'm sorry. They are. I know you all were friends."

"They were best friends. Before... before..."

"I'm investigating what happened to you and the other girls," I said carefully. "If you're up to it, I would love to talk with you."

She didn't respond. I gripped the phone in my hand, straining to hear. Had I screwed up? I shook my head, berating myself for answering the phone like that. It probably had taken a lot of courage for this girl to call me.

"Can we meet?" she finally asked.

"Sure. When and where?" Hope bloomed inside of me that we'd find a clue as to who had attacked these girls, bringing us closer to at least solving the crimes against them. Because our current investigation was going nowhere.

I could hear her exhale. Felt the weight of her silence. The internal debate she was most likely having. "Now. If that's okay? Otherwise, I might lose my nerve."

"Of course."

She gave me the address of a diner in Sandpoint. I texted Rachel to let her know where I was going and pulled back into traffic.

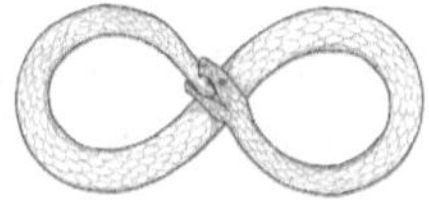

I ARRIVED at the diner fifteen minutes later and rushed inside, worried she might have changed her mind and not come. I scanned the thin crowd, kicking myself for not asking her what she looked like.

A few patrons sat at scattered booths. They stared out the large bay windows. No one looked up when I entered. Crap. She had left. Or not come at all. I pulled out my phone, ready to call her back, when I caught a young woman with a child signaling to me. She looked so young, light-skinned, with short brown hair framing her face. She gave me a hesitant smile, and the little girl next to her waved at me, her dark black curls bouncing with her energy.

I made my way to them.

"Nicole," she said when I stopped at her booth.

I nodded. "Can I sit?"

"Yes. Yes, of course." She had a thick, worn envelope in front of her, and her purse strap was still slung over her shoulder. She had either just arrived or was about to leave.

"Hi!" the little girl said, leaning over a paper kids menu with a red crayon in her hand.

"Hi," I said, smiling at her. "She's adorable," I said, glancing at Deidra.

She looked at the little girl with sadness in her eyes. "She is. I don't think I could go on without her."

I started to reach for her hand but stopped. It wouldn't be right to touch her without her consent. I understood that feeling more than anyone.

She looked down at my hand and gave me a sad smile. "I appreciate the effort." She met my eyes. "Cecilia was the strongest person I knew." She smiled with feeling then. As if the memory of her friend filled her with joy. "We felt so safe with her. God, she was fierce. And smart," she said, eyes rounding. "I loved being in her presence. And Gracie. She used to talk enough for all of us." She harrumphed. "The other girls at the school hated us. We were too smart. Too pretty. Too ..." She splayed her hands on the table. "Whatever thing they could make up."

She shrugged and looked at the little girl. "But that ..." She shook her head as if removing the memory. "I thought out of all of us, those two would make it." She bit her top lip, then let out a heavy sigh. "Cecilia texted me a few weeks ago, when summer classes started." She looked at me, eyes narrowed in confusion. "She said she smelled him again."

"Did she say anything else?" I asked carefully.

She shook her head. "No. Just that. When I asked what she meant, she didn't respond."

Deidra slid the envelope across the table. "After what happened, Ms. Peterson brought in this counselor to talk with us." A tear spilled down her cheek. "We couldn't talk about it. But—" She knuckled her chest as if trying to ease a sudden pain. "I needed to get it out of me. So I wrote Ms. Peterson a letter telling her what happened. And after I did, Vicky and I left. We were both pregnant by that..." She glanced at her little girl. "I lost the baby. I was so happy," she said, choking on her pain.

The little girl patted Deidra's cheek. "Okay, mommy. Okay." She wrapped her little arms around her, and Deidra closed her eyes, seeming to accept the comfort.

"When Vicky gave birth, she left. Leaving Madeline with me." She stared at me. "I almost gave her away. But now? Now I can't imagine my life without her." She eased out of the booth. "Come on, sweet girl. It's time to go." She scooped her up. Madeline laid her little head on Deidra's shoulder. "When you catch him, will you let me know?" she asked.

I reached out, and she took my hand, squeezing it. "I will." I held up the envelope. "Thank you for this."

She nodded and hurried away. Madeline waved to me as they left the diner. Her little round face seemed so familiar to me. But I couldn't figure out why.

I stared at the murder board and the sticky note I had tacked up to it.

Something is missing that should be there.

Only problem was, I couldn't for the life of me figure out what. It was as if my brain had gotten stuck, and I couldn't find a way past it because something about that item or person or clue or whatever had a missing piece that should be there.

Rae had already organized the clues we had and where they led to: nowhere. I'd read only the first page of the letter Deidra had given me. Just enough to know they hadn't seen their attacker. He'd worn a mask and had Gracie tie each of them up. And once he'd bound her, he attacked all four of them. A few times.

I finished going over the letter, then carefully folded it, hands shaking with rage the entire time. I'd give the letter to its intended recipient later. Hopefully with the body of the girls' attacker too.

One thing stood out to me, though. Each of the girls had said he smelled evil. And they would forever remember that scent. Diedre had opened the letter with that.

He smelled like evil, and we would always remember his scent.

It was an interesting thing to remember. Like the imprint of his odor was significant. Almost as if they might have smelled it before. Which meant they could have had contact with the man prior to him hurting them.

Cecilia's text to Deidre was also a clue, but without knowing where she'd smelled him again, I couldn't suss it out.

I sighed.

"Huh," Rachel said. I turned and looked at her. "Cecilia had dropped the Professor Thornton's class, but she started an online version a week later." She looked up at me. "I wonder why she did that?"

"She didn't drop any of her other classes?" I asked, an idea forming in my head.

She shook her head. "No. Just his."

"When?" I asked, my body buzzing.

"Right after the attack." She stared at me. "Do you think it was the professor?"

I shook my head. "No. He is too old. According to the letter, their attacker was around their age." I paused. "Could something about the professor have made her uncomfortable?"

Why was the little girl so familiar?

Devlin and Alek walked into the room. "Hey," Alek said, walking over and kissing my cheek. "Did you find what you were looking for?"

I nodded. "But if you don't mind, I would like to share it in front of your auntie."

He nodded slowly. "Okay. If you're sure."

"I am." I filled them in on my brief conversation with Deidra and showed them her letter.

Devlin sat down and stared at his hands. "That's gotta be rough." He shook his head.

It reminded me of Kara's situation. She, too, had been a product of rape. Only her mother hadn't left her in the hands of a loving friend. She'd let Kara's sadistic grandmother raise her to be an assassin.

"Any leads at Eddie's?" I asked.

"None," Devlin said, not looking up. "I found out he'd sent his grandmother to a facility in Georgia that specialized in training blind seniors." He looked up. "I think that's when Eddie started selling drugs. The facility is expensive." Devlin surged to his feet. "We need more theories, team."

"I got into Oscar's laptop, but there is nothing saved on it. Looks like a brand-new machine."

"I wonder what happened to his old one," I said, resuming my study of the board.

The front door opened, and the tantalizing aroma of pizza filled the air. "Hey," Marta said, setting three large pies on the table. "I wanted to bring dinner just in case." She walked over to the board. "I went through the photo albums. Nothing but family pictures." She pulled a photograph from her purse and tacked it to the board. "But I did find this." She pointed to the images of three boys huddled together with their arms around each other. "This is Oscar. I believe this is Dimitri. And this boy." She chuckled. "He looks pretty. Like the neighbor described. All that curly hair."

"Fuck!" I yelled, eyes widening.

"What?" Alek asked in alarm.

I shook my head. I couldn't voice it just yet. I had to confirm my suspicion first. Yanking my phone from my purse, I scrolled through the contacts, only to scream in my head. I didn't have a direct number for Leticia. Only the number for the school. I found Angela's number and called her. She answered on the third ring.

"Hello," she said.

I glanced at the clock. It was after ten. "I am so sorry, Angela. Umm ... First, thank you for giving Deidra my number. I met with her, and she helped tremendously."

"You're welcome," she said.

"I apologize for calling so late. But I really need to get a direct number for Leticia."

After a brief pause, she rattled off the number, and I thanked her and hung up.

Fingers shaking, I punched in Leticia's number. I glanced up and found everyone staring at me, eyes wide. Waiting for me to explain. I held up a finger, signaling for them to wait. Leticia answered on the fourth ring.

"Hello?"

I let out a ragged breath. "Leticia. Hi. It's Nicole. I am so sorry to bother you. I just needed to ask you a favor."

"Yes," she said, alarm in her tone. "What is it?"

"When we interviewed the professors yesterday, we noticed a wall of pictures. I was wondering if you could send me a copy of one of them?"

"Which one?" she asked. I could hear rustling. She must have been in bed. Or down in her workshop.

"It was a faculty and family photo from 2014."

She went silent. I strained, trying to pick up on any sound. "You identified him," she said finally, her voice a deadly calm. It wasn't a question. She must have suspected the man at some point. Must have dismissed the idea as well. Otherwise, she wouldn't have had Professor Thornton at her school.

"Yes," I said, confirming for her.

My phone alerted me to an incoming text. I checked and found the image I was looking for.

"I don't care what you do to Lionel. Although I hope you put a bullet in his head. But as for his son, Michael. Bring him to me." She hung up without saying goodbye.

"Michael," I said, looking at Devlin. He nodded, anger storming in his gray eyes.

I looked down at the picture. Just as Leticia sent an address. Blowing up the photo, I stared at the curly-haired boy standing next to his father.

He smelled like evil, and we would always remember his scent.

Now I understood why Cecilia had dropped the professor's class and why she might have smelled her attacker again. The smell she associated with evil must've been a trait, something passed down generationally, something in the blood.

"They live in the East Gate Estates community," I said, leaving the room. I had stowed the gun Devlin had given me in my drawer.

The entire team headed for the door.

Leticia had suggested I put a bullet in Lionel's head. Sounded like a great idea to me.

The fancy wooden sign, lit by ground lights for East Gate Estates, came into view. Professor Thornton obviously had no problem showing off the wealth he couldn't possibly have earned at the Peterson's girls school. It was brazen and a bit cocky. But then again, he must have believed he would never get caught. Working at an all-girls school while his son, Michael, preyed on the students.

I was pissed beyond all reason, and right now, I just wanted to take that anger out on someone. Preferably with a great deal of pain and bloodshed.

Alek turned onto the partially hidden road. His headlights carved a path of light into the dark. If only I'd had a sixth sense, we could have eliminated this man and his son last week. Right after attending The Daughters of the Vine wine and sex orgy. I needed to blow off some steam after that encounter. It would have been so nice to know that another enemy lay in wait just a short distance from Gavina Young's home.

We found the address. A long brick driveway wound toward a house that reminded me of a castle. It was missing only a moat with alligators swimming in its murky waters.

After parking in an alcove near the front door, we all climbed out of our vehicles and entered the unlocked house. Maybe they believed they were safe in this settlement for the rich.

Voices carried down the hall. We strode across the marble floor, me resisting the urge to spit on it, the others with their game faces on.

We stepped into a large dining hall and found our target sitting at a polished dining table, tucked into a feast fit for royals.

"You have got to be kidding me," I said, staring at the biggest cliché of them all: the villains sharing a meal while they talked business. Next, we'd be treated to an arrogant speech, followed by veiled threats, even though we held all the power.

"Ms. Fontane," Lionel Thornton said, watching the team spread out around them. "What are you doing here?"

Really?

Dimitri sat to the professor's left, his son Michael to his right, and another man I didn't recognize sat next to Michael. That man had a ledger in front of him instead of a plate of food.

"If an older woman wearing a scarf wanders out of the kitchen with more food, I might just start shooting." I sat down and groaned into my hands. I wanted bloodshed. At least some semblance of a fight. But instead, I'd walked onto the set of a gangster movie.

"I think they're here for me," Dimitri said with a smirk on his face. "Did that old woman send you here to collect her missing sheep?" He scoffed, then pitched forward, clutching his head. An orange mist circled his body, seeming to squeeze him in a vice. I glanced at Alek. His eyes had darkened, and a look of pure rage painted his face.

"I still have yet to understand why any of you are in my house," Lionel said.

I stared at him. "You can't be serious. You must know what Michael did."

He glanced at his son and shook his head. "I've already talked to him about that," Lionel said, as if his dear son had been caught stealing and a stern talking to was all it took to get him back in line. "When did you find out?" he asked, as if we really owed him an answer.

"Question is," Devlin said, "when did you find out? Let me guess," he continued not letting the man answer. "I'd say around a year ago, when he was taking up with his friend Oscar. The neighbor witnessed you scolding him."

"Giving him what for," Marta said. She looked around. "That scolding must not have included all his other illegal ventures."

"Who are you to judge?" Michael asked.

"I met your granddaughter," I said, staring at Lionel. I wanted him to understand the pain of what his piece-of-shit son had done. "The resemblance to your son is remarkable. Of course, it's a really good thing his victim didn't get a good look at him when he assaulted her and her friends. Otherwise, it would probably be too painful to raise that sweet little girl." I paused, my anger rising. "Do you feel any shame?"

His lips thinned. "I did everything I could to help those girls. But they refused me."

"They said he smelled evil. Now. Now I understand why Cecilia dropped your class. Your stench probably reminded her of the worst pain she ever experienced." I got up and stalked toward him. "You did everything you could?"

He glared at me as I moved closer. As if the weight of his stare could somehow stop me in my tracks. Fucking bastard.

A burst of power slammed into me.

The surge was met with the brick wall of my protective mark. I could still feel the sensation crawling all over me.

Lionel roared in pain, clutching his head as spittle ran down his chin.

I laughed. "Did you try to use your power on me?"

He swelled up from his seat and rushed me. I didn't even flinch. I welcomed his attack. I needed it. Bloodshed was the only answer in this moment.

"What the fuck are you?" he asked, voice filled with homicidal rage.

I cocked my head to the side, staring up at him. "Your accent has changed. I guess I should ask who you are."

He didn't answer. But he did avert his gaze and stare behind me. I followed his line of sight. "Do you know Alek?"

Silence. But something in his eyes said yes.

Magick flooded the air. A whirlwind of green, blue, and orange saturated the room.

"You should probably step back," I said, a smile on my face.

Of course, he didn't listen. He snatched me up, and again, I laughed. Confusion filled his face. I let my gaze go distant, found that ball of light at his center, and yanked it the fuck out of him. I crashed onto the floor, him on top of me.

Next thing I knew, he was airborne. Slammed into the wall by a raging Alek. I let go of his slimy soul and got up.

"She asked how you know me?" Alek bit out.

Lionel bucked and kicked at the wall. "By reputation."

Alek just stared at him.

"To answer your question on why we're here, we came for him," I said, as if Lionel's little petty attempt at hurting me hadn't taken place. "Dimitri." I pointed in the unconscious man's direction. "He has kidnapped four girls from their homes. Coerced two of them into killing their parents before they left. He is also responsible for the deaths of the girls we came looking for at the school. A place I'm sure you will no longer be welcome." I walked around the table and stood next to Michael. "We have also come to retrieve this one," I said, slamming my hand on Michael's shoulder. "So he can pay for the brutal rape of Cecilia, Gracie, Deidra, and Vicky."

Michael shoved back, knocking me down. He snatched up his knife and fell on me, intent on stabbing me. Like father, like son. The blade came down dangerously close to my head. I'd managed to shift out of the way just in time. I didn't reach for his soul. Instead, I grabbed that useless member between his legs and twisted it with strength and enough anger to pull it clean off.

His scream pierced my eardrum.

"Nikki, I don't think it's fair you get to fight everyone," Rachel announced.

"They seem to be targeting me," I said, shoving Michael off me.

I stood. Seriously, why were they just attacking me?

Lionel rushed toward his son. Rachel stepped into his path and punched him in the gut. He doubled over, and she blew dust into his face. Her chant filled the air. Lionel's skin sizzled; pieces of it slid off and fell onto his jacket.

The other man at the table had yet to move.

All of it was over too soon. For what these people had done, I wanted more. I wanted to tear into them. Toy with their souls. For Alek to break their minds. Our fight with the Dacian had been brutal. Shouldn't finding the ones responsible for so much pain be as well?

Lionel scrambled to his chair, holding his cloth napkin to his face. Alek shoved Michael into his chair. The men glared at both of us.

"Did they rebuff you?" I asked, staring at him. "Did they bruise your ego?"

Lionel groaned. "Don't answer her," he choked out. "Don't answer any of them."

"I don't think you understand the situation, sir," Devlin said. "We're here to make sure you all pay for your crimes."

"You're not the authorities. And you have no proof we committed any crimes. Our hands are clean."

"If you let me go, I can give you their books," the fourth man, who up until this point had been silent, said, sliding the ledger across the table.

Devlin picked up the offered item and stared at the black binder. "Like your boss said, we're not the authorities." His magick surged out, the book caught fire in his hand. He tossed it onto the marble floor and let it burn. "Alek. Are the girls here?"

Dimitri startled awake. "What—" he started, but Alek grabbed his shoulder and squeezed.

"Quiet," Alek said, his eyes going that dark shade. He lifted his head, magick pouring out of him. "There are several here."

"Are Nadia and Sophia here as well? Petronela wants to speak to them. And you too. About the murder of their parents," I said to Dimitri.

Dimitri's eyes darkened. "I don't know where those girls are. They didn't want to come when I invited them. And I don't know anything about murder. That witch won't lure me to her..." He slumped forward, obviously not having learned his lesson the first time.

I thought about that for a minute. So much of what we'd gone through in the past few days had been to find these two girls. To bring them and Dimitri to Petronela so they could pay for killing their parents. So, where the hell were they?

Something should be here, but it's not. No. I shook my head, completely aware everyone was watching me. Not here. Where?

I blew out a frustrated breath. "Okay. I guess we're done here. We'll just take your son and Dimitri, and the girls you have here as well. And I will let you finish your meal while the rest of your face falls off." I looked at Rachel. She smiled and made her way toward him. "Wait, Rach."

I walked over to Lionel and stood next to him. He glared at me, his face a macabre mask of melting flesh. Defiant till the end. Maybe I should have let him regale us with a speech. Maybe a veiled threat or two. But honestly, I was just too damn tired. And I wanted all of this to end.

"Ms. Peterson is aware you let your son rape her students. She suspected. Probably even questioned you. I am curious what you told her to convince her you weren't responsible. But it really doesn't matter." I paused. "She also wanted me to put a bullet in your head." He started to move. Marta handed me her gun, and I jammed the muzzle against his temple and pulled the trigger.

A fine mist of blood and gunpowder landed on my shirt and face. I grabbed one of the cloth napkins from the table and wiped it off me, happy that I hadn't missed. "She wants to kill you a little more slowly," I said to a wailing Michael. He didn't hear me, of course. He was too busy screaming for his father.

"*Sometimes you have to become a monster to fight another monster.*"

Leticia was right. I had become a monster.

Nine girls lay on mats in a large room upstairs. When we entered the room, they didn't even acknowledge us. Just lay there in a drunken stupor. We found Daniella and Ileana, the first of Petronela's girls to go missing, near the back.

Alek crouched and shook one girl. She slowly opened her eyes. "Daniella," he said. "Do you remember me?"

She smiled and stretched. "Didn't think I'd see you here," she slurred and reached for him. "Whatever price they gave you"—a grin spread across her face—"I'll waive it." She licked her lips. "You are gorgeous, Alexandros."

Alek was patient and kind to her, helping her up while I helped Ileana. It would have been so easy to say these girls had chosen this life, and if they wanted it, we should leave them here. And chances were, when we took them back, they might run off again. But I couldn't abandon them. Something in their lives had gone wrong and forced them into this situation. Or, as I assumed, Dimitri had sold them a bunch of lies and convinced them to take this path. Either way, we weren't leaving them here.

And while we wanted to rescue all the girls, we didn't have the space to take them with us. So, Devlin put in a call to Opal, while we put Daniella and Ileana in the back seat of Alek's car. Then we crammed Dimitri and Michael in the trunk.

Despite burning the ledger, Devlin still wanted us to find the drugs. So, while he questioned the accountant, we searched the house.

We found nothing. Which meant there were others involved in this scheme. It would have to be a worry for another day. We still had two other girls to find and no leads to follow.

I started back down the stairs and stopped at the wall of framed political figures. It had caught my attention on the way up, but I'd been too focused on getting to the girls. Now, I stood there looking at the strange array of politicians and country leaders throughout time. Was Lionel really this obsessed with the subject? Seemed a strange thing to devote an entire wall to. And, sadly, I couldn't question him about it. I'd already put a bullet in his head.

I sighed and continued down the stairs. I really needed to get some sleep. Or at least stop obsessing about unimportant things. When I reached the bottom of the stairs, I froze. Turning slowly, I walked back up the steps, heart pounding, until I reached the middle. In a brown frame, printed on yellow-tinged stationery, was the quote:

I learn a great deal by merely observing you, and letting you talk as long as you please, and taking note of what you do not say.
- T. S. Eliot.

Adrenaline flooded my body. It wasn't the wall or the weird obsession with leaders of the past that had caught my attention. It was the quote. Those simple words had dislodged the missing thread I'd been worrying over for two days.

I'd figured out what should be there but wasn't.

And it was at the place this all began.

A female Dacian guard met us at the gate. Alek spoke to her in hushed tones, signaling toward his car as well. I glanced at the sky, expecting to see the tapestry of souls I'd been drawn to when we left her a couple of days ago. Had it really been such a short time? It seemed as if we'd been searching for the truth for much longer. And all it had taken was a simple quote to bring the mystery into focus.

I'd spent the ride over ordering all my thoughts. Devlin had pressed me for answers, but I told him I needed time to fit the pieces together myself first. Marta walked up and joined me. I looked over at my friend, gun resting in a holster on her hip. She'd said from the start she wanted to deal with the person who'd poisoned the kids. I had to give her the opportunity. But it saddened me that she just may become a monster like me.

The Dacian guard walked out of the gate and followed Alek to his car. After retrieving Dimitri from the trunk, Alek and Devlin grabbed Daniella and Ileana from the back seat, and we followed the women into the carnival.

People in ceremonial robes moved about, cleaning up the last of the ritual items. The funeral pyres were ablaze, but no souls hovered above the dead. They must have moved on, having been woven into the tapestry. One day, I'd ask Petronela to tell me more about this intriguing ritual. That is, if she still wanted to speak to me after today.

Cristian met us halfway and took Dimitri from the guard. He pushed the man down to his knees and stood vigil over him while others came and took the girls from Devlin and Alek. Petronela strode over to us, with Alek's cousin Bria walking behind her.

They stopped near Dimitri and looked down at him. "He is the one who has done this terrible thing to my people?"

I shook my head. "He has done something terrible. But not what you suspect."

"Where are the others? Sophia and Nadia?" she asked.

I sighed, readying myself for the next part. "I believe they are still here."

Everyone gasped and turned my way.

"Cristian, where are the healer and his wife, Dawn?"

He stared at me for a minute. Confusion colored his eyes before he nodded. He looked around and then called over to the nearest person. "Bring John and his wife here," he ordered, then turned back to Petronela.

She continued to stare at me. I could feel the anxiety rolling off of her. "You have figured it out?" she said finally.

I nodded. "And I believe your recent weakness can be explained as well. But I need to get this out before we talk about it."

She nodded.

John and his wife walked over, brows furrowed in confusion. "Is there something wrong?" John asked. He glanced down at Dimitri. "You've caught him?"

I didn't respond. Instead, I just waited for him to finally talk to me.

Dawn stared at me, her eyes misting with unshed tears. She was going to put on a show. I was really not in the mood for that.

"You know," I started, fatigue, anger, and frustration warring inside of me. "I have spent the last few days wondering what was missing that should be there. For the fucking life of me, I couldn't figure it out." I looked at both of them, willing them to read my damn mind. I wanted to snap their fucking necks. "Then we solved a case we were not hired to solve." I pointed at Dimitri. "The one *he* is involved in." I glanced at Petronela. "Your hiring practices need to be improved." I shook my head. "I came across a quote that finally, finally jogged my damn memory." My voice rose, but I didn't care.

"'I learn a great deal by merely observing you, and letting you talk as long as you please, and taking note of what you do not say.'" I quoted.

"T. S. Eliot," Devlin said.

"Why didn't you talk to me, John? When Cristian came to get you, he told you I wanted to talk about the boys' deaths." I looked at his wife. "And you so helpfully supplied me with the information you thought I'd need. Probably took great pleasure in feeding me some bullshit."

Bria moved behind Dawn, and Alek behind John.

"Cristian said they fell asleep and didn't wake up. You said they had been found and you treated their symptoms, which you believed were caused by toxic shock. That story makes little sense. I believe what Cristian said was true. Which meant you had to be the one who killed them. What you described—" Marta handed me my notebook, and I threw it at Dawn. She flinched, stepping back, only to land against an angry Bria.

"What you described," I started again, "sounds a lot like foxglove poisoning. We didn't look in the one place it and the hemlock would be." Anger rose, boiling my blood and making my eye twitch. "Your damn trailer."

"I would never!"

I shook my head. "Save it." I pulled in a breath. My throat had gone dry, but I needed to continue. "What did you do with Sophia and Nadia?"

She stared at me, eyes rounded. "I don't understand what—" She grabbed her head and dropped to her knees. Power rolled through the small space we stood in. I looked at Alek. It wasn't him. I turned to Petronela and took a step back in alarm. I'd seen Alek's darkness. Had even been frightened by it. But nothing compared to the storm of power rolling off Petronela. It was a miasma of orange, gold, black, and silver. It wrapped around Dawn, squeezing her. The woman jerked, body twisting from side to side as blood flowed out of her eyes and mouth.

And then, it stopped, and Dawn sagged to the ground.

"Cristian. Alexandros. Please go and retrieve the girls from the water."

"I'll go," Devlin said, his face a mask of pain. He had checked the water's edge when we investigated. I knew he was berating himself. But he shouldn't have. It wasn't his fault. And, after we dealt with the two who were to blame, I'd tell him that.

John stared down at his wife. A look of resolve appeared on his face.

"Are you thinking about your part in all this?" I asked him. "Because you are the one to blame for it all. Your affair with Florin and with Larissa didn't go unnoticed, did it?" I paused, putting the last pieces in place. "Florin was first. At first, the love letters we found in her daughter's bedroom with 'liar' written on them threw me. I believed they might have been from Dimitri. But he only wanted their daughters. Why bother with the mothers? Then, when your wife killed her sons, Florin plunged into a grief she could never come out of. So you moved on to Larissa. Her murder was savage. A woman at the end of her rope, perhaps? Or maybe Larissa used her magick to fight back. Either way, Dawn killed her."

He shook, rage rolling off him. He didn't dare chance a look at Petronela. All his anger was focused on me. "You have no proof of this."

"Would you like me to crack open your mind too?" Petronela said, her tone deadly. "You have been preparing my tea as of late." She moved toward him, and he shrank back, only to run into Alek. "I wondered why I was having so much trouble with my power. I never would have suspected you. You and your wife are clever." She turned to me. "Continue."

I nodded. "It was the cabinet. It had been tampered with. I

started thinking, what if there were letters in there as well? The ones you'd written to Florin had been hidden in her daughter's room. So she couldn't get to those. Probably assumed Florin had thrown them away."

Devlin and Cristian came walking back, carrying the bloated bodies of two girls in their arms. They placed them on a nearby table. Devlin had tears on his cheeks. He was tormenting himself.

Dawn moaned and crawled to her knees. Only to be met with a gun to her head. She gasped, spitting blood onto the ground.

"You killed those children because you were angry that your husband couldn't keep it in his pants?" Marta asked.

Dawn's gaze shifted up, giving Marta a pleading look.

"You should have just left," she said and pulled the trigger.

Everyone went silent, gazes locked on Marta. She stared down at the woman she'd killed while tears streamed down her face. Before I could go to her, Petronela walked over and pulled my friend into her arms. "You are a mother," Petronela said. "For you, this is the worst of things."

Marta nodded against her shoulder.

"Do not fret for what you had to do. We all become the thing we hate sometimes. I, too, have had to kill." She moved back, gripping Marta by the arms. "Grieve the act. But not the animal. She does not deserve your tears."

Marta swiped her cheek and holstered her gun. "Thank you. And I don't grieve for her. I grieve for the children she killed. They didn't deserve any of this."

"I didn't know ..." John started, drawing attention to himself. Was he really trying to plead his case?

I walked over and stared up at him. "Yes, I believe you did. Why else would you go into such a rage at having to take part in a ceremony for people you claimed to hate? Yet have the robes on long before others did? You were the missing piece. But you couldn't talk to me, could you? Not with Alek or Cristian in the room. You had to distract them. Keep them from seeing your true motives."

He dropped his head, resigned.

Petronela stared at me. "You see so much," she said.

Oh how true that was.

"Thank you. For the work you did." She took in the rest of the team. "All of you." She paused and stared at Dimitri and John. "I wonder. Have the two of you ever had the chance to enjoy the attractions here?"

Neither man responded.

"Well. You will tonight. Cristian, please retrieve Unrie. It's time to open the carnival again. We have guests to entertain."

Rachel, who I'd honestly forgotten was there, stepped forward. "Are you going to hunt them?" she asked, her voice filled with joy.

Petronela smiled. "Yes. Would you like to join?"

Rachel nodded. "Yes, please. Dev, is it okay?"

Devlin nodded, a small smile creasing the corner of his mouth. I walked over to him and pulled him into a hug. "Don't you dare blame yourself," I whispered. "Understand, Boss Man." I stepped back and looked up at him.

He smiled at me. "Are you joining the hunt?"

"No. Are you?"

He shook his head.

I turned to Petronela. "Besides, I need to talk to Petronela."

"Oh," he said. "I need to be there when you do." He looked at Alek. "Are you joining the hunt, Alek?"

Alek smiled. "Yes."

"Marta?" I asked.

She shook her head. "I'm going to make myself useful." She glanced over at the people moving the girls, then made her way toward them.

We watched them for a while. They shoved Dimitri and John and a dazed Unrie out of the surrounding gate and into the park. A group of people, including Alek and Rachel, set off after them. I would have loved to hunt. Loved to practice my magick on them. But I'd already had my fill for the night. And before my throat went completely dry from overuse, I needed to speak with Petronela.

When everyone had set about their tasks, the old woman turned to me. "You and Devlin can talk to me in my room. I assume you have questions."

"Yes," I said, and we followed her down the path.

etronela settled on her dais and signaled for us to sit. I had always wanted to see this room, but now that I was actually in here, all I wanted to do was lay on her sofa and take a long nap.

"I feel like I've been talking all night long."

Devlin laughed. "You have. You've been proving to us just how valuable you are. Not that we didn't know it. This, your ability to see so much, is the reason Rachel was so adamant that you join the team." He smiled. "I'm so glad you did."

"Boss Man! You are going to make me cry in front of company."

Petronela laughed. "You two are like brother and sister."

"Yes, I know."

Petronela and I stared at each other. "Tell me, Nicole. Did you see the souls when you were last here?" She picked up an ivory pipe and lit it.

I opened my mouth, then closed it when I couldn't formulate a response.

She inhaled the smoke. "Would you all like tea? Or water?"

"As long as it's not the tea John made you. But yes, my throat is really dry. And I saw the souls. They... they called to me."

She smiled and nodded. "I figured they would. Your lineage being what it is." She turned to Devlin. "Did you open the container I gave you?"

He shook his head. "You told me it was a bedtime story. I figured I'd try after this case."

"Yes. A story your father should be able to read."

"You know about my father?"

"Umm ... I have met him," I answered, even though he hadn't asked me the question.

Devlin turned his gaze to me. "When?"

"Last week. When I went to talk with Ezra. They were playing pool together."

"What's his name?" he whispered.

"Killion Greyson. Horus." The delivery was blunt. But flowery was never my way of speaking. Although, I could have eased into it.

He nodded. "I guess she did name me for him." He leaned forward, resting his arms on his thighs. "He's followed me all my life. I could always feel his power. It was so similar to mine." He eyed Petronela. "You knew this?"

She nodded, a ring of smoke circling her head.

"How?"

"He told me," she said. "He worries for you. But fears getting close." She shook her head. "But I don't think you've come here for that." She studied me. "The soul's attraction to you is because of your lineage. But I swore to your father I wouldn't discuss this with you. I believe, however, you need to learn more about it. Your power is so unique. And left untrained, you could do a great deal of damage."

Someone walked into the room carrying a tray filled with tea and sandwiches. I smiled at the formality of it.

"How long do you think John was poisoning you? And how did you not know?" I asked her, taking the offered cup.

She took a sip of her tea and leaned back. "He started preparing my tea a few months ago. The impact on my power was not as significant as it could have been. But it did cause some trouble. My visions were hazy." She stopped suddenly, her eyes going a little distant. "Unless I actively look for it, I would not be aware of the danger someone poses to me. I'd grown too soft and stopped testing my people. That will end."

"You will drive them away," Devlin said.

She shook her head. "I believe John has been putting poison in my people's ears for a while now. He took to the Kotzurs and Ardeleans quite well. They were the leftover members of Tribe. His affairs with the women were a surprise."

"You had old members of Tribe among you. So how did you know Tribe wasn't involved?" I asked.

"When the original group was defeated, I allowed the Kotzur family and the Ardelean family to stay. They had shown genuine remorse for their actions. The others that were sent away did not. So, when they left the island, I hired the Dacian to hunt them down."

She looked at me. "How did you figure out they weren't involved?"

"It didn't fit. And felt more like a distraction than anything." I paused, then added, "Speaking of the Dacian, a group came after us. I believe they were trying to kill Alek."

She laughed. What in the hell?

"Such foolish people would send them after Alexandros. Did he destroy them?"

"Yes. But they hurt him," I said carefully.

She grew silent, her eyes lit up, and she smiled. "They are having such a wonderful time out there. I should have joined them." She looked at Devlin. "If you were there, Alek must have been protecting you. It is not a reprimand. Only an observation." She studied Devlin. "You have kept him from destroying himself. Thank you for that. One day, he will allow me to teach him about his gift." She looked at me. "Now, Nicole. We have reached the point where you ask your questions."

I pulled out my phone and found the picture of Tulare Island. "I believe you gave Devlin a half-truth when it came to the reason Tribe tried to kill you."

She nodded. "Go on."

I pulled up the picture I'd taken of the map of Tulare on my phone and showed it to her. "I found the original map of Tulare at the museum," I said, watching her. Her gaze remained on the image, but she showed no surprise that it depicted our island a great distance away from its current location. "At some point, the island started moving," I continued. "And then the land bridges appeared in the '80s. But despite that, it continued to move." I stopped. She met my gaze, and I saw a glimmer of pride in those eyes. "Then you arrived."

"Yes," she said.

"And it stopped."

I polished off my tea. The intensity of her gaze was going to make me lose my nerve. "So," I said, forging ahead. "How did you stop it?"

She smiled and then looked at Devlin. "You're right. She is observant." She leaned back. "The Ani'-Yun'wiya' were the first to be tasked with protecting the island and the Ark containing the soul of the Old One now referred to by a given name, Set. His brother renamed all the Old Ones so that they could rule over Egypt."

"The Ani'-Yun'wiya'?" I asked. "I thought the Cherokee were the first inhabitants."

"That is not what they call themselves."

"Wait. The island was made to hold Set, but how did they keep the Ark safe prior to the... Ani'-Yun'wiya' arriving?"

"They didn't need to. Not until one or more of the Old Ones broke their vow and started moving the island."

"Which ones broke it?" I asked, thinking of Lemuel Oren.

"I am not certain of all the players. But I do know Khnum is part of it."

"You know about Lemuel Oren?" Devlin asked.

She smiled. "He believes himself crafty. He is responsible for Tribe. But, back to your question. When the island kept moving, they populated the land bridges with more firsts and their descendants. The Creole and the Gullah Geechee." Her lips thinned.

"But it wasn't enough. So, I made a pact with the Historian and brought my people and the Houses of Power here, and coupled with the energy from the others, we stopped the island. We can never leave this place."

"Never?" I asked, my heart breaking at the sadness in her tone. She shook her head no.

"Firsts," Devlin said. "You've used that term before. Explain."

"After the *Nar al-nasaa* were created, the Architect and the Historian brought humanity into the world. I am the first of my lineage."

I sat back and stared at the old woman, who, if I believed what she was saying, had been around for thousands of years. "Alek said you've always been old."

She sighed. "Yes. I chose to give up my youth in a time when elders were respected. Now, the young respect no one."

"You told me you missed your face," Devlin said. "I didn't really understand the significance of that. Can't you go back?"

"No. None of us can. Tribe wished to kill me, despite that being a wasted effort. If I am removed from this spot, if my people and I stop feeding it power, Khnum will be successful in his mission to free his brother by moving the island."

"I thought it took all the Old Ones to create this island," I said. "And why would he want to free him?"

Petronela shook her head. "No. It took all of them to imprison Set. But only the most powerful of them made this island."

"Lemuel Oren is the most powerful of them?" I asked in alarm. We were so screwed.

Petronela laughed again. "No. Hathor, his sister, is the most powerful. And the most broken."

My brain decided at that moment to break. I was going into information overload, and if I didn't go and sit somewhere quiet by myself, I might break as well.

Petronela watched me. "The answers I gave you are because Devlin is here. I, along with many others, have promised your father we would not divulge this information to you. So take what I have told you and use that ability of yours to find more answers. I suggest asking your parents. Your mother in particular."

She turned to Devlin. "You, as I've said before, I can give answers. My door is always open."

Petronela and Devlin talked about his father. While I seethed at being denied the information I needed. Once again, I found myself trying to make sense of something. How was Hathor the most powerful? More importantly, how did she create the entire island by herself? It didn't say that in the scribe, *The Land Guarded by People of Colour*, that Thoth had penned. At least, I didn't think so. I'd have to read it over more carefully.

But the revelation of what Petronela said suddenly made Camilla's reaction to her sister's presence on the island make sense. She was scared of Hathor. And I didn't blame her for being so. I would fear anyone who could create an entire island as well.

So how did Lemuel Oren plan to get around his sister?

It was just after dawn when we arrived at the Peterson's all-girls school. Randall and Leticia were waiting outside when we pulled up. Randall had a wheelchair in front of him. I could almost view the sight of it as comical. It had a ghoulish undertone to it. After all, we were there to take Michael to the secret room in the walls so that Leticia could torture him in her pursuit of understanding blood magick.

And we were responsible for his delivery.

Alek parked, and Randall wheeled the chair to the trunk. I sat there for a minute, ordering my emotions and thoughts, while I tried to pretend we weren't doing what we were doing.

"Are we getting out, Nikki?"

So much for pretending. Rachel had opted to come with us. I'd thought, after her hunt through the carnival, that she would have wanted to go home with the others to rest. I was so wrong.

We both got out of the car.

Leticia walked over with a small, sad smile on her face. Without warning, she pulled me into a hug, and I actually hugged her back. Strange that I'd originally come here intent on bringing her down if we found out she was practicing blood magick. But, as fate would have it, we were instead on our way to becoming friends. Enemy of my enemy and all that.

I stepped away from her and pulled out the letter Deidra had written her several years ago. "I had to read it in order to find clues." She accepted it from me. "But I believe you should have it. She responded to the help you offered after their attack. Just not in the way you had hoped."

She stared at the letter. "I'll read it later." She ran her hand over the worn envelope. "Do you still wish to learn more about blood magick?"

I smiled. "Yes. But right now, I need rest. This case has taken a lot out of me." I turned to Rachel. "If you don't mind, my friend here wishes to learn too. Rachel, this is Leticia. Leticia, Rachel."

"I don't need rest," Rachel said. "I can stay and help you with Michael." She beamed at Leticia.

I put my hand on Rachel's shoulder. "Rach, honey, I think they have classes today. We can come back later."

She dropped her head and nodded.

We watched Alek and Randall wheel an unconscious Michael to a side entrance. I could be honest and say I'd hoped to be there when he woke up. To see the look on his face when he realized what was about to happen to him. And, yes, to try really hard to hear the song in the blood. But more than the song, I wanted to hear him scream. Beg for his life. Plead for Leticia to stop. The sick bastard had caused so much pain. He needed to suffer.

"Did he tell you why Gracie and Cecilia left?" Leticia asked.

I was all talked out, but I wanted to give her this explanation, at least. "I don't think they did." It had taken me some time to see through the charade to find the threads of truth. When we found them in that house, high on drugs, Cecilia had a gun with her. At first, I believed it was to protect the house and her and Gracie. But then, when I really focused on her behavior at that house, not to mention how she went about dealing with the pain of her attack all those years ago, there was really only one conclusion. Cecilia was a survivor. She would never have gone willingly to that place where dreams went to die. I believed they had been kidnapped, drugged, and left in that house, away from the other girls who had already accepted their fate.

And during her bouts of lucidity, she'd found a weapon to

protect her and Gracie. She'd made little sense when we were talking. But drugs could do that. It was her talk of dreams that really did it for me. And the leaving of all their possessions behind.

They had intended to return. Only someone had stopped them. Someone with mind magick.

We said our goodbyes and promised to return later, then headed home to sleep. Petronela had invited us to the ceremony to weave Sophia and Nadia's souls into the tapestry.

The Road Less Traveled

Devlin watched Marta examine the third puppy with the concentration of a parent looking for any hazard that might harm their child. He smiled at the small woman who'd given in to her daughters' demands for a dog. It might have been the fear of dying or just motherly love, but their quick trip to pick up a gift for Nicole had turned into an hour-long search for the right dog.

As he watched her, he thought about his own mother. It'd been a while since he'd heard her voice, and he would have been fine with that. Except... except... he'd had his own brush with death these past few weeks and learned the being watching him was his father. An Old One. If he believed she would be lucid enough to answer, he'd ask her how she had encountered the god and what had become of their union when she became pregnant with him.

"He's so sweet," Marta said, staring into the puppy's eyes as it tried relentlessly to lick her hands and face, tail wagging feverishly.

"He is," Devlin said, avoiding adding more. He'd given her a detailed opinion on the first puppy and knew what she needed was not his advice but time to sit with her decision.

He shifted the bag in his hand and smiled. Nicole would

either hate the gift the team picked out for her or love it. A part of him secretly hoped she hated it. If only to have a reason to spar with the woman who he'd come to view as a sister he never had.

Again, he thought of his mother.

She'd become a checkmark in his daily life. Her care and well-being just another item to cross off his list at night. In his mind, that was enough. For all he'd had to endure as a child, this was more than enough. All the pain, fear, and abuse he'd suffered. It was hard to let go of the torment. To see past all that and understand that his mother had been broken. If anyone was to blame, it was his father. All that time, Killion watched him and never intervened.

When he did finally meet him, god or not, Devlin would do everything in his power to make the man pay for that.

"I might need to get more items," Marta said, pulling him from his thoughts. "Puppies need a lot stuff." She wandered off, the puppy she'd obviously selected secured under her arm, in search of … stuff.

Devlin switched the bag with Nicole's gift to his left hand and pulled out his phone. He stared down at the device for a minute, debating if it was a good idea to call so early. It was barely seven in the morning in California.

Before he could talk himself out of it, he dialed the number and pushed down his fear.

"Devlin," his mother's caregiver's familiar voice filled his ear. "You're early today. Is everything okay?"

His breath grew shallow, and for just a moment, he was back in his room, listening as his mother screamed about an unseen enemy digging inside her mind. "Yes … yes, I'm okay." He pulled in a lungful of air and let it out slowly. "Is she up?" he asked.

Ruth didn't respond right away. "She is," she said slowly. "Do you want to talk to her?"

"If she's eating or in the bathroom or just…"

"Slow down. She's here. We just finished breakfast, and she's on the porch." She grew silent. "Today is a good day," she said finally. "A good day to hear her child's voice."

"Okay," he said and turned to find Marta standing behind him. She moved closer, took the bag from him, and handed him the puppy. He smiled at her through his tears. She nodded and stepped away.

The puppy wiggled in his arms, bathing his chin with doggy kisses. A moment later, he heard her. The woman who had terrorized him as a child. The woman who had wanted him to be immortal. The woman he could never stop loving no matter what.

His mom.

"My baby," she sang into the phone. "I've seen your face in a dream. Are you coming home soon?"

He let out a ragged breath. "Maybe one day... mom. How are you?"

"The sun is bright today. Ruth is taking me to see the ocean. I'll buy a new dress and make you a cake... I think we have..." He heard the phone drop and waited, but she never returned.

"Are you still there?" Ruth asked.

"Yes. She sounds okay."

"Mm, she is. She's been wanting to see the water. Says it's important to go to the water. Been saying that for a few days now."

Devlin froze. "When?" he asked, urgency in his voice.

"Since Sunday," Ruth said carefully. "Why?"

"No reason. Thank you, Ruth. I will call again later." His mind was racing.

"All right," she said. "I better go before she really starts making that cake." She hung up, and Devlin stared at his phone as the puppy continued to wiggle in his arms.

Marta walked over and took the dog from him. "Are you okay?" she asked. "Is your mother okay?"

He looked at her, temporarily unable to formulate words. But after a short while, he reassured her he was okay, and they headed out to make their way home.

As he navigated the streets of Tulare, a single thought kept circling his mind.

His mother had known he needed to search for the girls in the water.

I woke to the sound of laughter and the familiar scent of nachos. I smiled as I lay there, absorbing a bit of normalcy. Letting the weight of the past few days roll off me. Had it really been only three days? The case seemed to have taken forever to solve. I ran my hand over Alek's side of the bed. He'd made it again. Normal. Even our relationship was ... normal. Could I handle this unchaotic existence? Where I woke, did my job, went to bed if the case allowed, and had sex with the same man? A man who I was unable to admit my true feelings to just yet.

Maybe, I thought, rising. My stomach growled at me. I absolutely loved Marta's version of nachos. We used to make them together, Kara included, and watch reruns of *Columbo*. It would be nice if we could convince the team to watch an episode while we filled our bellies with ground beef, cheese, salsa, and a mountain of toppings. Stacked right, the chips should cave under the weight of all those delicious items.

Normal.

After getting dressed, I went out to find the nachos—and the team, of course. They sat in the war room, smiling at one another. A gold shirt box with a large red ribbon sat on my desk. I lifted an eyebrow in question. No one met my eyes, except for Devlin.

I had a bad feeling about this.

Hesitantly, I walked over to the box, expecting the worst. "You all got me a present," I said, glancing at Marta. Her head was down, eyes wide as she studied the paper in front of her. Alek wasn't any help either, his mouth constantly moving as if he were trying hard not to laugh. Rae chuckled under her breath. And Rachel beamed at Devlin as if the present was for her.

"Umm... I'm not opening this unless you all tell me what's inside."

Devlin caved and walked over, picked up the box, and handed it to me. "It's from all of us. You kept asking me to make you a superhero belt. But after this case, I believe this suits you much better. It speaks to your skills." He smiled, but behind that merriment, I saw a glimmer of worry.

"Okay," I said slowly, sounding out each of the syllables. "Thank you."

Carefully, I removed the ribbon from the box and opened the lid. Resting inside a bed of red tissue paper was a black coat. I pulled out the thin jacket and stared at it. A medium-length, button-down raincoat with a strap to tie around the waist. The fabric was thin enough that I wouldn't cook to death in it but also would protect me from the rain. Underneath the coat, I found a black beret.

My eyes widened. They had rendered me speechless.

"Do you like it?" Marta asked. "I ordered it this morning, and Devlin and I picked it up after we gave our statements to the police about the shootout yesterday."

"You paid for this?" I asked, still stunned. How was this a replacement for my superhero belt?

"With the company credit card, yes. I can exchange it if you want something different."

"We will discuss the fact that you have a company card and I don't later. First ..." I looked at Devlin. "How is this my superhero belt replacement?"

Everyone lost their composure and laughed. I shook my head and glared at them.

Devlin regained composure first. "Try it on," he said.

I was missing something. And then it hit me. "Seriously," I

said, slipping on the coat. "Was it the long-winded summation of the crime that convinced you all I needed this?" I smiled at the gesture. The coat actually felt nice.

"Yes," Devlin said. "You reminded me of the old movies I used to watch of Hercule Poirot. The way he put together the thinnest of clues. And Marta said you love Columbo." He grabbed my arms. I tilted my head up and met his gaze. "In all seriousness. I was worried about you. But you knew that. Then I saw you lay out a complicated case in a way that amazed me. We would still have been chasing clues, running down leads, and getting nowhere. You think outside the box. And in this case, we needed that. You don't need a belt. Or a gun." He leaned in. "You really don't need a gun." We laughed. "Your mind is your superhero belt. This coat. You can wear it if you like. But I think it suits you."

"Look in the pockets!" Rachel said, still beaming.

Devlin stepped back, and I searched first the outside, then the inside pockets. Resting in the inside pocket was a book. I pulled it out and stared at the notebook with "Nikki" written on the front. Next, I pulled out the glitter pen and groaned.

Rachel laughed. "I ordered that with my own money. You like it?"

My eye twitched. Was it too late to veto the name? "Yes, thank you all." I shook my head. "I guess I could make this work. Strap the dagger to my thigh. Wrestle my hair into the beret." I looked up at my team through tear-filled eyes. "Seriously," I choked out. "Thank you."

Against my expletive-filled protests, we all shared a group hug.

Once our plates were filled, we sat down to an episode of *Columbo*. When it was over, Devlin ran down the issues we would face. We told them about my theory and Petronela's confirmation of why she was needed on Tulare.

They had cleared the murder board of the recent case. Only a notecard with the Dacian's name remained. We needed to find out who had sent them after us. Or, as we assumed, after Alek. We also needed to have a long conversation with Ezra and Hathor. I might need them to provide me a charm to protect me from their crazy sister Camilla as well. I could add it to the collection already on my bracelet, next to the one to keep Set away from me.

There were many loose ends we needed to tackle. But I didn't mind. I had a brand-new coat and a purpose. And most of all... I had my own Tribe.

EPILOGUE

According to Alek, the Historian always showed up when disaster was looming. Yeah, well, I'd say an Old One moving the entire island of Tulare so that it joined up with North America all so he could free his deranged brother was a disaster in the making.

We pulled up to Luisah's just as the sun was beginning to set. I, along with Devlin, Marta, and Rachel, were in the car with Alek. Jonah and Kara followed in his truck.

Ten days ago, Luisah, the Historian, in exchange for information on Divine Evil, had made Devlin promise to return with his entire team. Her knowledge had helped us defeat Gavina Young.

At the time, I didn't understand that promise. Usually, she charged fees for the knowledge she provided. But like the promise she'd gotten from me when I was researching the Stewart family, I understood that the vow had weight.

We wouldn't refuse. It just wasn't an option.

I wore my new coat for the occasion. Rae had braided my hair, so it fit nicely under the beret. A few strands had escaped, but I liked how it looked. Along with the lipstick and the knife strapped to my thigh, I had become a sexy mastermind, and I loved it.

Later, me and Alek were going to my parents' house for dinner. It was way past time I talked to them about my power. Alek would be my buffer. Hopefully, they would give me the answers I needed. The ones my father had forbidden others to share with me.

The lights were on inside her shop, but the Closed sign was

still hanging from the door. We walked over, and I tried the handle. She appeared in the doorway. She smiled and opened the door for us.

We stepped into the familiar shop, and I inhaled its scent. Floorboards creaked under our combined weight.

"It is good to see you all," Luisah said, her hazel eyes radiating with power. I'd seen her true form before—an ancient primordial being capable of so much. She hid this power in the form of a middle-aged Creole woman.

"I've brought them," Devlin said.

She nodded and looked down the aisle.

A tall, dark-skinned man with an average build wearing a long gold and red robe walked out of the back room. He had light brown hair and eyes that looked like polished amber. Power rolled off of him. Filling the room.

I looked inside of him, trying to determine what kind of magick he had, and gasped when I didn't find a soul. What I found, resting in a bed of gold light, was a galaxy of stars, black holes, planets—too much power for my mind to fathom.

"Your ancestors never could see me. Despite my essence creating them," he rumbled.

I let out a shaky breath.

"Brother," Luisah said. "You will kill them with you power if you do not contain it."

He shook his head, and suddenly, I could breathe again. "I have not been around humans for quite some time. I apologize."

I glanced back at the others. Blood ran down their faces. I touched my own wet cheek and stared at the smear of crimson on my fingers.

"God?" I asked, my voice small.

He smiled, and everything inside of me burst behind a dam full of emotion. I laughed, I cried, and I reached for him. He took my hand and cradled it in his. He pulled a white handkerchief from his pocket and wiped my face. "Please. All of you, sit." It was then that I realized he wasn't speaking English. Yet I understood him. His voice, the tone and inflection, the words, all sounded like a song.

We sat. Luisah handed napkins to the others so they could wipe their faces.

"I am the Architect. But you may refer to me by the name my sister gave me. Bakari." He paused, taking a seat next to me. "My sister and I made a pact when we saw the destruction humanity could bring with only a little knowledge. She would not give her wisdom out so freely. But now, we must rethink that. Someone disturbed our little sister's Ark once again. They are bringing it here. We cannot stop this event." He looked at all of us. "But you can."

"Your sister," Alek said with fear in his tone.

Bakari nodded.

"Why?" I asked. "You're God. You can stop anything."

"We cannot interfere in the affairs of humanity. We are bound by the rules we have spoken into existence. To go against them now would destroy us and all we created."

"I don't understand," I said, looking between him and Luisah.

"I told you before, girl. We are bound," Luisah said, both anger and sadness filling her ancient eyes.

"Is your sister bound?"

They both nodded. "She can only influence. Like us."

"Who is your sister?" Kara asked.

I could have answered her. But I was too busy trying to fight through the sudden wave of panic consuming me. Alek had told me about the three gods responsible for humanity.

The Architect. The Historian. And the Harbinger.

Which meant Death was coming to our shores.

Acknowledgments

First and foremost, I have to send so much love to my husband. He has encouraged me in so many ways, and I will never be able to thank him enough for sticking with me on this journey. So many more books waiting to be written and it's not so scary when I have a great partner by my side!

Jess Moore. I can not begin to tell you just how much of a pivotal role this incredible human being played in getting Tribe to this space. Tribe was with a publisher. And I was comfortable with that. Happy, even. I wanted my entire series to be published by them. But things don't always work out like you want them to, and I had to make the difficult decision to ask for my rights back for both this book and the two previous ones. To say I was scared is an understatement. But what helped me gain the confidence needed to go at this alone was Jess. And while the back-end process of publishing is scary AF, I have the above two people in my corner, cheering me on!

Special thanks goes out to my family who are a constant source of joy and support! My Mom is forever asking if I'm writing. I love that so much!!

Now, I do have to send a special shout out to Midnight Tide Publishing. They folded me into their welcoming embrace, and I have to say I do love my new home. Thank you ladies!

To my new crew of editors! Jess who I trust to reign me in when I want to get all wordy! Meg aka the Comma Goblin. Yes, you deserve that name!! Kelli Lea Jennings, thank you for your careful eye on my work. Your notes were extremely helpful! And Desert Ink Editorial, I can't wait to work with you again!!

A special thanks goes to my readers, Zarina, Tina, Rita, Geoff, and so many more. I appreciate your constant support and joy at my story world and its many, many, many, MANY, colorful characters!

And to the new readers, Tribe has entered the chat! You might want to start with Lineage, but if you're starting with book three, then welcome to the family! I hope you can stay for tea.

About the Author

C. Vonzale Lewis is the best-selling author of the Blood & Sacrifice Chronicles and various short fiction. She resides in Hesperia, CA where she spends her days plotting the demise of her enemies. All her stories tend to be dark with a little mystery thrown in and some love to round out the mix. When not writing, she enjoys reading, spending time with her husband, and binge-watching British crime fiction.

Overkill by Lou Wilham

Sometimes the hunter becomes the hunted.

Overworked, and underappreciated, Eric Marcelino just wants to hunt the vampires plaguing Ironport, keep his students out of the field, and somehow make it home in enough time to get a full 8 hours of sleep. . . maybe 6.

Tony McMahon and his sister arrive in Ironport looking for a fresh start. Only Tony didn't count on the instant attraction he feels toward the Huntsman's golden boy, Eric, nor being drawn into an ancient prophecy set to end the Huntsman forever.

Something strange is brewing in Ironport. With bloodsuckers, the Council of Creatures, and his students breathing down his neck, Eric has to wonder if he's in over his head and if a potential boyfriend might be the final nail in his coffin. This is gonna suck.

Overkill is a mm paranormal romance perfect for fans of Buffy.

Available Now

The Kindred Few by Heather Kindt

Take a breath. Taste the fruit. Let out the scream you've held in for so long.

When the death of her mother orphans Mari, it shatters her perfect life in Avren, the beautiful city on the hill. Branded an Undesirable, she's banished to the unforgiving wilderness on the eve of her adulthood, forced into a life of servitude. It's in this forested world that she discovers the monsters in the fairytales she heard as a child are all too real.

Facing unpredictable dangers, a group of orphaned strangers named the Kindred Few adopt Mari into their fold. She learns the art of survival from her new brother and enigmatic commander, Bastian Hale. As they train for battle, they await the two prophesied saviors who will save them from Avren's iron grip.

But as ancient fae prophesies unfold, Mari learns a difficult truth.

She is one of the two destined to lead the charge to liberate the wilderness.

Available Now

Dreamwalkers by Leslie Rush

Between working in her mom's tarot shop and trying to graduate before her nine-year-old genius brother beats her to it, Vivian Night Hawk has only one escape from her tiny New Mexico town: the ability to control her dreams, a gift she inherited from her Apache father. But lately that control is slipping, stranding her in a nightmare that seems to follow her even when she's awake.

When she finds a jacket she suspects belonged to her dead father, Viv steps beyond lucid dreaming and discovers the electrifying secret of Dreamwalking--the power to control the dreams of others. But with it comes a deadly menace: a top-secret CIA plot that threatens her brother Brian. Sought out by fellow dreamwalker Lucas, who is convinced their fathers are still alive, Vivi ventures deep into Dreamland to find a way to protect Brian. As the bond between Vivi and Lucas ignites, the conspiracy linking them together closes in, and Vivi must unlock the darkest power of all--a power that begins with her father's quiet words: "Walk with me"

Available Now